TANGLE & FEN

TANGLE & FEN

Edited by
RACHEL A. BRUNE

CR⊙NE
GIRLS
press

ISBN: 978-1-952388-14-9 (print)
978-1-952388-13-2 (ebook)

Original Cover Art & Design by
James @ GoOnWrite.com

Published by
Crone Girls Press
Crone Girls Press Trade Paperback Edition August 2023
Printed in the USA

This one is for our readers. Thanks for walking through the darkness with us.

CONTENTS

BUBBLE BATH

A.V. GREENE

IF I IGNORE the thick layer of dust glinting in the slatted sunlight, our bathroom looks like we left just earlier this morning. The shower caddy still holds my half-empty shampoo and conditioner. Rob's curly hair is still knotted in the drain.

My daughter is still here too, wandering in small circles like she used to as a toddler. "Misty, NO!" I would snap while she rummaged through my makeup or tossed my earrings in the sink.

She's not interested in making messes like that anymore.

I'd felt like a bad mom when I couldn't wait for her bedtime to arrive. I'd feel guilty when we found ourselves in the drive-thru for the third night in a row, or when I plonked her in front of back-to-back Pixar movies so I could work. In retrospect, all that guilt is laughable, compared to what I carry now.

She's right where I left her when the transports picked up survivors four weeks ago. Rob's body has been collected, though. The stain in the corner looks like someone spilled a glass of wine.

I'd never wanted a gun in the house. I'd lectured Rob that we were much more likely to die from gun violence because of it, but I'd never dreamed I'd shoot him myself. Or that he'd beg me to.

I slide into the bathroom and edge around Misty. She's harmless now; Rob managed to neutralize her before she bit him. Her eyes have a glacial film over them, but I swear I can still see some of my little girl in there. It makes me doubt what I've come here to do.

Her hunger and frustration are apparent. I think about the way she cried as a baby and the panicky jolt it gave me.

I couldn't breastfeed. I'd thought I was done grieving for that, but I feel that same sick desperation lodging deep inside me now. I can't feed her with my body now, either, thanks to the neutralization.

I start the bath and adjust the temperature until it's just right. I don't know if she can feel pain anymore, but I don't want to take chances.

She always hated baths.

The Razoxyl comes in a white pouch covered in sternly worded warnings. The CDC is letting civilians give it to their families, provided they've been documented and neutralized, like Misty. Otherwise, they're hosing down most of the known infected. I've seen videos of walking corpses spasming in rage and pain before they collapse. I can't let her go like that.

The Razoxyl, most effective as an immersion therapy, is different from a bullet to the brain. It does more than stop the infected; it defangs the infection itself. Of course, it also destroys any other organic matter it touches. It's incredibly dangerous, and it probably saved the human race.

So here I am, preparing to give my little girl a bath.

Misty can't focus on much; her eyes loll around in their sockets. Sometimes she nods her head, like she's enthusiastically agreeing. It'd be funny if I didn't know she was trying to bite, if her lower jaw wasn't gone. Neutralized.

Afterward, Rob stood with his back against the wall. He was so brave until just before I pulled the trigger. He screamed, "Wait!" but I had already started to squeeze.

I empty the pouch of Razoxyl under the water and pretend it's her lavender-scented bubble bath.

This will be my last act as a parent. I'm going to do it right. I'm not going to lose my temper. I'm going to be proud of myself as a mom, this one time.

I gently grip her shoulders and guide her toward me. She shambles forward and lets me pull her dress over her head. It's the blue one with lace edging she'd picked out herself for picture day. Her fine black hair is plastered to her forehead and neck, and I brush it out of her eyes. She makes a mewling sound.

I think of all the ways I'd tried to lure her into the bathtub when she was a squealing toddler. We'd pretend to be whales, fish, mermaids. We'd squirt each other with rubber ducks. I'd trace the alphabet on her back with a soapy finger.

I don't think any of that is going to work now.

I imagine her screwed-up face when she got her first round of shots. I think about every scratch, scrape, the one awful night in the ER when she broke her arm falling off her changing table. The suffering on her face now is unmistakable. She's been alone and hungry, unable to feed herself thanks to the mangling we gave her back when we still hoped for a cure.

They say they can't think any more and they don't have any memories. I hope it's true, but I also hope part of her still recognizes me.

I sing our bath song to coax her in. "Oh, Misty the baby, Misty the baby, Misty the baby needs a bath!" My throat catches. Misty lets out a moan punctuated by a wet gurgle.

Without thinking, I dip a finger in the water to test the temperature.

It doesn't hurt, but my finger just...shrivels.

Misty steps up her moaning and backs away.

"No," I say. "It's okay. Sweetheart, it's okay."

I realize what I have to do.

When she was a tiny baby, the only way she'd take a bath was if I got in with her. She'd curl up on my chest and go to sleep.

And so that's what we'll do now.

I pull off my sweater, step out of my jeans, and gather her to me. She jerks a little bit, but she lets me ease us both into the poisoned water. I kiss her head and tell her I love her before we're both gone.

This much I can get right.

About the Author

A.V. Greene is a writer living in the Ozarks with her family and an assortment of carnivorous flora and fauna. Though generally a harmless garden pest, she is best handled with care, as the spurs protruding from her ankles secrete a mild neurotoxin. Her short fiction has appeared in *Apex*, *Uncharted*, and elsewhere. For more, visit avgreene.com or follow her on Twitter at @avgreenewrites.

TAKE FROM THE EARTH WHAT IS GIVEN

SCOTT BOWEN

I KNOW that you taste good. Certain muscles, like the ones along your spine, and the *quadriceps*, are delightful when cut into steaks and roasted very slowly, with a dry pepper rub. If you are in good physical condition, the best cuts of your body compare to good veal. If you're well fed, your marbled meat cooks richly, and is juicy. Long ago, I learned to enjoy both lean and marbled.

These days, however, my heart and stomach have been won over by a woman of such exquisite vegan talents that I have adapted to that life because of the flavors she can create. I mix with Lorrie's friends easily, eating what they eat, becoming their friend, because she can make things taste like meat. I don't connect with the politics of these foodies, though, and sometimes I have to smother the desire to bite a hunk out of one of them. My current range of cuisine offers the camouflage of the perfect lentil stew, or the zucchini-and-tofu lasagna, disguises that prevent everyone from ever possibly believing that long ago I learned how to field dress and butcher a whole human man.

My father and mother called it "forest meat." As far back as I can remember, we ate forest meat every winter. When I was a child, this seemed to be the most normal thing, just like canning beets and apricots, or catching snapping turtles to put into a soup. The men, who came from other places, began entering the forest in the autumn—men who sought to kill and eat deer and turkeys, but who may also be eaten themselves. My father was very keen on forest meat and prepared far in advance to harvest a big man for our winter meals, including our Solstice Roast.

I was nine when my father took me hunting for the first time. I remember the ghillie suits we wore to hide, so we could watch. My father had made suits for every terrain and vegetation: rocks, pine, hardwoods, thicket.

I also remember well the image of the first man I saw dead; the naked, bluish-white body of the fellow lay under the sumac branches in the low afternoon sun. My father had shot him with a pistol, the suppressor making the shot nothing but a loud *snap*. We took off our ghillies and put on our blaze-orange vests so that if seen from a short distance we looked like two hunters simply going about our business, the dead man not visible above the brush. We tethered the man's limbs to the lowest branches of the sumac, hanging him face down, pulling tight to stretch the arms and legs. I watched my father use a short, thick, very sharp knife to make careful cuts, starting with the leg muscles, removing section after section. He sliced out the glutes and hams. Then he cut out the straps, the thickest rib muscles, and sliced free all the shoulder meat, biceps, and triceps. The knife tip never pierced the tough sack of guts. He removed the head and hands and cut free the bone-bare legs. We wrapped the sections of meat in cheesecloth and stuffed them into our packs. Then we buried the head, hands, legs, and torso in different places. We walked out, making our way to the truck, the beams of our headlamps slowly growing brighter.

❄

I HAVE ALWAYS HAD a keen sense of smell, and a very good memory of odors. I remember exactly the odor of the red spruce in autumn; the odor of fresh rosemary, which my mother grew in the garden; the scented fur of the cat I had as a boy.

I can also remember so very accurately the odor of perfectly cut human flesh, with its hint of blood. It is a sweet, tasty smell, like the top of a fresh pound cake, but with a rusty-iron edge.

Sometimes I can smell the layers of flesh through a person's skin. When I roll in bed with Lorrie, demanding to kiss every inch of her, I cannot wait to slide my nose and lips along the underside of her thigh, so high that the top of my head is pressed into her bush of curly brown hair. And there, where my mouth is, I can bite ever so tenderly into the perfect spot and sniff her flesh with all my lungpower, smelling underneath her skin the layer of hamstrings.

I nibble and she squeals, and says, "C'mon, don't make me wait."

The life I lead now could never have been foretold in my childhood. Most days, I do not recall life before my late teens. Then the pleasant odors of something cooking will transport me in an instant: something in baked yams that suggests the scent of forest meat softened in a stew; the earthiness of a tofu-and-chestnut risotto that conjures the flavor of my mother's mincemeat pies; a marinated and grilled portobello mushroom that when cut reminds me, for just a second, of a flank steak of man.

No one around me at my girlfriend's dinners could possibly imagine what I see in my mind as we sit eating in her apartment dining room, the windows looking out to the treetops of Golden Gate Park. These intense gourmands of plant-based cuisine cannot even bring themselves to watch a true chef cut up a dead chicken on television. I keep my laughter to myself.

My mind reels back to quiet winter days:

With the big freezer full of forest meat—this hidden under a layer of venison and cuts of stray goats—my mother spent December inside our cabin cooking, as my father and I pretended to be mountain men so hungry it made us growl. We'd yell for food from the table in the little turret off the kitchen, where we ate all our meals. We'd howl from outside that we needed a meat cake. At night, in bed, I'd cry out that I was starving for a rolled-up slice of sausage. We laughed at ourselves and loved every minute of our winter life in that place of odors of smoke, spices, and roasting fat.

For seasoning, my mother used cloves, ginger, lovage, rosemary, cumin, and, her favorite, savory, which she had to buy at the store in town. Other herbs and seeds, the basil and rosemary and mustard, she grew in the garden and then dried, or she gathered them from the forest. Preserved apricots, rhubarb, raisins, and prunes found their way into meat pies. The winter that I turned thirteen, mother made for my birthday a magnificent chili. She ground the meat out of the rump of the biggest man my father had ever killed. He and I had needed two trips, back and forth, to bring all the meat to the truck.

My father was careful to take just one man every season. He thought he was being careful, anyway. He and I scouted for days on end. When we scouted, we dressed like any other deer hunter. We each had a license and deer tags, too, and would eventually tie each one to a whitetail's ear.

Scouting was something that took a long time. Finding or tracking another hunter in the woods was very difficult. The parcels of state management land were very big, the woods very dense. The adjacent federal land was even bigger. So, the most effective way to scout was to drive along a back road until we saw a lone vehicle parked in a pullout. My father and I would note this and park a distance away, then walk back along the road, wearing our woolens and orange vests, my father with a .50 Hawken slung across his back. He carried this black-powder gun, built from a kit long before I was born, because such a longarm was legal in any gun season, and that afforded us a lot of time. We'd find the path the hunter took from his truck, and then we would locate a good observation point, put on our ghillies, and take cover. Eventually we would see the hunter returning to his truck, and we could study him as he walked past us. If he were the kind of man we would prefer to have, someone not too lean or too small, then we'd return to look for him a second time, hiding again in our ghillie suits not far from the road. If we found him, my father killed him.

To learn to do the same, I had to practice sitting perfectly still in the woods, in one of the ghillie suits. This began the spring that I was thirteen. My father would come looking for me. He always found me, but one day he took much longer to find me, and he said, "Now you can learn to shoot."

I practiced with the pistol my father used. It was a Ruger .22 that he had fitted with a homemade suppressor and modified so it did not cycle itself. Semi-autos make a distinct noise when they cycle.

In the garage, I practiced rising from a sitting position in the ghillie and moving with a minimum of noise. I had to hold my arms away from my sides, moving bow-legged, so the strips of camo did not whisper together. I moved ahead two steps and shot a target hanging from the ceiling. The bullet shot into a stack of hay bales that blocked an open door. I had to get the whole motion complete in less than three seconds, or my father wouldn't let me go out alone.

My first season, I was allowed to scout alone. That was all. My father would drop me off in a spot where we had seen a truck, and then he would go scout another possible man. I scouted the same man two weekends in a row, and finally told my father that he was worth taking.

"Why do you think so?" my father asked.

"He's a larger man and looks healthy. I don't smell tobacco or whiskey on him," I said. "And I know exactly where he'll be. Sit with me today, and we'll get him."

My father studied me. He heard and saw how serious I was. He nodded. Looking back, I realized he had given me all the time I needed to reach this conclusion; he had not picked any man he had scouted himself. He had wanted me to make the choice.

So, very early one morning, in a hard frost, we sat in the dark, waiting. We had gone out ahead of the man, parking our truck a distance away and then getting into position. We heard the man's truck on the road. Heard the click of the cab door as he shut it slowly and carefully. Then we saw the tiny dot of a headlamp, colored red, bobbing through the trees. He came right to us, and passed us, and then my father rose and made the shot.

Both of us stood in silence, listening, waiting for the sound of anyone else, a hunting partner running late. We heard nothing. Far away through the trees, a line of orange light was visible.

I carried the man's pack and shotgun as Father dragged the man away from the trail and down a slope, into a curtain of vines hanging from locust trees along a small creek. By noon, the marks we left in the frost would be gone.

My father caught his breath. He put his arm around me. "You had that scouted perfectly, son," he said. "Next year, you'll hunt, for real."

We quartered the man, putting his legs, arms, and sections of his torso in our packs. My father put the man's feet, hands, and head in a bag that he carried separately. As we hiked, he picked spots where he hid these parts, stuffing a foot into a crevice in a rock wall, or pushing a hand up into the bowed-open side of beech tree. The head we buried in a rocky ravine. Later, my father burned the man's driver's license, hunting license, and wallet in the backyard fire pit. I watched the face on the plastic card melt into a runny mess.

Forest meat was supposed to age, hanging in a cloth bag for three or four days, depending on the weather. After that, we cut the meat off the bones and made steaks. The *vastus* muscles, *quadriceps*, and straps came off in long strips. The calves, *gluteus*, and shoulder muscles were hunks. We were always careful to clean up after butchering, and to make sure we never cut ourselves in the process. People have too many diseases.

To make her Solstice Roast, my mother took the largest, longest cut of leg muscle and dry-rubbed it with pepper, salt, thyme, rosemary, and a little garlic, then kept it very cool overnight. In the morning, she layered the top side with bacon and pine nuts, and then trussed it up with butcher's twine. Forest meat cannot be cooked hot or for very long, so it went into the oven just hours before the Solstice. The roast was sweet, and savory, and so tender that chewing it seemed almost impolite. My parents smiled at me and drank plum wine, my father getting red-faced and silly, reaching out to mess up my hair while we ate.

But before we ate, my father and mother took me to the crest of the hill, as they did every year, so we could watch the sun go down on the shortest day. When the bottom of the sun touched the Earth, my parents began the incantation:

We take from the Earth what is given,
As we will give ourselves to the Earth.
We eat what is here to be eaten,

As we ourselves will be eaten.
We eat what we must and what we can,
We who devour beast and devour man.

❄

THROUGH THE WINTER, we ate hamburgers made from ground rump. Sautéed medallions of meat cut from the straps. Delicious steaks of the biceps. Mother made a jerky, too, that she seasoned with peppercorns and bits of peach. I chewed this jerky while I went sledding.

Once I asked my father, "What's going to eat us when we're dead?"

"Critters," he said.

"And people will eat those critters?"

"Some of them, yep."

"Sometimes when I eat the meat, I think about what things the man must have said."

"Don't think about that. Just enjoy it. It's a sacrament."

"But only people speak. We don't eat other things that speak."

"Ever heard a deer grunt, or a bird sing?"

"Yes," I said.

"We eat a lot of things that speak."

❄

MOST RECENTLY, Lorrie made a dish she calls Mountain Gumbo, in honor of my geographic roots. It combines seitan, an imitation sausage called "Soyrizo," tomatoes, red peppers, and kidney beans. Its saving grace is the fresh thyme, delivering enough of an aromatic flashback to the wintry hills that I can make my way through the meal happily.

I devoured this at a Saturday lunch party. A number of Lorrie's lean, toned, yoga and running friends came over to her apartment, bringing their kale waffles, couscous, and lentil pâté. They also brought organic wine, which gives me a terrible headache.

As they ate, I studied their muscles: the *trapezius* of a woman runner; the thick shoulder of the long-haired yoga instructor all the women desire; Lorrie's excellent calves and glutes. I silently speculated at possible differences in flavor between the flesh of women and men, and the differences between various diets. I spread almond butter on a kale waffle and chewed it, nodding, visibly agreeing to its wonderfulness, although such stuff lacks so much in sheer edibility that I feel a pang of sorrow over my last winter in the Monongahela hills.

Child services finally came for me, as the police came for my mother and father. But not before Father and I had one last season.

My father asked me if I wanted to hunt a man that he and I had observed twice, in the third week of a warm November. I said that I did.

"You know everything you're supposed to do," he said. "And just be patient. If he doesn't show up, we'll go back tomorrow."

My father seemed nervous this time, something very much unlike him. I never found out why. Maybe he was worried about me because I was growing up and he thought I might want to see the outside world, and leave home, but I had no such desire then. Inside the unlit cab of the truck, we figured out a place to meet after my hunting: Father would go to that spot at noon and wait an hour, and if I did not appear, he would leave and then come back an hour before sundown.

He handed me the pistol. The weight and shape of that .22 forever impressed itself into my hand. I stepped out of the truck, into the cold, and tucked the pistol into the slash pocket of my orange hunting vest. Then I tightened my backpack, which held the ghillie suit, a canteen of water, and a small folding chair. My father looked at me, but he didn't say anything. I nodded and smiled and stepped away. He drove off.

I stood on the road until he was out of sight, and then I moved into the trees. Sunrise had just begun, and I saw the other hunter's truck parked off the road, almost against the trees. This fellow was already on his stand and surely heard our truck. I was careful to move slowly, quietly, until I found a good place in a small cluster of cedar trees along the scant trail that the man had used. I could see faint lines of his boot tracks here and there in the soil. I set down the folding chair so I could lean against a cedar, facing the way I had come. I took off my vest and stuffed it in the backpack, and then pulled the ghillie suit over my head, fitting my arms in the sleeves and then pulling the hood closed so just my eyes were uncovered. The hem of the ghillie suit hung to the laces of my boots.

Sitting on the chair, I was close enough to the trail that I knew I could rise and fire in one quiet motion. I held the pistol on my lap. The morning was cold, and I was glad I had worn my woolens.

I waited all day. I wondered about killing this man. I wondered how he might taste. I recalled that he was a tall man, with a belly, and would probably be very good. I imagined I had already killed him. I did this to still my nerves, so that when the time came, I could shoot without hesitation.

Endless thoughts brought on sleep, my mind filled with a dream that was much more odor than vision: fresh dough, rosemary, cloves, meat, cinnamon, sweet potatoes, squash. This reverie relaxed me so much that I nearly fell sideways out of the camp chair. Catching myself, awake, I heard movement.

Listening, I quickly realized the man was coming back down the trail. He was dragging a deer. I heard clearly the sounds of such exertion, yet I could not recall hearing a shot. A gray light coming through the clouds filled the trees. I held the pistol by my side. Out of the corner of my eye, I saw the man come along on the trail, laboring a few steps at a time with the weight of a large deer. He was humming with a tone of pleasure. I was immensely hungry. The man came even with me and did not notice me at all, his gaze set on the trail ahead. I smelled his sweat and the odor of his boots. He moved a step past me. He had his rifle slung across his back. I stood but did not raise the gun.

I thought of the incantation. I thought of winter nights with warm food. I whispered, "*We take from the Earth what is given.*"

The man heard me and turned halfway around, looking into the trees, looking for a person to match the voice. He saw my arm move and turned his head to face me. I fired at his forehead and hit him square. In that instant I saw that this fellow was not the man my father and I had watched. This was someone different. I did not recognize him as I stood looking down on his body. He had fallen on his side.

The heavy clouds hid the sun. I guessed at the hour of day:

almost noon. I hauled the deer into the space between the cedars where I had sat. It was a good buck, size-wise, but with skinny antlers.

I took off the ghillie suit, stuffed it in the backpack with the pistol, and put my orange vest back on. Then I took the rifle off the man. It was a really nice gun, and I hated to make it disappear, but I hid it deep in the brush. Then I dragged the man by holding his ankles, pulling him with all my might through the brush. I did not go very far. When I found a small clear space in the dense thicket, I did as I had learned: I stripped the man of every bit of clothing, hiding all that, and put his wallet, keys, and hunting license in my pack. I took the batteries out of the man's cell phone and GPS unit and put those devices in my vest pocket. I tied his bootlaces together and slung the boots over my shoulder. Then I went to see if I could find my father.

I walked down the road until I saw my father's truck parked along a stand of tall hemlocks. I slipped into the brush, waited a moment, and then I whistled. I heard his answering whistle. The sky was dark enough that I flashed my headlamp three times. Father came forward quietly, and I held up the boots for him to see. He nodded and smiled, but neither of us acted excited. We were doing something essential, the work of surviving. The day was dark, and quiet. The forest road was empty.

My father gestured at the hemlocks. I climbed one as high as I dared. In the dangling clusters of needles, I tightly wrapped the intertwined laces of the man's boots around the base of a branch, shoving the boots inward on their sides. Then I climbed down and we walked together into the woods.

As my father looked upon the man I had killed, I could tell something was wrong. Finally, he said, "I know this man."

"He's not the man we watched," I said. "I didn't realize until I had shot him."

"Why did you shoot him in the forehead?"

"He heard me and turned around."

"What?" He said this loudly, louder than we spoke in the woods, and he must have been angry.

"He heard me say the incantation. I spoke a line of it just before I raised my hand."

"Why didn't you just think it?"

"I must have just whispered it loudly enough. I'm sorry."

My father shook his head. "It doesn't matter now."

"Why isn't he the one we saw?" I asked.

"He must have borrowed his friend's truck and hunted in his friend's stand."

"Who is he?"

My father didn't answer. He handed me the knife, and I handed him the GPS, wallet, and phone, and then he went to find the buck.

The solidity and thickness of the man's legs surprised me. Even as sharp as the knife was, I had to press hard, sawing downward. I managed to do both legs, and the hams and glutes, without great trouble. The man's genitals were like a goat's. The smell of muscle and blood was overpowering. At first, it roused my hunger, but then settled it, and even repulsed it, as if I had gorged on the entire raw man. The odor of the blood was a thick scent of rust and syrup. The shadowy light distorted the colors of the man's body, everything a weird red, purple, and gray. I struggled with the muscles that ran along the spine, the ones that my mother cut into small medallions and sautéed. These came out ragged, incomplete. I was embarrassed.

In the mid-afternoon, my father returned, dragging the gutted deer. He must have sat with the buck, waiting, giving me time to do everything myself. We wrapped all the sections of forest meat and stuffed them in our backpacks, and then we hid or buried the man's leg bones, hands, head, and torso. As we worked, we heard the sound of a truck engine coming up the road. It stopped where the man's truck was parked. The engine cut off, and then two doors slammed.

"We'll have to find another way out," my father said. "Let's leave the deer. We'll get the packs in the truck, and then we'll come back for the deer."

We bushwhacked our way to the road, moving slowly so we made little noise. We had to cross a ravine below the roadbed, and I nearly fell backwards with the weight of my pack.

Father and I jogged down the road to the truck. I had sweated a lot while dressing out the man, and my legs and armpits chilled in the air as I ran. My father opened the back of the truck, and we shoved our packs inside. Then he closed it softly and locked it.

"I put my tag on that deer," Father said, "so we need to get it. We can't let anyone find it."

"Let's go," I said.

"If we meet those men, whoever they are, I'm telling them the buck ran a long way after I shot it, and it took us all morning to find it. I let you field dress it."

I nodded.

We walked back up the road, and then across the ravine. I didn't think I could have found the buck on my own, but I knew my father would find it. He grabbed the front legs, and I grabbed the back, making sure not to touch the scent glands at the joint, and we started a clumsy walk.

Doors slammed in the distance, and the truck engine started. The noise traveled across, in front of us, and as it moved up the road it slowed down. The men were looking at our truck. They sat there a while, and then drove on. But when my father and I were on the road, we saw the truck coming back.

"I'll talk to them, if they stop," my father said. "You know what to do if they talk to you."

I said, "Yes," intending to do it perfectly right. To this day, I do not know what gave us away. We both had blood on our clothes, me much more so.

Just as we carried the deer to the back of our truck, the other truck pulled alongside us. A big white man leaned out the driver's window and called out. My father walked over to talk to the man face-to-face.

"Nice deer," the driver said.

"Thanks. He's nice and fat," my father said.

"I don't know if I know you, but I think I recognize you," the man said, sounding both jovial and suspicious.

"I'm Charlie Suttree," Father said, and gestured toward me—"that's my son, Karl."

The man looked at me. I looked at him but did not nod or wave. I couldn't see clearly the man in the passenger seat, but he was also large.

"You seen anybody else out here?" the man said to my father.

"No. Saw a couple trucks parked but didn't see anybody."

"Where were you hunting?"

"This part of the unit," Father said, pointing over his shoulder to the woods on the other side of our truck.

"Didn't see anyone?"

"No. Why?"

The man studied my father for a moment. "Just looking for a friend, is all," the man said. The other man in the truck said something, and he and the driver talked quietly back and forth. The drive looked at my father again, saying, "Did your boy shoot that buck?"

"No. I did."

"With what?"

"My old fifty-cal."

"Fifty?"

"My old Hawken," Father said.

The men studied my father and me a moment longer, and then the driver put the truck in gear and sped away. We put the buck in the bed of our truck and drove off in the opposite direction, neither one of us speaking. My father did not like other people, and surely those men did not seem to like us. As a precaution, we stopped along the road, and he loaded and fired his flintlock into a distant tree, and then rubbed some black powder on his hands. At least his gun smelled like it had been used.

"Just remember everything I've taught you if strangers come to the house," Father said. "Do exactly the way your mother and I taught you, understand?"

I said that I did.

Some days later, my father, mother, and I again hiked to the hilltop to watch the sun go down, and we chanted again as a family. Their voices remain in my head, repeating over and over those words that defined us and bound us as one.

The Solstice Roast came out of the oven as wonderfully and richly as it ever had. The house smelled of onion and meat, black tea and bread, pumpkin, cider, and whiskey. I went to bed every night stuffed full, warm, and happy.

Just before New Year's, I was fixing a door on the side of the barn when I saw a line of cars come up the road quickly and fill the space in front of the house. I wanted to run, but I held steady, remembering everything I was told to do. I at least owed it to my mother and father to be dutiful, and so I was.

❄

YEARS, miles, schools, psychologists, foster parents, and many bland meals have long since separated me from that life in the woods. A horde of unremarkable people, their parade of mushy faces blending in my memory, thought they had taken the wild, weird child out of me, never fully explaining to me what I already knew: that I might never lose my taste for what I had eaten. My identity was kept a secret. My name was changed. My father was killed in state prison, and my mother died in another state prison, or so I was told—I never went looking or asking, as much as I wondered.

I might have seen my mother and father while they were being arrested at the house, but I don't remember. As far as my recollection works, the last time I saw them was in the light of the setting sun.

I sometimes wish they could eat a meal with me now, and understand how I use mushrooms and cumin, walnuts and lentils, or prunes and filo dough to keep myself in a certain way, to be this man who has this woman. Father might say, "Do you think you'll marry this girl?" and I'll say, "I should. She likes me and she likes to cook."

Indeed, I should marry Lorrie, if only to be able to nibble on her for the rest of my life—just sink my teeth lightly, gently, into the roundness of her hip or the beautiful slope of her shoulder, and dwell on the taste and scent of her. I make love like a man savoring a meal he can smell but not swallow and must imagine what it is to chew.

After we've rolled around in the bed on a Sunday morning, we shower, dress, and begin the ritual of the kitchen. She calls some friends, and then she describes to me the foods that they will bring. The yoga instructor lately has been baking a heavy bread with small hunks of yam and cranberry in it, and I think how wonderfully a slice of forest-meat ham would taste on that.

As they all gather, and talk, and taste, I fill my mouth, thinking of carved flesh crackling in a pan over a fire. I whisper to myself:

We eat what we must and what we can,
We who devour beast and devour man.

About the Author

Scott Bowen lives and writes in southeastern Pennsylvania. He is the author of a short-story collection, *The Midnight Fish* (Morris-Lee Publishing), and a satire, *The Vampire Survival Guide* (Skyhorse). He has written the annual April Fool's story for MidCurrent.com and has published previously in *Hospital Drive* (the literary journal of the University of Virginia Medical School), TheHorrorZine.com, and HelloHorror.com.

https://www.linkedin.com/in/scott-bowen-51296212/
https://www.facebook.com/scott.bowen.982
https://twitter.com/Beaufinn

CROSSROADS

MADISON ESTES

10 mph

RUST CRUSTED the edges of the beige car door, infecting the metal springs with orange and brown granules. Thomas's biceps bulged as he jerked it open. The Camry protested.

Ehhhhhheeeeeeeeeeee!

"Not this one," he said.

"The squeaking will go away with a little WD-40," Ruben replied, patting the hood like he would a dog's head.

"The squeaking won't go away until the door falls off this old piece of junk." Thomas shut the door, another shriek filling the air. "I need something bigger anyway."

The L.A. sun beat down on them as they strolled through the auction lot. As an actor, Thomas saw sunscreen as an investment in his future rather than a luxury, and so his pale skin was spared the sun's cruel wrath. Ruben was not so careful, and the bright summer day reddened his ears and shoulders.

The police auction was far bigger than Thomas expected. They'd checked in with the front desk (the window of a broken-down prison bus), filled out paperwork, and received a bidder card and auction list.

They spent the morning walking the yard, looking over each car with a fine-toothed comb. Ruben owned a junkyard and lived and breathed used cars. The Camry had been one of a dozen cars Ruben suggested that Thomas passed over.

"Yeah, wouldn't be easy to fit a car seat in there anyway," Ruben said. "You gotta think about things like that now."

Thomas scowled. "I guess." The words *As Is* floated around in Thomas's head as he passed dozens of signs reminding him all sales were final.

No refunds, he thought as the ultrasound flashed in his mind. *No returns. No going back.*

"It's not like we have to get one today," Thomas said. "I've got time."

When they came across the Porsche, Thomas almost passed it up. Not because of the state it was in, but because the mere fact that it was at a police auction made him suspect it was too good to be true. Thomas nudged Ruben anyway.

"What about this one?"

Ruben frowned. "A Porsche?"

"Look at the highest bid though. That's less than the Camry."

"Which means it probably won't run."

"Yeah." Thomas frowned. "But couldn't you fix it, or buy it off me for parts and make a profit?"

Ruben nodded. Without hesitation, Thomas made a bid. He and Cindy had nine months to get a safe car. He would sacrifice his dream condo, new headshots, late nights at The Echo and Skybar, if he could just have this one thing, this one remnant of the life he wanted. He could face what was to come if he had the Porsche. He would make the necessary compromises of his time and money, he would give and give without end, but he would not give this up. This was for him.

❄

20 mph

"I can't believe you came back with a Porsche." Cindy's hands were on her hips, and she glared at her boyfriend.

"Hear me out."

"We need a family car."

"And we'll get one. We're both going to be working when we move to the suburbs. We're both going to need cars," he said. "And there is a backseat in this. It's not the greatest; it's not President of the PTA mom material, but we can squeeze a baby back there if we have to."

"Did you just hear yourself? 'Squeeze a baby back there'?" She crossed her arms.

His hands rose in surrender. "Maybe that wasn't the best choice of words, but you get my point."

"Sure, let's just throw the baby back there with your stupid dumb-bells and gym gear."

"Why put him in the backseat at all?" Thomas scratched the back of his head and gave a little shrug. "We'll just chunk him in the trunk with a baby monitor."

"You mean a cell phone; baby monitors are so last gen."

"If he needs us, he'll text, right?"

"We're going to be great parents." She smiled. He wrapped his arms around her, planting a kiss on her cheek, then on her lips. He smiled into the kiss, and for a moment, his worries washed away.

❄

30 mph

As Cindy's belly swelled, so did his anxieties. His parents were gone, not that they had been there for him when they were alive. One pill popper and one drunk meant that he'd faced decades of broken promises and empty seats on opening nights. His grandmother had raised him, and her one piece of parenting advice to him before she passed away was, "Don't have children. It's not in our blood."

Thomas had done the best acting of his life in the past few months, pretending he felt as happy as Cindy and her parents. Sometime during the second trimester, Cindy began to show so much that every time he looked at her, all he could see was their future. Crying, tantrums, stress, messes, financial strain. But also, glittery cards on Father's Day, hugs, teaching his son or daughter how to fake cry their way out of a ticket. (Thomas had never been good at sports, and a father has to teach his child something.) His moods flipped like a tossed coin spinning in the air. Except when he was inside the Porsche—everything made sense in there.

He liked driving around the streets of L.A. like a bigshot, but he truly found serenity driving outside of L.A. where there was less traffic. His foot tapped the accelerator, and he passed the speed limit of 65 mph. He watched the speedometer pass 70...75...80...

"Don't have children."

85...

"It's not in our blood."

90...

"What do you know?" Thomas said. "You raised a fucking druggie."

95...

"You weren't there for me either, you fucking bitch. No one was."

100...

Several yards ahead, he saw a woman cowering in the street. Her screams filled the air. He slammed on the brakes. His knuckles whitened as he grasped the steering wheel. The car jerked to a stop.

She was gone.

He took a shaky breath. He stepped out of the car, looking everywhere for her, even under the car. When he got back into the driver's seat, he noticed the glove compartment had opened when he hit the brakes. He found a few pieces of junk mail he'd thrown inside, and a white rag inside. His forehead glistened, and he felt clammy. He grasped the rag to wipe perspiration from his face. As he unfolded it, he realized it wasn't a rag at all, but a baby onesie, with dark red stains across it. A deep male laugh echoed from the backseat. Thomas dropped the onesie on the floorboard as he spun around to look behind him. Nothing.

He picked up the onesie and tossed it in the glove compartment, then shut it. Shaken, he started the car and headed home. When he glanced in the rearview mirror again, he nearly swerved off the road.

The seatbelts were strapped in.

❄

40 mph

THOMAS BLEACHED his hair in the bathroom the next day. On a whim, he decided to go blonde instead of dying the grays out of his hair like he usually did. As he wiped some of the dye off with old rags, it reminded him of the onesie.

As soon as he'd gotten home the night before, he'd tried to put the whole bizarre drive out of his mind. He'd shoved the onesie in the trash and washed his hands afterwards. He didn't think it was likely, but he had to ask Cindy if she'd put the onesie there. He called and asked her about it after he finished washing his hair.

"No, I've barely been in your car," she said. "I know that's your mancave-on-wheels."

"Ha-ha. Very funny. I was just wondering how it got in there." He went to the garage to inspect the car.

"Who knows?" Cindy said. "That's the best part about buying things secondhand. All the fun little surprises you find."

He circled the Porsche like a cop sizing up a suspect.

Cheater was scratched into the driver's door.

"I have to call you back." Thomas's heart pounded. "Someone is on the other line. Could be work."

"Okay, I'm almost home anyway. See you soon."

This was just what he needed. Cindy had already been glancing over his shoulder when he was on the phone, throwing him suspicious looks whenever he mentioned going out at night. He couldn't say he blamed her. His mind hadn't been right since he saw that little plus sign on the pregnancy test. Cheating wouldn't be a huge leap considering he couldn't predict his own behavior from day to day.

The problem was that he wasn't having an affair, nor was he even entertaining the idea of it with anyone. He'd flirted with a few girls at the clubs, but never gave any one girl enough attention to think it meant anything. There wasn't anyone who would resort to vandalism to get back at him.

He grabbed a soft cloth and toothpaste and tried to buff the scratches out. His knees ached as he kneeled on the concrete, still buffing away when Cindy came home. He tossed the cleaning equipment in the corner and stood awkwardly when the door opened, trying to shield the word from her view.

"Hey."

"What the hell is that?"

A sigh escaped him. "I have no idea how this happened. I just…" He stopped when he noticed she was looking at his hair and not the car.

"Okay, Slim Shady. And is that toothpaste on your shirt?"

"Oh, yeah. I was just buffing the car." He turned to lean on the door, hiding the markings from her again.

She rolled her eyes. "You know, I'm starting to get a little jealous of that thing."

"Don't be silly." Thomas gave her a kiss on the forehead. She took his hand and he let her start to lead him out of the garage. When he glanced back, the word was gone. He pulled away from her and examined the door. His finger trailed along the metal, searching for the etchings. Cindy groaned.

"Oh my gosh, really? You buffed the hell out of it. It looks great. Are you going to admire it all night?"

He shook his head. "Of course not. Let's go inside."

❄

50 mph

"I MISS GETTING CARDED," Thomas whined as he and Ruben left the bar.

"Don't we all?" Ruben supported Thomas as they made their way to Ruben's truck.

"Hey, did you ever want to be in a band?"

"No, the only instrument I ever took to was the triangle, and there's not a huge demand for triangle-ists. Come on now, in you go."

Ruben dropped him off a little past midnight. Thomas staggered to his front door, laughing when he rang the doorbell. He couldn't remember the last time he'd been so drunk. It was the kind of drinking he was supposed to have been doing in his twenties and thirties when he was hopping from bar to bar using parties to meet people in the business instead of enjoying himself. He felt like he'd made up for twenty years in one night.

He tried to stick his key in the hole and giggled when the door opened.

"Hi, baby. I'm drunk."

"I heard." Her tone was clipped. "Ruben let me know he was dropping you off."

He zigzagged his way to the couch. The room spun like a tilt-a-whirl. Cindy stood next to him with her arms crossed.

She looked at him, and in that moment, he knew that she saw him as he really was. Not the life of the party, the B-list actor, the charmer who could talk his way into parties and out of tickets. Not the comedian or the guy with connections. She saw beneath the Porsche and the ridiculous new hair and the late-night drives and his sad need to hit every bar and club in L.A. before the baby arrived. She saw that he was a scared little boy in a grown man's body—an almost forty-year-old man, for Christ's sake—and he could feel shame and embarrassment radiating off of her. She shook her head and threw a blanket and pillow on their couch. He nodded, unable to meet her eyes. His stomach twisted as she continued to give him a look of disappointment, worse than anything she could have said. He had been flirting, not with another woman, but with the idea of being without her or their future child. And he had been caught.

"Thomas."

He closed his eyes, preparing for her to ask him what the hell he was doing. She placed one hand on her belly and the other on his leg.

"Do you hate us?"

"What? I... No," he said, placing his hand over the one she'd put on his knee. He squeezed her hand. "I love you."

"Then stop acting like your life is about to be ruined. Before it actually is."

She went into the bedroom and shut the door. The sound of the door locking echoed, as did her muffled crying.

❄

60 mph

IN THE MORNING, Cindy made pancakes and coffee and didn't mention the night before. He was grateful the Porsche was still at the bar. He didn't want to see the physical manifestation of his midlife crisis. Knowing the car was across town felt like a weight being lifted, although he didn't dwell on why he felt so much better with it gone.

He ditched an audition, and they spent the day together. They watched television, made love, decorated the nursery, and discussed baby names. They left behind the unpleasantness of the night before.

Ruben came over mid-afternoon to drive Thomas back to the bar to get his car. Thomas couldn't explain the mixed feelings stirring in him as they entered the parking lot and he saw the green Porsche sparkling in the sunlight. He'd anticipated that someone could have vandalized it overnight, but it looked like someone gave it a professional cleaning instead.

His stomach turned. Something told him not to get behind the wheel.

"Meet you back at the house?" Ruben said.

"Sure." Thomas stared out the window, making no move to exit the truck.

Ruben eyed Thomas up and down. "You okay? You look pale."

"I'm fine." Thomas got out and into his Porsche. His chest constricted. The air was wrong. It was heavy and solid. He rolled the window down and gasped. The drive home was bearable with the windows down, but he felt inexplicably exhausted once he got home. When he walked in, Ruben was setting the dining room table.

"That smells really good, Cindy," Ruben said. Thomas operated on autopilot. He greeted Ruben. Sat down. Ate. Listened to their banal conversation.

"I appreciate you inviting me to dinner. You know I cook about as well as Gordon Ramsay fixes cars."

Cindy laughed. "That's really funny, Ruben."

It wasn't that funny, Thomas thought. He grimaced when she hugged Ruben goodbye after the meal was over. Their hug was a little too long for his taste.

"You're fucking him, aren't you?" he said once Ruben was out the door.

"What?"

He knew it was insane the moment the accusation flew from his mouth. He chuckled. "I'm kidding, babe."

"What's gotten into you?" she said. An excuse was already forming in his mind, but he pushed it back. Her words scared him because something *had* gotten into him, and she used to be the person he could talk to about those kinds of things. He bit his lip. Maybe she still was.

"It's the car. I think there's something wrong with it."

"What?" Her eyebrows furrowed. She couldn't understand how the car connected to what had been happening to him. How could she? He didn't understand it himself.

"Maybe, like...a carbon monoxide leak. Not enough to make me pass out or die, just enough to make me feel funny, you know? I never should have gotten a car that was sold as is anyway. I don't fix cars like Ruben."

Cindy nodded. "Have Ruben take a look at it, or just sell it." She didn't reach out to him or hold him. He took her hand. He sighed in relief when she didn't pull away, although she didn't try to get closer to him either.

"Yeah, I should just sell it." He kissed her hand. "Everything is about to get a lot better."

She gave him a small smile and kissed his cheek. "I think so, too."

❄

70 mph

THOMAS DIDN'T OFFER to sell the car to Ruben, didn't want to involve him in whatever it was that was going on. He put an ad up on Craigslist and took the first bid. Thomas would still be making a grand in profit, but mostly he was just grateful the car would be off his hands.

As per the buyer's wishes, they met in a public place. Thomas introduced himself and shook hands with the potential buyer. He looked way too young to be buying a Porsche, probably mid-twenties, although everyone not on drugs looked younger in L.A. But Thomas didn't care to figure out the guy's financial situation. Cash was cash. He was just glad to be getting rid of the car.

"I bought this car in 'as is' condition, and that's how I'm selling it too."

"It runs though, right?"

"Absolutely. You want to go for a test drive?"

"Sure."

Thomas hesitated. He didn't really want to get in, but he didn't trust the kid not to drive off with the car. He opened the door, got in the passenger seat, and buckled up.

The kid got in and Thomas handed him the key. He tried to start the car.

Errrrrrrrraaaaahhhhhhhhhhhhhhhh ti ta ta ta.

Errrrrrrrraaaaahhhhhhhhhhhhhhhh ti ta ta ta.

"Sorry, dude. I'm gonna have to walk away from this one," he said, getting out.

"Wait!" Thomas said, but the kid was already on his way back to the car he came in. Thomas tried to get out, but the door wouldn't open.

"Let me out. Let me out, come on."

"You don't want out of this car, Thomas. You want out of this life, and I don't blame you one bit."

Thomas spun around and looked into the backseat. A man was sitting back there in a three-piece suit, legs crossed, arms resting on the backs of the seats.

Thomas's eyes widened and he froze. "Who the fuck are you?"

"I'm Rick Stanson, and once upon a time, I owned this car."

"Get out. Or let me out," he said. "Now."

The man chuckled. Thomas recognized it as the same laugh he'd heard during his strange drive.

"You were there," Thomas said, "when I almost had that accident."

"That was a good night. And between you and me, it wasn't an accident. At least not the first time it happened."

Thomas closed his eyes, seeing the woman's figure cowering under the headlights. He shook his head. "That really happened?

"Yes, it did, and it was one of the best nights of my life."

Thomas's mouth dropped open.

"She deserved it," Rick said. "That homewrecking bitch ruined my life. I offered to pay for an abortion. She didn't want one. I offered to pay her rent and all her expenses, a well-kept mistress, and visit her and the child regularly. A second family. She didn't want that. I offered to let her go off on her own and raise the child and still financially support her. Do you know what she did? That whore told my wife everything, the sneaking around, the expensive gifts, the business trips that weren't business trips. She even showed her letters I wrote. She held nothing back; nothing was sacred to her. She said she did it because she wanted her child to know their siblings, that the secret had to come out, but I know she was just jealous and wanted to ruin my family so I'd be stuck with her. Well, I showed her, didn't I?"

"Jesus," Thomas said. That woman's screams came back to him. He looked over his shoulder, expecting her to pop up and bang against the side window. He took a shuddering breath.

Rick went on casually. "I like to think about what she might have felt in her final moments. Fear. Defeat. Regret. I remember the feeling of her striking my front bumper. The sudden impact jolting me forward, the seatbelt yanking me back. I can still see exactly how far the car threw her.

"She didn't move after I hit her the first time, but she wasn't dead, so I drove over her again, slowly crushing her under my wheels. I still think about her bones breaking under the weight of this car, the crevices in the rubber tires filling with blood. Her screams. Her hair stuck in the grill.

"I felt two bumps when I drove over her the second time. First, I crushed her, then the car bounced and tilted a bit higher—that's when I knew I'd crushed *it*, that I'd turned her baby bump into an indentation."

"Stop." Thomas winced. He tried to open the door again, to no avail. As he pulled the handle harder, his grip weakened. His chest tightened. He gasped, jerking on the handle again.

"They didn't replace the tires, just hosed them down," Rick said. "Everything in the car is 'as is.' If you sprayed luminol down there, it would light up like the Fourth of July."

"Just let me out. This has nothing to do with me."

"Oh, but it does." He leaned forward. "You'll see."

Thomas kept yanking on the handle. The car interior began to shift around him. The driver's window doubled, then quadrupled. He turned his head. The last thing Thomas saw before he passed out was Rick Stanson's beady eyes peering at him from the backseat.

❄

100 mph

THOMAS AWOKE to children's voices blaring from the radio, singing a familiar nursery rhyme.

"*The people in the road go thump, thump, thump,*
thump thump thump, thump thump thump,

The people in the road go thump thump thump,
As they fall down."
He hummed along, dimly aware those were not the correct lyrics.
"The bones in the bodies go crunch crunch crunch
crunch crunch crunch, crunch crunch crunch
The bones in the bodies go crunch crunch crunch—"
He shook his head and rubbed his face, trying to wake himself.

"That's my children singing, you know." Rick grinned at him in the rearview mirror, the smile of a proud father. "I only get to hear their voices on the radio now. Do you know what that's like? An eternity away from my own children. Hell isn't hot enough for her. I hope that's where she is now. If I deserve it, so does she."

Thomas shook his head again, still dazed. Darkness was all around him. Streetlights shined from above. He must have been asleep for hours. It felt like the car was doing donuts even though they were parked. The singing continued.

"The baby under the tires goes squish squish squish—"

"Stop it!" Thomas yelled.

"I miss my children," Rick went on. "My real children. Not the bastard that whore carried inside of her. Probably wasn't even mine."

Thomas choked, the air hot and heavy. He tried opening the door again. When that failed, he beat on the window.

"Let me out!"

"You have a one-track mind, don't you? You haven't even figured out why it's so hard to breathe in here."

Thomas met Rick's eyes in the rearview mirror. He turned his head and found the backseat empty. Rick smirked at him in the mirror.

"Can you believe that whore had the nerve to speak to my children? My wife might have planned to tell them in a gentle way, but Susanne got to them first. God knows what she told them. My children hated me. I had nothing to live for after she ruined my life, so I ended it in this car. Gassed myself. But it doesn't have to be like that for you. Not all bastard children have to ruin lives."

"Cindy and the baby aren't ruining my life." He concentrated on breathing. *Inhale,* exhale. *Inhale,* exhale. His lungs refused to cooperate, just as they did when he forgot his lines on opening night, or when he saw that pink plus sign on the pregnancy test all those months ago.

"Aren't they? What are you going to miss out on because of them?"

As he thought about the future, he didn't see as many missed opportunities as he did before. He didn't care about not having time for auditions or money for clubs. He just wanted to be there with Cindy and their baby. He wanted to let her squeeze his hand when the baby came. He wanted to know if he was having a son or a daughter. He wanted to hold his own flesh and blood.

As if reading his thoughts, Cindy's name appeared on the radio display as the car called her.

"No," he whispered. "No. Please, no."

"Hello?" She sounded like she just woke up. "Thomas, where are you? I thought—"

"Call the cops! Call 9-1-1. I'm being held hostage." Thomas banged the buttons on the steering wheel, trying to end the conversation.

"Hello? Thomas? I can't hear you."

"Hang up and call 9-1-1."

"Hello?"

"Oh baby, thank God I got ahold of you," Rick said in a voice that sounded just like Thomas. It came from the speakers. "Meet me outside of town. I'll text you the location. There's no time to explain. I need your help."

"Okay." Her voice trembled.

"No!"

"And Cindy," Rick said in his perfect Thomas voice. "I love you."

"I love you too. See you soon."

The call ended. Rick, suddenly appearing in the back, crawled over the divider into the passenger seat. The car started up and rolled forward.

"You're not the only one that can act." Rick smirked. Thomas grabbed him by his suit jacket and threw him against the dashboard.

"What the hell did you do?"

"I'm saving you. You'll thank me someday."

"What have you done? What are you planning?" The car swerved as it made an abrupt right turn. Thomas fell over, still holding onto Rick's jacket.

"It's almost time," Rick said. "It's July tenth. The day you become free."

"What's so special about July tenth?"

"It was the day I became free. In my case, death was freedom. But for you, death will only be the beginning."

"This isn't happening. This isn't real."

"Oh, it's real. As real as that baby trap, as real as crushed dreams and potential. My life was over the moment Susanne spilled everything to my wife, but yours doesn't have to be. You have your whole life ahead of you. That bitch wants to take it all away. She's jealous because you have talent, real potential to do something with your life, and she'll never be anything special. She got pregnant to trap you. Most 'unplanned' pregnancies are entrapment. History is full of poor saps stuck with manipulative women because they were too good to walk away from them. You're not going to be one of them."

"If you kill her, I go to jail and my life is over."

"Nonsense. That's why we're meeting her far away. It will be quite easy to clean up a body hit in the middle of nowhere. This car cleans up after itself, in case you haven't noticed."

"Don't do this," Thomas said. His grip weakened.

"It's already done." A maniacal grin spread across Rick's face. He went on and on about his mistress, and all Thomas could think about was Cindy, how she was almost due, and she was driving out to meet him in the middle of the night no questions asked because she was concerned about *him,* scared for *him,* because he hadn't been himself since he got the car, or even before then.

He wanted to cry. He'd failed her. He'd been failing her for a long time.

"If you don't want to watch, just go to sleep. When you wake up, this will all be over."

"No." Lightheadedness set in, threatening to knock him unconscious again. He straightened up.

"You can't have her." As the words left him, he realized he misspoke. "*Them.* You can't have them."

He grabbed the wheel and yanked it to the right, steering them headfirst into a tree.

❄

0 mph

CINDY SCREAMED at the top of her lungs for the second time that day. The first had been when she found her boyfriend's car smashed into a palm tree. Their last conversation played in her mind, how final it seemed, and between contractions, she wondered if he'd driven into it on purpose to escape them.

He'd seemed so happy the past few weeks. She knew a lot of people who committed suicide were, because they knew the end of their problems was in sight, but she hadn't thought he'd been that conflicted about parenthood. They'd made plans for the future. He wanted his child. Didn't he?

Pain shot through her abdomen, and thoughts of the collision ended. All she could think about was the fact that she was alone. No one had expected the baby to come for another two weeks. Thomas was supposed to be there, her parents were supposed to be there, and she was by herself in a strange hospital bringing a fatherless child into the world.

She screamed again, and after one more aching push, her baby boy screamed along with her.

❄

RUBEN CAME THE NEXT DAY, after her parents and friends left to get some rest. Bouquets and stuffed animals covered every surface of the room. All the flowers and teddy bears made the hollow look in her eyes seem worse somehow.

"I'm sorry, Cindy."

"Me too."

"That fucking car." Ruben shook his head.

"Do you think the car malfunctioned?" She clutched the bedsheet. He hesitated.

"I think it was a bad car." His hairy, plump hand rested on the bed's handrail. "He loved you. He was selling that car for you, because he was coming to his senses. It was an accident."

She nodded. After Ruben saw the baby and offered congratulations as well as more condolences for Thomas, the nurse took the baby to the nursery so Cindy could rest. When she woke up, she went to check on him. A man she'd never met before was looking into the nursery, focusing on her son.

"It looks just like him," he said, shaking his head.

"Who are you?"

"A man without children." He turned to her and smiled sadly. "And now a man without a home. Without purpose."

His gaze returned to her baby. He smirked.

"He'll be a handful. You keep him close, won't you? Children must be kept close. They can be taken from us at any moment."

"I want you to leave. Right now. I'm calling security."

He nodded toward her and turned to go. He walked next to the window into the blinding sunlight and vanished. She blinked, certain that her eyes were playing tricks, but did not see him walk down the hall or hear his shoes on the tile floor. He was there, and then he wasn't.

Just like Thomas.

❄

INSURANCE DECLARED the car a total loss. Ruben bought what remained of it once it became available for salvaging and took it to his junkyard. The walls of the baling press closed in on the broken windows, the unhinged doors and crushed hood. What remained of the Porsche curled in on itself like a swatted spider's legs folding against its body. When the machine finished compressing, it ejected the metal through the hole in the side. It was hard to believe so much devastation could come from something that could be crushed into the size of a small refrigerator. As Ruben stared at the heap of metal, he felt like he'd avenged his friend's murder, killed a killer rather than simply crushed a couple tons of metal into a compact form.

He waved away one of the approaching forklifts. The employee furrowed his eyebrows and shrugged.

"I'll take care of it myself." Ruben stared at the metal with a sense of wariness. He had a spot picked out for it, a grave he'd dug just for the sole purpose of putting it to rest.

"This one's not for sale."

About the Author

Madison Estes is a freelance editor and writing instructor at The Writing Barn. She is a recipient of the 2020 Ladies of Horror Fiction grant and the Mystery Writers of America Helen McCloy scholarship. She is the editor of *Road Kill: Texas Horror by Texas Writers Vol. 6.* She lives in southeast Texas and has three dogs. She runs a hybrid horror-tube/authortube channel on YouTube. You can find her on Twitter @madisonestes or Instagram @madisonpaigeestes or visit her website: authormadisonestes.wordpress.com.

SOCIAL MEDIA LINKS

Amazon Author Page: https://www.amazon.com/Madison-Estes/e/B07B7M9ZGB%3Fref=dbs_a_mng_rwt_scns_share
Instagram: https://www.instagram.com/madisonpaigeestes/
Twitter: https://twitter.com/madisonestes
Facebook: https://www.facebook.com/madison.paige.estes
Website: https://authormadisonestes.wordpress.com/
YouTube: https://www.youtube.com/channel/UCmB7qxgKgHqbETdıiwUXrlA

THE WAY THIS WILL END

ANDY RAFFERTY

I

"I'M READY," Mia said.

Angie glanced up, her fork halfway to her mouth. "Sorry?" she said through a mouthful of scrambled egg.

"I'm ready," Mia said again.

Angie frowned, then her expression softened. She swallowed.

"Are you sure?" she asked carefully. Mia nodded without saying anything more.

"Cool," Angie said. She looked down at the remains of her omelette, then back up at her wife, half a smile on her face. "Cool," she said again, and continued eating.

2

An hour after breakfast, Angie was working on the boat in the wooden shack she always referred to as the garage. Checking the engine, checking the wooden hull, making sure everything was in order. Once she'd finished, she made sure all her tools were clean and in their assigned spaces.

She closed up behind her, locked the door, and hung the key on a nail she'd hammered into the doorframe. She stood with her hands in her pockets for a few moments, staring at nothing in particular, then started back towards the house.

She glanced over towards the far bank and froze. A pack of the dead were shambling along in the shadow of the trees. A dozen of them, some still wearing the tattered remains of army fatigues. Most were naked, their livid skin twisted with signs of conflict. One had no arms, another was missing its jaw.

Even now, after all this time, her instinct was to run. She fought it down. Movement might attract one of them, if it happened to look in her direction, and while there was little chance they would make it across the water or up the steep cliffs, it was not worth taking any risks at this stage.

She watched them pass, trying to keep her breathing steady, half-wishing she had her rifle. She knew it was pointless to take potshots at a pack like this, and that all she would be doing would be risking drawing the attention of more of them. But it would be something. Sometimes the only way to keep the numbness from swallowing her was to do something. Anything.

But in the face of that horror...it was all one in the end, she supposed.

Once she was sure the pack was gone, she resumed walking but couldn't stop glancing over at the far shore and checking to make sure there were no more. It was some time before her heartbeat subsided back to its normal rhythm.

3

They'd been lucky, obviously. For a given value of lucky.

Even when the first stories had started on the news, Mia could already see which way the wind was going. They'd had one terse conversation, sitting in front of the 24-hour news, and they'd wasted no time. The car was packed and ready to go within the hour and that meant they left the city well ahead of the panic.

They'd seen pictures, while there was still television. Miles-long jams of cars and vans, the shrieking of horns and swearing of drivers and passengers turning to anguished screams as the apocalypse caught them sitting on the motorway. People jumping from overpasses. Fire devouring the living and the dead.

By that time, they were safely—relatively safely—at Harry and Liz's house. Mia's brother welcomed them with tight, quick hugs, his eyes wet, talking lightly about how it was nice of them to visit and they could stay until the situation was resolved.

It was clear that Liz was putting on a brave face for the sake of her family, but she didn't share her husband's optimism that this was all going to be over in a couple of weeks. She and Angie had finished off a bottle of wine together on the back patio the night they arrived, and talked about the things they'd read on the internet until long after their respective spouses had collapsed exhausted into their beds.

Harry and Mia's other sibling, Ian, was supposed to be picking up their mother from the nursing home outside Exeter. He wasn't answering his phone. Harry said it was probably just a problem with the network or something, but it wasn't clear who he was trying to convince. They'd seen pictures on the news of people attacking telephone masts, convinced that it was 5G that was to blame for the troubles. Harry had waxed lyrical about morons making the situation worse. Angie kept her thoughts to herself. People were afraid, and grasping at straws, and she privately thought it would probably all be the same in the end regardless.

They never found out what happened to Ian, or to the sparkling elfin woman Angie remembered from the wedding, wearing a brand-new hat and bursting with pride as she carefully led Mia down the aisle, clinging to her daughter's arm.

That nice house in the nice rural village nearly became their tomb, of course. Again, it was Mia who got them moving. The night of the last broadcast from News 24, there'd been a blazing row about what they were going to do. Harry was adamant that they were safe here, and Mia just pointed out over and over that there was nothing between them and London except wide open spaces, and roads. Towards the end

Harry broke down, nearly struck his sister, desperate not to abandon the house because it was where Ian would be bringing Mum. Mia had shouted at him that Ian was dead, that their mother was dead, and that if they didn't move, they'd all be dead too.

Angie and Liz had to separate them, try to be voices of reason. They could leave a message for Ian, tell him where they were going. He could catch up with them. They couldn't afford to take the chance, not with the children to think of.

4

Mia was in the kitchen when Angie came in, writing at the table. Angie didn't tell her about the pack— she never bothered her wife with news of the dead unless she absolutely had to. She stood in the doorway for a few minutes, watching Mia write. Her tongue protruded as she concentrated, occasionally blowing at an errant strand of loose hair that kept falling forward over her eyes.

She looked very tired, and it made Angie's heart ache to look at her like this. She opened her mouth to say something, then thought better of it and crossed the kitchen to stick the kettle on the hob, making a little more noise than she needed to as she scooped instant coffee and dried milk into mugs. When she turned round, her eyes were quite dry.

"What do you fancy for lunch?" she asked. "I thought I might go through the cupboards, sort things out. Label things. You know, in case..."

Mia didn't look up from her work.

"In case...?"

"Well, you know. In case anyone comes by after we've gone. Other survivors. If I was scavenging, I think it'd be a great help to know what was where. 'Specially if I was in a rush or whatever."

Mia finished what she was doing and put her pen down. She took a moment to pin some loose strands of hair back behind her ear before answering.

"Do you think that's likely?" she asked quietly.

Angie shrugged.

"Not really but...you never know. It's not as if we can take it with us when we leave."

"Fair, I suppose." Mia contemplated her wife thoughtfully, took the proffered cup of coffee, but didn't drink anything. "You'll probably want to clear out the perishables," she said after a moment or two. "Anything open. Just leave the tins and the sealed stuff, otherwise things will rot. Also make sure that the plastic bottles are labelled properly. Don't want people mistaking Domestos for something if they're in a rush and..."

"Do you want to do it?" A slow smile crept across Angie's face.

Mia echoed her smile, a little ruefully. "Sorry, love, sorry. I can't help myself. No. No, I'm going to go and say goodbye to the chickens."

"Are you sure they're going to be alright?" Angie asked. The chickens and their eggs had been a godsend, and she didn't want to see them come to any harm. Neither of them did.

"They'll be fine," Mia reassured her. "There's no predators here for them to worry about particularly, and they're not stupid. They'll have somewhere warm and dry to sleep, and the run of the island. Ellen will look after them."

Ellen was the largest of the chickens, a bossy, blustery bird who brooked no nonsense and ruled the chicken run like a benevolent dictator.

"Cool," Angie said. "You do that, and I'll make a start in here. I've already seen to the garage."

Mia pecked her on the cheek as she went past, taking her coffee with her.

5

In the end Harry and Liz's neighbours, a pleasant couple called Daphne and Miles, had come with them. Three cars in convoy making for the coast. It was Daphne who'd suggested that they get off the mainland, put some water between them and trouble, and even Harry had seen the sense in her suggestion. They'd made a game of it for the children, packing the cars up at four in the morning while the kids were still yawning and struggling to get dressed.

Even so, they'd almost left it too late. As they were pulling out of the village, there had been a sound of shattering glass and a scream, dark shapes moving quickly through the narrow streets. Mia had wanted to go back, to try and help, but Angie had refused, putting her foot down.

Something had loomed ahead of her through the darkness, a black shape outlined briefly in the orange glare of a streetlight, and she'd run it down. It was probably one of the dead, but even if it hadn't been... She dreamt about that night from time to time, and in her dream she was alone in the car and she woke up from those dreams sobbing.

They'd made it to the coast, and they'd found a boat, and they'd crossed the narrow span of sea to the island and the holiday cottage that Daphne and Miles's old friend had told them they could use any time they wanted. They'd been expecting to find their friends there, but the island was deserted. Everything neat and tidy, but no signs of life apart from the chickens, a belligerent and unfriendly goat, and some raucous gulls.

Television ended for good about a week after they reached the island. The radio continued for another few months, then it, too, went silent, drowned in a despairing chorus of white noise.

They were self-sufficient for a while. The island had a generator and plenty of supplies. Once a month they'd make a careful, quiet foray onto the mainland to supplement their stocks with whatever they could find, marking off the little villages and isolated hamlets on the map Harry kept pinned to the corkboard in the kitchen.

Sometimes these raiding parties went without a hitch, the settlements they visited having been evacuated one way or another. Sometimes they didn't. Nineteen weeks after they'd reached their island sanctuary, they were looting a service station when Miles opened the wrong door at the wrong time and a dozen ravenous horrors poured out and over him, tearing and biting and ripping him into ribbons of tattered flesh and broken bones. The others barely made it back to the car.

None of them were prepared for Miles's death, but Daphne seemed to take it in her stride. She listened as they explained what had happened, and she cried—they all cried—but she seemed to put a brave face on it. They all knew the risks.

It was Angie who found her. She'd brought up a cup of tea and some biscuits and stood outside the bedroom door for five minutes, gently tapping. In a way she'd known after the second rap with no response what had happened, her stomach twisting like she was going down in a fast elevator. Daphne had taken an overdose of sleeping tablets. There was no note. There was no need.

6

They had a light lunch and chatted quietly about what they'd do afterwards. Mia wanted to pack up the camping equipment from the attic and bring it downstairs, which inevitably resulted in Angie humping boxes down the stairs while Mia sorted through clothes in the bedroom, packing up the wet and cold weather gear into plastic boxes they carefully labelled and stacked in the kitchen.

After they finished, they took a shower together, using up the last of the hot water. Then they went out to pay their last respects to Daphne, buried in the shadow of the apple trees behind the house. Angie brought out the wedding photo in the silver frame that had been in the lounge since they'd first arrived, and left it propped up against the trunk of the tree.

Then they settled down with two bottles of wine, the last of the precious frozen pizzas, and the cassette player.

Curled up on the couch in the living room as the sun went down, they talked and listened to music, and laughed together like they had in the days before everything fell apart.

7

With Daphne and Miles gone, something changed in the house. Harry's temper deteriorated. He shouted at the kids, at Liz, at Mia. He never shouted at Angie.

In the end she took him aside and told him to get a grip, and his eyes blazed and for a moment she thought he was actually going to hit her and then he burst into tears. She didn't quite know what to do with him, held him awkwardly while he sobbed. As long as she'd known him, her brother-in-law had been absolutely certain about everything and now... It was upsetting seeing him falling apart.

They soldiered on for a few weeks. Harry stopped coming with them to the mainland. They never talked about it. It made things a little more difficult, but they coped. Their raiding trips were taking longer and longer, as they were forced to push further and further afield. They talked briefly about trying to go inland, rather than pick at the villages along the coast, but neither of them wanted to risk that. Not yet anyway.

Sometimes they were forced to spend the night away from home. On nights like that, as they huddled together on a flat roof over-looking the quayside or barricaded themselves in an attic behind locked doors and stacked furniture, Angie couldn't sleep for the terrible dread that ate at her insides. The certainty that they'd become overconfident, that this was the night the dead would come in force and break down the doors and end them the way Miles had ended... But they survived.

8

Six weeks after Miles and Daphne left them, Harry announced he and Liz were leaving too. He pointed out the army base on the map. He was certain there would be people there. Safety. Stability. Mia and Angie were welcome to come with them—should come with them—but if they didn't want to, he'd be sure to tell the army where they were so they could come and collect them.

Mia tried to talk them out of it, but he was adamant.

"At least leave the kids here," she begged him at the last. "If it's safe, you can come back for them. Please, Harry."

He refused to listen. The next morning as the sun was rising, they took the boat across to the mainland. Harry and Liz and the kids bundled up against the cold winter air, with packs full of stuffed toys, and sleeping bags, and the ham radio that had not picked up any signals in months.

They left most of the supplies—Harry was confident they wouldn't need much, and joked that if they did, they'd just hit a Tesco Direct. He was all smiles now, making the children laugh and treating it all like a great adventure. But Liz didn't laugh.

The night before they left, Angie and Mia both tried convincing her not to go. She refused to listen, and became more obstinate the more they argued.

"If there's nothing there, we'll just come back," she said, repeating herself until she lost her temper and went to bed with a terse: "Thank you for your concern, but we know what's best for our children," and a curt: "Goodnight."

Everyone said their goodbyes on the dock, and as they drove off, a light dusting of snow began to fall. Mia insisted on waiting on the quayside for the rest of the day, just in case they came back, just in case they needed the boat to get them to safety on the island. But they didn't, and as evening started to darken into night, Mia finally gave up and they rowed back across the water.

"Maybe they'll be alright," Mia said, talking more to herself than to her wife.

"Maybe," Angie said, not believing it.

9

Two years they stayed on the island, and then Mia started finding it more and more difficult to get up in the morning. She did her best to hide it from Angie, but without much success. They'd sat at the table as Mia calmly, matter-of-factly in her best bedside manner explained the likely situation, the likely prognosis. It was not good. In some ways, the lack of emotion in Mia's words had hurt Angie more than the grim fact of her decline.

They'd fought, not like the blazing rows of their younger days but a cold, harsh fight of bitten-off words and carefully channelled anger and a frustration that had more to do with the unfairness of it all than anything else. In the end Mia relented, gave Angie a list of things to look for, and begged her to be careful.

The trip to the town had been... It was bad. Even now it was bad. Angie'd very nearly failed to come back, but ultimately she was lucky, and she made it in and out again, and she made it back to Mia. She even managed to get some of the drugs she'd gone for, and for a little while the situation improved. Mia was back to her usual self.

Neither of them made the mistake of thinking it would last, and Angie had the dull certainty that next time she would not be coming back from the city, and that Mia wouldn't let her go anyway.

So they talked.

10

The generator fell silent a little after nine o'clock. Angie lit some candles.

"Are you sure?" she asked again, practically whispering.

"Yes," said Mia again. "You don't have to..."

Angie cut her off, kissing her forehead. "We said when we went, we'd go together. You can't leave me alone with the monsters."

They lay together on the sofa for a little while, wrapped around each other, just breathing and listening to the sound of their hearts. If there were tears, they were quiet ones.

"I think it's time to go to bed," Mia said eventually.

Angie hugged her tightly, nodded, took her hand, and together they went up the stairs for the last time.

11

The house is quiet, now. If you listen carefully, you can hear Ellen in the yard bossing the other chickens around. Everything is in its place, stacked neatly, labelled. Everything is still.

At the top of the stairs, four precisely placed drawing pins fasten a note written in a neat, careful hand to the firmly closed bedroom door.

ONLY SENTIMENTAL ITEMS WITHIN.
PLEASE TAKE ANYTHING ELSE YOU LIKE, BUT LEAVE US IN
PEACE.
GOOD LUCK.
MIA AND ANGIE

About the Author

Andy Rafferty writes for a live-roleplaying game company; his job involves coming up with scenarios designed to make people fight. In his spare time, he tries to come up with stories that make people afraid. He lives in Lancashire with his partner and a cat and thinks there should be more sad apocalypse stories.

LINGERING TRINKETS

TARVER NOVA

WAY on the edge of town, just before civilization gives way to corn-stalks, the antique shop sits lonely. Its gravel parking lot is empty, lit by moonlight. The only sign of life: a single shaded bulb above its front door, casting a cone of light and moths at its stoop.

The door jangles as six-year-old James and his Papa enter the shop. The smells hit James first. Wet wood, like Papa's old barn after a rain. Festering dust, like Nana's closets. Still packed with her things, so long after she left.

The shop is claustrophobic, long but not wide. Stained glass lamps line the walls. To the left stands a shop counter, unmanned. The wall behind it is plastered with posters from eras far older than James. The right wall hosts intricate cuckoo clocks, tick-ticking in a flurry, all the way down the shop. Between the two walls: tall, gnarled-oak book-shelves knot the length of the room, each overflowing with antiques large and small.

A door groans from the back, and a withered man hustles along the clock wall. Younger than Papa, but as eroded as his antiques.

"Mister Olsen," calls the shopkeep, his voice crunchy like the parking lot. "I see y' brought your grandkid."

The men shake hands. The shopkeep reaches past Papa and locks a deadbolt high on the door.

"Meant to close up already," he says, but he flashes them a yellowed smile. "But for you, Mister Olsen, I'm always happy to chat."

The shopkeep rounds his counter and settles in. Papa leans on the counter casually, as if the shopkeep is an old friend. They start talking about old cars.

James stares at the junk on the shelves ahead. He sighs.

The men look to him.

"Something wrong, James?" his Papa says.

James shuffles his feet. "No, it's just..." He shrugs. "This looks like stuff only Nana would like."

The shopkeep laughs, startling James.

"Y' know what, kid?" he says. "You're *right*."

He waves James over and slaps a knee. James demurs. He doesn't know this man.

"It's fine, James," his Papa says, nodding. "He ain't gonna hurt you."

So James has no choice. He crosses his arms and approaches. The shopkeep pulls James up on his knee. He smells of mildew and cigarette smoke. Dirt has burrowed under his nails.

James distracts himself with the shopkeep's counter. An antique metal register, so old the numbers are worn right off. A rotary phone. An antique black safe. But he pauses when he spots something not so antique. Sitting atop the safe, there's a gun. Polished and gleaming. Something primal builds in James, a deep-rooted unease he doesn't fully understand—

"Listen, kid," the shopkeep says. "Your Nana? She *loved* this place."

"Really?" James says. "Papa, is that true?" Papa gives him a pursed smile and a nod.

"Could hardly drag her out of here," Papa says. "This was practically her second home." He looks out to the antiques. His eyes glimmer in the dim light.

The shopkeep snickers. He ruffles James's hair. "In *faaact*," the shopkeep says, "after your Nana went missing...didn't you drop off some of her trinkets, *Papa*?"

"Well, yes," Papa says, head drooping. "Couldn't bear to keep 'em around." He rubs the shine out of an eye. "Though look at all those antiques. It's like she's still with us."

James blinks wide. "So I might find her old things here?"

"Maybe," the shopkeep says. "Maybe they're all sold off." He scratches a sandpapery cheek.

James stares at the shop with a newfound awe. It feels suddenly like a treasure hunt: any one trinket could be Nana's.

The shopkeep chuckles to his Papa. "Well, see that glitter in his eye. Might got a little antiquer for a grandson!" He pats James's shoulder. He leans in. "Or are you a little shophand? Wanna work here?"

James wiggles, and the shopkeep lets him hop down.

"Ah, get to it, kid," the shopkeep says. "Even got a toy section, back corner."

The shop feels brighter now. Flickers of metal catch the wan light ahead. James shuffles into the winding bookshelves, weaving for the back corner. Papa's voice follows: "And we ain't got cash to buy!"

On the first shelf: a model tractor, a tiny cabinet of curiosities, a snow globe. No organization. They're only family because they're old. He's so distracted, he trips on boxes at the foot of a shelf. Dust wafts up, and he waves a hand to disperse it.

He feels his Nana all around him. So many things he'd show her. A ship in a bottle. A frog statue with a felt top hat. She collected items like these: different and exciting and weird. *My little magpie*, Papa called her. *My little bird*.

To think he might be looking at the same trinkets she once owned.

In the back corner, a single lightbulb hangs above. Unlike the unstained bookshelves in the rest of the store, all the toy shelves are painted, each a solid color, forming a dried-out rainbow.

Toys are scattered about, little scenes left from past playtimes. All worn, all dirty, but the rust and the cracked paint only make them more interesting. And in the very corner, wedged between shelves, stands a full-size traffic lamp, nearly as tall as James.

He squats down and grabs a race car. Pushes it back and forth, testing out the wheels. They squeak, but spin well enough. So he lines it up, gives a hearty "*bruum-bruuuum*," and shoves it on its way. It rolls past a one-eyed teddy bear, a mechanical cowboy, a plastic doll. Clatters across oversized puzzle pieces before catching a wheel on an abandoned book. It flips, crashing upside-down against the bookshelf.

James laughs, but as he stands, he hears a tiny bell ringing from the shelf. The car must've roused another toy.

He finds tin bird figures on flowery pedestals, each no wider than James's palm. One white bird, one black, facing each other. The white bird is moving. It dips forward and back on its pedestal, and its wings flap. With each forward dip, it pecks at a flower, which rings a tiny bell inside. Gears within the pedestal click and whir.

He smiles. "I'd get this for you, Nana," he says softly.

Just as he turns away, the bird starts hitching, flapping in short bursts. Slow, then fast. Slow, then fast, its gears inside whining, making a strange sound. Almost like speaking.

Heeeh-mee… Jiih-meh… Ji-mmy…

A name that only one person called him.

James stares wide-eyed at the bird.

"…Nana?"

The bird stops, its beak inside the flower. Papa's laugh carries from the front of the store. James looks up a second, sees that no one's coming. He leans in.

"Nana, if it's you…" he says, at a near-whisper, "flap right now."

The white bird flaps, only once. Punctuates the movement with a single *ding* of its bell.

James gasps, swooping the tin bird against his chest.

"Nana!" he says. His words spill out. "I missed you so much. How are you doing this? What are you doing here?"

He holds it back out and watches it in awe. The white bird titters. It flaps, as if ready to buck right off its platform. As the bird churns, a hitch catches in James's chest. His smile collapses.

"I'm glad you're here," he says. "But… I wish I could talk to you."

Dust wafts gently away from the bird. It stills.

"…Nana?"

The bird doesn't move. James feels tears creeping—but from a bottom shelf nearby rises a low warbling. In the darkness, there's a doll in a crib, its eyes closed. James spots it, and the eyes flick open, staring blankly at the ceiling.

The warbling builds until it congeals into two words: "*Love... You...*"

James smiles, brushing a hand at his eye. "I guess we can play together, at least." Still holding the bird, James kneels to the crib and starts rocking it. "Hello, Nana."

The baby doesn't speak again, but James spots dust wafting. It crosses to the other shelf and settles around a metal cowboy atop a rusted metal horse, hand to its hat. The cowboy tips its hat.

"*Howdy, pardner,*" it says, an octave too low. James smiles, but the voice still shakes his emotions loose. He swallows hard. There's that primal feeling again, that ancient instinct something's not quite right. It builds in his chest—

James plops to the floor and gives a big sigh to shake off his jitters. "Let's play together, Nana." He grabs the overturned car, gives a hearty "*bru-u-u-m!*" and drives it around.

The dust sweeps under a nearby bookshelf. Two toy cars roll out, their wheels squeaking like mice.

James brightens. He crawls along the aisle, weaving around the mess of toys, *brum-brum*ming as he goes. To his delight, the cars follow, dust tailing them like exhaust.

They flit between each other like they're dancing. Then one jumps ahead, swerves—and crashes right into his.

He flinches, putting a finger in his mouth instinctively until he registers that it didn't get pinched.

"Nana!" he says sternly. "Be careful!" He slinks away from the cars. He sulks. Then he looks to the drifting dust.

"...Are you okay, Nana?" he asks. "Is something wrong?" His audience of toys don't speak. He holds the bird close. Then: he's awash in green light.

He startles. The traffic lamp in the corner is on, a bloom of green. James blocks it with his free hand, and the light starts to flicker, off and on and off again.

"Okay, okay," James says. The light blinks off. James thinks.

"Green. You're...you're okay?"

The light doesn't return. He's about to speak, but then—*red*. Now the stop light is on. The bird figure starts plucking at the flower again.

"So you're *not* fine?" James asks. "What's wrong? What's it like where you are?"

The dust spreads. Then, a plastic ticking behind him. A circular toy with an arrow in its center now spins around peeling pictures of weather. The arrow lands on a snowy scene. "*Winter! Brr, it sure is cold out!*" it sings.

James holds the bird close to his chest. Rubs its base, breathes on it for warmth. But the red light starts flashing again, faster this time. He sighs, looking around the toys. "Nana, what do you want?"

Nearby toys spill onto the floor. He inches away as the flashing quickens.

"Nana...?" he says.

The circular toy again: "*It sure is cold out!*" Its arrow spins, shaking the toy—and soon the other toys are shuddering too. Shelves and shelves of them: shifting, whirring, loosing rust and dust. It all gathers to a low moan as the toy lands on a rainy scene. "*Get your umbrellas, it's rainy!*" it warbles.

"Nana, I don't understand—" James says. The traffic light flips green, and flashes faster.

The arrow toy whines as it goes too fast for itself. It screeches back to the cold scene. The voicebox struggles to keep up. "*Whhuurruld out!*" it says. The arrow whips back to the rainy scene. "*Get youhhrrr...*" One spin, back to the snow: "*ruuhh out!*"

The bird in his hand rocks fiercely.

"Okay, Nana," James says, leaving the toy corner, "I, uh... I gotta show you to Papa."

The dust gathers around him, the toys talk and groan and shake ever more. Up, up, into a piercing grind—

As if Nana is screaming—

"The hell you doin' to those toys, boy?" the shopkeep calls. James freezes in place. The toys silence.

"S-sorry, sir," James says. "I didn't mean to!"

"James, I swear," Papa says, "If you break any of this nice man's goods... Why, imagine what your Nana would think!"

James turns back to the dead scene. Not a toy stirs. The traffic light is off. He blinks.

"I won't do it again!" he calls.

He leans to the bird. "Okay, you don't wanna talk to Papa," he says in a near-whisper. "Just...please don't scare me."

A terrible thought comes to James as he steps over the toys. Maybe he doesn't want to play with Nana after all. The thought feels dirty, even as it cements. He sits down cross-legged, the bird in his lap. He watches the dust swirl around it.

Nothing feels right.

"Nana... Why did you leave me?"

A long silence. Then: two tiny glowing eyes on the shelf. A robot standing by the traffic light shifts its arms, up and down. It twists from its hip. With every movement, its eyes flicker.

"Where'd you go?" he asks it. "Where are you now?"

Around him, James hears a soft hissing. A doll squishes up, its air releasing. A chorus of dolls around him all release, until their breaths make a sound: "*Hhheeeerrrre...*"

James blinks. "You're *here*?"

The robot grinds its hip, turning. And it extends a lone arm downward. The arm nudges back and forth, as if pointing.

"The floor," James says. "You're...here? Where—" He looks around. Along the opposite wall, the one with all the cuckoo clocks, he spots a door—same one from which the shopkeep had emerged.

The robot waves its arms up and down at James. The circular toy spins its arrow again. "*Hooooooold ooooon,*" the toy moans, "*to your hats, it's windy out there!*"

But James is already off to the door. "It's okay, Nana," he says. "I'm coming for you."

He doesn't hear the toys groaning, doesn't see the stop light flicker on again, blinking faster and faster and faster.

James nears the door and finds a sickly glow along its right edge. It's cracked open.

Holding Nana close, James pushes on the door. It creaks louder than he wants. But he only hears Papa laughing heartily.

Nana churns her gears, fidgeting on her stand.

"Shh," James says. "You'll get me in trouble again."

Nana quiets, though her gears purr. James pulls the door slower, until it's open just enough for him. And he slips on through.

The other side is just a small wooden landing, and to the right, a stairwell of uncut planks to the basement.

Each stair protests like the door had. Smells build with each step. Soggy scents, like the neighbor's dog. Mustiness. And freshly turned dirt, like the first day of Papa's harvest.

James quickens down the last steps.

The dust swirls thick. The floor is compacted dirt.

Cardboard boxes line either side of the basement. The tops of some boxes are open, and antiques poke up. Yet more antiques are littered around. The sea of boxes leave just a narrow path to the back of the basement. At the other end, a light flickers.

"Nana," James says. "You're down here, right?" He starts down the alley of antiques.

The bird churns again, low and rough. He holds it closer, and it struggles against his chest, tiny gears clicking. In a box up high, an action figure rocks its arms. A few steps farther: a music box plucks a few notes. A few farther: a shuffling at his feet. He jerks away, thinking it's a rodent. It's a doll, her head turning to him.

James passes into the back. To the left, the source of light: a lit lantern sits on an antique workbench. A blue tarp covers the dirt floor below the workbench. On it, antique tools of all kinds: saws, wrenches, hammers. Along the wall hang ever more tools. They seem to jitter on the walls in the flickering lamplight. His eyes follow them across the back, further and further away from the light—until he spots the ground on the right. At first it looks like three piles of antiques, spaced neatly around three shallow piles of dirt.

As he approaches, he sees them clearly. The left plot has an old fancy sword, military medals, and an ancient photo frame of a young man in an army suit. The plot to its right has a toolbox, a hand drill, and a photo of a young man sitting atop his car.

The last plot has a handmade floral quilt. Same as the one that once rested on Nana's bed. A glass lamp—the one that Nana had read by. And Nana's very own glasses.

In the photo frame, a photo of a dressed-up couple. James picks it up, and even the frame feels familiar. The man is seated and wearing a suit. The woman stands with hand on his shoulder, wearing an elegant white dress. *The* dress. As Nana had told it, she'd sewn the whole thing herself. The lace veil had given her so much trouble. But she was so proud of it.

The basement stairs creak. James stumbles away from the plot, just as a voice calls: "Boy, the hell you doing down here?"

Only now does James realize that Nana's bird is rocking on its station as if to fly right off. He hides Nana and the picture frame behind his back.

The shopkeep stomps down the aisle of antiques, a scowl cracking his face.

"This area's private, you little—" the shopkeep stops, bites his tongue as Papa rushes down the stairs, limping from rushing his bad knee.

"Sorry, sir," James says, "I was just looking at your tools—"

Papa reaches the basement, but the shopkeep puts a palm out to him. Papa stops halfway down the box alley.

"It's alright, Mister Olsen," the shopkeep says. "Little James here's coming right along." With his other arm, the shopkeep beckons fiercely. "Ain't ya, boy?"

James nods, and rushes forward. The shopkeep puts himself between the box alley and the plots. Papa curls a stern hand on James's shoulder, already pulling him back for the stairs.

Against his Papa's pulling, he holds up the frame. "Papa, look," he whispers, "I found Nana."

Papa looks to the picture. Freezes in place. His hand tightens on James's shoulder, then drifts for the frame.

"Nice visit, Mister Olsen, but I think it's time you both ship out," the shopkeep calls after them. James hears him moving another tarp. "I'll see you round soon, I'm—"

Papa looses a sound that James has never heard—a sigh, a gasp, a sob, all at once. The shopkeep quiets.

"Where... Why..." Papa says. He turns to the shopkeep with the frame in both hands.

The shopkeep holds a tarp over the plots like he's tucking them in. He's already covered the first two, but the third—Nana's—is still exposed. Her quilt, her lamp, her glasses are plain to see.

Papa stammers. "What... What is this?" He points at the shopkeep. "What have you *done*?"

The shopkeep's face contorts in a flurry of emotions—he goes wide-eyed, he gapes, he squints. Then, his face clears. The emotions swirl away like the last water in a bath. He lets go of the tarp. He rolls his shoulders. Locks eyes with Papa. And he smiles, like an old friend.

"You know," he says, moving along the back wall. "I generally only collect *antiques*." He pauses, pulls down a crowbar. "But I guess some young blood won't hurt, *just this once*."

Papa gasps. "James," he says. "*Run*."

James goes stumbling as the shopkeep charges, crowbar held high. Papa catches the crowbar in his hands, and he cries out as they wrestle for control.

James knocks into antique boxes. They tumble down behind him. The antiques crash and cry out.

"*Mama, mama*," dolls cry.

James hits the stairs at a run, holding Nana against his pounding heart. Over his shoulder, he sees the shopkeep push Papa back, against the boxes.

Now on the ground floor, James rushes past the clocks. Their ticking blends into a wall of sound. He reaches the front, throws himself against the front door—and it barely moves. He remembers, looks up, and sees the deadbolt. It's far above his reach.

He knocks on the glass. The sky is bright with stars, and the road is empty. Moths flutter around the lone light above.

James runs for the desk and drags the chair out. Only halfway to the door, he hears stairs pounding.

He slips into the shelves just as the shopkeep shoves the door open. Heavy boots stomp along the clock wall to the front while James creeps to the toy area.

The shopkeep stops at the front. Then, he sighs. "Door still locked, I see," he says. "Boy... Let's have ourselves a little chat."

James reaches the toy corner. In the dim bulb light, he skims the haunted trinkets for anything that can help him. From the front, a gun cocks.

"Nana, help me," James whispers. He cradles the bird close to his chest.

The shopkeep's footfalls approach the back, slow and heavy.

"Nothing to worry about, boy," the shopkeep calls. "Everything's gonna be just fine."

Nana starts to churn, gears growling low. The bulb hanging above the toy corner flickers—and then goes dark.

"Funny little trick," the shopkeep says. All the bulbs in the shop fizzle and die. "What the hell?" He stops, and James holds his breath in the newfound black. He sees only floating dust and the edges of shelves. The dust seems thicker now, tempting James's nose to sneeze.

"Damned old knob and tube wiring..." the shopkeep mutters. He clears his throat. "Listen, boy. You don't have to hide..." His footsteps resume. James peeks around the corner. The shopkeep's gun catches the light.

From the front of the store, a little voice calls: *Mama!*

The shopkeep pivots. "Boy?" he says. "It's no time to be playing with dolls."

The doll calls out *Mama!* again, and the shopkeep heads its way. Behind James, the street light flashes quick: a single burst of green. James crosses the shop.

He reaches the wall of clocks, which tick out a cacophony. The shopkeep swears, and something across the room goes clattering.

Mammerrr... the doll utters.

James creeps for the front of the store. The heavy footsteps make for the toy corner. "Look, boy, this won't be so bad," the shopkeep says, his voice suddenly delicate. "You'll be with your Nana again...and your Papa too! Don't you want that?"

James doesn't want that at all. He looks back into the darkness—and his foot catches a heavy antique. He trips onto a pile of boxes. The dust kicks up high.

James rights himself and coughs hard in the dust. The shopkeep calls: "Come here!"

The heavy footsteps pound over. James rushes for the front. The shopkeep rounds the corner, raises his gun—

The wall erupts in noise as all the clocks chime the hour. James ducks into the knot of bookshelves.

The shopkeep yells over the chaos: bells ring, cuckoos pop from their homes, melodies sing.

Nana's bird begins to churn in James's hands.

He winds through the shelves. It's easy to get lost here in the middle of the store; the shelves weave around each other without order. The shopkeep yells somewhere behind. Then, he throws himself against a bookshelf, which crashes sideways. The bookshelf slams into one right behind James, toppling like dominoes. Another yell from the shopkeep: another bookshelf topples, its antiques clattering before it, too, smashes against its neighbor. James runs for the front, as another bookshelf goes falling.

James reaches the last shelf just as it topples toward him. He stumbles, then falls, landing in the open floor in front of the shop counter. He spins back. The shelves are all toppled. Dust collects like a raincloud above.

As the clocks still chime, the shopkeep jumps atop his fallen shelves.

"Look what you made me do, boy!" he says, arms wide. "This is why I collect *antiques*. This is why I don't bother with children."

The dust between James and the shopkeep builds and builds, forming a long shape.

James moves to get up, but the shopkeep raises his gun.

"You've made enough of a mess." He cracks a wide smile as the dust coalesces around him. "Time to join your ol' Nana."

The light catches the cloud just so, and a figure seems to emerge. Long, thin, wispy. The shopkeep spots it. Though he keeps his gun trained on James, his face contorts. "What the hell...?"

The dust takes further shape, and finally James recognizes it. The long dress, plain but elegant. That tricky lace veil. *Nana.*

She floats between James and the shopkeep, her dress of dust flowing in a wind of her own making. Her hair is like fire, smoking about her head.

The shopkeep rears his gun with both hands. She drifts for the shopkeep, her hair flaring wide, her arms out.

The shopkeep yells: a bullet shrieks over James's head, shattering the front door. James scrambles for cover.

Nana moves unhalting, and the shopkeep stumbles across his fallen bookshelves, further into the darkness. He raises his shining gun again. Fires two more shots through Nana. The bullets whorl through her, and the dust dances as if laughing. The holes fill with the dust the shopkeep kicks up. And still Nana nears.

"Get back!" the shopkeep yells over the chimes of the clocks. "Get back!" Further and further into the darkness. Two more shots, the flashes catching the shopkeep's ever more desperate face. They reach the back corner. The shopkeep screams out in terror. They're so far back, James can't see a thing.

A last shot rings out. The clocks all stop. A heavy *thump* against the floor.

James is still in the sudden silence. There's only the dust swirling gently over the bookshelves, the sound of crickets trickling through the broken glass. Then, one by one, the stained-glass lights flicker on. All but the one by the basement door.

James stands. He spots Nana's bird lying near him, so he plucks it up. He looks for the back.

"Nana?" he calls. The dust coalesces in the middle of the store, and there's dust-Nana again, her figure blurred. Still in her wedding dress. Though he can barely make out her face, he thinks he sees a smile. She gives him a gentle wave, and then her arm points to the front desk. Her form dissipates to nothing.

James nods. He drags the shopkeep's seat back over, pulls the rotary phone close. And he dials *911*, just like his Nana always taught him.

❄

THE HEAT from the police car's vents is refreshing, a distraction from the flashing red-and-blue of the cop cars in the gravel parking lot.

"Look, kid," says the policeman. He holds a steaming cup close to his face. "We're getting ahold of your parents. But whatever you saw in there..."

"It's okay," James says. "Nana kept me safe." He spins the bird in his hand. The gears no longer churn, but that's okay. He knows that Nana's not with it anymore.

The cop sighs and looks out across the corn fields.

Over the scanner, a voice: "*Gonna need Forensics to the basement here...*"

The cop turns off the scanner. "Let me get you outta here," he says. "There's snacks at the station—"

James sits up quick. "Wait!" he says. "I need to return something. Nana will be mad if I don't." The police stammers, but James is already out.

Two detectives talk by the shop door, now propped open with an antique lamp. Behind, the policeman stumbles out of his car, yelling and spilling coffee on himself. The detectives barely have time to look before James slips through the door.

He runs for the toy corner, away from all the officers gathered by the basement door. The back wall's shelves are still standing. There, he spots the black bird. He places Nana's bird next to its friend. Makes sure they're set. He nods. Steps over the bookshelves back to the waiting policeman.

The officer sighs in relief, his eyes darting for the basement door. He brushes the coffee stains on his sleeve. "Your Nana raised you well, didn't she?" He puts himself between James and the commotion, and rests his hand on James's shoulder. And they head out into the cold.

❄

THE TWO BIRDS sit lonely in the corner, lit by the wan light. The police are busy across the store, but it's quiet here.

The white bird hiccups, and then begins waving its wings. It rocks for a few cycles, and then stops.

Then, the black bird hiccups. Churns, as if getting used to its gears. Then it, too, rocks for just a cycle.

There's stillness again. Then, both the white and black birds begin flapping and whirring at each other. The police don't notice the little display. But that's no bother. The birds are happy to flap just to each other. Cheery in their own little world, in the corner of the antique shop way on the edge of town.

About the Author

Tarver Nova is a spec-fic writer and professional night owl in New York. His stories are found in *Baffling Magazine*, Air & Nothingness Press, *Daily Science Fiction*, and other fine places. He is an associate editor of the fiction podcasts PodCastle and CatsCast. Find him at tarvernova.com or show him your cats on Twitter @tarvernova.

THE OTHER JACK

SAMANTHA BRYANT

Jimmy's room wasn't really a room. Mom called it a partition. She found some smoky plexiglass somewhere and used it to divide the long narrow room at the end of their trailer into two tiny bedrooms, each barely big enough for a twin bed and a narrow chest of drawers that was also the desk and the nightstand. It wasn't much, but it gave him and his brother a little illusion of privacy, something that mattered more now that his brother was older and didn't want to share a room, let alone a bed with his little brother.

Jimmy had to pretend he didn't hear a lot of things these days, especially if Mom wasn't home. He'd never tell, of course. Brothers didn't rat on each other, even if the girls were mean or the smoke smelled weird.

But he missed the nights when Jack would turn a light on the plexiglass wall and make shadow puppets for him, or press his face against the wall, smooshing it comically and getting them both in trouble for wild laughter. When Jimmy was feeling lonely, he'd flatten his hand against the glass and his brother would do the same on his side, making a double image of their two hands, shaped just the same even if Jack's was a lot bigger.

Lying on his bed drawing, Jimmy heard a tap on the glass. He jumped. He hadn't thought anyone was home—he was being a big boy and taking care of himself like he had to sometimes.

But maybe Jack was home after all.

Jimmy looked over his shoulder. A hand pressed against the other side of the glass. He laid his own over it on his side of the wall, and Jack spread his fingers wide so Jimmy could compare the size of his hand to his brother's. Jack was almost ten years older than Jimmy, so catching up was taking a long time, but he felt sure his hand was bigger than it had been the last time. Pleased, he knocked three times, their secret signal for happiness. Jack didn't respond.

The hand moved away, and Jimmy went back to his drawing. From time to time a thump made him glare at the plastic wall, and once he thought he heard a girl's voice, but he just turned the music up louder and kept drawing. The cat-man he had invented was having an undersea adventure this time, and Jimmy was having a hard time getting the bubble helmet to look the way he wanted. After a few tries, he threw the wadded-up paper at the wall in frustration. Maybe he'd finish the pirate ship one instead.

There were two hands on the wall now, pressed flat enough that Jimmy could trace the lines in the palms. Jack was pushing hard, like he wanted to come through the plexiglass wall instead of climbing over the bed to get to the hallway like a normal person. The makeshift wall scraped against the ceiling, groaning like the train cars that shook their trailers at night. Jimmy smacked his hands over his ears and gritted his teeth. "Stop it Jack! You'll get in trouble if you break it."

The pressure released. Jimmy watched the shadowy figure rock back and forth. Even over his music, he could hear the huffy breathing that probably meant his big brother was really mad. Jimmy curled up, hugging his legs with his arms to make himself into a ball.

Jack could be crazy sometimes, but Jimmy could usually get him to stop before it got too bad. Jack was still huffing and puffing, but he wasn't moving anymore, and Jimmy relaxed a little. Just as he was thinking about picking up his drawing again, the hands clenched into fists and pounded against the wall, making it scrape and groan and shake ominously. Jimmy yelled. "Stop it, Jack! Stop it!"

The pounding stopped abruptly, and at the foot of his bed, the door opened. "Stop what, Squirt?" Jack leaned in, still wearing his fast-food tee shirt with the happy cartoon chicken forming a thumbs-up out of his feathers. He was holding a crinkled-up bag with the same chicken on it.

"J-J-Jack?" Jimmy pointed at the wall behind him, wordlessly. The Other Jack started pounding the plexiglass again, and Jimmy thought the fists might be bleeding now. His mouth went completely dry.

Abruptly, Jack had him by the armpits and was pulling him out of the room. His space-cat comic fluttered away and slipped under the dresser. Before he could cry out, he was outside the trailer, standing barefoot in the chilly night, gravel digging into his feet while Jack fumbled with the keys to the beat-up station wagon.

Jack picked Jimmy up like he was a baby and slung him into the front seat, where he was never allowed to sit and slammed the door. Before either of them had even put on their seatbelts, Jack was backing up fast, flinging gravel against the metal sides of the trailers.

Jimmy cried, "Where are we going?"

Jack didn't answer him. He was on the phone, talking fast to someone. He said their address—Jimmy had memorized it for kindergarten so he recognized it—and said there was an intruder. Jimmy didn't know what that meant, but Jack sounded scared, and it was making him scared, and he thought he might throw up.

Jack said he didn't know where their mother was, but that was silly because Mom was at work. She'd had to go in before his bus came home. That's why Jimmy was being a big boy and staying by himself until Jack got home, just like he'd promised he would.

Jack said other stuff, too, but Jimmy couldn't understand—it was hard to hear over the squealing inside his head. He hummed really loud to calm himself down, but that was hard to hear, too, like his voice came from the other side of a wall instead of inside his own head. The car spun around in a circle.

Then, his brother was shaking him, telling him it was okay, but he was crying when he said it, and Jimmy didn't believe him. Jack was too big to cry.

There were blue lights flashing and a woman with a flashlight and a clipboard. Her big eyes blinked slowly while she talked to Jack. Jimmy hung onto his brother's shirt and peered around him at her, but she didn't look at him.

She pushed them down behind the car when someone started yelling and then a loud bang shook the little tree Mom had bought in a pot last Christmas. An ambulance took someone away. Jimmy wasn't allowed to see. Jack held him too tightly, kept Jimmy's head pressed against his chest.

It was a long time before Jimmy got the full story of the night his mother died and he almost died, too. If Jack hadn't gotten home when he did, the bad man would have killed Jimmy.

They told him his mother was a hero, that he was lucky. She'd trapped his father in Jack's room with her. It didn't make sense because Jimmy's mom always said that he didn't have a dad because they didn't need one. They were enough, just the three of them.

But Mom lied.

Jimmy did have a daddy after all. His name was Jack, just like his big brother, but he wasn't the right Jack. He was the other Jack, the bad one.

They said he was dead now and couldn't hurt anyone anymore. But Jimmy wasn't sure. He saw his hands against windows all the time, everywhere he went, pressing to come through. They'd told him he didn't have a dad and he did, so why should he believe them now?

About the Author

Samantha Bryant writes superhero and horror stories, which one depends on whether she wants to save the world today or watch it burn. She is best known for The Menopausal Superhero series of novels, which asks why young people should have all the fun. When she's not writing or working the day job, Samantha enjoys family time, old movies, baking, gaming, and walking in the woods with her rescue dogs. You can find her on Twitter and Instagram @samanthabwriter or at: http://samanthabryant.com and subscribe to her newsletter at: http://eepurl.com/bwgsxD

A YOKE OF IRON

GABRIEL TUGGLE

A WALL of silver mist and fog clouded the parking lot, obscuring Lawrence's view of the school. Through murky patches he caught glimpses of brick, an ancient two-story building with concrete trim, front windows opaque like the ocean at night. Unseasonably dark and gray and cold for this late in spring, Lawrence thought absently while his loafers clicked across the pavement. If one had met him in the fog, it would've seemed he emerged from thin air.

A comma of black hair fell across his forehead, still scarred with the ghosts of teenage acne over a decade behind him. He pushed it back with a hand calloused, aged, the hand of a grown man no longer nimble or thin with youth. And driven into the hard planes of his face, visible in the sharp contours were the remnants of angst, which never really goes away. Instead, it becomes mature, becomes hatred and anger and bitterness within the adult world.

But Lawrence Allen's most illustrious feature was his eyes. It wasn't that they lacked color or vivacity, nor that they were primal or evil or even empty. But they were the eyes of a machine dealing in calculations and analytics, especially when it came to other people.

He stood at the bottom of the front steps, looking up the stoop at the barrier of red doors. He imagined legions of students pouring out on a Friday afternoon, sixteen-year-olds hurrying to antique sedans, lovers hand in hand, athletic types strolling in packs—all shoulders and no brains. But right now, it was empty, and he was the only one waiting in the silence. I went to this school, he thought, during a time of George Bush and Blink-182 and PlayStation. A time when Tony Hawk was a common answer for, "Who's your favorite celebrity?"

The school looked no different than it did in Lawrence's memory. Somewhere within this man was the boy who had attended here, a low-energy boy of great height and minimal weight, a boy more awkward than the sum of his peers. For three years, Lawrence fought for a place, a purpose within the school, but he gave up late in his junior year after the baseball team dunked his head in a toilet bowl full of urine.

He mounted the steps and marched toward the open door, an unblinking eye on the building's face. The hallway within was a chasm, its farthest point dark and suspended in shadow. On the left, the front office stood vacant for the weekend behind a wall of glass. A staircase bent up to the second floor, and corridors stretched into the reaches beyond where classrooms waited in silence for Monday morning. For some reason, Lawrence did not want to think of them, those rows and columns of empty desks. A cold finger touched the base of his spine, and his skin broke out in goosebumps.

A sandwich board was propped a few feet away, bearing the message, "Welcome Class of 2005! Reunion in Cafeteria. Food and drink provided."

He wandered toward it. Lockers passed in a blur on either side. The trophy case was nothing but a glimmer of gold and silver cups.

A cloud of dust and paper wads kicked out of an adjacent hallway. A broom shuffled just behind it. Lawrence swerved hard to the left, spun around to meet a gaunt-faced janitor in a gray jumpsuit. "Bill" was stitched upon the breast in cursive. Only a balding man of sixty could've been named Bill, and the janitor fit the description.

"Startle you?" he chuckled, a dry sound like bones dancing in a coffin.

"Yes, but you're fine," Lawrence said. His drumming heart told a different story.

"Here for the reunion, I reckon?"

"That's right. I'm going the right way, aren't I?"

"Mhm. Guess it's been a long time, ain't it, Lawrence?"

"Long enough for me to forget my way around, if that's what you mean. This place always felt so big when I was—"

Bill raised his brow. "When you was what?"

"How did you know my name?" Their voices echoed far in the wide caverns of Shy Rock High, drifting seamlessly between arched ceilings and polished floors.

Again the janitor chuckled. "I may not be a teacher, but I know things about this place. Hear things. See things. Think of me like the caretaker. I'm not real noticeable, which is the way it should be."

"I don't even look the same. You couldn't have recognized me."

"I never forget a face. God-given talent."

"But that was over ten years ago."

Bill's warm expression turned grim. "It's been sixteen years, Lawrence, since you and me last met." The many lines of his face were accentuated in the dim light, as if carved with a knife.

And didn't Lawrence recognize him? A background character occasionally lurking with a cart of trash, a shadow salting the sidewalks, cleaning chalkboards. An immortal, almost legendary figure is a high school janitor, one who does not age or speak often, who could only ever wear a blue collar, but is a mainstay of their workplace.

Bill was familiar, but he, like the school, appeared no different than in Lawrence's memory.

He backed away from the janitor's glare and excused himself. He hurried toward the reunion with sweat beading on his temples. He didn't look back, but he had the unmistakable feeling that he was being watched, that Bill's stare bore into the back of his head.

Just past the gymnasium, locked and dark and eerie, a blonde woman met Lawrence at the cafeteria door. The smooth ridges of her face held no wrinkles yet, but he could tell she was his age. Her features held the distinct fatigue of a thirty-something. "Long time no see, Mister Allen," she said, smiling with wide, blank eyes.

His breath caught. The only thing that kept him from running in the opposite direction was the possibility of seeing Bill again. She touched his arm, cocked her head to look at him.

"Lauren?" he asked. "Lauren Wheatley?"

"That's me," she said happily.

Lawrence had a vague recollection of asking her to prom once. Strong recollection of her saying no.

He glided past her with a nod, and the cafeteria swallowed him. The ceiling was full of wooden rafters so high up that they were never cleaned. If a paper plane ever jammed in a crevice up there, it did not come back down.

Balloons attempted to brighten the dull room. A curved banner hung on the opposite wall, welcoming graduates. Streamers and ribbons spiraled overhead. Confetti scattered across the floor. But none of it could make up for the depressing gray light spilling in from the wall of windows at the far end.

Speakers played music from his youth. Songs like "In Too Deep" by Sum 41 and "I'm Just a Kid" by Simple Plan. Songs before smartphones, when the Internet was only accessed from a giant white desktop in the family office. Hearing them, Lawrence could've been seventeen again.

Most frightening of all, for some reason, was that every table was empty save for one in the center of the room. Only eight people gathered around it. Their voices muffled and droned in the large space so that Lawrence could hear no individual words. But they seemed lively enough, and so he took a few steps closer until someone noticed.

"It's Lawrence! Look who it is, fellas."

The other heads spun around, some chewing hotdogs, some with soda cans lifted to their mouths. Smiles spread like an infectious disease.

Lauren Wheatley closed the door behind them and led Lawrence to an open seat at the table, a gentle hand on the small of his back.

"Man of the hour," a smartly dressed Korean man said, clapping Lawrence on the shoulder. "Welcome back."

"Say, what is all this?"

"It's our class reunion, buddy," a broad-shouldered fellow replied. "You didn't forget about us, did you?"

"I know I graduated with more than nine other people. Where are they? Where is everyone?" He motioned to the vast cafeteria around them, feeling lonely and agoraphobic. The entire room was without color, without life. Even the decorations were now drab, as if from a faded photograph. And the people around him, they were vibrant by comparison, present and grounded in the moment. He thought he was dreaming, but he glanced down at his hands, studied the lines and freckles, the bump of his knuckles, and knew a dream could not be so vivid.

"We're the only ones that you invited," the Korean man answered.

"I didn't plan this."

"Oh, he's so modest," Lauren Wheatley said, beaming.

"Dammit," Lawrence said. His hand clapped the tabletop. "What is all this? Who has a sixteen-year reunion anyway? Why such a specific number?"

"We get together every year," Jimmy Hettinger spoke up. Lawrence recognized him immediately because of the thick-lensed glasses he wore, which magnified his eyes and made him look surprised all the time.

Spiders crawled in Lawrence's clothes. He writhed in his seat, shuffled his feet, clenched and unclenched his fists on the table. Sweat poured off him in buckets now. The music was not playing anymore. Perhaps there was never any music at all. There was the hum of quiet, the rush of blood in his ears. The former students stared, unmoving, smiles not adding anything to their emotionless eyes. He recognized them one at a time, named them in his mind. Drew Blackwell, Jensen Hamilton, Steven Carver, among others. They seemed too young for their adult bodies, children playing dress-up in their parents' clothes.

"Listen." The Korean man, whose name was Jason Mun, gestured with an open palm. "Tell me this, Lawrence. What did you do today?"

"Well, I..." And then his sentence trailed away to nothing. "I guess I... Say, is this some kind of trick question?"

"Just answer."

"Well, I don't remember. I just started walking through that fog. And I wandered into here."

"You don't remember because there was nothing else."

"But what about work? I had to go to work, didn't I?" Lawrence's heart raced. Black blotches pulsed across his vision. He realized he did not work. Did not have a job. A home. Did not even have a car. He'd emerged from the fog as if a baby being born. No one answered him, because his understanding was evident enough on his pallid expression. "You're crazy!" he screamed at no one in particular, rising from the table. His chair left black skid marks on the floor. He backed away without resistance. "You're all crazy. That's what you are."

Breathing heavily, he dashed for the door.

And it was locked.

In the murky reflection of the glass, he did not see a man, but a boy. A teenaged boy who wore black combat boots to school, who parted his hair in the middle, who weighed a hundred and twenty pounds soaking wet. His height did not save him from torment, for Lawrence Allen was still a loser, a title not even worthy of a capital L. Eruptions of acne peppered his narrow face, on which a mustache had just started to blossom. His voice was no longer as deep or adult when he screamed, when he raised his bony arms and pounded on the door.

He had never aged, and any indication that he had was an illusion to make this encounter easier.

Bill the janitor stood on the opposite side and stared into the cafeteria as if spectating a caged animal.

"Bill, let me out. In the name of God, let me out!"

"What's your hurry, son? Memories catching up with you?" Although on the other side of glass, his voice came through clearly, as if spoken directly into Lawrence's ear. As if inside Lawrence's mind.

"Shut up! Just shut up!" He tried the door again. Bolted. Locked. "I never did anything wrong."

"Because of you, boy, those kids never grew up. I never saw my wife again. We never left this place. None of us. And we're stuck here. Together."

"Do you have any idea what hell I went through for four years here? Any clue? Do you know what this school did to me?"

"And you think murder is a fair response?"

"No, I never—" In his trembling hands he held a 12-gauge shotgun, gunmetal black as night and well-oiled, wooden stock and pump glossed to a high shine. Lawrence tried to throw it away, but the firearm was welded to his hands. It was impossible to tell where his flesh ended and the gun began.

The cafeteria stunk of acrid smoke and a coppery stench like old pennies. And what he'd believed to be music earlier was actually the fire alarm, ringing, blaring its one-note scream on the world, loud enough to mask shouts of pain and terror.

"Turn and look at it, Lawrence," Bill whispered.

The reunion façade was gone. Had never been there. Would never be there. Nine bodies lay at random about the room in pools of blood. Limp hands held onto textbooks. Unseeing eyes peered under cafeteria tables. Boys and girls who would grow no older, who would never go home, never change clothes, never attend college. And forever in time they would be suspended here in this moment, regardless of how long had passed or how old the survivors grew. And Lawrence Allen would remain with them.

Except this time, he could not take the easy way out.

He racked the pump of the shotgun, but it was empty. All his shells lay spent on the ground, twirls of smoke rising from them.

"In this room, boy, you did unspeakable things. Said unrepeatable things. In this room you thought you were God."

The bodies got up. Soaked red and flesh torn by gunshots, the students stood to face him. Bones creaking, open wounds squishing, mashed heads cocked to the side, they shuffled to him like a run-over dog shuffles toward its owner. They chanted his name through lips that weren't there.

He turned to Bill. The janitor was collapsed on the floor with a hole in the center of his chest, but his eyes were not dead. His expression was alive and conscious.

"And in this room, you escaped punishment."

A few feet away, slumped, was Lawrence. The top half of his head was gone, and the wall above him was painted red.

"No," was all Lawrence could muster. For the first time, he realized he was not actually here, that none of them were, for an anguished mind never leaves its corpse even after the flesh and bone turn to powder. And those broken thoughts remain on repeat for all eternity within the coffin.

But the jury, the students, could not alter their verdict, for they were dead and would never have another opinion. Dead, yet they still came forward. Still crowded around him. They could not speak, but only moan in agony, mimicking their final breaths years earlier. The sound wreaked hell within Lawrence's ears.

He shrieked as they closed in, groped and clawed for him. He dropped to his knees, feeling every death, every bit of pain inflicted that day, every ounce of grief or sorrow or remorse. But Lawrence did not die, would not die, for this is what he'd wanted. To be infamous, and infamous he was.

❄

A POLICE CAR patrolled the block around the abandoned school. Its brakes squeaked. Its spotlight flicked on, illumining a trio of young boys in the dead shrubbery. They screamed in unison, voices cracking, and bolted off down the sidewalk. The bushes shivered where they'd just been.

"Get away from there!" the officer barked from the passenger seat. "Go home!" He turned off the light and leaned back inside the car.

The other officer eased off the brake and let the car roll onward. They'd made laps around the old school ever since nightfall and had caught a dozen young people trying to sneak inside.

"What the hell is wrong with kids these days?" the driver said.

"Probably think it's haunted. Want to go inside and see a ghost or graffiti their name on the wall or some damn thing."

"Probably is haunted. Tell you the truth, place gives me the willies."

The school loomed across the empty parking lot. Even in the darkness one could see its smashed windows, dilapidated and moldy brick, cracked pavement where weeds shoved through. It had sat empty for sixteen years now, and on every anniversary Shy Rock Police drew straws for who had to keep watch.

"Why don't they tear it down?" the driver mused. "Why leave it? It's an eyesore. And the worst kind of tourist attraction."

"Maybe," the other officer said, nodding, "they leave it as a reminder. Like a warning."

"Imagine your kid died there, Everett. Imagine having to drive past it everyday and see it."

"They didn't tear down Auschwitz either, you know."

The driver shivered in spite of the warm night. "Whatever you say. Couldn't pay me to set foot in there."

And the police car continued making laps, continued its crawl around the block.

They would return the next year.

And the next year.

And the next.

About the Author

Gabriel Tuggle has many loves–VHS collecting, woodworking, PlayStation. But none hold a candle to books, so much so that he received his degree in English from the University of Kentucky in 2020. He currently lives with his wife and dog, Biscuit.

Twitter: gabriel_tuggle

Instagram: partyoftuggle

GOOD BONES

JEFF SAMSON

THE HOUSE at the end of the lane.

It sure sounds like the premise of a horror story. But you wouldn't think so by looking at it. I certainly didn't.

There's no pair of third floor attic windows peering out like watchful eyes. No darkened entrance stretched in a ghostly yawn. No decrepit foundation or wildly overgrown lawn or wrought iron gate teetering around it. Just your average three bedroom, one and a half bath, twelve-hundred square foot Dutch Colonial with a modest covered porch, a shingle roof a few years past its twenty-year guarantee, and solid early 20th century craftsmanship throughout. A house with good bones.

Good bones.

I'd never heard that expression before buying a home. It sounded like something my nana would have said with an air of piety and Old World superstition. But as I learned, it's actually a common term in realtor speak, used to make fixer-uppers more attractive by romanticizing their better features. Plaster walls and ceilings. Old growth, wide plank flooring. Solid cherry trim and cedar shake siding. Appointments that are now trendy and costly but were wholly unremarkable a hundred years ago.

In fact, the only thing outwardly remarkable about the house at the end of the lane is that it's the last of its kind—the only original structure still intact on a street where all of the others have been bought, bulldozed and rebuilt as mansions whose foundations take up most of the quarter-acre lots on which they rest, and whose great rooms could swallow whole the perfectly good homes they replaced.

The other remarkable thing about the house at the end of the lane, while much less outwardly so, is that not more than six months ago, it looked exactly like the rest of the three-story monstrosities on the street, complete with seven bedrooms, five and a half baths, a study with floor-to-ceiling bookcases and a ladder on a track, a circular driveway in the front, and a sprawling Brazilian Ipe deck and bluestone patio leading to a waterfall-fed pool in back.

If that strikes you as confusing, don't worry. You're not alone.

❄

MY FIRST CLUE that something wasn't right came the day we received our certificate of occupancy.

We'd just suffered through a week of final inspections at the mercy of a gentleman whose criteria for a pass or a fail seemed mostly to do with which side of the bed he woke up on that morning. But after a day of having to uninstall and reinstall every ceiling fan in every room to prove they were properly anchored, he'd at last given us his begrudged blessings.

We weren't due to move in for another week. But our twins, Sofi and Sebastian, were with the in-laws for the night, and Cora wanted to celebrate. So we drove over to the house, just the two of us.

"What did you have in mind?" I asked.

"For starters?" she said, producing a bottle from under her seat. "Polishing off this Barolo."

"I'm with you so far."

She leaned in, so close her lips brushed mine as she spoke.

"And making love in every room in the house."

I did a quick tally in my head and came up with twenty-one, assuming we were including the pantry. And if I knew Cora, we were.

"That's an awful lot of rooms, you know," I said.

She shrugged. "What's your point?"

As we were walking back to the car, our stomachs full of twelve-year-old wine, our forty-eight-year-old backs and knees a little worse for the wear, I happened to glance back at the house. Two things occurred to me then. The first was that making love in every room was a hell of a lot easier in a two-bedroom apartment in Williamsburg. The second was that I counted three gables on the third floor where, only a few hours earlier, I'd counted four.

❄

I wish I could say I didn't spoil the evening.

"But you can't keep looking at me sideways and casually explaining it all away and then act surprised when I start getting upset, Cora."

"I'm not trying to make you upset. I'm just trying to make sense of it."

"Because I'm not making sense?"

"No, I didn't say that. I just think you're stressed. Between the build, the move, your taking on more responsibility at work. Your plate's never been this full. It's a lot, Terry. A lot to keep...you know...together."

"So now I'm cracking up."

"Again, I didn't say that. But I do think it's highly unlikely that the gable just disappeared into thin air. And that it's a heck of a lot more likely that you're simply mistaken."

"No."

"That you're just remembering something from an earlier set of plans."

"No."

"Or a rendering that we wound up not going ahead with."

"No."

"And that's why you can't get your stupid gables straight."

"Wow. That's really sweet of you, Cora."

"*That's* what I think."

"Yeah well, you're wrong."

"Yeah well, you're being an asshole."

On we went like that. Cora incapable of running out of explanations. Me unwilling to accept even the possibility of a single one. An irresistible force and immovable object, steadily dragging what should have been a beautiful night down a spiral of stubborn pride and pettiness, the bottom of which saw her suggesting I might be having a senior moment. And me exploding in a fit of righteousness about how cold and unfunny it was to say a thing like that given how I'd lost my father to early onset Alzheimer's, which, I felt the need to remind her, was a hereditary disease. And her saying what a shame it was that I inherited his shitty temper instead of his sense of humor. And the two of us driving back into the city with not a sound passing between us but the steady hush of the AC and the faint mumbling from a talk radio station neither of us cared enough to change.

❄

"I'M LOOKING at the same docs you are."

Alan didn't even try to mask the aggravation in his voice. And I couldn't blame him.

On the heels of my blowup with Cora, I'd torn apart the bedroom looking for the blueprints that turned out to be on my workstation in the living room, where she'd said they were all along. Unsatisfied, I called up every email exchange and attachment between myself and our architect, Alan Fine, hoping—and fearing—I'd find not so much what I was looking for, but what I'd been seeing all along. And again unsatisfied, I'd called him on his personal cell—a number I imagine he'd given to me in the confidence of knowing I'd never use it unless absolutely necessary and that I wasn't a stark raving lunatic—just after eleven o'clock on a Thursday night to set the record straight. But he only confirmed what was becoming painfully clear.

"And I can tell you beyond a shadow of a doubt," he said, "that nowhere, at any point in the process, did I share a blueprint or rendering or even a sketch, for that matter, with four gables."

"I see," I said. But I didn't. "And you're sure you're not...forgetting anything? I mean, we run into version control issues all the time at—"

"Version control?" he fired back. "You know, Terry, if I didn't know you were such a kind and thoughtful guy, I might have found that insulting."

"I'm sorry," I said. "I'm just...this whole thing is driving me a bit mad. Which is driving Cora a bit mad."

At that he let out a long sigh.

"Look," he said, his tone already softened. "You've probably just been too close to this thing for too long. You're an ad man. You know how it goes. You spend days and weeks and months looking at a piece of work and you think you know every bit of it by heart down to the littlest detail. Then one day, you take a step back and you see something you've never seen before. And for the life of you, you can't figure out how it could have been there all along, right under your nose. But there it is. Where it always was."

It was my turn to sigh.

"I know," I said. And though I still wasn't satisfied, I felt I'd already taken up more of his time than I deserved. "I know and I...I'm sorry and I'm sure you have more important things to get to."

"Terry, it's no bother. Happy to help you...uh...verify."

I would have thanked him and hung up. But there was something in his hesitation. A nervousness of sorts that I couldn't ignore.

"Everything all right?" I asked.

"What's that?" he said, absently.

"Is everything—"

"Oh!" he said. "Yes, fine."

But I could sense there was more. So I gave him the time.

"It's just," he said at last, "well, I hope you won't take this the wrong way. But after revisiting your plans, I'm actually a little surprised, at least from an aesthetic standpoint, that I went with three gables instead of four."

✳

A WEEK LATER, I wasn't any less uneasy about the gable that, for all I could tell, had either vanished into thin air or had never existed in the first place—a detail that didn't really matter since both scenarios made me the crazy one. Nor did it matter that I couldn't put it to rest. Plans had been made. Steps taken. Bodies set in motion. There'd been mortgages signed, down payments made, movers booked, furniture purchased, kids enrolled in new school districts, and a hundred other decisions and revisions. And that's to say nothing of the full year and a half of our lives we'd devoted to bringing our dream home to life. If there had ever been a threshold for bailing out, we'd crossed it long ago.

Besides, our now previous apartment of five years had been leased to new tenants the moment we informed our landlord we were moving. And if I'd suggested moving in with her parents until I sorted myself out, Cora—who was by now very much over my newfound obsession— would have killed me slowly.

And if it sounds like I'm trying overly hard to justify the fact that I did what anyone else in my situation would have done and proceeded to move my family into our new house out of the purest of hopes of making it our new home, it's because I am.

✳

IT REALLY WAS A GREAT HOUSE.

Spacious and bright and open and flowing, yet so delightfully private where it needed to be.

Cora and I finally had a master suite together and a pair of home offices apart. Sofi and Sebastian, while insisting on still sharing a bedroom, so tirelessly explored the house and yard and semi-deep woods, you'd think their previous residence had been the *Château d'If*. And the pool, which I'd initially resisted putting in, was proving to be the best decision we'd made.

The twins spent the better part of every day in the water, which meant they crashed early and slept like the dead through the night. And I'd taken up swimming laps every morning, which Cora was thrilled about since I'd resisted every other workout suggestion she'd thrown my way for the last five years. And despite how often I'd been making use of the wet bar in the great room, the pounds seemed to be coming off around my midsection. Or, in Cora's words, my spare tire had sprung a slow leak. As someone with a touch-and-go history with working out, I was fairly impressed with myself. In thirty days, I hadn't missed a morning swim.

❄

ON DAY THIRTY-ONE, the twins were racing in from the backyard as I was walking out. They took one look at me and howled with excitement.

"Beach day, beach day, beach day," they were shouting, first separately then in perfect unison as was often the case with them, sometimes to eerie effect.

"Beach day?" I said, squatting down to their level and furrowing my brow to the extreme. "Who said anything about a beach day?"

"You're dressed for the beach, Daddy," Sebastian said, pointing at me.

I did a quick once-over of myself in my board shorts and bare feet. "Well how about that? I guess I am."

Again they howled with delight. And again their shouting synced up. "We're going to the beach! We're going to the beach! We're going to the beach!" Stretching "beach" into a singsong "bee-each."

"Sorry, kiddos. I hate to disappoint you, but we're not going to the beach today."

"Daddy!" Sofi whined, making my name last way too long until Sebastian joined her and stretched it out even more.

"Oh, come on now, you two." I stood up and gestured outside. "Who needs the beach when you've got a p—"

And immediately, I understood why the twins had thought I was dressed for the beach. Why that word had lodged itself in my throat. Why my palate flooded with acid. Why every hair on my body seemed to bristle with current at the same time. And why it suddenly felt like I was hovering tenuously a few inches above the hardwood floor beneath my feet, as I gazed out between my open arms upon an uninterrupted stretch of lime green lawn.

❄

AS YOU CAN IMAGINE, that put a bit of a damper on our homeowner honeymoon phase. You could also imagine what happened next.

There were checkups and tests and consultations and more tests. There was a lot of referencing my family history and speculating as to whether or not I was falling victim to the same disease. And with not a single examination or diagnostic test revealing anything of note, there was a lot of head-scratching. Which meant there was a lot of talking to therapists and filing scripts and popping pills.

Every now and then, I'd think I was starting to feel...better. The oppressive dread that hung over my days would lighten. And my nightmares would ebb to things less brutal and cruel. But then I'd wake up to a blank wall where a window used to be. Or a walk-in closet now too small to set foot in. Or one half of a two-car garage simply gone...and the newly-leased Land Rover that had been parked inside along with it.

I'd scream for Cora, and she'd come running. I'd ask her if I was remembering something that wasn't. And her answer...and the way she'd shake her head and bury her face in her hands and cry and speak in a low, slow, defeated tone...would always be the same.

"Terry," she'd say, and pause, as if waiting for me to return from whatever state or realm I'd slipped off to before continuing. And when she did, she'd say every word as if it were followed by a period: "Everything is as it should be."

And it would be my turn to collapse.

"I'm sorry, Cora," I would say between sobs. "I'm so sorry."

Because it was all I could say.

Because something, whether from the outside in or inside out, was bent on breaking me down. Piece by piece. And I didn't know what it was. Or how it was doing what it was. Or why.

All I knew for sure...all I understood...was that I couldn't do anything about it.

And so all I could say was *sorry*.

❄

THE NIGHT it made me understand, I was woken from an increasingly rare peaceful sleep to a rumbling. A deep groan that seemed to be coming from everywhere around me. Deepening by the second. Growing evermore intense. So intense I could feel it resonating inside me.

I drew myself up, rested my shoulders against the headboard, and rubbed at my eyes with my palms. And when I forced them open wide, I found myself staring at our darkened bedroom. Mercifully unchanged. But vibrating. Shaking back and forth and up and down so hard and fast it turned everything into an all but indistinguishable blur. And ramping up in time with that ravenous groan threatening to rattle my heart from my chest.

I turned to wake Cora, somehow still asleep. But as my hand reached for her shoulder, a sound wrenched me from my bed and sent me hurtling towards my bedroom door. A sound that pierced the incessant drone like a hot knife. A sound primal and terrible. A sound no father should ever have to hear.

In a heartbeat I was racing down the hallway towards the twins' bedroom door. But for all my exertion, my feet shifted and sank beneath me as if I were running on sand. Halfway down, the door had dilated to the size of a laundry chute. But with every step, the hallway expanded like a concertina, drawing its end farther and farther away from me.

Another handful of strides more and it wasn't much bigger than a mail slot. But even as my legs screamed with effort, the whole house shifted and twisted about me, sending me careening into the wall at my left, my right, over and over again, like I'd been picked up and spun around and set down and made to run.

And as I reached the end at last and clutched for the brass knob, my fingertips found only the flesh of my palm before my head met the wall.

✳

"YOU CAN ALWAYS TELL a good house by looking at its bones."

That's what our realtor had said to us when she first showed us the house. Standing in the foyer, scanning the downstairs with narrowed eyes, she'd balled her hands, curled her arms, and her typically cheery tone was suddenly grave with what I could only call reverence.

"This house has good bones."

It seemed an odd thing for her to have said at the time, seeing as we'd made it very clear we were looking for something to tear down and rebuild.

But in hindsight, she was more right than she might have known.

Every now and then, one of our neighbors will ask us if we'll ever get around to redoing the place, commenting how nice the neighborhood would look if our little house was more aesthetically in line with the others on the street.

And I smile and agree and say it's something we're considering.

Every now and then, Cora will talk about how nice it would be to start a family. How it would give us an excuse to go through with the renovation we've been putting off for what seems like forever, and start making this house feel more like home. And we'll slip into our little ritual of trying out names.

"I keep coming back to Sebastian," she'll eventually say.

And I'll smile. Even as I die inside.

"And if it's a girl?" I'll ask every time, just so I can hear her name beside his.

"Sofi," she'll say, nodding certainly. "I keep coming back to Sofi."

Still I'll smile.

And when I find the strength to speak again, I'll remind her what a good thing we have here with just we two.

What a great home we've made together.

How everything is as it should be.

In this house at the end of the lane.

About the Author

Jeff Samson makes a living as creative director in the ad industry and writes horror stories to stay wholesome and sane. His work can be found in numerous publications, including *Nature Magazine, Cast of Wonders, Perihelion, Lore,* and *Stories We Tell After Midnight Vol. 2.* Jeff lives in the great Garden State of New Jersey with his wife, two kids, one dog, and no cats.

SUSURRATIONS

CAROL GYZANDER

JUNE 1

Greg and Jane sat at the kitchen table of their rural Virginia home, just outside the Washington, DC metropolis, staring at the Excel spreadsheet on the laptop before them. Empty coffee cups showed how long they had been reviewing the numbers.

Greg swiped his hand across his face, pushed away the laptop, and sat back in his chair. "Well, we paid the mortgage for June on time. And we got Kenny off to his year abroad. But unless I can get another job, and fast, next month..." He shook his head. "And advertising jobs are not falling in my lap right now. Who's gonna hire someone who just turned fifty-five?"

"I know, hon." Jane put her hand on his arm and squeezed. "At least my paycheck covers utilities and food. I think working at the library is important, but they sure don't pay like it is."

"Well, we can sell the house. Tell Kenny he's done with college. Or... do something creative."

"Creative? What do you have in mind?" She sat back and raised her eyebrows.

"We have the chickens out back, right?" At her nod, he went on.

"And we buy mealworms at the feed store every week to give them more protein. Ever wonder where those mealworms come from?"

"What? No. I never even thought about it. What are you suggesting?"

He grinned in a way that made him look more his son's age. "I was poking around online and came across a site that tells you how to build a bug farm. To raise mealworms and sell them. I mean, lots of people raise them just to feed their own chickens, but if you scale up, it says there's a decent market out there for them."

"You're serious?" She pushed on his arm and chuckled. "You *are* serious. Bug farmer to the stars?"

"Sure! Just think how many of our friends around here also have chickens in the backyard. Organic everything is the rage these days." He leaned forward and reached for the laptop. He pulled up a site that showed a picture of black beetles, and another of a mass of one-inch long, slender tan worms with no heads piled together in a dish. "Here's the site. *Tenebrio molitor* is the Latin name for the darkling beetles."

She frowned. "*Tenebrio*? That means...seeker of dark places. Or, figuratively, a trickster. That doesn't sound promising."

"Trust my lovely librarian to know the old Latin name. They prefer a warm and dark environment, so I thought I would set up in the barn loft out back."

"Really? You can use the barn?"

"You'll see. I have to get some trays to hold them and purchase the starter worms. At the feed store, or even buy them online, but you're supposed to get them from reputable US suppliers so that they haven't been treated with any chemicals, or else they could injure the chickens."

Jane shrugged and laughed. "Okay. I never figured you'd go from advertising maven to chicken feed producer. You never cease to amaze me, hon."

"And it's not just chicken feed! Pet stores sell these mealworms to reptile owners as well. A whole hidden market." His eyes lit up. "We can pay for everything I need to get started, and maybe the next three or four months of the mortgage while I get rolling, by taking a loan on our 401(k) plan. So, I think it's worth a shot. What do you say?"

"Take a loan? On the retirement plan? But if it fails, we'll be left with next to nothing."

"Yeah, I know, but I really think I can make a go of this." He smiled broadly. "I'm so sick of the nine-to-five rat race, but I tell you what. I've learned so much from doing *other* people's advertising campaigns that I know I can market this home business like nobody's ever seen before."

"Oh, hon, I haven't seen you excited in months. Borrowing against the retirement plan makes me nervous, but let's give it a whirl."

"I was hoping you'd say that. I'll start ordering stuff tonight and get things set up as soon as possible. But no peeking...I want this to be my surprise project. I kind of feel like I need to make good on my responsibilities as the breadwinner."

"It's funny. I'll be tending my chickens in the bottom of the barn, and you'll be tending their food in the loft. Here, you can start by getting me more coffee, Mr. Breadwinner."

He grinned as he grabbed her mug, went to the counter, and put another pod in the Keurig machine. "You bet! But seriously, no peeking out there until I'm set up."

Standing at the fridge while waiting, he idly toyed with rearranging the little poetry magnets their son had given them for Christmas one year, each with a word on it. They had made a game of writing haiku to each other.

Stick with me, baby
Infinity and beyond!
Best is yet to be

When she came over to get her coffee, her breath caught when she read the words. Blinking back tears, she gave him a hug that turned into a kiss and led them upstairs.

❄

JUNE 15

After preparing dinner, Jane hauled the overfull garbage bag out of the kitchen container, tied it up, and headed out to the garbage cans. "Gosh darn it, this is supposed to be *his* job. But *noooo*, he's too busy setting up the new bug empire."

She lifted the outdoor garbage can lid and prepared to hoist in the bag. Something caught her eye, and she stopped before depositing her burden.

"What on earth is all this?" She pulled some mailing wrappers out of the can and scanned the labels covered with Russian characters. "I thought he was supposed to use reputable US suppliers?"

Keeping one out of the can, she hefted the kitchen garbage in, closed it up, then turned and headed toward the barn.

As she moved toward the stairs with the wrapper under her arm, she passed by the chicken wire run that connected to the room in the barn they used as a chicken coop. She greeted her favorites. "Hello, Henrietta. Hello, Marjorie. How are you two lovelies today?" They squawked, then went back to pecking at the ground.

She stopped at the base of the loft staircase. "Greg? Greg, are you up there? I'm coming up!"

His head appeared at the top of the steps. "Oh, hey there. I was just about ready to give you a tour, anyway. Come on up!"

She stopped at the top of the stairs and looked around, mouth agape and eyebrows raised. "Wow! No wonder I haven't seen you for two weeks. You've been busy! What is all this stuff?"

He took her free hand and walked her around the room, showing her the various fish tanks in a row, each with a screen over the top for ventilation and a couple of inches of wheat bran that served as both food and bedding for the mealworms.

"It's like butterflies. First, mealworms pupate and become darkling beetles, which lay eggs that hatch into more mealworms. It's supposed to take a couple of months to cycle through all those stages, but each female will lay lots of eggs. So I'll have lots more mealworms in a few months!"

She bent over the nearest aquarium, watching the residents wriggling through the wheat bran. It looked like living sawdust. "So, they eat that and live in it, too? That's wild. But what do you do with all the beetles once they've laid their eggs?"

"That's the neatest thing." He grinned. "They don't live very long, and all the larvae just eat their bodies after they die. So, no muss, no fuss, no messy cleanup!"

"Eew. That's nasty. You give your life to make the next generation and get eaten as thanks for your effort. Creepy."

She wrapped her arms across her chest. The crinkling reminded her of the wrapper she carried. "Oh, hey. What's this all about? I saw a bunch of these in the garbage. I thought you said you had to get them from a reputable source, and you couldn't trust international providers? I can't even read this label, so I have to assume that's international."

He ducked his head, looking sheepish. "Well, that's true...but this provider got a good rating from several online forums. You know how much time I spent researching it all. Trust me. It'll be fine."

She frowned, then shrugged. "Well, you're the bug farmer. I'm just the chicken keeper here. Speaking of which, I need to check the ladies to see if they have anything for us. Is there still room in there for more eggs?" Her hand gestured to the old fridge at the back of the loft.

"Well, I have it set up now to hold the new crop of mealworms. Is it okay if we keep the eggs inside the house from now on?"

"Oh, you bet. I don't want to mix my food with *their* food. But, hey, I forgot we had some magnets out here, too." She walked to the fridge and rearranged the tiny magnets to make a poem.

He put his arms around her waist from behind and read aloud over her shoulder.

> *I love you so much*
> *We'll always be together*
> *For eternity*

Greg laughed. "Aaw, lovely. That's a much nicer poem than the ones I can usually make!"

He sobered and put his chin on her shoulder as he hugged her tight. "Thanks for trusting me, Jane. I mean, about this bug-farming stuff. I have a really good feeling about it all. Next, I have to start designing the packaging material and the marketing."

"Well, for that, you are *definitely* the expert. Congratulations, honey, this is all really impressive." She turned and gave him a hug and a kiss, then headed down to check the chicken coop for eggs and bring the chickens in from their outside enclosure for the night.

❄

JULY 15

"Greg! Greg?" Jane dumped her bag on the side counter in the kitchen and took a quick tour around the house. It was her late night at the library, and she was hungry. The room was tidy, and there were none of the wonderful aromas she'd come to expect when getting in from the late shift.

"Honey, did you make any dinner?" No answer.

Muttering, she headed out the back door toward the barn. The chickens scrabbled around in their run as she passed them in a hurry, not even stopping to greet them. She banged the door open to the barn. "Greg! Are you still in here? It's late!"

He poked his head over the edge of the loft. "Oh. Yeah. Sorry, I forgot to start dinner. But come on up, and I can show you something cool."

"Honey, come on. You've been in here so much! Can't we do this tomorrow?" No answer. "Greg?"

She tried to relax so that she wouldn't stomp as she headed up the steps. Stopped at the top and took a deep breath. "All right, I'm here. Show me the cool thing, and then I want to eat. I'm starving."

"I've got a bunch of mealworms to harvest already! Watch this. They said in the forum that you just put a piece of apple in the bin, and in a few minutes, all the mealworms are attracted to it and latch onto it with their mouths." He took the screen off the top of the first bin, propped it on the old wooden chair in the aisle, and tossed in a few apple chunks.

She came over next to him and watched the surface of the wheat germ start to move, slowly at first, until it was undulating with waves of mealworms wriggling toward each apple piece. Jane crossed her arms and hugged herself as crawling worms attacked more and more of the fruit.

Greg reached in and picked up a chunk, lifting it in the air with the attached worms squirming. Jane gagged and took a step back.

"Oh, my God. That's nasty. And what on earth happened to your fingers?"

Greg moved the apple into a smaller container and then held up his hand, looking at the multiple bandages on his fingers. "Oh, it's nothing. I, uh, just scraped them on the screening and figured I should cover them for safety. No worries. But isn't that cool to have more worms so fast?"

"Yeah. What's up with that? You said it would be multiple months before we had mealworms to harvest."

Greg fished out the other pieces of apple. "The guys in the forum who recommended this supplier have some great advice. Good tips on better, uh, nutrition to make them grow faster."

"Huh. Interesting, I guess." She stood with her arms wrapped tightly about her body, not touching anything around her.

Her gaze traveled out the barn window at their home. "Wow. It gives me the heebie-jeebies to have the house so close to all this." She shivered. "Okay, I need some dinner. Are you coming in?"

"Yeah, let me just show you the new packaging. A guy is coming from the pet store on the highway to pick up mealworms tomorrow." He grabbed what looked like a Chinese food carton from the floor, shook one of the apple pieces over the open top, and grinned in satisfaction as the mealworms dropped off into the container. When it was full, he folded the top closed and held it up for her to see.

The bright red carton bore a white square label on it, and in the square, she read the words "Early Worm Gets the Bird."

Greg grinned. "What do you think? Catchy, right?"

"I guess. Worm gets bird? Maybe creepy is more like it. But you know the marketing and advertising side better than I do."

He placed the container with a dozen others in the fridge and closed the door. She stared at the magnets on it.

> *Your pulsating love*
> *Commitment is the answer*
> *Leave the world behind*

She frowned and pointed at it. "That's weird. Why would you write that? 'Leave the world behind'?"

Busy filling the next container, he didn't answer her.

She stared at him with one eyebrow raised, then brushed her arms off with her fingertips as she turned on her heel and headed down the steps. "Dinner. Now. Coming?"

❄

JULY 17

Jane talked to the chickens as she tended to them in the chicken coop before work that morning.

Put feed in each trough and fresh water in the automatic waterers. "Here you go, ladies."

Collected the chicken poop and used bedding materials to place in the compost pile. "I don't know why he can't do this. He's out here pretty much all day anyway while I still have to go to work."

Checked for eggs. Another half dozen, which she planned to take into work. The kitchen fridge was getting full now that she couldn't use the one in the loft—and there were only so many eggs you could eat. "Thank you, ladies." Shooed them out of the coop into the run outside. "Out you go."

As she headed for her car, Greg came stumbling out the back door, shielding his eyes from the morning light. "Oh, hey. Have a good day." He started toward the barn.

"Honey, will you be able to get the lawn cut today? It's getting long." Jane gave a little lopsided smile and a shrug.

"Oh, uh, I don't know. My fingers are kind of sore." He waggled his hands, showing even more Band-Aids than before. "I guess I'm just clumsy with the screens. But I'll try."

He sketched a wave and headed into the barn. Jane stared after him for a few moments, then got in her car and headed for the library.

❄

LATE THAT NIGHT, she was alone in the house after dinner. Greg was still outside. She was restless, unable to read or enjoy TV.

She missed her husband—even when he was around, all he did these days was read the online forums.

She looked out the bedroom window as she brushed her hair before bed and saw him through the barn window, sitting in the dim light of the meager overhead bulb. Just sitting and rocking. Staring at one of the bins and what she imagined must be the roiling mass of worms it contained. She closed the blinds and went to bed.

❄

JULY 19

Cleaning up the kitchen after dinner, Jane smiled. At least they had eaten together—he had prepared a lovely, rare steak on the grill—and were watching the nightly news as usual.

She touched him on the shoulder. "Can you bring the dishes over, hon?"

Greg continued the conversation as he passed her the dishes. "So, the production rate is so good that I need to increase the number of bins. I needed to get some even bigger trays and make it more efficient. Already ordered them, and they should get here tomorrow." He beamed.

"That's great—" Jane broke off as she noticed the headline of the upcoming story on the local news: "Reptiles face down owners."

The newscaster posed in front of a suburban house. "And now, for our nightly interesting moment, some reptile owners in Leesburg report being cornered by their two pets. They say the pair of iguanas climbed out of their cage and stalked them across the room, extending their tongues in a threatening manner."

The image changed to show a middle-aged man and his young son standing indoors in front of an aquarium with two large iguanas inside.

"I don't know what got into them," the man said. "I've never seen them behave like that before. It's like they were a team, herding and hunting us. Then they just went back to normal. I don't know; maybe they were just hungry."

Jane clutched at Greg's arm. "Look! On the shelf over the aquarium."

The image on the television zoomed in toward the iguanas, showing a red Chinese food container partially hidden behind them. The words "Early Worm" were visible over the top rim of the aquarium.

"What on earth?" Jane turned to look at Greg. "Do you think...?"

Greg cleared his throat. "Huh. No, just some kind of coincidence. Nothing really happened, anyway. They always look for weird stories for these human-interest segments."

He turned away, jostling the elbow of her hand that held the sharp steak knife.

"Careful! Oh, crap." Jane dropped the knife in the sink when she saw the bright red blood on her index finger. "Dammit."

His eyes widened. "Jane, I'm so sorry! I wasn't paying attention. Here, rinse it off, and let me put pressure on it."

He guided her finger under the water, then whipped a clean handkerchief out of his pocket and applied it to the cut, pressing firmly for a minute while he held the wounded hand over her head. He brought her arm down and peeked to ensure it had stopped bleeding.

"Are you trying to take after me? I thought I was the clumsy one." Folding the bloody handkerchief carefully, he tucked it in his pocket and guided her toward the powder room. "Come on, let's get it bandaged."

She gave a wry grin and followed along to be patched up. When she was all set, she sat back down on the couch in front of the bay window in the kitchen and laid her head back.

Greg finished the dinner cleanup and then slipped out the back door.

Looking idly out the back window, she saw him pull out the handkerchief as he crossed the lawn toward the barn. Then, a moment later, she saw the light come on in the window upstairs.

❄

J*ULY 25*

Jane did her usual morning routine with the chickens, then noticed she was out of mealworms to give them for their every-other-day protein treat. Sighing, she headed to the loft to get more from the fridge.

Something skittered in the corners when she stepped into the loft, and she paused for a moment, but didn't hear anything else. She started across the room. There were now many more bins, six feet long and three feet wide, laid out in a grid at the far end by the refrigerator.

A slithering sound came to her ears from all around as she crossed to the fridge, and she shrank away from the bins on each side. The activity got stronger as she passed each one, and she shivered.

She was about to open the door when she stopped dead and stared at the magnets.

> *Join us deep inside*
> *As one among the many*
> *Become one with us*

"What the hell. Where does he get this stuff?" She yanked open the door, grabbed an "Early Worm Gets the Bird" container, and slammed the door shut before heading back down to feed them to her ladies.

As she entered the coop, they all quieted and stared, heads tilted to the side, until she put the mealworms into several piles on the floor. All the hens regarded her with an intense, unblinking gaze until she backed out of the coop. Once the door closed behind her, they rushed at the wriggling heaps, grabbing the mealworms and gobbling them down. She watched as they devoured them all, goosebumps on her arms despite the warm weather, then headed to work with a frown.

That evening, she went to bed alone yet again. She felt so fretful that she took a sleeping pill, but woke in the middle of the night from a sound sleep, her heart pounding in her chest. She clutched the covers with both hands and looked, bleary-eyed, to Greg's side of the bed. It was empty.

She heard a rhythmic squeaking sound. Looking back to the foot of the bed, she saw Greg sitting in a chair, staring at her, with his head tilted as he rocked back and forth. Groggy, she blinked her eyes a few times and pulled the covers over her head, slipping back into sleep.

❄

JULY 29

Home from another late night at the library, Jane chatted to her ladies as they squawked and milled about the coop. She reached into the first nest, pulling out sticky pieces of broken shell. "Hey, is one of you ladies getting too fat? Crushed your own egg? Poor thing!"

She wiped her hand off on a rag and felt around in the next nest. Pulling out an intact shell, she smiled—until she realized that it felt too light. Looking more closely, Jane discovered a hole pecked in one end of the egg. She merely held an empty shell. It slipped through her fingers and crashed to the floor, the pieces scattering across the coop.

"What...what's going on?" She rummaged frantically for the next, only to discover the same thing.

When she checked each nest for eggs, she discovered that all of them had been pecked open. Her hand flew to her mouth. A chill ran down her spine when she noticed the stillness behind her, and she turned around.

All six birds stood lined up, facing her across the center of the chicken coop. Then, stepping in unison, they advanced toward her with their beaks slightly open, their outstretched heads tilted to the side, and their gaze fixed upon her. Their clawed feet scratching on the coop floor made the only sound.

"What the—" She took a step backward and then another as the birds stalked her across the space. She swung her head from side to side, looking around for something to help. Her gaze lit on the half-full container of Early Worms, and she grabbed it off the shelf.

Sprinkling a pile of them on the floor away from the door, she breathed a sigh of relief as the chickens broke formation and dove in to gobble up the mealworms, tossing and flinging some up in the air in their eagerness to consume them. Then, while they were occupied, she bolted out the door and shut it behind her.

"The hell with the eggs. What was that all about, anyway?" She realized her hand shook as it rested on the chicken coop door.

"Greg? Are you...are you up there?" She headed upstairs.

Entering the loft, she saw his back as he sat in the rickety chair and leaned over one of the bins. He didn't look up as she walked around to his side; he held his hand over the bin, squeezing blood out of a cut on his fingertips into the bedding. Worms roiled over each other, writhing to get to the blood spatter.

Jane stopped still, clapping her hands over her mouth as she gagged. Greg didn't even look up as she turned and ran down the stairs crying.

It was hours before she went to bed alone, covers pulled up tight around her neck.

She awoke in the middle of the night to an odd sensation. She sat bolt upright in the bed and pulled the covers down to see dozens of mealworms wriggling across her abdomen and under the sheets. She shrieked and jumped out of bed, frantically brushing them off her. "Oh my God oh my God oh my God."

Greg's side of the bed sat untouched.

"Greg! Where are you?" When there was no answer, she turned and looked out the window to see the dim light still on in the barn.

She ran down the steps, shoved her feet in shoes, and dashed out the back door toward the barn. She charged up the steps to the loft and into the middle of the grid made of bins but stopped abruptly when she saw him in the chair next to the largest bin in the corner by the refrigerator.

His Band-Aids lay discarded on the floor next to him. He used the sharp knife to cut his finger yet again, and the mealworms roiled beneath the dripping wound, diving at the blood splatter.

She averted her gaze, catching sight of the same poem on the fridge. It still gave her the creeps.

Join us deep inside
As one among the many
Become one with us

"*Greg!* What the hell is going on?"

This time he noticed her. He stood and turned, frowning.

"I'm sorry, Jane. I tried to get you to be part of us. But you haven't been listening." He advanced toward her down the row with his head forward and tilted slightly to the side, the bloody knife in his outstretched hand.

"Hon, you're freaking me out. You look just like the chickens did earlier. Hon? *Greg!*" She backed toward the steps.

He moved too quickly and blocked her way to the staircase. She stopped, one bin between them, then backed up a row and moved the opposite way through the maze of bins toward the window. He followed, moving one row forward and parallel to her movement. She whimpered and went the other way, hoping to get around him to the steps.

As she passed his row, he lunged forward and grabbed her by one arm with his free hand. Her husband pushed her toward the giant open bin, holding the knife to her neck. She cringed at the feeling of his hot breath on her ear. When they reached the giant bin, he spun her around and backed her up so that her legs pressed against the edge, the susurration of the worms filling her ears as they swarmed to the surface. Ready to receive her.

His back was to the fridge, and as she twisted to the side, trying to break free of his grasp, she looked over her shoulder at the roiling mass of mealworms in the big bin.

Then her gaze fell upon the magnets on the fridge door.

The words had changed. It was no longer a poem.

Push him in.

She did.

About the Author

Carol Gyzander writes and edits horror and science fiction. She focuses on strong women with twisted tales that touch your heart. She brought a female focus to her Bram Stoker Award®-nominated story, "The Yellow Crown," inspired by Robert W. Chambers' world of the twin suns. Her cryptid novella, *Forget Me Not*, occurs near Niagara Falls in 1969/1939. She has stories in the cosmic horror edition of *Weird Tales 367* and *Weird House Magazine* Volume I.

She co-edited the *Even in the Grave* ghost story anthology with James Chambers. The reversal of Roe v. Wade inspired the latest horror anthology she co-edited with Rachel A. Brune, *A Woman Unbecoming*, which presents stories of women's rage, power, and vengeance and benefits reproductive healthcare services.

Carol is one of the HWA Chapter Program Co-Managers, the Co-Chair of the HWA NY Chapter, and co-hosts the online Galactic Terrors reading series. Find her at CarolGyzander.com

THE WAREHOUSE

MICHAEL J. MOORE

SEATTLE'S MAYOR, Doris Curry, will later claim during a press conference that children have no business wandering the SoDo district unsupervised, and though Jamarse's mother shares the sentiment, she works weekdays at Cortez Grocery on Beacon Hill and can't afford a babysitter. It's an ideal arrangement for a twelve-year-old, unable to understand his own struggle against the weight of poverty, so he deviates most days after school. He's only been caught once when she came home early on a Friday. She whipped him until his dark skin turned pink, but her belt didn't change a thing because Monday afternoon, he and his friends went to Chinatown and purchased three dollars' worth of rice candy with a handful of change they found in the ashtray of a parked car.

It's mid-spring, sunny, and nearing 3 p.m. when Jason Callahan sweeps a clump of dishwater hair from his eyes and boasts of an abandoned building he and his older brother nearly broke into over the weekend. Jason, being the token white boy of the trio, tends to live up to the unspoken expectation that he also be the craziest.

"Yo ass wasn't 'bout to break into shit." Tre waves him off as an old town-car growls past, leaving an expanding cloud in its wake. It fogs up Jamarse's wire-rimmed glasses, so he pulls them off, causing the surrounding industrial buildings to morph into a collection of blurry silhouettes. Wiping the lenses with his T-shirt, he sets them over his nose, and the world comes back into focus. The SoDo is located close to downtown, but outside of morning and evening rush-hours—and the quarter-mile radius surrounding the local Costco—traffic is generally thin, as there isn't much reason for anybody not working in one of the countless factories to traverse the district. It just so happens, however, to be located between the boys' school, and the neighborhood in which they live.

Jason says, "My brother's idea, dude. Not mine. But that don't mean I wouldn't'a did it."

They're just walking past a Krispy Kreme, and Jamarse's stomach growls as the smell of exhaust slowly dissipates, replaced by the sweet aroma of caramelized sugar and cinnamon. His backpack seems to grow heavier with the awareness of his hunger.

"Either of you have any money?" he asks.

Both boys glance at him like he has a slug on his face, and then resume their conversation.

"I guess I can believe that. Yo brother crazy as hell. You know what I heard about him yester—" Tre peers up into his eyelids, "actually I think it was last week."

Jason sighs. "Man, if it's about him getting jumped at the bus-stop—"

"'Course it's about him getting his ass whooped. You know Dig over on Forth and Union?"

"You mean your cousin?" Jamarse offers.

Tre, ignoring the question, pats an itch out of his braided hair. "He said yo brother just walked up like it was a family reunion and started using the n-word. Even yo ass ain't that dumb."

"Man—" Jason shakes his head, "you know he didn't mean it like that."

"He white. Ain't no other way *to* mean it."

Jamarse's gaze drops to the dusty sidewalk just in time for his shoe to evade a lump of greying gum. Tre tells Jason he and his siblings only live in the hood because their mom's a crack-head, and the exchange begins to fade in and out as Jamarse considerers heading home to peruse the stock of ramen noodles and boxed mac and cheese in his pantry. He's been reprimanded more than once for sharing food with his friends, and he's sure if it happens again, it will be his ass. So as Jason taunts Tre, claiming that not everybody has a pastor for a dad, Jamarse tries to think of a tactful way to ditch both of them.

He figures he can easily spin a tale of how his mother, whom he knows his friends have no desire to encounter, will be home early from work. The tricks to lying, he knows, are preparing for cross-examination and assuring one isn't later caught by inconsistencies in one's story. The narrative needs to be carefully crafted before it's delivered, so that's exactly what he's working on when Tre suggests he has more gangster in his little pinky-toe than Jason can achieve in six lifetimes.

Jamarse's thoughts drift to a box of Pop-Tarts in the cupboard above the sink. They came from the foodbank, and though they taste like brown-sugar—rather than one of the flavors he prefers—they're still Pop-Tarts. However, fantasizing about the food in his home won't get him there any sooner, so he opens his mouth to inform his friends he'll be parting with them once they reach the Central District, and before he can get a word out, Jason says, "Whatever, dude. If you're so hard, let's see *you* break into a building."

"You mean the one yo dumbass brother tried to get into?"

"Sure. Why not?"

"Well, if it was so easy, why didn't y'all get in?"

"We would have. A cop drove by, though, so we just cut out. We're gonna go back next weekend."

"Then why you trying a get me to do it right now? Y'all got some freaky white people shit up in there? Something gonna jump out and try and eat my black ass? Man, ain't falling for no—"

"Man, if you're scared—"

"What—nigga? Scared'a what?"

Though Jamarse is a straight-A student, he often struggles to understand the social interactions that take place around him. Still, experience has taught him that once the s-word has been uttered amongst boys, there can be no backing out for anybody within earshot. So, taking a deep breath, he pushes all thoughts of food to the back of his mind and listens quietly to the conversation that, seventeen minutes later, will lead him into a dirty alley which he has passed five days a week since the beginning of the school year, but until today, never paid a second glance.

It's some kind of warehouse, and Jason is right because though there are no bottom floor windows in which to peek, the surrounding silence suggests it is, indeed, abandoned. It appears to be four or five stories high, and constructed from dark-gray concrete. Across the alley sits a building that Jamarse knows houses storage units, with two green dumpsters against its outside wall.

Along the way, they encountered a bone-thin blond woman with no teeth and a wrinkled neck, who offered to show them her tits for five dollars. Jason laughed, while Tre spit on the sidewalk and called her a crackhead. Jamarse ignored her like he often did panhandlers, as they tended to frighten him. The experience was the topic of conversation amongst his friends until they reached their destination.

Now they all stand staring at a dirt-caked metal door with no handles. It's painted gray to match the wall, and the bottom corner is bent slightly outward. Jason says his brother did that with a hammer.

"What?" Tre shrieks. "What the hell he doing carrying around a hammer in the SoDo?"

"I don't know, dude. After he got jumped, he just—I don't know. We going in, or what?"

"Man, there ain't no handle."

Both boys glance at Jamarse, as if he will have the solution. He does.

"It's gonna take two people."

"What?" Jason asks, though Jamarse knows he understands, and likely had the same discussion with his older brother.

Still, he explains, "Someone's gotta pull that corner out while someone else crawls through. Then, he can open the door from the inside and let us in."

Jason takes a deep breath. "What if it don't open from the inside?"

"It will."

"I ain't doing it," Tre asserts. "Last thing I need is one a y'all niggas letting that thing go while I'm halfway through and taking off my head."

"Whatever dude," Jason sighs. "I ain't doing it either, so unless Jamarse wants to volunteer, let's get the fuck outta here."

"Man, you would put it on Jamarse, wouldn't you?"

"What's that supposed to mean?"

As the boys argue, it occurs to Jamarse that they're both attempting to strategically pass the blame onto him because neither actually want to break into the building. And though neither does he—in fact all he really wants is to go home and eat—he desires even less to be the scapegoat. So he slides out of his backpack and instructs Tre to pull on the corner because he's the stronger of the two.

"You sure?" Tre hesitates.

"Just hold it as tight as you can, okay?"

Setting down his own backpack, Tre takes hold of the metal and grunts as he wrenches it, and Jamarse examines the opening.

"It's not big enough."

Tre's eyes expand for a fraction of a second, and then he loses his grip, causing the metal to snap back so hard the report echoes through the alley like a gunshot. It seems to ring out from Jamarse's chest, and expand into every inch of him, pressing goosebumps out from within.

"I can't pull it no further," Tre complains, examining his palms. "And that shit digging into my hands!"

Cringing, Jason scans both of the alley's entrances.

"It's too staunch," Jamarse states.

His friends lock eyes, and then stare blankly at him.

"The metal's too sturdy. It's gonna take both of you."

So Jason sets down his backpack, both boys pull, and once again Jamarse peers at a triangular opening through which he now believes he'll be able to squeeze his thin frame. Without hesitation, he drops to all fours and thinks of the container of sweetened orange juice in his refrigerator.

"Come on, nigga," Tre grunts. "This shit ain't easy."

Jamarse shakes off the thought, and crawls toward darkness, realizing now that he'll need to crouch lower and maneuver his body slightly sideways in order to fit. Taking a deep breath, he reaches in with one hand, planting his palm on a dusty cement floor, poking his head through, and thinking, *It's too dark in here. I'm gonna need a light.*

Tre is the only one with a cellphone, so Jamarse prepares to back-track in order to request it of him, but then something wraps around his wrist, and he feels his heart leap into his throat because it's cold and scaly and he doesn't have to see it to know it's a snake. It's thick, and he can feel muscles flexing beneath its rough skin as it swiftly tightens around him like a noose.

Jamarse gasps, and he's about to scream, to jerk back his hand, but then it's pulled out from under him and his face collides with the dirty pavement. He sees red, and though there must be pain, there's no time to process it because he's pulled like a piece of thread through the opening. It snaps shut behind him so loud his ears ring as darkness consumes him.

❄

AT FIRST, all Jamarse can hear is the squelch inside his skull. It's pitch-black in the building, and he's dazed, but the cold and dusty floor against his stomach and cheek informs him that he's lying prone and the hem of his shirt is slightly elevated. Something solid and sharp rests under his left thigh, which he thinks may be a rock, but before he's considered it any further, it occurs to him that there is still a huge snake coiled around his wrist. A trembling moan escapes him as he scrambles, first to his hands and knees, then to his feet. He shakes his forearm, finding it lighter than expected. Still, he reaches with the opposite hand and presses his fingertips against his own smooth skin, relieved, yet aware that if the reptile is not stuck to his body, then it must be nearby on the floor.

He knows he needs to move, but instead finds himself checking to confirm his glasses are still on his face, and contemplating whether or not it's even possible for a snake to pull a boy through a door. But it felt like a snake, and moreover, if not a snake, then what?

Move, he thinks. *You need to get out of here. Now. Feel along the surface of the door until you find the handle, and then get the hell out.*

As he's having this thought, the ringing in his ears subsides, and he hears the voices of his friends mere feet away, yet separated by brick and metal.

"Jamarse!" Tre's voice is muffled.

"Oh, man!" Jason cries. "Oh shit! Oh shit! Use your phone, man! Call nine-one-one!"

Then they're drowned out by a sequence of guttural explosions that Jamarse quickly recognizes as the frantic, deep bark of a large dog. An angry and aggressive one at that. It echoes inside the building, and though this makes it nearly impossible to locate its source, it's growing louder, which means it's getting closer.

Finally Jamarse screams, and he's never heard his own voice reach such high volume or pitch. He backs into the door, curling into a standing fetal position. His voice somehow transcends that of the dog's, and once he's expelled every bit of air from his lungs, he sucks in a gasping breath and becomes aware that the animal has stopped barking.

"Jamarse, my nigga!"

"What the hell are you doing, dude? Call nine-one-one!"

Now the dog is growling, and doing so directly into Jamarse's ear. It must be massively tall, and so close Jamarse can feel its warm breath on his neck, so he bolts upright and the back of his head collides with the door, causing a hot flash of pain to shoot down through his body like lightning.

Then he's in motion, sprinting through the darkness because behind him is a snake, behind him is a dog, and though it's inevitable he'll collide with a wall or a piece of unseen industrial machinery, this is favorable over being consumed by dangerous creatures.

But he doesn't run into a wall or an assembly line. Rather, something catches his shoe and though he can't see the floor, the wind against his face tells him that it's coming at him rapidly. Jamarse is falling, falling, falling. He readies his palms to catch the pavement, but instead they touch wood.

Recognizing the feel of a staircase, he climbs to his feet and locates a wall, constructed of splintery plywood. He doesn't take the time to consider his situation until he's already climbing the steps, and thinking, *This is better. Safe. Safer than down there, at least. And what the hell just happened? How could a snake pull me through that door, and why is there even a snake in this building, let alone a dog?*

But the dog has, at some point, gone quiet, and Jamarse no longer hears his friends yelling about nine-one-one. The trek smells of sawdust, and a hint of light from above catches his eye, prompting him to pick up his pace. It grows in intensity as he approaches, and soon he can see the top step and the floor that lies beyond.

※

IT'S CARPETED.

He emerges into a hall that extends to the left and the right and seems abnormally long in both directions. There are doors along one wall, and windows on the other. They're spaced about a dozen feet apart and let in enough sunlight for Jamarse to see that he's now in what appears to be a row of offices. The scent of sawdust has disappeared, replaced by some sweet-smelling air freshener.

The carpet is clean. White. So are the walls. This area has been maintained too well to be in an abandoned building, but somehow he finds no comfort in this. He must discover which of these windows—if any—overlook his friends, get it open, and call down to them.

If it doesn't open, he thinks, *I'll break it.*

First he looks right. Then left.

Left. Left is right. That's the direction you came from.

He turns his body just as a raspy voice calls behind him.

"Hey! Pst!"

Nearly jumping out of his shoes, Jamarse spins on his heels and beholds the blond woman with the wrinkly neck. She's wearing the same white blouse and baggy blue jeans in which he saw her earlier.

"You wanna see 'em or not?"

With this, she reaches up, takes her shirt-collar in both hands and wrenches in either direction. The cloth rips down the middle, exposing a set of sagging breasts that hang over a stomach strewn with flabby, loose skin.

Jamarse stands frozen as she begins to laugh and then breaks into a coughing fit. She drops to her knees, clutching at her throat, until finally, her stomach heaves and a ball of slimy, grey hair falls from her mouth to the floor. It unravels, crawls onto four tiny legs, and before it has taken two steps, Jamarse recognizes it as a rat. The woman continues to cough and heave, as the rodent scurries toward him, but Jamarse is done watching. He turns and sprints the other way.

A wall is visible up ahead, and it appears the hall curves to the right, but it's still too far away for Jamarse to comfortably anticipate reaching. Instead, he stops and reaches for one of the doors on his left. The handle is metal, and coldness indicates there must be a freezer on the other side. Still, he twists, and pulls it open, running into a room that's slightly darker than the hall, and pulling it shut behind him.

❄

IT'S HIS BEDROOM, only it isn't, because his bed, his dresser, every surface is covered in a thick layer of dust. His mother stands in the middle of the room in a pair of red sweats. She's wearing her wig, which gives the illusion of straightened, highlighted hair, and staring down at him blankly. Jamarse finds no comfort in her presence because her right hand is clutching the tail of a thick green snake. It's wriggling and flicking its tongue, attempting to break free, but his mother is just too strong. This must be the snake which forced him into this place.

She says, "What did I tell you about not coming straight home after school? Now I'm about to whip your little black ass till it bleeds, and you're begging me to stop!" She raises the snake as if it is her belt, and it locks eyes with Jamarse, then hisses.

Jamarse feels his bottom lip curl as tears pour down his face. His mother takes one step, then two, and he turns, wrenches the door, and runs back into the hall.

＊

HERE IS THE DOG, standing mere feet away, and Jamarse hates that he now recognizes it. It's thin and muscular, with a coat of short, black fur. A Doberman pinscher. Staring death at him and baring razor-sharp teeth. The same teeth that left a scar on Jamarse's right calf when he was nine. When this dog belonged to his next-door-neighbor. But this dog was put to sleep for attacking him, and though he knows this can't be real—none of it can—he also knows that it is.

Behind the canine stands the wrinkled woman, her breasts fully exposed. She stares at him, a maniacal, toothless smile stretched from one ear to the other. Then Jamarse's mother steps from the bedroom, still holding her snake and the floor begins to vibrate under his feet. In the distance, he hears a noise like the ocean's waves, and then water appears.

It comes from around the corner, pouring in so deep he knows it will flood the hall and he'll drown—not only because he can't swim, but because there will be nowhere *to* swim. Without thinking, Jamarse chooses another door, runs through it, and slams it shut.

＊

HE'S in an office which he knows well. One in which he's been every month for the past two years. This is the office of Dr. Cavil, who is white, with a round belly and a graying beard, and who now sits in his armchair across from the couch. Like Jamarse's bedroom, it's dark and dusty in here. Books are arranged meticulously on one shelf, and assorted toys on another.

Dr. Cavil smiles and says, "Jamarse, I want to talk about something with you. Would that be okay?"

The sounds from the hall have altogether vanished, and because this fact ushers with it a comfort that Jamarse doesn't wish to lose, he tells the doctor it's okay.

"You know, Jamarse, no two people are the same, and often it's our differences that unite us." He leans forward, rubs the back of his neck with one hand, and then sets it in his lap. "There's nothing wrong with you, and I think it's important that you understand that. I believe you have a condition that's been associated with some very prominent people. Some have even had a great impact on the world."

Only now does it occur to Jamarse that this very meeting has happened before. That he's reliving the worst day of his life, because it was the day he learned, at ten-years-old, who he truly was. Rather than letting Dr. Cavil finish, he says, "I know. I'm autistic. I have Asperger's Syndrome."

But Dr. Cavil says, "You *had* Asperger's, Jamarse, but things have changed. Why don't you take a seat on the couch, and we'll discuss your new condition."

Jamarse doesn't want to sit. He doesn't want to talk. All he wants is to get out of this place, so he turns, opens the door, and flies back into the hall.

❄

IT'S EMPTY.

No dog.

No mother.

No tits.

No water.

Jamarse sprints back the way from whence he came, and then down the stairs, emerging into darkness and seeming to glide until his hands touch the metal door. It flies open and he bursts through to see Jason and Tre, who both jump, startled and screaming in unison. Their high-pitched shrills echo through the desolate alley as Tre's phone falls from his hand, onto the pavement.

"Oh shit!" Jason cries. "Did you see that? Did you just—"

"'Course I saw it, nigga!" Tre responds through tears. "The damn door done opened itself!" He leans down to pick up the phone and only then does Jamarse see another boy. One which he's beheld in the bathroom mirror every morning for as long as he can remember. He's sprawled out, facedown, on the ground. His head is inside the building. His neck—swollen and craned unnaturally.

Tre puts the phone to his ear, sobs, "Yeah. Yeah, I'm still here. I don't know, man. It don't matter. I think he dead. I told you already! The door snapped shut on his neck while he was trying to crawl through! What? I don't know! I don't know how to explain it! Damn! I don't know the damn address neither!"

I'm dead, Jamarse thinks, finally achieving some semblance of calm. *I'm dead and my fears have somehow managed to follow me into the afterlife. This is like living a nightmare.*

But his fears, it seems, are all inside this building, and now he is not. So maybe he'll be all right if he stays outside. Or maybe he can make his way back to the Central District. Back to his home. To his mother who will never whip him again.

Before he's finished having this thought, however, the sound of growling echoes from inside. Then the terrible dog steps from the darkness, snarling and drooling over its teeth.

Run. Run now. You need to run now.

But the animal lunges first, catching him by his leg—the same leg it bit when they were both alive—and even though he's dead, it sends a wave of pain up his body. He cries out and tries to pull free, but this only causes it to bite harder as it drags him back inside.

About the Author

Michael J. Moore is the bestselling author of the Stoker shortlisted, *Highway Twenty*, as well as *Secret Harbor, Nightmares in Aston: Wicker Village, After the Change,* and *Cinema 7*. His short stories and nonfiction have appeared in dozens of magazines and newspapers, and he currently has a small handful of film projects in the works. Follow him at: https://michaeljmoorewriti.wixsite.com/website, on Facebook at: https://www.facebook.com/michaeljmoorewriting, or on Twitter at: https://twitter.com/MichaelJMoore20.

THE DEMON CORE

SCOTTY MILDER

Los Alamos, New Mexico. May 21, 1946

THEY CALLED it *tickling the dragon's tail*, and Louis knew better.

Fermi even sat Louis down not a month ago, pinned him with that severe Roman gaze, and said: *You'll be dead within a year if you keep doing the experiment that way.* But Fermi was older than Louis, and European. He had an old-world, old man's way of looking at things. He was more comfortable drifting serenely through the halls of the University of Chicago, issuing precise little nuggets of genial wisdom, than he was scraping through experiment after dusty experiment out on this pine-studded plateau, way at the ass-end of nowhere at all.

Louis and the other young fellas saw themselves as gunslingers. Sixty years ago, and just a little bit south of here, Billy the Kid was still rustling cattle and shooting holes through anyone who got in his way. Louis came from Winnipeg and hadn't sat a horse in his life. But he was still a gunslinger. He even went out and bought the boots to prove it.

Tickling the dragon's tail. They all knew better, but they did it anyway. Knowing that at any moment the dragon could turn around and eat them up.

They called the core "Rufus." Louis didn't know who came up with that. It was six grams of plutonium-239—tarnished like a chunk of weathered cast iron, but pulsing with a hot malevolence that—even after Louis's four years on this mesa—filled Louis with religious awe. Louis was a Jew, and even though he gave up on religion around the time he learned to read, the vague notion he still held of God remained satisfyingly Old Testament. The plutonium-239 was proof, as far as he was concerned. A substance like that could not be the work of a loving Father. It was the God of Vengeance sending His thunder down from Sinai, rendered in burning metal.

The way the experiment is supposed to go is: you set the core into a half-spherical beryllium tamper. Then you *oh-so-carefully* lower a second tamper over it. The tampers reflect the neutrons back into the core. They don't have anywhere to go so they just pinball around in there. Too many neutrons tripping over each other like drunks at a bachelor party, and the damn thing goes *prompt critical*. That's what you want to avoid. That's when the dragon rears up and bites.

The point is to see how close you can nudge Rufus toward prompt critical without tipping it over the edge. Neutrons and gamma rays aren't anything to mess around with, so protocol says you lower the upper tamper over the top of the core only after placing shims along the bottom tamper to maintain the gap. You watch the monitor to see how all those drunks are doing in there. Once satisfied, you remove the second tamper.

That's the right way to do it. The *safe* way to do it. But that isn't the way gunslingers do it. Billy the Kid never played it safe in his life.

So what Louis did on that day—the last true day of his life—was: he held the upper tamper with his left hand, forgot the shims altogether, and instead stuck a little screwdriver into the gap with his right. He slowly inched the screwdriver out, letting the gap *close...close...close...* Trusting that screwdriver the way old Billy trusted his Colt single-action revolver. Louis tried that analogy once with Thomas, who immediately came back with: *Didn't Billy the Kid get shot and killed when he was twenty-one?* Louis scowled and swatted his friend's shoulder. *You're no fun*, he said.

Today, it wasn't Thomas but Alvin standing behind him. Louis was heading back East. Gunslinger or no, he was done with this place. He was sick of all the dirt, the trees, the yapping coyotes, and the nights lying awake in his cot listening to the wind howl and thinking about all the people he'd helped to kill. He'd wanted to leave once the war was done, but the military bureaucrats and government pencil pushers wouldn't let him. *I'm one of the few experienced bomb putter-togethers they've still got, I guess*, he told Thomas bitterly after the word came down. But now he was finally headed back to Chicago, where he was going to teach the next generation of gunslingers how to shoot right from the hip and not miss. Alvin was supposed to take over.

Alvin peered over Louis's left shoulder, watching Rufus with hungry, curious eyes. This was the final test before it was to be shipped off to Bikini Atoll, which the generals planned to blow off the face of the earth. And, as much as Louis wanted to wash his hands of this place, he still wished he could be there. He'd been at Trinity. There was a great picture of him to prove it: standing next to "the gadget," as they called it, sunglasses perched on the bridge of his aquiline nose, his unbuttoned shirt displaying a tanned and leanly muscled torso. He looked *sexy* in that picture, like a Como or a Sinatra rather than just another too-skinny Jewish scientist from Canada. It wasn't so much the open shirt as the look on his face. Stoic, windblown confidence. The confidence of a gunslinger.

Trinity was big. Bikini was going to be much, much bigger.

"That's the same core that killed Daghlian?" Alvin asked nervously.

"Sure is," Louis said, easing the screwdriver out another millimeter. Alvin wasn't quite the gunslinger the rest of them were. Probably because he was married. That was okay. Alvin would be careful.

"Wow," Alvin said.

Louis's eyes bounced between the tamper and the monitor. The drunks were getting very rowdy in there. "Be a pal and wipe the sweat out of my eyes, wouldja?"

Alvin pulled a handkerchief from his back pocket and mopped at Louis's brow. "So, what happened there?" he asked.

"Where?"

"With Daghlian?"

"About what you'd expect. Harry had the core in a stack of tungsten bricks," Louis said. He eased the screwdriver out another hair. The monitor emitted a series of startled chirps and pops. "Same idea; the tungsten bounces the neutrons back into the core. Daghlian was almost done when his hand slipped. One of the bricks fell. That was that."

"Well," Alvin said, and swallowed.

"Don't worry," Louis said. "I've done this dozens of times."

"How many times did Harry—?"

"Shut up." Another millimeter. "Where you taking her this weekend?"

"Huh?"

Louis had about half a centimeter left to play with. "Your wife, you dummy," he said. "Isn't it your anniversary?"

"Oh," Alvin said in that maddeningly benign way of his. "Right. I suppose." Elizabeth worked in Metallurgy and was probably smarter than Alvin and Louis put together. They married back in Chicago before the war. She followed Alvin out to the mesa in '42, and someone finally found a way to put all her smarts to work. She was stolid where Alvin was airy, and had a blunt, practical sense of humor that left her husband generally flummoxed. Louis didn't think she'd take kindly to having their anniversary forgotten.

"You *suppose?* Friend, you're gonna wake up Sunday morning and find yourself in the doghouse."

"Lizzie's not like that," Alvin huffed. "She understands how busy I am. She's busy too."

Louis snickered. He moved the screwdriver. The monitor chirped. A quarter centimeter now.

"You just wait," Louis said. "Write down the time and date you told me that, and in a month when you're still sleeping on the couch I'll point back and say that's where the whole thing went *fakakta.*"

"The twenty-first of May, nineteen hundred and forty-six," Alvin said. "Fourteen hundred and thirty-nine hours—"

Louis snickered. "Where you gonna take her?"

He felt rather than saw Alvin shrug. "Probably down to the Teahouse."

Louis made a *tsking* sound. The Teahouse was Edith Warner's place, an adobe hut at the bottom of the mesa, right on the bank of the Rio Grande. Any further than that, and you needed permission from the Director. The Teahouse wasn't much, but Edith made a damn fine chocolate cake.

"It's your *anniversary*, Alvin," Louis said. "Everyone goes to The Teahouse." An eighth of a centimeter now; the noises coming from the monitor began to sound like a warning. "Get a pass, take her to Santa Fe, have dinner at El Farol or somewhere, maybe some dancing, then a nice romantic stroll around the Plaza."

"You think?" Alvin asked.

"Sure, sure," Louis said happily. His life—or all useful parts of it, anyway—would be over in the next fifteen seconds. "You'd be hopeless without me, fella. Hopeless! Take her out to that big gazebo on the Plaza and kiss her like it's your very first date. Who knows? You play your cards right you—"

A door *boomed* outside, rumbling like distant thunder. Maybe that's all it took—that eighth-of-a-second distraction. Or maybe his hand just twitched.

Either way, the result was the same. The screwdriver slipped. The tampers snapped shut.

A sour taste flooded Louis's mouth. Blue light crackled across his corneas. He shuffled to the left, blocking Alvin's body with his own. *He's gotta take Lizzie out this weekend for their anniversary*, he thought madly. Of course, there was no way that was happening now.

Alvin was shouting. So were Young and Kline, who Louis had completely forgotten were in the room. It all sounded very far away, buried beneath a ringing in Louis's ears. A ringing, and another sound warbling gloomily beneath it. Heat lanced up his right arm, as if his veins had filled with fire.

It happened in less than a second. In that second, behind the blue glow, Louis saw...*something*.

He batted the tamper away. It hit the cement floor with a resounding *bong!*

Louis's eyes felt swimmy, floating around their sockets like loose bubbles through surging water. Blood rushed in his ears. His lungs felt sloshy. His stomach was slowly twisting into a hard knot.

I saw something, he thought. *I saw—*

He looked down at Rufus, peeking innocently up from the bottom tamper. Just a hunk of metal, no bigger than a doorstop, tarnished like cast iron.

"Oh my God," Alvin said. He sounded like he was choking.

"Well," Louis said thoughtfully. "That does it."

❄

Los Alamos, New Mexico. May 30, 1946

"Lucky for him he's almost dead," Percy said. "If he wasn't, I'd kill him."

Thomas grimaced. "Percy. Please."

Percy shrugged, not apologetic in the least. Thomas supposed he understood. Shit rolled downhill, the saying went, and most of the shit from this incident had landed right on Percy's head.

A rainstorm lashed the plateau, kicking up mist and sloshing buckets of water across the Willys's windshield. Thomas could barely see the black shoulders of the Jemez Mountains to the North and West, hulking into a dead gray sky.

"You know it was the same core that took out Daghlian last year," Percy said.

"Rufus. I heard."

"They're not calling it Rufus anymore," Percy said. "They're calling it the Demon Core."

"Oh Christ," Thomas said. "Really?"

Percy shrugged again. "Not me," he said. "The boys. Not that I think they're wrong. Send the damn thing back to Oak Ridge and melt it down, that's what I have to say on the subject."

The Willys sluiced through mud, tires skittering. "How's Alvin?" Thomas asked.

Percy's already serious mouth narrowed down to a hard line. "He should live," he said.

"And Schreib? Young and Kline? They were all in there too, right?"

Percy nodded. "They'll be okay."

The Willys rolled up to the camp hospital, a long one-story building, indifferently constructed. Water streamed off the galvanized iron roof, splattering in glistening waterfalls to the gravel. Most of the windows were dark, but orange lights flickered behind a couple of them. Thomas wondered which room they'd put Louis in.

"You coming in?" Thomas asked.

Percy shook his head. "He asked for you, not me," he said. Percy and Louis never got along; Louis looked at Percy as a nanny and a scold, and Percy saw Louis as a reckless showoff. Turned out Percy had the right of it.

"Have you seen him at all?"

"I stopped in yesterday, when they said he was doing better. I..." Lightning spidered out of the slate sky and exploded across the mountains. "I thought it best to leave him alone today."

"Okay," Thomas said, and squeezed Percy's hand. Percy squeezed back gratefully. Then Thomas opened the door and stepped out into the deluge.

By the time he got into the lobby, the suit he'd been wearing for the last sixteen hours was sodden through. Wind howled through dark plank walls. Two caged bulbs hung by their cords from the rafters, gently swaying. Thunder boomed. The lights flickered. Like just about everything on the mesa, the building seemed like a series of shacks haphazardly tacked together. The army threw these up quickly, and only now—through the Director's constant lobbying—were they beginning to establish a permanent presence on the mesa. Eventually what had been classified "Project Y" until only a few months ago might turn into an actual town.

A pretty WAAC nurse (*Betty? Betsy*) sat behind a metal desk, thumbing through a weeks-old magazine. A radio sat on the shelf behind her, tuned to the jazz station in Santa Fe. Doris Day crackled out of tiny speakers; Thomas thought the song was "My Dreams Are Getting Better All the Time," but it was hard to tell through the static. Another whipcrack of thunder, closer this time, and the walls shook. Betty/Betsy glanced up fearfully. Then she saw Thomas and smiled.

"Doctor Weinraub." She pushed her chair back. It made a horrid scrape across the concrete. Thomas winced. "Oh my, you're soaked. Let me get you a towel—"

"I'm fine," he said, and forced a smile. "How're things looking?"

It was hard to tell in the dimness of the light, but it seemed to him that she paled. "They thought yesterday there might be some improvement. He was even awake and joking a little bit. But... He took a bad turn in the night."

Thomas nodded. "I heard he asked for me," he said.

"Did he? I wouldn't know, Doctor Weinraub. Perhaps he said something to his parents."

"And how is Doctor Graves?" he asked. "I heard he'll likely make it."

She nodded, although she didn't look too sure. "Likely," she said.

"Young and Kline? Schreib?"

"Doctor Schreiber is fine. He got the least of it. Doctor Kline and Mister Young should make a full recovery."

"Thank you," Thomas said. He turned and entered the hall. It was even darker than the lobby, and closed around him like a dry throat. He picked up the first smells of the place: disinfectant, sickness, an undercurrent of rot and death that made him want to gag. He'd always hated hospitals.

Closed doors slid past, small windows black and staring. He knew these rooms were likely empty, but he still felt the press of watchful, idiot eyes tracking him.

He rounded a corner. An elderly couple sat in two metal chairs outside a room at the end of the corridor. The man's head was bowed. The woman stared ahead, her hands clasped in her lap. *This really is bad*, he thought. He knew it, of course, had since Schreib called him the day it happened. But seeing these two collapsed old folks sitting there —so like his own mother and father back in Minneapolis—brought it all home. *They wouldn't have let in his parents if they didn't think it was already over.*

"Hello," Thomas said.

The man looked up. A plain black yarmulke sat atop a bald, liver-spotted head. Large, milky eyes crouched inside bruise-purple sockets. The man's cheeks were dusted with several days' growth of beard. Thomas's people were assimilated Jews who drove on Saturdays, celebrated Christmas alongside Chanukah, and weren't averse to a couple strips of bacon with their eggs. But Thomas knew the tradition. *He's already in mourning*, he thought.

"Hello," the man said, and seemed to shrink a little. "Are you a doctor?"

He thinks I'm here to deliver more bad news. "No, no, well...yes, but not that kind of doctor," he said quickly. "I'm Thomas Weinraub. I work with your son."

"Oh! Yes. Louis spoke of you often." The old man's gravelly voice was inflected with something Slavic. Maybe Russian. "My name's Israel Slotin. This is my wife, Sonia."

He extended a shaking hand. Thomas took it and tried not to recoil from the sour dampness of his touch.

The woman looked up. "I'm surprised we haven't seen you before," she said, and didn't bother to hide the reproach in her voice. "Louis told us you two are very close."

Thomas's cheeks burned. "I was in London for a conference. I was only able to get back today."

She made a small noise.

Israel was smiling. "My son was asking for you last night," he said. "I'm very glad you came."

"I got here as quickly as I could," Thomas said. "Is it...?"

He stopped, unsure how to continue.

"Is it as bad as they say?" Israel finished helpfully.

"Yes."

Israel nodded. Thomas saw, for the first time, that he held a leather-bound book in his lap. The Torah, open to the Book of Numbers. "I'm afraid so. I think our poor boy has seen his last sunrise."

Sonia made a tiny growling noise but didn't say anything.

"I'm so sorry," Thomas said.

"We all are. Go see my boy. He hasn't wakened at all today, but who knows? Louis has tremendous willpower. Has since he was a child."

"That he does," Thomas said, and allowed himself to smile.

"I think he's been hanging on just for you."

"Thank you."

Thomas looked into the room. The window was smudged and nearly opaque; a pale light glowed inside.

※

Los Alamos, New Mexico. May 21, 1946

Louis bashed through the metal doors and stumbled out onto the loading dock.

Someone—probably Kline or Young—had rushed across the road to the main lab to get the dosimeter badges. The badges were unhelpfully locked in a box at the far end of the facility. Of course, they were all supposed to wear them during the experiments. But Louis never did. Because he was a gunslinger.

They aren't going to do any good now, he thought as he leaned and gazed balefully out at the dirt road. If he'd been wearing the badge in that critical second when he caught the blast, it might tell him something. Maybe, at the very least, give him a rough idea of how long it was going to take for him to die.

The canyon floor was carpeted in piñons. A big wall of yellow cliff rose beyond them. It had a craggy, broken look. A couple army trucks rumbled by like beetles, happily unaware. The next days opened up before Louis like a grim mystery. What would it be like, to bake from the inside out? To feel your intestines turn to slurry, your lungs to phlegm-filled char? What would it be like to watch as your skin opened up and dissolved right before your eyes?

He supposed he was about to find out. The scientist in him almost relished the upcoming discovery. The rest of him just screamed.

I saw something.

Louis took a deep breath and felt a hitch deep in his lungs, where things were already going very, very wrong. The world felt watery and insubstantial. He bobbed along in its current. He tried to fix his gaze on a single point: a sign just across the road. It read "OMEGA SITE: TECHNICAL AREA 18." He knew this because he saw that sign every day. But just now he couldn't read it; it kept bouncing around in his vision like a rubber ball. *Vertigo*, he thought. *That's one of the symptoms. How many rads do you think you took? Five hundred? A thousand?*

He leaned against the post and vomited.

I saw something.

Whatever it was, it was fading like a dream. It left behind an impression of vast immensity. It was like standing at the base of a mountain in the dark; you can't see the mountain, but you know it's there and the knowledge of all that rock looming above you...it presses down...down...*down*...

His mind tried to grasp at whatever it was, to stitch a simulacrum out of the cascade of images that had flooded into him after the screwdriver slipped. It skittered out of reach. He closed his eyes and saw a bivalve mollusk, an ebon tower, a fathomless lake, a spinning neutron star—and a deep, colorless darkness.

He felt a gravity, not pulling him toward *it* but rather it toward *him*.

He heard something too: an atonal and distant fluting, a collision of notes like a hammer against glass. It felt ancient. Alive.

Outside, he thought.

He shook his head and immediately regretted it. His stomach roiled again, and he gagged. The thought didn't feel like his own. Or, at least, not entirely.

It's outside.

It wants inside.

He choked down the bile and blood that was even now bubbling up from the core of his now ruined body. It all happened so fast. But that half-second seemed to span aeons.

He leaned on the railing and looked up into the sky. It was cloudless and blue. The sun seemed to pulse inside that dome like an electromagnetic wave. A bird called somewhere, a low and lonely *whoo-whoo* from distant trees, and it took Louis a moment to realize the *whoo*s fell in syncopated rhythm with the pulsing of the sun, and with banging of a screen door somewhere, and with the ebb and flow of the breeze against his skin.

There was a door somewhere. That door was shut. What Louis did, when he let those spheres snap together, was open it just a crack.

Behind him, someone said: "Louis."

He spun around. He saw not Young or Kline but Schreib standing there, wide-eyed and holding a dosimetry badge. He hadn't even known Schreib was at the site today.

"Let me see it," Louis growled.

Schreib handed Louis the badge. It was green plastic, with a little raised bubble at the top. A glowing crystal sat inside the bubble.

"Where was this taken?"

"I propped it up against the core."

Louis looked at Schreib, aghast. *"You went in there?"*

Schreib shrugged. He looked pale, but otherwise okay.

Louis looked down at the badge again. The glow was faint, but distinct. This had to mean, no less than three minutes after the incident, the core was still kicking off at least five hundred rads. *Double or triple that for me*, he thought.

"Thank you," Louis croaked and handed the badge back.

"We've called the hospital. They're sending an ambulance for you and Alvin," Schreiber said. "Probably for Young and Kline, too."

"And you," Louis said. "You went in there."

Schreiber nodded. "And me."

Louis's legs felt weak, rubbery, but the rest of his body thrummed with a peculiar energy, as if he'd just plugged himself into an electrical socket. It was probably the adrenaline. Probably.

"You know I'm not getting out of that hospital," he said.

Schreib nodded. "I'm going to go call the Director."

❄

Los Alamos, New Mexico. May 30, 1946

What hit Thomas first was the smell. It was sharp and antiseptic, but beneath it lurked the copper tang of blood and the slow cooking of meat.

The room was large, with a single bed pushed into the far corner. A sconce above the bed kicked off a warm, yellowish glow. Darkness swallowed everything else. Rain pounded the metal roof, sounding like the charge of an army. Thunder boomed. The light flickered.

Thomas wasn't aware that he was moving toward the bed. It seemed instead that the room was contracting around him, irising him forward like a pupil.

"Oh," Thomas said. "Oh, Louis."

Louis somehow looked both swollen and emaciated. The flesh melted away where he needed it, ballooned where he didn't. His hair was coming out, leaving just a few black clumps protruding from the wet soup of his blistered scalp. His hands lay by his side. They were plum-colored and tumescent, swelled to twice their normal size. Open sores leaked viscous jelly all up and down his arms, his chest, his throat, his cheeks. Flayed lips ripped back from bloody gums. More blood smeared in Rorschach patterns across his teeth.

There was a chair next to the bed, and thank God for that, because if it hadn't been there Thomas thought he would have collapsed. He knew what to expect. But knowing wasn't the same as seeing.

"Louis," he said again. Louis, who rode pillion behind Thomas on his BSA B21 as they cruised up and down the narrow dirt tracks spiderwebbing the Jemez. They'd ridden, smelling the pine and the petrol, feeling the wind lick their skins and trying to ignore the crush of all those black volcanic cliffs pressing in around them. Eventually they came to the caldera. It was a vast green expanse ringed by mountains, with a dark dome rising out of the center. *Jesus,* Louis said when Thomas let the motorbike drift to stop, *there isn't anything that looks like this in all of Manitoba.* Thomas laughed. *Nope,* he said. *Not in Minnesota, either.*

Thomas reached out and took Louis's hand. It was filled with feverish heat and felt like gripping wet sausage. But he didn't let go.

Louis's eyes opened and rolled toward him. Burst capillaries filled the sclera, turning them the dull red of old brick. The irises had gone inky black.

"It has a name, but I didn't catch it," Louis muttered. His voice was a croak, but Thomas nevertheless caught the words clearly.

"What? What had a name?"

"I didn't catch it," Louis said. "It tore away. I can't say it."

"Louis. It's Thomas. Can...do you know that I'm here?"

"Thomas," Louis said, tasting the name like something unfamiliar.

"Yes. It's Thomas."

"Thomas," he said, and blinked. His eyes were leaking something yellow and thick. "Thomas, that you, pal?"

"It's me."

"Is it gone?"

"What? Is what gone?"

"The core? Did they..." He coughed, spraying droplets of blood. "Did they take it to Bikini?"

"Not yet," Thomas said. "They've got to let it cool down first."

A gray tongue darted out like a worm.

"You can't let them," Louis said.

"What do you mean?"

"Something in the core. You gotta...*gotta*..." His eyes drifted shut. Thomas feared he'd gone back under. He gently squeezed Louis's hand.

"Louis," he said. "What are—?"

The eyes snapped open. They spun around the room, unfocused and wild.

"It's got a name, pal, but you can't say it. It's like cotton on the tongue. Sticky."

I'm losing him, Thomas thought.

"You gotta stop 'em, pal," Louis went on. "You gotta. They can't take the core. They can't take it to Bikini."

"Okay, Louis," Thomas said. "Okay."

"Something in the core. You hear me?"

"I hear you, Louis."

Louis licked his lips again. He slowly shook his head.

"I don't know how it got in there," he said. "Unless the neutrons, they're like stars, and I think it lives behind the stars, you know? Between."

"Okay," Thomas said.

"It wants in, you get me? It's looking for a way in."

"Okay. I get you—"

Louis's head sprang off the pillow. He gripped Thomas's hand, squeezing so hard that Thomas yelped and tried to pull away.

"No, you *don't*," Louis hissed. "Go out and look. But you gotta look *between*."

"Sure," Thomas said, managing to extricate himself from Louis's grip. "Look between."

"I didn't catch the name," Louis said. "It tore away. Don't ever say it."

"I won't, Louis."

"Promise me you'll never say it," Louis insisted.

"I promise."

Louis sighed, apparently satisfied. His head flopped back to the pillow.

"Melt it down," he said. "I don't think it can get in if you melt it down. But go see it first. Otherwise you won't believe me."

"Go see what?"

"The core," Louis said. "That fucking core."

❄

Los Alamos, New Mexico. May 21, 1946

By the time the ambulances got there, Louis had vomited four more times. It ripped out of him like liquid fire. By the third time he saw thick ropes of blood in it.

He could feel his mind starting to fragment. Schreib said something to him. The big fella driving the ambulance said something to him. He said something back. He had no idea what.

The ambulance rattled its way out of the canyon, each jostle falling in perfect time with the pounding that was tearing apart Louis's skull. He squeezed his eyes shut, wondered if maybe he was screaming.

The ringing finally stopped. But that other sound was still there. Distant flutes, all braying the same shrill note.

As the road smoothed and the ambulance turned toward the bridge, the note became a voice. Silky. Insectile.

By the time the ambulance pulled to a stop at the hospital, the voice was whispering a name.

❄

Los Alamos, New Mexico. June 4, 1946

A soldier sat in the little wood shack right where the dirt road snaked off the mesa and plunged into Pajarito Canyon. The soldier looked at Thomas's ID, bored, and waved him through.

The night was cloudless, but there was still a pulpy wetness in the air. Thomas wound the pickup into the canyon. Its headlights sliced across yellow canyon walls, so different than the black ones carving their way through the Jemez. Thomas wasn't a geologist, but he couldn't help but wonder at how much the landscape could change in just a few short miles.

Frank Munn's voice scratched out of the radio, crooning "A Little On the Lonely Side." Static swallowed the song as the truck descended.

Thomas came around a curve and braked for an elk. It stood in the middle of the narrow road and regarded him with the imperiousness of a king, before moving slowly off into the piñons. Thomas thought about what Louis would have said. He probably would have talked about shooting it. It was his fixation on gunslingers.

Thomas's heart clenched at the thought of his friend, now safely buried in the family plot up in Winnipeg. Thomas saw Louis's parents one more time. Israel looked broken, hunched over and stumbling like an overloaded mule. Sonia helped him toward the airplane, and there was love there, but it was hidden behind a wall of rage and grief that twisted her features into something almost inhuman.

Maybe it's getting time to move on, he thought. He could go back to Princeton, where he had a tenure offer waiting for him. *This place is spoiled for me now.*

Thomas switched off the radio. The truck rattled along the bottom of the canyon until a sign swam into the headlights: "OMEGA SITE: TECHNICAL AREA 18."

The building was two-storied, long and nearly windowless, with gray cinderblock walls and a flat asphalt roof. Another, smaller building tumbled out of the piñons like a boulder. It was shingled in white boards and had a small loading dock and big steel door painted blue. Building 1. That was where it happened.

Thomas shut the truck off. He sat there for a moment, listening to the engine tick. Somewhere, deep in the canyon, coyotes yapped and snarled. Fighting over a rabbit, probably.

Thomas opened the door and got out.

❄

SOMETHING IN THE CORE.

Thomas didn't know what that meant. He didn't know, precisely, why he was even here. Louis never came awake again. He died later that day, with his intestines leaking out like diarrhea. Thomas stayed with him until the end. Then he'd gone to the administration building and looked up the records for the core. It was inventoried as "HS-7, R-3," fabricated at Oak Ridge at the same time as those used at Trinity and in the bombs dropped over Japan. He saw a note from the director indicating that HS-7, R-3 was still too hot to be considered safe for use in the *Able* test at Bikini. The note continued that, after careful monitoring, the core might conceivably be used in the *Baker* test three weeks later.

Thomas tried to put it out of his mind. The gamma particles had been tearing Louis's brain apart. Whatever he was talking in those final hours was nothing but nonsense.

But it stayed there, niggling away at him. *Something in the core.* What could that mean?

Go out and look, Louis said. *But you gotta look between.*

Thomas walked up to the main building and slid his key into the lock. He turned it. A deadbolt clunked inside.

Way off in the canyon, a coyote screeched triumphantly.

❄

THE CORE WAS LOCKED AWAY in a big lead-lined drawer. The word from the Director was clear: no one was to go near it until it had cooled.

Thomas gazed at the wall of drawers. Thin moonlight trickled in through one dirty window, painting them in striations of oozing silver. Thomas thought about turning the light on, but didn't.

He closed his eyes.

You gotta look between.

Something scurried across the parking lot outside, claws scrabbling against gravel. A bobcat, maybe, or another coyote.

Between the stars.

Another scatter of pebbles, followed by a throaty snarl. Something yipped. It didn't quite sound like a coyote.

BEHIND the stars.

Howls rose suddenly in a desperate chorus, some near and some far. Something *bonged* off metal. Probably Thomas's truck.

Behind.

Outside.

He opened his eyes. He stared with a dawning, terrible awareness at the drawer. It was toward the bottom of the wall, labelled "HS-7, R-3." Some wit had drawn a pair of devil horns across it in chalk.

Whatever it was, it was in there, tugging at him.

When the coyotes started howling, something buzzed across his mind like a wasp. He saw a field of ionized blue. A churning ball of fire. Fire that filled the world.

And there were flutes.

Two of them, he thought randomly. *The first one lies in the deepest black and slumbers. The second one spins around it. It plays its flutes to keep the first one asleep.*

If it wakes...

If it wakes.

They can't take it to Bikini.

❄

IT COULD BE DONE, he realized as he piloted the truck out of the canyon. He still felt the pull of the core, and whatever lay beyond it. But it was slipping away like the thinnest gossamer.

It could be done. All he'd need to do would be to fudge a few monitor readings, keep the Director and all the military brass thinking that the core was still too hot by the time the *Baker* test rolled around. Two months. It could be done.

After that, it would just be a matter of paperwork. Requisitions and reports, shuffling the thing from one place to the next, until it made its way back to Oak Ridge.

I don't think it can get in if you melt it down.

The sun feathered the distant horizon, leaking gold into the black sky. The truck rolled across the bridge and back into the main camp, which was just now trying to stir itself awake. It would be the opposite for Thomas; he needed a few hours in his bungalow to sleep off the jetlag. Then maybe he'd be able to come up with a plan.

He switched on the radio. Johnny Mercer wafted out of the radio: "On the Atchison, the Topeka, and the Santa Fe." Thomas hummed along and thought about what he'd seen. Nothing, really. Impressions more than images. And that sound. That hollow trill of distant flutes.

There'd been that tug. Malevolent. *Insinuating.*

Let them blow up another core, he thought. *It makes no difference to me.*

Johnny Mercer was asking if he heard that whistle from down the line, figuring it had to be engine forty-nine.

I hope I did it right, Louis, Thomas thought as he sang along, telling Jim he better get that rig, whoo hoo hoo...

I looked between, he thought. *Like you said.*

Sleep well, pal.

About the Author

Scotty Milder is a writer, filmmaker, and educator living in Albuquerque, New Mexico. He received his MFA in Screenwriting from Boston University. His award-winning short films have screened at festivals all over the world. His feature "Dead Billy" is available to stream.

His short fiction has or will appear in various horror magazines and anthologies.

He teaches film at Santa Fe Community College, Sol Acting Studios, and the Seattle Film Institute. He is also the co-host of "The Weirdest Thing" history podcast.

You can find him online at scottymilder.com or at: www.facebook.com/scottymilderwrites.

THE OLYMPICS OF CORPOREALITY ALONG ROUTE 206

MIKE ROBINSON

IT WAS ABOUT seventy years after Kirkwald's death that Carter Morgan met him in the flesh—so to speak.

Carter lived only several miles from Route 206 and had certainly heard the stories. All rather hackneyed, in his opinion (and as the only teacher in town with a PhD, that he'd use words like *hackneyed* in actual conversation only widened the social moat between him and many others in nearby Briggsville). The tales struck him as refashioned Halloween yarns: apparitions wafting through dark woodland, or repeating over and over their heartbreak leap from the bridge to Sherman Creek below.

Most prominent, though, was the phantom hitchhiker, the Spectral Staple of Route 206, a man by the name of Gus Kirkwald whose speeding jalopy had tumbled fatally down a particularly steep incline. That was December 8, 1941. As lore had it, he'd been on his way to enlist, to "punch back at the Japs." So all-consuming was his excitement that he'd taken little heed of the newly established signs warning of hairpin turns.

Planting himself by the side of the road, Kirkwald then jutted his thumb to infinity, ever-hoping to complete his journey and fulfill his noble aim for Uncle Sam—embodying, as some locals boast, Brig-gsville's patriotic fervor.

Seven decades later, Route 206 was paved and painted, though of course it maintained its sinuous, steep-edged curves and narrow gloomy corridors overhung by groping trees, where even high beams struggled to pierce the midnight shadows. There was a Feeling here, or Vibe...as if the road itself were conscious of every vehicle trickling across its back, allowing most—*most*—of them safe passage.

Woe to the unlucky lottery winner, though, for whom it decided to buck off into brambly oblivion, to send crushing, spinning, careening.

Or, in Carter Morgan's case—flying.

❄

A CAR WAS COMING. And not a particularly healthy one, judging by the dinosaurian throat-clear of the engine.

The two men stared at one another, separated by road and a forty-yard stretch. Kirkwald had the general territory of the giant oak tree; as expected, it took only seconds before Carter could no longer see the bark of tree through him.

Any flesh-and-blood driver, heading down this road as Carter figured he must have once done (memory remained foggy), could certainly be forgiven in assuming Kirkwald a fellow of similar constitution: a traveler with a charming, old-fashioned taste in clothes, perhaps, and hoping for a lift, if only to relax his thumb.

It remained a mystery to Carter how such lightness could feel so *heavy*. Apparently, he'd been stuck here for almost a year now. Yet his body remained unformed. What was the holdup? He'd never been the slow student. His gifts—astonishing for Briggsville, maybe above-average all-round—had rocketed him on to Brown University, bounced him abroad to Cambridge, ricocheted him to UCLA, after which, in passing on two professorships, he'd returned in a charitable bid to teach earth science at Briggsville High.

At this very moment in his...post-life, of course, he didn't remember all this. But the experience teased him from the cloud of his subconscious, frustrating him all the more.

Right now, he was a breath, trying to lift a brick.

A feather, trying to move a rock.

Mist, aspiring to muscle.

Carter tried to draw energy from every lifeform he could, the surrounding grass, passing bugs, whispering plants or ancient trees. Meager calories, though. Sometimes there was a deer or a rabbit, but he could never snatch much from them. They moved too fast, with all the enviable agility and freedom of being physical, and he was anchored here, held by the weight of circumstance beyond his understanding.

And that was just the...*material* side of things, one could say. According to the brief, somewhat patronizing advice Kirkwald had given him, one also had to summon the *mental* stamina. Most importantly, the certainty of one's existence. The absolute entitlement to some kind of definition in a universe looking to just sweep you out of the way.

"An identity," Kirkwald had said, standing over him, when smoke from Carter's car had dwindled. "You're now a spot of dye dropped into water. You could easily dissolve. You have to fight for your color, to fight for *there*-ness...if you got the moxie."

Kirkwald's dialect and vocabulary had struck Carter as an awkward mishmash of different eras. When he himself learned to speak again (kind of), Carter mentioned this.

"Makes sense," Kirkwald replied, with a nod. "I've seen many drivers over the years. Heard 'em. Smelled 'em. Felt 'em. Quite an awesome bit of sampling seventy or so years will getcha."

The word "sampling" rang strange and ominous, but Carter didn't press.

Presently, Carter kept trying what he could, to punch *through*, to assert and to hold himself as a form that looked *there*.

At least for a few seconds.

Faint impressions of him started to materialize—the lightest of the lightest clothes, the palest of the palest skin—but it was no use. The vehicle with the dinosaurian throat-clear, an old Ford pickup, drifted deferentially over to Kirkwald who looked as *there* as ever, as photographable as a goddamn mountain.

As Carter had witnessed multiple times now, driver and hitchhiker exchanged inaudible pleasantries, and the driver, wearing a neighborly grin, leaned over and unlocked the passenger's side door of his pickup.

Kirkwald climbed in and shut the door.

The truck lurched, then shuddered off. With maybe only an arm and a half visible, and the roughest sketches of legs and a torso (God knew what had come of his face), Carter could only watch as the truck passed and Kirkwald winked at him—the arrogant wink of an adolescent, lording privilege over a child.

❄

OF COURSE, it was Kirkwald who had the ability to mosey on over toward Carter's area, never vice versa. He always had some energy, or *juice*, as Kirkwald called it: reserves of what he'd siphoned from any number of generous drivers. Drivers who, by now, had either gone on to tell their tale, adding yet another thread in the large yarnball of lore about Route 206, or since drowned their encounter quietly in beer.

Often, Carter felt like just a set of eyes. A forgotten echo.

"How ya holdin' up over there?" Kirkwald stood in the middle of the road, hands in the pockets of his old blood-stained slacks. Night had fallen, and the frogs and crickets sang to one another.

Carter almost didn't want to answer. He resented Kirkwald. At first, the man—who felt older even though death had frozen him at an age several years Carter's junior—had himself seemed annoyed at Carter's presence, probably because he'd had to share this territory. This had resolved into a climate of, quite literally, "You work your side of the street and I'll work mine," in which Kirkwald had offered only scant bits of advice before effectively ignoring Carter. In time, though, it seemed like he'd come to relish the one-sided comparison. Competition, even.

"I," Carter said, already winded. Earlier, a snake crossing Route 206 had been run over and injured. As it drowsily slithered within reach, Carter had stolen the rest of its waning energy. "Need. I feel—"

"Like you could blow away with the next breeze?" Kirkwald said. A smile stretched his face, his teeth forming a tiny crescent moon in the shadows. "I get it. I do."

Carter wanted to ask, *Then why don't you let me have a fucking* driver?

Then—the purr of a nearby engine. Headlights splashed across trees, zoomed closer and the car passed right through Kirkwald, who didn't flinch.

"It's funny, y'know," Kirkwald said. "Between mine and yours, there've been many other wrecks 'round here. Even at our very spot. But you're the first to stick around. Well, second, after me. There's gotta be a reason."

Carter just listened, as the night settled in deeper, darker.

"For me?" Kirkwald went on. "I'll admit: it's survivalism. I've heard bits and pieces about me trying to make the army recruitment center. How stupid do they think I am? I may no longer have a brain in the traditional sense, but I sure as hell know the war's been over for a good seventy-plus years. And the Japanese make fine cars now. Christ, I've *ridden* in them." Kirkwald's legs were no longer visible—he'd softened more into something of a human-shaped effluvium. "But as freaky as this world can be, it's *something*. Y'know? A raft in the ocean isn't ideal, but, by golly, it beats what's underneath."

Carter considered the sheer force of the will to exist. Thirteen billion years ago, it was enough to blow impossible smallness into impossible bigness. And with the soul of Gus Kirkwald, it was apparently enough to endure year after year of roadside repetition, of flagging down drivers and rumbling off...only to whip-snap back to his post along Route 206, by that big ancient oak tree.

"At least I get to talk to all sorts of people," Kirkwald said. "And taste 'em. I once got three weeks' juice out of a college senior. Didn't need to hitch all that time, really, but I did. I like the faces."

One thing Carter found remarkable: Kirkwald's ability to gauge time. Assuming the man's general accuracy, how did he do it, if not by any device beyond the sun and moon? It wasn't like he had a running watch. Did he just keep mental track of every day? Maybe. Maybe that was something to do between rides. To literally pass the time.

Another car was fast approaching. Kirkwald grew starker, his legs visible again, his cloudy definitions straightening.

"I think you were feeling fear," Kirkwald said, "when you crashed. Why? I don't know. You positively soared over that edge. Almost like you wanted to die with abandon."

If he had any semblance of a face, Carter imagined it'd be frowning. Why would he have wanted to die? To mire himself here, as some whisper of a self, clinging to debris?

The car rolled into view, lights blazing. It slowed as Kirkwald stood in the middle of the road, hands raised. Then, with a roar and a shrieking chorus of squeals, the car rapidly accelerated and sped off, swerving around Kirkwald but grazing him with the side-view mirror.

A wave of something thick and tingly struck Carter. It was like substance poured over him, like wet sand he could use—briefly—to give himself form. His hands, arms, legs and torso shimmered into view. All still transparent, all still cold, but more *there* than he ever remembered since this whole ordeal began.

Kirkwald turned back to him. "Oh well. Can't win 'em all."

With his heightened energy, Carter was able to ask, "What was *that*?"

"I think the driver recognized me. She got all—"

"No, that..."

"Oh, that burst? That tingling? That's fear, man. Yeah. The fear."

Carter didn't say anything. He was too lost in the feeling, studying the firmer impressions of his hands.

"Sometimes you get a savory burst like that," Kirkwald said. "You scarf it up and you don't even need the ride." He inhaled, long and mindful. "And it *is* savory, isn't it?"

More than just giving Carter a physical (metaphysical?) high, this wave of sensation seemed to jostle loose, vague memories in him that contained similar fear. They were moments of chest-burning panic. Thundering drum-pounds of dread. He'd experienced it before, surely, as had others around him—younger ones, somehow. Yet he couldn't dredge up anything more.

❄

THE ENERGY BOOST from the terrified driver lasted only half a day or so —*that* was easy enough to tell. Kirkwald had returned to his post by the oak tree, and Carter had resigned himself to his usual weakness, to being one bar of signal, if that.

Then came the drunk.

Carter turned at the rustling behind him. He assumed it a deer, which could always sense his presence and never allowed him to get close. He was about to turn back to that chronic view of Route 206 when he heard the *tink* of dropping glass, and a low, dyspeptic, "Ugghh..."

He glanced down the road. Barely visible, Kirkwald sat against the oak tree. It looked like he was meditating, or napping. Resting, regardless. He hadn't heard anything.

The man stumbled from the bushes and collapsed a few yards from Carter like some gift plopped down from above. His clothes were ratty, and a ball cap with camo designs clung to a shock of dark, matted hair. By the whirlpool of the man's energy, Carter figured the booze had had one or two accomplices in the pipe, pill, or even needle.

The main thing: he was still alive.

Carter made it halfway to the drunk before weakening. He needed a quick fill-up. *Dammit.* The souse was utterly passed out, but time was still limited. Either he'd wake up and wander off, or he would die. Both options rendered him useless.

He waited what felt like hours. The man snored on, soft and sloppy, while Carter snatched upon what *juice* he could—a cloud of gnats, several blooming flowers, a worm, a younger tree.

Inch by inch.

Eventually, he gathered enough to get him the rest of the way to the drunk. He knelt, placed his hand on the back of the man's neck.

The man snored: "Unngghhh... *Unnngghh*... Unnggh..."

And Carter drew.

And drew.

It was like a faucet that started weak and needed a moment to kick in. The man's energy crackled into Carter. He felt like an empty container, being filled. Substance flowed through his limbs, and, in doing so, made them *limbs* again.

Soon the trickle became a current, pulpy with some of the drunk's own memories or emotions but for the most part clean. Clean fuel. Clean energy. Clean *life*. Or something like it.

"Unnnghh..."

Thoroughly engrossed in this "sampling," to use Kirkwald's terminology, Carter relaxed all notice of the wider spaces in the man's pulse, the twitches in random muscles, the snores that dwindled to suckles of air and then, at last, to silence.

He only noticed the change when he studied his own body, which *was* a body! Clothed (dirt and blood-streaked jeans, likewise-stained hiking boots), and hairy-armed (bad scratches up and down) and all flesh-colored and flesh-heavy, too—maybe not as much as before, but it was something.

It was a *there*-ness!

Then Carter glanced down and saw the drunk's ashen pallor, the pathetic tongue hanging out his mouth, the eyes dumb. He withdrew his hand like someone who'd just touched a hot surface.

For a while he stared at the dead man. He almost felt too good, too rejuvenated, to feel guilty.

"Shit," he said. "I'm really sorry."

Maybe you saved him, said a voice. Yes. From the purgatory of being yet another stuck soul, crowding up Route 206.

He returned to his post—then continued walking into the road, waving at Kirkwald who, on seeing him, looked like someone (there was no other way to put it) who'd just seen a ghost.

❄

It happened that afternoon.

As forever-amusing Fate would have it, the milestone car was a small red two-seater, big enough for one driver, one passenger.

The contest unrolled in a manner more gentlemanly than Carter might have expected. He and Kirkwald both, of course, exerted themselves, flashed their thumbs and their smiles, pretending the other simply wasn't there.

Yet for all Kirkwald's seasoned posturing, all his seventy-year-old skill, the little red two-seater bypassed him and rolled straight for Carter, pulling up across the road. The driver, a youngish, bearded man with the window down, beckoned him over enthusiastically.

Carter hurried to meet his ride, glancing only once at Kirkwald, whose eyes were narrow, his expression stony.

"Where you going?" the driver asked with a wide grin.

"Away from here," Carter said. *Hopefully.*

"Sounds like a plan. I'm your ticket. I'm Adam, by the way."

"Carter." He went around the car and climbed into the passenger's seat.

The car purred off. He lost himself in the different-ness. New trees! New signs! New curves! New views! And he thought that perhaps this was the beginning of a snowball; he was on the inside track now, able to build on what he'd gained. Could he actually get enough energy to break that snap-back gravity effect that always seemed to return Kirkwald to his post? Not that Kirkwald ever seemed to complain.

Carter thought: *The jackass wants to stay.*

"Those're some nasty scratches there," Adam remarked. "On your arms."

Carter studied his forearms and hands. "I was in an accident. Got a little roughed up."

"Hmm. Sure about that?"

Carter looked at Adam, whose smile had never left his face. Something danced in his eyes.

"What do you mean?" Carter asked.

"You sure those aren't scratches from, say...someone's nails?"

Carter remained silent, confused. He couldn't refute this, exactly, as he still didn't quite remember, but—

"I'll narrow it down," Adam said. "From the nails of a young sopho-more? A female sophomore whom you...tutor?"

"Huh?"

The smile remained. If Adam were accusing him of something, he wasn't doing it out of malice or vengeance. The vibe was one of excite-ment. Like a fan meeting his idol.

"I know who you are," Adam said. "You're Carter *Morgan*. The biggest predator little Briggsville ever made. The nerdy pervert. Chased out of town. Sent careening off Route 206. Mangled into mush."

A chill overcame him. "What? No..."

"Why do you think I pulled over for you? You're a fucking legend! And you're still around!"

"Stop it!"

They were approaching another curve. Carter lashed out and grabbed the steering wheel and yanked it. Even with his heightened energy, though, the effort was hardly as easy as it might've been with a fully material hand. Yet Adam didn't seem to resist much—in fact he *laughed*, and, in frantic glances, as they veered off the road and bounced and crashed and hurtled toward the edge, Carter saw more of whatever danced in the man's eyes.

Whatever it was, it was terribly exotic. A swirling dusk.

Inhuman.

The red two-seater went flying, sailing over shrubbery before crashing head-on into a tree, pinwheeling down farther, vomiting glass and oil and shedding rubber and paint and metal. Carter felt the shock and jolt of every collision, some electric simulation of bodily pain.

When the car had crumpled to a stop, Carter emerged amid the brush. Adam lay motionless over the steering wheel and dashboard, teeth missing, blood flowing out his mouth and down his scalp and from his nose, the cartilage of which was torn back to his skull's nasal slits.

Gruesome as the scene was, it was not what ultimately fixed Carter's attention. That honor went to the massive shadow-thing, blacker than black, that now towered above the car. He recognized something like eyes, something like a monstrous, humanoid shape, but recognized most of all that this had been the source of Adam's strange, unmitigated smile, and the unnerving, excited dance in his eyes.

Though Carter Morgan, even when growing up in churchgoing Briggsville, had never entertained a religious bone in his body, he knew. He was looking at a goddamn demon.

The shadow-thing moved toward him. He heard a voice, cut like a blade through his head.

Savory, isn't it?

And then the afternoon became black. Blacker than black.

About the Author

Born and raised in Los Angeles, Mike Robinson is the award-winning author of ten books and dozens of short stories. His work has received honors from Writers of the Future, the Maxy Awards, *Publishers Weekly's* BookLife Contest, and more. He is also an editor, screenwriter, hiker, cartoonist and dog parent. See more of his work at www.mike-robinsonauthor.com.

GO

MATTHEW KRESAL

THE KNOCK WOKE Andy Wilburforce with a start. He felt the sensation of something rushing toward him in an instant of terror. Then it was gone, leaving him bewildered and damp with ugly sweat.

The knocking came again, this time from the door beyond the foot of the bed. And, now, with a man's voice following in its wake. "You okay in there?"

"Yeah." Coming out of his sleep, Wilburforce was still trying to remember the nightmare. Only it slipped away, grains lost in the sands of time. Instead, a new question presented itself in a whisper. "Where am I?"

"It's time to get up, buddy." Wilburforce heard the man outside the door chuckle. "Get dressed and come eat some breakfast. You've got a big day ahead of you. How do you want your eggs?"

"My what?"

"You know, for breakfast? It's traditional, you know."

"Over easy," Wilburforce replied, trying not to sound shaky. The chuckle from the other side of the door told him he'd gotten away with it. "I'll be out in a couple of minutes."

"No problem. You know where to meet everyone at, right?"

"Yeah." Wilburforce stifled a yawn. He threw back the blanket and put his bare feet down on cool linoleum flooring. The breeze of a small fan hit his bare arms as it blew with unnerving quiet. With a flip-flop of feet, Wilburforce crossed the room and turned the fan's knob to the off position.

"Where am I?" he asked again. He looked around the ill-furnished room, dominated as it was by the bed where he had slept. The lamp on the nightstand was still on, casting a hard yellow glow to the four corners. There was also a small table and chair arrangement that caught Wilburforce's eye, drawing him across the room.

A white shirt lay draped over the back of the chair. Wilburforce had thought it was a dust cover at first until he noticed the outline of the sleeves. He picked up the shirt and turned it over, finding it to be a polo shirt with a collar lined in red. On the left breast, stitched in black letters, was his name. Below it was a patch depicting a Space Shuttle flying away from the Earth, leaving a yellow trail behind it, all set against the backdrop of an American flag.

A sense of urgency came over him, a feeling he didn't understand. Noticing a pair of khakis and dark socks in the chair, he decided to put the clothes on. Wilburforce sighed, slipping the polo over his head.

"Good of you to join us!"

Wilburforce blinked at the man's words. He couldn't recall how he'd entered the brightly lit dining room, given he was putting on his shirt a moment ago. The thought was soon lost as he looked over the people seated at a large white table. On the longest side were four chairs, three of them taken by two middle-aged men and a dark-haired woman in her thirties. On the edges were two people to a side. A mustached dark-skinned man with glasses and a balding but amiable man took up one end. On the opposite side sat an Asian man and a white woman with curly brown hair.

"How are you feeling?" the man in the center asked from behind a flower arrangement full of patriotic colors. Wilburforce smiled, offering a friendly wave.

"Tired, but I'll be okay."

"I feel you," the man replied.

Getting close to the table, Wilburforce noted that everyone wore the same clothes as he was wearing. All of them had matching white polos with red trim around the collars. Though the styles differed, even the pants were the same color.

"Am I in a cult?" Wilberforce wondered aloud, realizing he'd said so louder than he meant to have. He almost froze in mid-step until those assembled gave a warm laugh at his remark.

"We do kind of look like it, don't we?" It was the woman with brown hair who said it from one side of the table.

"You know NASA and their traditions," responded the balding man on the opposite end of the table. Wilburforce stopped off at an odd angle to the table. Everyone looked familiar, but he couldn't place them.

"Sit down," the man in the middle said to him, nodding toward the empty chair next to him. The man spoke in a tone that was charming and authoritative. "They're bringing your food out now."

"Thanks." Wilburforce took the offered seat. Sitting down, he caught sight of the name stitched onto the man's shirt.

Scobee.

"How's the weather looking?" the dark-haired woman, *Resnik*, sitting on the other side of Wilburforce inquired in between mouthfuls of steak.

"It's cold," Scobee replied with a shrug, lifting a forkful of eggs. "Like record cold outside."

"Did you see about the citrus crops?" the Japanese man, who had *Onizuka* stitched on his shirt, piped up from his side of the table. "I caught it on TV when I got up. Farmers were lighting fires in trash cans trying to keep the fruit from freezing."

"Can you imagine what orange juice will cost in a few weeks?" The man with glasses, *McNair*, said, raising his glass of juice, causing everyone to break into laughter. Those around the table reached for their juice at once, except for Wilburforce.

Lost in his thoughts, it took him a moment to realize all eyes were upon him. Wilburforce blinked, a nervous chuckle escaping his lips. "Sorry, I was just wondering what I'm doing here."

"Don't sweat it," the lighter-haired woman told him with a friendly smile. "I've spent months now asking myself that same question."

Another laugh passed through the group. Even Wilburforce joined in this time, picking up his glass of orange juice. As he raised it, he looked with everyone else toward Scobee.

"Drink it while you can, folks!" Scobbe laughed. A chorus of chuckles and "Hear, hear," swept over the table. After everyone took sips, Scobee raised his glass again. He tipped the cup toward the smiling, excited woman who had comforted Wilburforce moments before.

"To the star of this mission: Christa."

"To Christa!" was the cry around the table. Wilburforce joined in as a chill traveled up his spine. He steadied himself, the shiver having come close to making him lose grip on his glass. An echo of memory sat there, like a word on the tip of his tongue.

"Hey." Scobee nudged him, startling Wilburforce. "You sure you're feeling alright?"

"I'm not too sure, myself." Wilburforce tried to make the confession seem lighthearted. "Feeling a bit nervous, I guess."

"First flight jitters." The fellow on the other side of Wilburforce, a guy named Smith based on his shirt, chimed in. He flashed a bright, comforting smile. "We all get them. Don't you worry about them, okay?"

"It's not that," Wilburforce protested. Then, too late, he realized that he didn't know what "it" actually was. He let out a long sigh, rubbing a hand through his short salt and pepper hair. "I've got an odd feeling, that's all. It's like this sense of—"

"—deja vu?" McNair jumped into the conversation, throwing the phrase out with ease. "It's the training. We've done this so many times it's hard to believe that, finally, they're going to let us do the real thing."

"Sure." Wilburforce realized that his plate of eggs was sitting in front of him, getting cold. "I'll feel better if I eat something."

"Of course you will," Scobee said.

Wilburforce picked up his fork and used it to cut off a flappy bit of white yolk. Taking a bite of it, he wondered how it could be so tasteless.

"This might sting a bit," a new voice said. Wilburforce stood up at the voice, turning his head as a white-suited technician came into view. Wilburforce blinked rapidly, trying to figure out how he'd gotten here from the breakfast table. Feeling cool air on his chest, he reached up and realized the polo was gone. He stood in a white room, bare-chested, half of what seemed to be a powder blue tracksuit covering him from the waist down.

The sting, like rubbing alcohol against a wound, came without further warning. A soft, child-like "Oooh," escaped Wilburforce's lips. The sound elicited a chuckle from the technician.

"Told you so," the technician said, still chuckling. "The good news is that we'll know if your heart stops beating in orbit."

"Here's hoping that doesn't happen!" someone else, maybe Smith, laughed, starting another round of chuckles. Wilburforce smiled and laughed, though he didn't feel like it.

"You can go ahead and put the rest of the suit on and zip up," the technician told him. "It's cold outside, so stay warm."

Wilburforce started to zip up the thick suit, only to unzip it partway through to get his arms through the stiff sleeves. Finally pulling it into place, he looked down the length of his body, noticing the same patch as before on one side of the suit. It was the one on the opposite side that made him take a sharp breath.

Wilburforce

Astronaut

"I'm not an astronaut," Wilburforce muttered. He turned around, finding the rest of his one-time tablemates identically dressed in the same powder blue suits. The cult thought crossed his mind again for the briefest of moments, replaced by another thought.

"I'm not an astronaut." Wilburforce's words ended up quiet, even to him. He took a breath, ready to launch a protest. To say, with conviction this time, that he didn't belong here.

"Okay, folks," Scobee announced, waving an arm forward like an advancing cavalry officer of old. "Let's get to work!"

A set of doors opened, leading out into what Wilburforce presumed was a hallway. He took another breath, determined to remain behind. Yet, his feet moved of their own accord. He wanted to cry out, like a prisoner going to their execution. The moment after, he was in line behind the astronauts, next to go through the door.

Wilburforce found himself somewhere that was not a hallway. Instead, it was another room, more cramped this time, but again decored almost entirely in white. Two more technicians in white suits stood by a black and white entryway. Not a door, more like a hole in the wall. Beside them, now wearing a helmet, was a solitary astronaut.

Wilburforce turned around, looking back the way he'd come. "The doors," he gasped, surprised that his mouth was working now. "Those aren't the doors I walked through."

"We got you something," he heard one of the technicians say with a soft Southern twang. Wilburforce moved back toward them, expecting the man was speaking to him. Instead, they were still with the other astronaut. They held out an apple for the astronaut; one of the women, based on the laugh from inside the helmet.

"That's sweet of you," she replied between laughs. "Save it for me when I get back?"

"We will. Good luck to you, Christa."

There was a wave between the trio. As the astronaut climbed into the hatch, helped by the other technician, Wilburforce moved forward. The remaining figure in white took a helmet off the rack. It was white with a blue and red stripe down the bottom edge and, in the front, a black visor to cover the face.

"Here we go."

Wilburforce said nothing even as the nagging thoughts of protest remained at the back of his mind. The helmet was like a clamshell, closing around his head in an embrace at once firm but gentle. All noises faded into some impossible distance for a few seconds until a radio squawk went off in his right ear.

"Radio check," the technician said. Wilburforce watched as his lips moved. "How do you read me?"

"Five by five." The words came almost second nature to Wilburforce, leaving him surprised by his actions. Before he could speak again, he was in motion, bending down and sliding through the hatch.

Wilburforce was startled for an instant by what he saw. It was like a scene out of a movie he'd seen years ago with everything turned sideways or upside down. He had the sensation of walking through a room while standing on its walls.

"Here's your seat," a technician said, pointing to an unoccupied seat off on its own. "Let's get you strapped in."

With movements that felt rehearsed and honed with experience, Wilburforce did as commanded. He sat in silence as the straps fastened and tightened around him. He looked around the cabin, catching sight of three other crewmembers a few feet away, already in their seats.

"All set," the technician said at last. The man gave Wilburforce a thumbs-up before stepping away. Wilburforce raised his arm, trying to get the technician's attention, trying to stop things. Only he was gone too soon to effect rescue.

Wilburforce sighed, putting his head back against the seat. A rumble sounded as if a mythical giant yawned out of deep sleep. Wilburforce's eyes snapped open as his stomach tightened. A determination made itself known within him, causing him to lift his head.

"Hey!" Wilburforce cried out, hoping it would get broadcast over his headset. Someone had to hear it somewhere, didn't they?

"Visors down!" Scobee's words crackled in his ears. Without a second's hesitation, Wilburforce reached up as ordered. He felt the plastic beneath his fingers, and he slid it down, the black plate coming down over his eyes.

"How did I know that?" Wilburforce wondered aloud. No one took notice of the question. Annoyed and desperate, Wilburforce asked again. Barely a syllable in it, another sensation drowned it out.

The shaking made Wilburforce think of paint spun around in a mixer. It combined with a lurching motion for a moment, offering a brief illusion of freedom. Then came a force which pushed Wilburfoce against the seat, as if that giant's powerful and unseen hands were pressing down on him.

"You've cleared the tower," a calm voice said over the headset. Wilburforce again wanted to speak out. He knew, though he didn't know how, that this wasn't where he was meant to be. Even so, he knew it wasn't like turning an airplane around and going back to an airport. He was trapped now.

The voice squeaked in his ear again. Calm, yes, but this time with an air of contained excitement to it. "*Challenger*, you're go for throttle up."

"Roger, go for throttle up," came Scobee's reply. Hearing the word made Wilburforce's blood run cold. Memories piled on like the force of gravity, and he knew in a terrifying instant what was about to happen.

"No!" he screamed, possessed with fear. "Don't do it! We'll all die!"

"We already did." No sooner had Scobee said the words than the force of gravity lifted off of Wilburforce's body. The shaking stopped, and the Shuttle seemed to level off. Wilburforce opened his eyes and stared at the seven astronauts all crowding around him.

"What are you talking about?" Wilburforce lifted the visor, getting a better look at them. He knew them all now. Their names and faces, the lives they'd led. "I know what's happening. Today is January 28, 1986—"

"—the day we died." It was the raven-haired woman, Judith Resnick, who spoke the words. Next to her, Ronald McNair stepped forward.

"We didn't have to, did we?"

"It was the O-ring," the balding Gregory Jarvis spoke as he shook his head. "It burnt through the side of the external tank, causing it to explode while full of fuel."

"Seventy-four seconds into the flight, we lost both space and our lives," Ellison Onizuka informed him, no longer the friendly soul from breakfast. "Because of you."

"Because of me? Why me?" Wilburforce demanded of his accusers. It was Smith, the mission's pilot, who answered.

"Because, Andy Wilburforce, you decided to launch."

The astronauts faded, as did the cramped confines of the Shuttle. Wilburforce found himself in an all too familiar conference room, sitting next to a speakerphone set-up. He looked up at a wall where figures and a chart were up on a screen. Memories of a time and place long ago in his life haunting him.

"We've delayed twice already," he heard himself saying. "And now you want us to do it again?"

"This isn't because of a bad forecast or a hatch handle," a frustrated man on the phone was saying, his voice crackling with the height of 1980s' technology. "We're talking about the cold hard facts."

"You mean cold, specifically?" Wilburforce mocked the man. But his debating opponent wasn't laying down yet.

"The data we have recommends against launching tomorrow. We're talking about fifteen or more degrees below the coldest launch to date."

"Then we'll set a new record." Wilburforce laughed, shaking his head. "Hell, we're having a teacher go up, so why not set another record while we're at it?"

"That's why we're asking you to reconsider," the man on the phone pleaded. "We built the solid rocket boosters, didn't we? And we're telling you that we cannot guarantee that the rubber O-rings will hold in place."

"What do you want me to do?" Wilburforce growled, throwing his hands up in the air. "Wait until April?"

"No, of course not. Wait a few days for the weather to warm up."

"'Wait a few days?' I don't know if you're aware out there in Utah, but that teacher's gotten the press out here all hot and bothered. We delay and say, 'Oh, we're sorry, it's too damn cold,' and Johnny Carson's jokes will lead to budget cuts. You've seen *The Right Stuff*: 'No bucks, no Buck Rogers.' Well, my friend, we don't go tomorrow, and there will be neither."

"And if you do launch," the man bellowed back at him, "you'll have seven dead astronauts. There's no way I'd get on the Shuttle tomorrow."

"Lucky for you, I'm not asking you to."

"Would you get on that Shuttle?"

"You're damn right I'd take that risk. Now good night." Wilburforce punched the "end call" button so hard it shook the entire speakerphone. He took a deep breath, shaking his head, as there came a knock on the door. Wilburforce turned toward the door.

"Come in!"

The door opened, and Scobee walked in. Not Scobee the astronaut in his flight suit, but wearing a nice gray suit. There was a smile on his face, though there was a worried look in his blue-gray eyes.

"Sorry to come bug you, Andy," he started to say. Wilburforce held up a dismissive hand as he stood up.

"Not at all, Dick. What's on your mind?"

"The cold. It's freezing out there, especially given we're talking about Florida. I want to go tomorrow as much as anyone, especially with the press boys here to see Christa go into space."

"Whatcha trying to say?" Wilburforce watched Scobee. The astronaut considered his words before finally speaking again.

"Are we sure it's wise to launch?"

"Dick." Wilburforce put a friendly hand on the astronaut's broad shoulders. "I've been looking into things. The contractors say we're good. So rest assured, come tomorrow morning, we're go for launch."

"You're certain, Andy?" Scobee looked Wilburforce in the eye. A look of trust and hesitation paired with that question. Wilburforce could only smile.

"You just get a good night's rest, will you? If things get too cold, we'll abort."

Scobee smiled, a laugh coming from behind it along with a nod. "You say so, Andy. See you when we get back then, okay?"

"Yeah." Wilburforce let go of the astronaut's shoulder. "See you then."

Wilburforce closed his eyes. When they opened again, he was back in the Shuttle's lower deck, surrounded by the *Challenger*'s crew. A sigh passed his lips.

"I didn't see you again," he said after a long pause. Raising a hand to his face, he felt the helmet's hard plastic instead. "I got to see your remains and the wreckage when they came back to the Cape. What I wouldn't have given to have not seen all of that."

"You could have done something." It was the other woman who had spoken, the schoolteacher Christa McAuliffe, the one the press had loved so much. "But you were so keen for the press and the praise you let us die instead."

"No!" Wilburforce cried out. He took a deep breath, speaking his next sentence with slow, forceful delivery, his eyes closed. "I made the right call with what I knew at the time. I'd do it again if I had to."

"Is that so?" Scobee asked of him. Wilburforce nodded his head in the affirmative, not wanting to look them in their faces. "Then we have nothing more to say this time."

"'This time?'" Wilburforce opened his eyes. The seven astronauts in their powder blue suits were gone, the Shuttle's lower deck back as it was before. Wilburforce let out a long exhalation, his heart pounding in his chest and the blood rushing in his ears.

"What a damn night," he said with an exhausted laugh. "What a stupid nightmare."

Wilburforce's laugh grew less shaky. It raised in volume, and he pushed his head back against the seat. All he had to do was to wake—

A boom filled his ears for a split second. Everything was in motion the next moment as cold, stiff air pressed against Wilburforce's entire body. He reached, grabbing for the straps like he was on a rollercoaster. He wanted to scream, but he could scarcely breathe through clenched teeth.

Opening his eyes, Wilburforce looked to see paper and plastic debris hurtling through the air around him. Feeling the cold air coming from his left side, he turned his head, his muscles twitching and aching as he did so. There was a gaping hole in the wall next to him, looking out on a bright morning and blue ocean. An ocean that grew ever closer at an increasing speed as his section of the Shuttle fell out of the Florida skies.

"Hell." The word escaped his lips as the sea claimed him and the *Challenger*'s crew. He wanted to say something more at that moment, but they were out of reach.

❄

THE KNOCK WOKE Wilburforce with a start. He felt the sensation of something rushing toward him in an instant of terror. Then it was gone, leaving him bewildered and damp with ugly sweat to start a new day in a hell of his own making.

About the Author

Matthew Kresal was born and raised in North Alabama though never developed a Southern accent, weirdly enough. His anthologized fiction includes "The Aurora Affair" in Belanger Books' *A Tribute To HG Wells* and the Sidewise Award-winning "Moonshot" in *Alternate Australias* from Sea Lion Press. His first novel, *Our Man on the Hill,* was published in May 2021 by Sea Lion Press. He is also the author of the *Dark Skies* volume in Observe Books' Silver Archive series, separating fact and fiction for that 1990s conspiracy thriller/alternate history TV series. You can follow him on Twitter @KresalWrites and on Facebook at facebook.com/KresalWrites.

DEMON IS JUST PROTECTOR SPELLED WRONG

ANJUM N. CHOUDHURY

MY MOTHER USED to scare me into obedience with stories of the demon hag. Rakkhosh Buri was always on the hunt for naughty children. She'd snatch them from their beds in the dead of night, bury them under her dangling bosom, and whisk them away to her secret lair, where she broiled them over a spit for breakfast.

I was always a good girl. I know I was. But that didn't stop my mother and the maids from draping enormous bras, shapeless and stained yellow with age, over my headboard as I slept. I saw the Rakkhosh Buri's untamed hair, her craze-blown eyes, her long salivating tongue, and her bare breasts everywhere. In the way branches clumped outside my window. In upholstery patterns. In bricks on the side of buildings. In dust bunnies, and litter on the street-side.

The memories sprang up, unbidden, as Anis slammed the car door shut.

"For God's sake, Nikki," he hissed. "I told you to bring Ruby along, didn't I? I'm not hauling a diaper bag around all day."

Zayne danced on the balls of his feet between us. "Papa, let's go," he whined.

"Your son is seven years old, Anis," I retorted, jabbing the bag at him. "It's just a towel and change of clothes."

Anis waved me off and headed out of the parking lot. Zayne skipped after him.

"Zayne," I said, catching up with them. "Keep this with you, then. Make sure you don't lose it, okay?"

"No." There was an edge to his voice. He picked up his pace. "If *you* can't do it, you should've brought Ruby."

My breath caught in my throat. I knew he didn't mean it to sound like it did (he was just a kid, after all), but that didn't stop my teeth from gnashing together.

I watched my son take my husband's hand as they wove through the sea of sedans to the resort's entrance. The space between them, the way it shrank and widened, had a curvaceous form. Seeing it always raised the hairs at the back of my neck, but lately it incited something else— clarity of mind combined with a desire for absolute control.

I brushed it off. I wasn't my mother. I'd vowed to be Zayne's friend, protector and savior—his *rokkhokh*, as we said in Bengali—when he was born. Vowed that he'd be free to be a regular kid. Parenthood— well, motherhood—wasn't meant to be easy, and I certainly wasn't going to resort to cheap scare tactics for my own convenience.

The resort where Anis's corporate family retreat was taking place constituted of a vast stretch of undeveloped land with a line of small bungalows at the far end. Zayne made a beeline for the pond, and Anis strode over to a cluster of his colleagues. I deposited the backpack on the bank for Zayne's convenience. He ignored my instructions to keep an eye on his things, stripped down to his swimming trunks, and leapt into the water.

The image the ripples evoked in his wake made me draw a sharp breath.

I roamed food and game stalls erected across the grounds in search of a familiar face. The spouses I was acquainted with were holed up in one of the bungalows with the air conditioning jacked up to full power. The conversation was practiced and robotic. Traffic getting here was awful. Everything costs too much. The children had no regard for their Bengali cultural heritage, and were watching too much American television. The stresses of corporate life were making everyone fat.

Everyone had diabetes, and everyone was in competition to consume the most pills.

I endured patiently until someone brought up the only thing that mattered—summer report cards. I didn't even need to say Zayne had come second in his class. The mothers of his classmates who were in attendance did it for me. They commended my Zayne for his sharp mind, and me for my Midas Touch with him.

This. This was what motherhood was about. Zayne was a star. All because we gave him everything he needed. Everything he ever wanted. And we never sowed stupid fears in his head.

I lost interest when the conversation shifted to tales of others' children. Excusing myself from the bungalow, I got a drink from one of the stalls and idly tracked Zayne frolicking about the pond. He was faster and stronger, not to mention a better strategist, than the other children. Most of them didn't have what it took to handle his personality.

"He's beautiful, your boy," a woman said beside me.

I didn't recognize her. She was small and elderly with thinning russet hair that had gone white at the roots. Her lips were stained red from a long habit of chewing betel leaves. The blouse under her faded saree was natty and ill-fitted like the one our neighborhood road-sweep wore. A flash of the face I often saw in her broom shot a violent jolt through my hip.

"Oh, ha!" I said, settling into a composed smile. "Yeah, he has his days."

"His age?" Her teeth flashed black and yellow between her red lips.

"Seven going on eight."

"Ah. That's a good age. A crucial age."

I detected a note of concern. Probably nothing, but I didn't like it.

"Tell me," she continued, "would you like me to take him off your hands?"

"Excuse me?" I asked, my voice pitched high.

I stepped away as she turned to face me. One of her irises was a cloudy blue, almost indistinguishable from the eye's white.

"You heard me, dear. I can take him off your hands. Love him. Look after him. Raise him to be a good, caring man."

Kidnappings of affluent children were not unheard of, but I'd never imagined it being so upfront.

"I think there's been a misunderstanding," I said, taking a moment to steady my legs and gulping to wet my parched throat. "My husband and I are both very well-connected, you know. If you come anywhere near my son, we'll start by getting security to throw you out."

"Oh, it won't come to that." The woman tilted her head and looked at me through her lashes like a beloved aunt telling me I knew what I did wrong. "But if you think you've got it under your control, I'll give you some more time."

She gave my cheek a light pinch. The heady perfume of betel leaves and chewing tobacco excised sight from my vision. I was suspended mid-air one second, then back with my feet on the ground the next. When the putrid haze passed, she was gone.

Blinking furiously to reorient myself, I sprinted to the pond and ordered Zayne out of the water. He refused, then pretended not to hear my subsequent appeals. I persisted till my throat turned hoarse and the grounds grew quiet.

Anis appeared at my side. He placed a firm, warning hand on my shoulder. I wondered if he'd try scaring me with stories about Rakkhosh Buri as well.

He pretended to admire Zayne's confident strokes. "You're making a scene."

"I don't care. There's a woman here. She just threatened to kidnap Zayne."

"Don't be absurd, Nikki. We know everyone here." He gave my shoulder a final, painful squeeze. "Now, get yourself something to eat. Maybe you'll be able to think straight then."

I glowered at him as he returned to his circle of colleagues, then looked at my son. There were beings more frightening than Rakkhosh Buri in the world. Duty required me to serve and protect them uncon-ditionally.

❄

I KNEW it was Zayne's fault when the boy appeared at his mother's side, shivering in his swimming trunks with his hands clasped over his stomach. I didn't know how or why, but I knew it was him. I sat stock-still as parents leapt from their seats to inspect the extent of the boy's injuries and extract the name of the culprit from their own children.

Circling past them, I found Zayne by the pond with Anis towering over him. The latter flashed reassuring smiles to the growing number of bystanders. I, of course, was not worth reassuring.

"What the hell is this, Nikki?"

Zayne's bare torso was dotted with mud. Her likeness lurked in the spatter—Rakkhosh Buri's. But then I was conditioned so thoroughly, I saw her in everything. Tearing my gaze away, I looked at the object Anis was pointing at on the grass. A boning knife with an ivory-colored handle. Its tip glistened a deep red.

"See, he took it out of his bag," a small, excited voice behind me panted. "Rony said he'd tell, but he said he'd share if he didn't. And then—"

I kicked the knife away and bent down to Zayne's height. "Zayne, where did the knife come from? Did you hurt Rony?"

I would've gladly accepted a denial. But he said nothing, and that was incriminating enough.

There was no remorse in his eyes. No fear. Because that's how I'd raised him. I'd promised he'd be protected. Always.

It was a misunderstanding. The knife wasn't even ours.

"Well?" I asked the gathered parents. "Is someone going to tell me how the children got hold of the caterers' knife? Who even hired these people?"

One mother began, "My daughter saw—"

"Zayne's not that kind of boy," I proclaimed. "Smart boys like him don't do things like this."

"Nikki makes a good point," Anis added in a genial voice. "The boy's just come second in his class. You don't think he'd be stupid enough to stab his friend with so many grown-ups around, do you?" He clapped his hands together. "Lighten up, you all. They're just kids. And Rony's fine, isn't he? It's just a scratch. Whoever's responsible, I'm sure they've learned their lesson. Come, don't let something like this ruin the retreat. The board will never authorize another one if we do."

Nervous chuckles rustled through the mob. They dispersed, leaving me alone by the pond-side.

✳

WE DROVE HOME IN SILENCE. Our irate faces startled our live-in house-maid, Ruby, as she let us in. Zayne shoved past her to the sanctuary of his room. I waited for Anis to do something. Anything.

Naturally, he did nothing.

Shaking my head in response to Ruby's questioning look, I locked myself in the bathroom, and tried scrubbing the day's stink off me.

Later, I settled down with my laptop across from Anis at the dining table. Our apartment had a narrow train-style plan: dining and family areas dead center with living and guest room to one side, master and second bedroom to the other. Low, red-brick arches separated the compartments to make cooling in the summer easier. We rarely used the living room when it was just the three of us, so I found it odd to see Zayne's silhouette hunkered down there in the semi-darkness.

"Zayne?"

He didn't respond.

"Zayne," I sighed, rising to my feet. I didn't want him punishing himself like this.

I switched on the overhead light and nearly choked.

Scratched across the white wall, in black, brown, red, and blue crayon, was a monster. A ring of some kind with wheat-colored clouds stuffed into its middle. Under it were two spindly wheat-colored blades that were crossed like a half-realized coat of arms. Over it all were two hovering moons—one black, one blue. A nest of brown-red snakes sprouted around it.

Rakkhosh Buri.

But how did he know about her?

"Hey! Stop that! Zayne, I said stop that right now!"

He continued with greater vigor.

I halted his hand, clawed the crayon out of his clenched fist, and yanked him to his feet. "The wall is not for drawing. We buy you plent—"

He tried to wrench free.

"Plenty of very expensive sketchbooks for that. This—this is unacceptable! Unacceptable, understand?" I released his hand to grab him by the shoulders. "Zayne! Do you understand?"

"Nikki, that's enough," Anis said, coolly, from the dining table.

"No, I've had enough!"

I collected his crayons and held them out of his reach. "You're not getting these back till you say sorry."

Zayne glared at me.

"Nikki." Anis rose from his seat.

I wouldn't look at him.

"Say sorry!" I said again.

Zayne's face wrinkled like a soggy paper towel. "I HATE YOU!"

He stormed off to his room, and locked himself in.

"Great." Anis shut his laptop. "I hope you're happy now."

He withdrew to the bedroom, switching the family room lights off on the way. Ruby's head poked out of the kitchen, but instantly retreated.

Tell me, would you like me to take him off your hands?

The words were spoken there, in the room.

But I was alone. I was always alone.

I gazed at the desecrated wall. Rage gave way to grief undercut by shame. I'd done everything to be his *rokkhokh*, but the fear had seeped in anyway.

My knees buckled from exhaustion. I switched the living room lights off. Dim fluorescent light from the street outside flooded the apartment. I dragged my feet to the family room and collapsed on the couch.

❋

IT WAS pitch dark when I came to. Dark enough for old fears to come knocking again.

I crossed the family room and stopped short of knocking on Zayne's door. He was muttering something inside. To someone. A woman. Likely Ruby. She spoke in hushed, comforting tones—that familiar melodic swing one slips into while coddling children.

There was nothing strange about Ruby spending her evenings cooped up in Zayne's room. There were times she spent hours painting and playing board games with him. Sometimes Zayne got it in his head to teach her the English alphabet. Other times, she just watched him play video games. Zayne was inconsolable one time when she got pneumonia. We needed Ruby to keep Zayne out of our hair, and she'd won his complete trust to accomplish that. I was grateful to have her.

But she must've been the one to tell Zayne about Rakkosh Buri, and that was unacceptable. If she was employing any of my mother's tactics to scare my son, I had to put an end to it.

Ruby's voice amplified, but it wasn't coming from Zayne's room. It sounded from the far side of the apartment. Casting a cursory glance at Zayne's closed door, I followed the strain through the dark, claustrophobic, seemingly never-ending tunnel I called my home.

The indistinct hums took shape. Formed disparate words. Then full sentences.

You don't have it under your control, do you, dear?

A shadow patch materialized in the gaping cavity before me. Zayne's drawing. Filtered through darkness, the demon hidden in his ham-fisted strokes loomed more prominent. More menacing. Its unblinking eyes locked with mine.

Nikki. I won't ask again. Come, it'll hurt less if you accept it.

"I'm his *rokkhokh*," I mumbled, so quiet, I couldn't even hear myself. "I won't put fear in him. I won't."

A little fear is good, dear. The demon on the wall seemed to be pulling closer despite my feet staying planted in one place. *A little fear brings respect for order, and a little respect molds the man.*

Memories flashed—of waking in a cold sweat in the dark, of trembling for accidentally speaking out of turn, of Anis glaring at me from across a crowded room, of Zayne on the brink of another tantrum. The unfairness of it all lit a fire in my lungs.

"Fear invites more fear. My son will not be weak."

No, dear. That he will be. That and something much worse.

Enough. I switched the lights on. As if on cue, the streetlights outside lit up as well.

I tried Zayne's door. Locked.

"Ruby!" I banged. "Ruby, open the door this instant! Ruby!"

"Auntie?"

Disheveled and bleary-eyed, Ruby leaned against the door to the kitchen, stifling a yawn. She frowned as she looked me over. "Auntie, what's wrong?"

I looked from her to my fist against Zayne's door, slack-jawed.

"Oh." I backed away from the door and composed myself. "No, I needed a word with you. About what you've been telling Zayne."

Ruby straightened. "What I've been telling Zayne?"

"Look, I know you must believe in rakkhosh buris and all that where you're from, but I don't want you teaching Zayne that stuff, understood?"

"Rakkhosh Buri?" Ruby burst into laughter. "Auntie, Zayne wouldn't care about that stuff even if I told him. The witches and spider...things in his video games are a lot more disgusting."

Witches and spider-things. Maybe that's what he was trying to draw.

I half-chuckled, half-sighed in relief. Zayne was a bright boy, but an artist he was not.

"Okay. Well, so long as you're not telling him anything scary. Go back to sleep, Ruby."

❄

I CONVINCED myself the drawing on the wall was Zayne's way of sorting through his feelings about what happened at the retreat. He'd been accused of stabbing Rony, yes. But, hopefully, he'd realized I always had his back.

I let the drawing be for a few days, until I was sure he'd moved on. Then I bought a large jar of mayonnaise, and told Ruby to clean the hideous thing off the wall with it while he was at school.

Big mistake.

Zayne collapsed to his knees and let out a bloodcurdling wail when he saw the empty wall. Ruby tried to placate him. His screams only worsened.

Worried the neighbors would come knocking any moment, I tried to strike a bargain with him. I offered him his favorite Belgian chocolate ice cream. Fried chicken. Pizza. A double feature. New sneakers. An extra hour of video games. Paintball on the weekend. No after-school tutors for the rest of the week. There was no consoling him.

He was a rabid animal, baring its crooked teeth, spitting venom, leaking tears. He cried out and pummeled my stomach with a vengeance.

Enough.

I plucked him by the ear and dragged him to the kitchen. I swung him into the storeroom where we kept our dry foodstuffs and bolted him in.

Ruby flinched at the ensuing thuds against the door.

"This is my house," I asserted. "He's left me no choice but to discipline him the old-fashioned way."

I waited for Ruby to plead Zayne's case, but she lowered her gaze and returned to her chores.

❄

ANIS WAS TOO preoccupied with himself to notice Zayne wasn't at dinner. He didn't notice how the occasional thud from the kitchen made me jump in my seat, or how Ruby looked like she was guilty of committing murder.

I sat there, at the table, long after Ruby cleared the dishes, and Anis went to bed.

I'd made a terrible mistake.

How could I call myself his *rokkhokh* if he started fearing me?

I had to make peace. Extend an olive branch of some kind.

I got Zayne's crayons from his room. If he needed the drawing on the wall to work through his feelings, I would give it back to him.

Halfway into my replication of his monster, the electricity went out, shrouding the apartment in complete darkness. My eyes adjusted quickly, and I continued as though guided by an invisible hand. A ring stuffed with wheat dough. Crossed, rickety blades underneath. Floating black and blue moons on top with a bush of russet snakes suspended over it. Then I made my own additions by connecting the disparate shapes with curved slopes.

Zayne was on the floor with his knees hugged to his chest when I unbolted the storeroom door. He recoiled at the sight of me. In fear.

But I would be his *rokkhokh* again.

"Zayne, baby, I'm so sorry."

He twisted away from my touch.

"The drawing's still there. Just as you left it. Why don't you come see, hmm?"

His eyes shined bright in the dark as they widened, first in disbelief, then in restrained glee. Scrambling to his feet, he swerved past me. He inched towards the monstrous patch of darkness on the wall, ran his hand over it and said something under his breath.

This time, I knew I hadn't moved. It was the dark form, the manifestation of every one of my childhood nightmares, that came to me. The bush of russet over the two moons sprang free of the wall in a matted cloud. Almond-shaped molds formed around the menacing moons and peered out at me. A betel juice-smeared mouth pulled up in a red, black and yellow smile. The crossed swords solidified into legs which straightened to find footing on the floor. The ring above it became arms which cradled bare breasts. Breasts which drooped down to her knees when released.

Rakkhosh Buri.

"Zayne," I found my voice. "Zayne, get away from her."

Too late. She set a skeletal hand on his head. He folded to the floor.

"Zayne!" I screamed, sliding to him on my knees. "Zayne!" I shook him. Nothing. "Zayne, baby, wake up!"

"He'll be all right, dear," Rakkhosh Buri said, the echoes of her voice laced with compassion. "He needs to be asleep for the journey ahead."

I cradled him to my chest. "What've you done to him? What do you want?"

"The inevitable," she said. "I told you, Nikki. I told you, I'll take him if you don't get things under control."

"Take him? He's *my* son. Who the fuck are you to take him?"

Her ancient eyes bore down on me. "You know who I am, Nikki. You've always known."

"Well, I don't need you. I'm not my mother. I don't resort to cheap scares to keep my son in line."

"No, you don't do anything at all." She sighed. "Trust me, dear, it's best this way." She bent down. Her betel-juice scented breath lapped at my face as she spoke. "After all, *rakkhosh* is just *rokkhokh* spelled wrong. And in your case, the reverse is also true."

I rocked back and forth, pressing Zayne deeper into my chest.

"And now that you've failed to warn him about me"—she clawed my hands off of him—"he will come to love me more than he ever loved you."

"You're insane!" I shoved her away. "Get your hands off my son! Anis! Ruby! Get here, quick! Hurry!"

Rakkhosh Buri pulled me upright by the shoulders. My feet lifted off the ground. "Nikki. Accept it. It'll ease the pain."

She released me. My feet tried to find the floor, and my arms tried to flail, but my muscles were paralyzed. Hot tears sprang from my eyes and sweat drenched my clothes as I exerted everything I had left in me.

Rakkhosh Buri pulled something out from the folds of her bosom. Something ivory white with the gleam of metal. A knife. Its tip poked the rib under my breast. She tilted the blade to press its sharp edge across my flesh.

"Please," I sobbed. "Please, don't do this. I'll protect him, I promise."

"No, dear," she said. "Your sort of protection is no protection at all."

Blinding pain chased the swift stroke across my flesh. A different kind of darkness ensconced me this time. One so final, even demons would beg for mercy from its clutches.

❄

I HAD nothing to say for myself when they found me unconscious on the living room floor. No explanation why Zayne couldn't be found.

My chest didn't show the slightest hint of the wound Rakkhosh Buri carved into my flesh. No blood. No scar. Just pain. The permanent kind that drilled deep into the realm of loss and shame.

She'd called me a *rakkhosh*.

I'd failed.

And what did the relief I felt say about me? What sort of madwoman was I for not fearing the repercussions awaiting me?

I didn't have an answer. Nothing besides, "We're never getting him back."

About the Author

Anjum N. Choudhury is a Bangladeshi author of speculative fiction. Her high fantasy novella, *The Divining Thread* was published by HarperCollins India in 2022, and her work has appeared in *Selene Quarterly Magazine*. For news about her latest releases, visit her website www.anjumchoudhury.com or follow her on Twitter @AnjumWrites, or Instagram @anjumnchoudhury.

BROKEN PLATES

JARA NASSAR

NAOMI CURSED under her breath as the key fell down for the third time. She picked it up. Her bag promptly slid off her shoulder. She crammed the key into the keyhole, grabbed her bag and stumbled a little as she entered the building. Once inside, she pushed the switch for the over-head lights, but they stayed dark. Broken again. Naomi hitched the bag back up her shoulder and made her way up the shadowy stairs.

Her mouth felt itchy and dry. She ran her tongue over her teeth, trying to get rid of the fuzzy stickiness the drinks had left her with. Maybe she shouldn't have had that last glass of rum and coke, and defi-nitely not the two vodka shots that had followed. Luckily, she had declined joining the tequila rounds. She had never liked the stuff anyway.

Naomi had left Hannah's house in high spirits, feeling contentedly tipsy and well prepared for the exam awaiting in the morning. Brian and Hannah had booed her for leaving early, but judging by the pres-sure that had started to mount behind her forehead since she had set out for the long walk back to her apartment, her departure had been at the right time. During the day, the path from Hannah's house along the forest was shaded in warm tones of green and brown; at night, the trees and lawns seemed to loom closer over the path, stretching skeletal branches towards passersby. Naomi disliked taking that road when she did not have all her wits about her, even though the most interesting thing to happen in this part of town was someone drunkenly driving their car into a lamppost some months ago.

The back of her neck prickled. Naomi found herself climbing the stairs to her floor softer than usual. *Why that, stupid?* she asked herself. Who or what would be listening in the middle of the night? The house was large and full of anonymous student housing with numbers rather than names on the front doors. People did not linger in the halls, but made their way quickly to their respective rooms. She was alone.

Once at her floor, she stepped softly through the hallway. It was near impossible to see where she was going, but she had lived in this apartment for several months now and walked this path innumerable times. Her mouth itched worse than ever. She needed that glass of water, maybe several. *This darkness really is something*, she thought. It was impossible to discern any color; even the bright pink of her jacket looked gray and lifeless in the shadowy gloom.

Absentmindedly, Naomi touched the colorful fabric. Brian had teased her about it earlier. *Legally Blonde goes sports nerd, but without the good hair*. They always made fun about her studying too much, obsessing over grades and results. Control freak, Nathan had called her. She scowled. It was quite ridiculous to call someone a control freak after two unplanned shots of vodka. No matter how much they meant it in goodwill and laughter, the teasing still felt like tiny skewers stabbing through her skin. She hitched the strap of her bag up her shoulder more securely and hurried down the dark hall, eager to wash away the residue of alcohol and mockery.

Naomi unlocked her apartment, hung her jacket next to the door and kicked her shoes off, rubbing her cold hands. Her corridor was even darker than the hallway had been. She flicked the switch, then remembered the light bulb had blown last week.

Leaning against the door, she waited for her eyes to adapt and thought of the next day. Hannah and she had been poring over the practice questions when Brian and Nathan had appeared, supposedly to study for their respective tests as well. Naomi couldn't quite remember when the alcohol had entered the picture. Her head throbbed dully as she thought of the exam. As a sports major, most people thought she didn't have to study at all, just play every game under the sun and eventually become a sour-faced coach for kids' soccer teams, yelling at six-year-olds because her own career as a professional athlete had failed. And of course, there was the rumor that she had just chosen the course to stay close to her friends, *your actual family*, as her mother always said, only half-joking. She resisted the urge to roll her eyes just thinking about it. So what if her friends had happened to get accepted into the same university, that just happened to teach one of her main interests? She didn't even know if Hannah, Brian and Nathan would have managed to stick together without her. They were all terrible at organizing, but she didn't mind making sure they saw each other at least once a week. Someone had to take on the job.

Naomi shuddered. She was starting to have a hot, churning feeling in her stomach. *Oh please, no throwing up*, she thought. She hated vomiting, the building feeling of queasiness beforehand, the knowledge of what was about to come, the inevitability of it, the cold sweat on her forehead, the wet sound of sick hitting the toilet or, in unlucky cases, her shoes, the breathlessness afterward, the waiting for more, the sour taste it left in her mouth. But she hadn't drunk that much. Surely the uneasy feeling was just a passing thing.

Naomi turned the handle of the kitchen door, quieter than necessary. *Dumb girl*, she thought. Whose attention could she possibly catch here? She slipped silently into the kitchen. Normally the windows across the door let in light from the street lamp on the corner. This night, the room seemed to be darker than usual, the shadows longer, stretching towards her.

Flipping the light switch here too changed nothing about the darkness. Naomi frowned. The light had been working perfectly fine last night. She stretched to tap the lightbulb above her head, but in mid motion she had the sudden feeling someone was watching her from behind. She whipped around, fists raised. There was nobody there. The room lay shadowy and still, the hallway motionless. Naomi resisted the urge to charge into the hall, instead letting out a long breath. *Calm down*, she told herself. *It's just the stress of the test and the aftereffects of the booze. You're imagining things.* The sound of the running tap rang loud in her ears as she fumbled for a glass of water. She drank hastily, suddenly wanting to return to her room as fast as possible. The cold water cleared her mind, settled in her stomach and washed away the sticky sensation in her mouth, but failed to do the same to her sense of unease. Naomi set the glass down, wishing the clink on the table wasn't as loud in the silence of the night. Carefully, she moved back into the dim hallway, which seemed somehow even darker than before. The pitch black betrayed nothing of her surroundings. She crossed the distance to her room in one stride, finding the handle with the ease of someone who has reached known territory, slid into her room and closed the door behind her.

Naomi tripped over a chair. Her thigh slammed into the armrest and sent it spinning away, screeching on the wooden floor. The sound rang unnaturally loud in her ears. Right in front of her, she saw something freeze.

Movement is easy to detect—humans are wired to sense it. That's why children stand rigid behind a thin curtain when playing hide and seek, convinced that their stillness will hide them from view. Of course, the senses can still play tricks, especially in low-stimulating environments. As if the brain gets bored and so the eyes and ears throw in some made-up stimuli to keep it entertained. But still... Something had just stopped in its tracks right in front of her.

She opened her eyes wide, straining to see. Her room, too, was incredibly dark; it was impossible to make out a single thing. What on earth had she just seen? Surely her tired and alcohol-befuddled brain was just imagining things. Playing a trick on her, like seeing faces in dark trees and empty street corners. *There's no one here.* Who should it be? She lived alone. Was it possible that a burglar was looking for something worth stealing and had been caught off guard by her coming back? The tight knot in her stomach however told her that what she had sensed was no burglar, but something more sinister.

Her eyes watered from staring. In one quick movement, she kicked up her foot. It swished through the air unopposed. She stood still once more, fists curled, thoughts racing. If it was a burglar, they wouldn't have been able to retreat this quickly without her hearing it. And yet... better double-check. She reached out her arm and swiped it in front of her, a movement carrying more confidence than her heart felt, as if to convince herself that she really was alone.

Her hand connected with something soft, dry, and completely unrecognizable.

She reeled backward, almost tripping as a wave of panic hit her.

That wasn't possible. There was nothing in this room that felt that way. She waited with bated breath, but there was no reaction. But still, she hadn't imagined touching whatever it was. Had she?

She could call out. Say something. Surely it was just her friends playing a trick on her. Hannah had the spare key after all. They had all bundled into Brian's car, overtook her on the road and hid in her room to play her a stupid joke. They had even unscrewed the light in the kitchen for extra effect. It wasn't the first time they had played a prank on her. They would think her panic funny. It was a completely reasonable explanation, but why had they not broken the silence yet? They would have reacted to a slap across the face.

The thought of making noise suddenly terrified her more than anything before. She scrambled backward, away, away, away from this unnamed, unknown horror. Her back slammed into the door at a weird angle, the handle jabbing into her spine and sending an unwelcome sting downwards. Her blood pounded in her ears. The shock and pain of the impact made her lose her balance and she fumbled to stay upright. Something told her it would be a very bad idea indeed to meet this thing, whatever it was, on the floor.

Naomi froze, breath catching in her chest. *If I don't move, it can't hear me*, she thought wildly. But what was it? What was lurking in the darkness right in front of her? She waited, stock still, straining her eyes and ears for the slightest clue.

Nothing.

Her stupidity hit her. The light. How did she not think of it, why did she not do the simplest thing in the world and turn on the light so that she could see what it was in the room with her...so that she could see that nothing was there, she corrected herself. That it had been a leather jacket under her fingers maybe, or a sports bag.

Slowly, silently, she reached out her hand to the side. The seconds seemed endless. She reached for the switch, praying she would get to it before anything could get to her. Still, not a sound.

The light switch was at the height of her ribcage; her arm bent uncomfortably upwards. The only thing she could hear was her ragged, shallow breathing. The thing, whatever it was, was completely silent. *Maybe it's gone*, she thought feverishly. *Oh please, let it be gone... Let me turn on the light and see nothing but an empty room... Just turn it on... Come on now...*

But her fingers remained frozen. A part of her, a very loud part, screamed, DON'T FLIP THE SWITCH DON'T DO IT. Her feet were glued to the floor, and she still couldn't see or hear anything, as if she had been plunged underwater.

And then something moved mere centimeters from her face.

She screamed but no sound came out as she sensed more than saw the thing curling back a wide mouth, the deadly centerpiece of an inhuman grin, a grin that split wider and wider. All the hairs on her body stood on end as it stretched and grew; she wanted to run, but her feet were rooted to the floor, her brain empty but for the thundering thought that she would never leave this room, never see the light of day again as the thing came closer and closer, emanating a warm, putrid smell of rotting oranges and something deeper, fouler.

Her hand slammed the light switch, causing the large lamps above her to burst into life, the shining white light that showed her...

Her room, just as she had left it.

Naomi blinked and gasped sharply. Her gaze traveled around the room, over the desk piled high with books, the scruffy sheets on the unmade bed and the random clothes strewn throughout. The lamps overhead were made of milky glass, glowing dully. The walls were painted eggshell white, the floor made of dark wood. It was all as it had been.

Wait. When she had left, she could have sworn everything had been, if not spotless, then at least not dirtier than usual. But now there was dust on the floor and cobwebs hanging from the ceiling. Something else was wrong too. She swept her eyes around the room, but she couldn't put her finger on it. Her heart picked up its pace again, her hands growing slippery with sweat. Then she realized what it was. The window, which should have been on her right, was missing.

Her gaze flew to the other side, where the door to the bathroom had been just hours or maybe a lifetime ago. There was nothing there but a stretch of blank white wall splattered with a dark liquid. The splatters spread the length of the wall, oozing slowly.

Eyes fixed straight ahead, she slowly slid her hand from the light switch—the last piece of normality—downward behind her. She felt nothing but a seamless stretch of wall. The door was gone.

Naomi whirled around and flung herself against the wall, battering it with her fists. Her voice came back with full force, and she yelled louder perhaps than anybody had ever yelled before. Her fists slammed into the wall where the door should have been, so hard she felt her bones must break. The light behind her started to flicker. She pounded at the wall, screaming in terror and pain, and finally the plaster gave way.

Hope is such a fickle thing.

Naomi slammed her fists into the crack, forcing more rips until finally, a small hole appeared. In that exact moment, the light behind her died, plunging the room into complete and utter darkness.

She tore at the hole her fists had forced, blood trickling down her hands, the rough plaster shredding skin from bone. If needed she would tear down the whole damn building. But just as the hole was large enough for her shoulders, the thing returned. One second it was gone and the next it was back, looming behind her with its wretched grin. If she could just get out...

But she knew she wouldn't. She knew just as she pushed herself through the hole that she wouldn't make it. The sickly smell of decaying seaweed grew stronger behind her. She could not see but knew, just knew, the thing was leering again, showing off row after row of teeth to a blind audience. Naomi pushed herself into the hole, headfirst, her skin scraping along the rough plaster, her legs kicking in an attempt to ward the thing off. She felt a rush of hot, humid air on the back of her neck. Revulsion coursed through her body. A pearl of manic laughter grew, not aloud, but directly in her head as she tipped forwards, arms outstretched, waiting for a landing that wouldn't come as she fell and fell, the maniacal laughter ringing in her ears.

With a sharp crack, she landed flat on her back. Her head slammed into the floor and, for a moment, lights danced in front of her eyelids. The force of the impact knocked the air straight out of her lungs and, judging by the sound and the piercing pain that followed, splintered some ribs as well. For a second she could do nothing but lie there, completely winded, the adrenaline coursing through her body like after the final sprint of a head-on-head rowing race, the other boat's and her blades almost kissing, Brian and Nathan yelling from the side-lines, losing grip on the oars on the last stroke, them slamming into her body, making her sick to the stomach. Her breathing was all she could hear in the silence. Her fingers throbbed dully, shock numbing the pain. She should check on them, and the rest of her wounds, but for the moment she stayed still, her mind oddly blank. What had just happened?

She tried to open her eyes but found it impossible. The memory was there and then it wasn't, flashing in front of her closed eyelids like stroboscopic light at a concert, bright and then black, never long enough to discern what was going on. Colors, shapes, sounds that could not have been—or had they?

Naomi turned her head to the side as if to dodge the memories or dreams pouring into her. Her eyes flew open. At first, she couldn't make out anything, but slowly her eyes adapted, showing her a stretch of concrete floor. She squinted. The floor spanned further and further with no wall in sight. Where was she? What had she been running from? Was that sweat she was drenched in? She had gone home, took off her shoes, and then?

The memory ran through her mind like water through cupped hands. She raised hers to her face and rubbed vigorously as if to press sense back into herself. They felt wet and sticky. Horrified, Naomi traced her face, searching for the wound, until she understood the blood was coming from her fingers. She spread her hands out and stared. Her fingertips were ripped into bloody tatters. Two fingernails were missing, the others chipped and bleeding. A gash ran down the length of her palm, with more scratches echoing it on each side. She remained frozen in place, transfixed. A rational part told her this was the effect of the shock, that these bloody hands really were her own and she should get to safety quickly. But the voice seemed to be talking to her from the other side of a massive wad of cotton candy wedged inside her skull.

Realizing she couldn't stay there forever, she stood up. Her surroundings blurred and came back into focus. She looked around.

It seemed to be the foyer of her dorm. The stairs were covered with a thick layer of dust. The usual noises of a building inhabited by hundreds of students, the comings and goings, the steps and laughter and phone calls to exasperated or worried parents echoing down the staircase, all were gone. Yet she knew she was not alone. Other, uncanny watchers were lurking behind the walls. The thought had barely come to mind when she noticed an itchy, fuzzy sensation in her mouth. She would go home and pour herself a nice big glass of water.

Naomi crossed the foyer and started up the stairs. Walking upwards she glanced towards the dark window. Without really knowing why, she directed herself towards it. As she stepped closer, it seemed to expand and retreat. The linoleum floor elongated under her feet. She walked faster but the hall easily followed suit, expanding to match her every step. Naomi broke into a run and far away the window was as large as the entire wall, stretching left and right out of sight. She was sprinting now, her breath burning against her broken ribs. The pain made her head spin and still she pounded on, eyes fixed on the glint of black glass which now shrank as the floor continued to expand. From all sides, blank wall engulfed the glass, like rainclouds taking over a sunny summer evening. Almost there. The glass had already dwindled to half her height and continued to disappear. She reached out her hand and had just enough sense to slow herself before slamming into what was now a solid stretch of wall. She pressed her hands against it and ran them over the canvas, but it did not yield. Panting, she laid her forehead against the wall. It felt cool on her sweaty skin. She was just about to push a strand of hair out of her eyes when the faint light that had been coming from downstairs flickered and vanished.

The change sent a jolt of hot fear through her body. Naomi turned abruptly. But instead of her dorm staircase, she found herself at the foot of the stairs in Brian's cellar. A shiver ran down her spine as a memory tried to come to the surface. She could feel it struggling, like a swimmer against an upwards stream, but the river was too strong and so the swimmer was swept away without a sound.

She had hurried down the stairs, terrified of what lurked in the stale air that smelled mustier with every step. Monsters live here and rats, ready to tear your eyes out and eat them for breakfast. The grownups thought the kids silly, if they thought of them at all, but for them this cellar was something to be avoided at all costs. Unless of course, you had lost a bet.

Brian's and Nathan's snickers rang from the top of the stairs. They had been the ones to suggest the game. Whoever came up last in a race around the house had to go into the cellar and bring back some oranges as proof. They all knew she was the fastest runner, always had been, so of course, she'd agreed. What she hadn't known was that Brian and Nathan had dragged the baby pool right to the middle of the path that ran around the house. When she came charging around the corner, far ahead of the others, she'd tripped and landed face-first in the water while they overtook her, laughing wildly. Hannah had sat aside, refusing to play along. Later she admitted that she had known of Brian's and Nathan's scheme, but had thought it was a little joke, there were no real monsters in the cellar, were there?

She protested, but a bet was a bet. And so she descended into the stale, dark cellar, careful not to look at the shadows that lurked in the corners, watching her. The orange crate was at the back of the room, in the shadows between two large shelves.

Eyes fixed, she walked towards it. Looking down from a much greater height, the oranges appeared smaller, but still tantalizingly bright and juicy. She hesitated, then bent down to pick one up. As soon as she touched the fruit it crumbled in her hand. The dust settled on the underlying oranges, which in turn dissolved. Within seconds, the entire crate was filled with nothing but a thick layer of dust. She stared at the gray residue on her fingers. The shadows came closer, looming over her. Whispering laughter filled her ears, mingling with Brian's and Nathan's laughter from the top of the stairs. A cold finger ran down the back of her neck. Naomi whipped around and ran. The laughter rang through the room, reverberating from the shadows behind her and her friends before her. She charged up the worn stairs and through the door.

Naomi stopped in her tracks. She had stepped into Hannah's kitchen. Her friends' quiet laughter still reverberated from the walls, their voices lower now, older. Her cheeks flushed red hot. Brian and Nathan were talking in another room, making fun of her as they so often did. Hannah laughed along. Naomi walked over to the sink and stared down into it, gripping the countertop. Hannah's pretty flowered plates were soaking inside, the remainder of their dinner still on them. Her fingers traced the winding vines and felt the knot of fear in her stomach suddenly loosen. How proud Hannah was of these plates. *And they call me soft*, she thought, the warmth from her cheeks creeping to her neck and ears. They call me a nerd and a know-it-all and Hannah won't stop bragging about some stupid plates. They are supposed to be my friends, but all they do is make fun of me. I don't need them. To hell with all of them, and to hell with these ugly damned plates.

Her head was on fire now, red anger overriding all other emotion. Her fingers gripped the plates, blood and dust from her torn fingers seeping into the soapy water, turning it pink and gray. It stung in her open wounds, but she tightened her grip as her thoughts raced like beat dogs. *They don't like me*, she thought. *They never liked me*. They just needed someone to laugh at, someone who will lie down and do whatever they want. But not anymore. *Never*—she pulled the plates out of the sink—*ever*—she lifted them high up over her head, water running down her arms—*again*.

The plates broke against the metal sink with a crack that seemed to come from far away. The shards cut deep into her already destroyed hands as every last flower splintered beyond recognition.

Blinking, she stared at the wreckage. Specks of bloody, soapy water landed in all directions. The droplets on her face stung in her eyes. What had happened? Hannah would be inconsolable; she loved those plates.

Something told her she did not want to be here when Hannah found out. Breathing flatly, she turned on her heel and headed towards the door, oblivious to the pain in her hands and the laughter still reverberating from the walls, deeper and more sinister this time.

Naomi grabbed the handle and pulled, but it was stuck. She wrenched at it with both hands, the knot in her stomach growing. The laughter from the other room came closer. Any second now, they would step into the kitchen and see the plates scattered across the floor, and she would have finally proven herself for what she was: a nutcase, completely and utterly unworthy of their friendship. Naomi whirled around and crossed the room in three strides. The plates crunched under her feet. The sound made the knot in her stomach tighten and rise, pressing against her throat. She pushed the door to the living room shut and leaned against it, looking around. The room was covered in porcelain splinters and bloody water. The knot in her throat clenched like a fist. The window across from her was gone, replaced by a blank stretch of wall. The overhead light reached less far than it should, leaving the wall in darkness.

This darkness, however, wasn't stable. Instead, it writhed and pulsed, advancing towards her. Wisps of complete and utter black reached for her, slithering along the walls like eerie snakes. One of them ran along the ceiling and started wrapping itself around the light, dimming it further and further. She stared, unable to move.

From the darkness, a mouth unfurled, sharp teeth glistening with saliva. It grinned at her, stretching until it was almost as wide as the room itself. Then it spoke.

"What are you doing here? We thought you had left."

Her fingernails pressed sharply into her palms. The thing in front of her continued to speak with Hannah's voice.

"We were happy you left. It gets so boring when you're here, so boring. No wonder nobody wants to be around you."

The words drilled into her brain, drowning out all thought, suffocating her, and all the while, the thin strands of darkness inched closer.

"Honestly, could you blame us? Look at you. You broke my plates. I knew you were jealous of them. Nobody is allowed to have nice things around you, you have to ruin everything. You just don't care."

Brian's and Nathan's voices joined Hannah's.

"I wish we would have just gone to different kindergartens. Then we would never have been stuck with you."

"Sure wouldn't. We could spend our time with people who don't have to ruin everything, you know?"

"Somebody a bit more interesting, you mean?"

Mockery dripped from Nathan's words like juice from the mouth of a child biting into a ripe peach.

"More interesting and all around just a bit more appealing. Someone who is actually fun to be around."

I am fun to be around, she tried to say, the paper-thin words incapable of passing her dry throat. *That's why we're friends, because you like me.*

But the realization that the voices were right crept on her like the wisps of darkness creeping across the room. She had known it as a kid and, no matter how hard she tried to forget, she knew it still, knew that it was true, that she was boring and annoying and wouldn't it be best, easiest, if she just went away and let them be happy without her?

The laughter started again, reverberating around the room.

"This is precious. Sorry to burst your bubble, I didn't know you actually thought we enjoyed being around you."

The knot in her throat grew so large she could barely breathe. The darkness slithered over the broken shards like the vines they had depicted.

"Sometimes," Hannah's voice said with a dreamy air, "sometimes I hope you'll just leave and never come back. Just disappear."

She watched as a vine wrapped itself around her ankle. *Just disappear.*

"So many options. You could get hit by a bus. You could fall down the stairs. You could drown in the lake, remember that? How much easier life would have been if you had just stayed in that lake forever."

But that isn't right, she thought. *My friends would never say something like that*. They don't want me to disappear or get hit by a bus or fall. That time I nearly drowned, they were the ones who pulled me out. This thing doesn't know anything about me or them. The blood rose in her face as the words finally dislodged themselves from her throat and she screamed:

"Liar!"

The vine around her leg contracted, almost throwing her off balance. Naomi yanked her leg upwards but it was no good. The thing let out a howl of mirth and surged forward. She stomped on the vine, sending another wave of pain through her leg, but it worked: as soon as she severed the connection, the vine disappeared.

More were advancing from every side. She rattled the doorknob, but it didn't budge. The laughter echoed behind her, and the voices that were not her friends' rang out louder than ever: "Finally, she's running! Did you not know we only kept you to make fun of you?"

The door didn't yield to her slamming fists, so she turned, every nerve in her body on fire. To her horror, a form began to manifest in front of her. The vines grew up the walls, engulfing the entire room. The writhing darkness hid the shards on the floor. Out of the mass, vines sprung. They wound themselves around her wrists, ensnaring them. She struggled and tugged, but they pulled her downwards. The fall sent a jolt of pain through her broken ribs. The last thing she saw before the darkness engulfed the ceiling, drowning out the last light, was the wretched grin once again hanging inches from her face.

All light eclipsed, she struggled against the ties holding her down. The voice whispered: "You know it's pointless. You've lost. Just give in. Some even say it's painless."

A thick strand curled itself around her neck. She yanked at her hands, but they were completely engulfed in darkness. It crept up her body like icy water, compressing her ribcage, the sensation so strong that for a moment she saw bursts of light before her eyes and her gut wrenched as if she were falling. Her head ached from the sound of the laughter and the vine slowly constricting her neck. Naomi raised her arms as if dragging them through syrup and scrabbled at her neck. To her surprise, the pressure was momentarily relieved. She opened her mouth for a gulp of air, but there was no more air. Instead, the darkness flowed down her throat. It tasted of rotten seaweed, of dust and something deeper. The restriction on her chest was so tight she drifted in and out of consciousness. She tried to cough, choking. The pressure in her head mounted as if it was stuck underwater, weighed down by concrete. The thing laughed softly in her ear.

As she struggled, memories flashed before her eyes. Brian standing awkwardly at her door with homemade soup when she was sick with the flu. Hannah helping her review her notes again and again before a test. Nathan sitting in detention after he had punched someone for calling her a controlling cow. All three of them, kids again, standing at the side of the lake as she dove, yelling for her to come back.

With tremendous effort, she kicked her legs downwards and pushed herself off the floor. Her head now thumping with lack of oxygen, she reached upwards.

The thing howled in rage and surprise. The noise pierced her ears, but she could see her friends standing above her, frantically reaching out their hands to pull her out of the water. The thing tried to rise with her, but she kicked downward in a powerful stroke. Her foot connected. The thing howled again, but it seemed to be coming from farther away. She rose faster now, the darkness less opaque. The icy water made her legs lose all feeling. Her lungs pressed into her broken ribs, the pressure in her head almost unbearable, driving all thought from her mind until nothing was left but numbness, beautiful, tantalizing numbness. Her head was a balloon rising softly, and it would carry her if she just let go.

Don't let go...

Her friends' hands were almost within reach. Her head felt as if it must burst. Underneath her, the thing gave a final shriek as she grabbed hold and broke through the surface.

About the Author

Jara Nassar is a German-Lebanese-US-American writer, performer and anthropologist interested in boundaries and blurring them. She writes poetry, plays, and prose in German and English, interwoven with Levantine Arabic. Her works have been published in *NEVER WAKE Anthology*, *Wizards in Space*, and *Glitter*. You can follow her work on Instagram under the handle @jaramachtsachen and on her blog dasreisekind.wordpress.com.

MOONLESS NIGHT

JIM D. GILLENTINE

IF THERE IS a physical record of that night, you would need the King's own security clearance to read it. It certainly isn't in the history books. But it happened, and I know. I heard the screams, saw the blood. My name is Jeremy MacArther, and I was there.

I was nineteen in 1942, a little over a year after Britain had entered the war. I had received my orders to report for duty for King and country on March 4 of that year and although I was terrified of going to war, I believed in the cause. My father had served in the Great War in the trenches of France in 1916 and I was not going to disappoint him or the family honor. I arrived at Aldershot to begin my training with many other young men either frightened of battle or anxious to prove themselves in it. I had been assigned to the 1st Battalion, Border Regiment in the infantry of the British Army. My regiment was housed in the North Camp of Aldershot's base, and that was where I met him.

His name was Joseph DeWard, a tall chap at six feet and, although not massive, his body was chiseled like the statue of David. His black hair was as dark as midnight and his blue eyes surely had captured several young ladies' attention.

I must admit I was very attracted to him, but...it...was something I really shouldn't have thought of. If it was discovered that I had those types of thoughts... Well, I'm sure you could guess what could have happened to me. Joseph was my bunkmate, and although quiet at first, he was friendly. If you were respectful to him, that is.

Harry Garter found that out one day. Although, looking back, it was partly my fault.

I was getting my breakfast tray in the corporals' mess. The line was long, and I was tired, and when I turned to go to my seat, I didn't make it. As I walked past the table where Harry was sitting, someone tripped me. I fell forward and landed on the floor, my tray spilling out everywhere.

"Will you look at that!" Harry shouted. "Jeremy here forgot how to walk."

There was a wave of laughter from the men in the room as I stood up and tried to brush off the food stuck to my green uniform. I looked around and saw that there were no higher-ranking soldiers in the room for the moment. It would explain why Harry decided to test my strength. Maybe it was the laughter of the men, or the smug look on Harry's face, but I went for a joke of my own.

Without much thought, I knelt and took the eggs off the floor and smeared the food on Harry's face. The laughter in the room stopped, and Harry stood and grabbed my shirt.

"So! Ya think ya funny?" Harry asked, shaking me.

"Think I'm funny?" I answered. "Chap, my mother is funnier than your jokes."

Harry drew his massive fist back, and I knew it was going to hurt more than it was worth. Harry threw the punch, but it never landed on its intended target. A hand suddenly stopped the fist from landing an inch from my face.

Joseph had appeared out of nowhere and was standing next to Harry and me.

"Don't hit him," Joseph said quietly. "Please."

Harry tried to pull his hand free from Joseph's grip, but it didn't even budge. The room was quiet as everyone was watching the two men, looking at each other.

I feared the two would go to blows at any moment, so I quietly whispered to Joseph. "He's not worth it! So, let it go, please."

Joseph let go of Harry's fist and he backed away. Harry left the mess in a rush, and Joseph sat down.

I cleaned up as much as I could off the floor of my breakfast and went back to where my friend was sitting. "Harry is trouble, Joe," I said. "He's twice your size. Don't mess with a bull like that."

Joseph cracked a small smile while he toyed with his food. "I'm not too worried about that," he said. "I just didn't want to see you get hurt."

Those words made me feel a little strange inside. "Well... I...I'm very grateful that you feel that way. But I heard what our commander did to those two men that left camp without leave last week. No need to go through that for me."

Joseph smiled, pushed his tray over to me and stood. "Anything is worth helping a friend out."

He started to walk away, but I called to him, "Hey, you haven't eaten your breakfast."

Joseph just smiled with a slight wave of his hand. "I'm not hungry, you can have it. To make up for the food Harry cost you."

Before I could say another word, he left the mess. I was flattered that Joseph felt close to me, but I couldn't shake this thought that I was feeling something more for him than I should be.

And, to be honest, this was the third time he hadn't eaten a single thing at mealtime. I was very confused, about his behavior and how I felt for him.

❄

THE REST of my stay at Aldershot was thankfully uneventful. I didn't have any further trouble from Harry thanks to Joseph's intervention. But the man still would give me dirty looks from time to time.

I also couldn't stop the feelings that I was beginning to have for my friend. It was far more than his dashing good looks or his incredible body. He had a kind nature about him. He would listen to you and truly seemed to listen to what you had to say. He...well...he seemed perfect.

Far too perfect, and that frightened me. Hell, I had a young lady I had on mind to chat up when I got back home.

But now, Joseph sent my mind into a whirlwind of doubt. I sat in longing for the handsome stranger, which he truly was in many regards. I had asked Joseph several times where he was originally from and had grown up as a child, but he always avoided that question and did his best to change the subject.

Until one day, we were in the mess on clean-up duty. Somehow the conversation turned to why we were there, and he grew quiet, but slowly began to tell me what had happened.

"I was living in Coventry, and the bombings left the town in total ruin. But the hospital was hit worst of all," he said, cleaning the table off with his washrag. "The upper floors were destroyed, so they moved everyone down into the basement level."

His hands clenched into tight fists. I stopped sweeping the floor and came closer to my friend. "Listen," I said, trying to say something to help him. "If it is too much to talk about…"

Joseph waved his hand at me and sighed. "No, no," he answered with a grim smile. "It needs to be said out loud. Being quiet about it doesn't help. I've found that talking helps me get the nightmares out."

He sat on the bench by the table and inhaled deeply. "There was a bomb that hadn't gone off on impact and was in the ground. It was deep enough that they could lay a piece of wood across it so people could walk across. It was going to get removed, but…"

Joseph paused and took a deep breath. "The bomb exploded and caused the first floor to collapse into the basement," he said, shaking with anger. "I volunteered to help clean up and try to save some of the survivors, but…there were so few."

Joseph buried his face into his hands. "I found a baby. Crushed. The poor thing couldn't have been more than two days old," he said quietly. "That was when I decided I was going to help stop this madness, in any way possible."

I did my best to comfort him. I understood his anger, because I had felt it myself, being in London during the Blitz. Seeing your home being reduced to rubble will change you.

"I understand how you feel," I said, holding his hand. He squeezed my hand slightly, and the wave that I felt gave me a pause.

"Thank you, my friend," he said.

We heard someone coming toward us and got back to work, but we smiled at each other again.

❄

I MADE it through my training and was assigned to the infantry. To my secret joy, Joseph was assigned to the same regiment. I was so happy that we would remain together to face the war side by side.

I wasn't going to be facing the dangers of war totally alone; he was with me as we were to be shipped to France. The Germany army had run roughshod over the country, and we were doing our best to fight back against them. It was 1944 by the time our regiment was near Burgundy, trying to out-flank a German division.

We were sleeping in camps at night and marching during the day. It was hard, but I had Joseph with me to help ease the burden. I had kept my true feelings hidden still, but it was growing harder to keep them to myself.

One morning, I woke up in our camp and noticed that Joseph wasn't there. I looked around the quiet camp, and there was no sign of him anywhere. I needed to take a piss and went into the woods, but before I could unzip myself, there was an outbreak of gunfire in the camp.

I gripped my rifle in my hands, and I heard shouted orders in both German and English. I froze for a second, fear coursing through my blood. Even though I had seen some combat this was different. I was alone, cut off from my comrades, and didn't know which way to turn.

Before I could take another step, four German soldiers appeared in front of me. They raised their rifles at me and began shouting at me. I could feel my heart beating out of my chest.

"Waffe runter! Hände hoch!" the one in the front kept shouting.

I dropped my rifle and held my arms up. All my bravery was gone, outgunned and outnumbered. One of the German soldiers picked up my rifle and hit me in the stomach with the stock.

I went to my knees, the wind knocked out of me. I was shaking, terrified of what they were going to do to me, and I couldn't hold my piss any longer and let it out. They were laughing at me and getting ready to fire.

Then I heard a familiar-sounding voice speaking German. "Lass ihn gehen! Geh jetzt, wenn du noch leben willst!"

It was Joseph. His mouth was covered in blood, and he was holding a dead rabbit. All eyes were on him now as he walked into the clearing.

His rifle was still slung over his shoulder, and his face was completely calm. He smiled at me and looked over at the soldiers.

They shouted at him, rushed him and hit him on the chest with the barrels of their rifles, He dropped the rabbit, but he kept smiling, taking each blow like they were nothing but pats from children. He held his arms out and stepped forward shouting at them in German, pointing at his chest and smiled even wider.

To my horror they opened fire and filled his chest with holes. He fell to the ground, blood pouring out of dozens of bullet holes in his torso.

The soldiers turned their attention back to me, and they pointed their rifles at me again. But before they could open fire, I heard a growl of anger.

The Germans spun around, and there was Joseph on his feet again, grinning like the Devil.

He grabbed the lead German by the shirt and neck. Just one fluid motion, and I heard the crack of bones snapping.

Joseph used the dead man as a shield and slammed into the other three men. He struck one man across the jaw and the man's head jerked around to his back. He fell to the ground and didn't move anymore.

Joseph threw the dead man he was holding at the remaining two soldiers. As they tried to catch the body by reflex, Joseph grabbed them both by the throat and smashed their heads together. They fell to the ground with a sickening sound of crushed bones.

He knelt beside me. I recoiled at the sight of his blood-covered hands.

"Jeremy..." he said quietly. "We have to get the hell out of here! There is no telling how long we have before more show up. We have to get back to the regiment, and I need to get a change of shirts before I'm seen like this. They had shot our guards and I can smell more coming!"

I knelt there, frozen.

"Jeremy, please!" he pleaded. "Get up!"

He grabbed me and forced me to my feet. He poured some water from his canteen into his hands and washed the blood off his face. He stripped off his uniform shirt and his blood-covered white undershirt.

His flesh was perfect. Not a single bullet hole, just a coating of blood.

I reached out and touched his chest, but I still couldn't believe what I was seeing.

"How is this possible?" I asked, finding my tongue at last. "What are you?"

He inhaled deeply and opened his mouth slightly. His throat was vibrating with a strange clicking sound, and he closed his eyes.

After a few seconds, he grabbed my arm and lead me into the woods. "I'll explain everything to you later," he said quietly. "The Germans are retreating, and we need to get back to the camp before it's too late if it isn't already."

"H...how do you know they are in retreat?" I asked.

Joseph turned his head to look at me. "I smelled it. And my sense of sound-sight let me know."

"Your what?" I asked.

"Think of it as being able to use sound to see things like a bat. *Echolocation* is what I think it is called by scientists. Now no more questions! I'll explain it all to you later, I promise."

We made it back to the camp undetected. The regiment was still on alert from the ambush, but he was able to get us back to our tent and get himself dressed.

I was still in shock at the horrible things that I had seen, but for now, I was going to try to listen to what Joseph had to say. He had saved my life, so I owed him.

❄

WE FOUND out that we were very lucky with the attack. Three soldiers had been lightly wounded. We broke camp and marched on to our next location. Our mission was to try to disrupt the supply lines going into Burgundy.

I hadn't spoken to Joseph in two days, but that night it was our turn to stand guard. We slowly marched on the border of the camp, and the silence between us was like a wall. The October night was chilly, and I was doing my best not to just run to the commanders and tell them what I had seen the other day. That this *thing* wasn't human, and yet I still felt like I did. I was so torn inside.

"So," Joseph said, breaking the quiet. "I wanted to say thank you for not saying anything about the other day."

I remained quiet, listening.

"I knew I could trust you, that is why I saved you. So, thank you..."

"What the fucking hell are you?" I whispered. "You should be dead! They shot you at point-blank range, and you got up like they had hit you with spitballs in primary school!"

"So many questions," Joseph said. "Where to begin?"

"Please don't play games!" I hissed through my teeth. "What are you?"

"That could take far longer than we have time to discuss about it." Joseph answered. "But, as you may have guessed, I am not human."

"I figured that out when you took six shots to the chest and got back up!" I said, doing my best to keep my anger in check. "But *what* are you?"

Joseph looked around the camp; he made a weak smile and shrugged his shoulders.

"I am immortal," he said, looking back at me. "I have been walking this world before your race took its first steps. This form you see... Well, it is what I look like most of the time."

We started walking again, keeping an eye on the surrounding woods. My friend, this thing I thought was a man. This beautiful body I had admired wasn't even human.

We stopped to each take a drink from our canteens, and I looked at him, still uneasy. "You—are you a vampire or werewolf? I've heard of the old legends. I mean I saw that American movie *The Wolfman,* but..." I asked, but Joseph quietly laughed.

"No, no. I'm not those things, please...that movie was such an insult to the old tales. But I think some of those stories are most likely because of me. I am unique, the only one of my kind. Give me time, I will tell you everything I can."

We started to walk again, and there was only one question I had left at the moment. "Um, about the rabbit?" I asked. "It looked like..."

"Yes, I was eating it raw," Joseph said with a sigh. "Cooked food makes me sick. I can force myself to eat it to put up appearances, but I require raw flesh and blood to feed me."

"I see," I said. "Have you, well...you know?"

"Eaten a human?" Joseph asked.

He smiled at me, and I could swear in the moonlight that his eyes flashed red as he looked at me.

"What do you think?" he said, smiling at me.

"I think I'm done asking questions for now." I didn't really want to know.

❆

OVER THE NEXT FEW DAYS, Joseph told me more about himself and his past. It seemed like it was combination of letting me know the truth, and a confession of old sins.

"My race was here before man. I look like a human, but I am far more than that. The form you see now is not my true form."

"What is your true form?" I asked, a little afraid of the answer. We were both on watch, and the chill night air and cloudy skies seemed to set the mood for his stories.

"It looks... Well, imagine a great wolf, black-furred and huge." He looked like he was trying to smile. "But not quite like that. I have been told I look like a winged demon, dark, terrible. But, that is just one legend about me. In all honesty, I prefer the tales of my human-looking side. A few heroes have been based off some of my deeds."

I thought about this for a moment, then decided to ask what was really on my mind. "Why did you do it?" I asked.

"Do what?"

"Save me."

Joseph looked at me, and he had a hurt look in his eyes. "Do you really have to ask, my friend?" He then smiled, and things seemed so much clearer now. "Do you need to?"

"No, I don't. Thank you," I answered. "For you, I will stay quiet." He then lightly touched my face and brushed my face.

"Thank you, my friend," Joseph said. "I am glad you are here with me."

"And I with you, Joseph," I said, smiling.

❄

WE FOUGHT our way to the Upper Rhine in about a month, and a small offshoot formed an inlet where we were able to gather water. While we started to hole up for the night, Joseph and I went to fill our canteens.

I began to lose my fear of him over the last few days. In fact, the mystery of him, his power, it had begun to excite me.

We were down by the lake, filling our canteens and the canteens for some of the other men. The sun was setting, and the sight of its rays on the water was breathtaking. The dancing light made the area look far more beautiful than it should with the war all around us. The air was crisp coming off the lake, but not too cold. I looked across the lake and could barely make out the shoreline of Germany. We were going into there tomorrow night, and that meant we would be in full enemy territory.

I took a deep breath and tried to concentrate on the job of getting the water jugs filled. I noticed Joseph was watching me, and his hand rested on my shoulder.

"You okay, Jeremy?"

I tried to manage a smile, but I failed. "I'm... Oh, never mind." I brushed his hand off of me, still fearful at that moment of being seen. I stood, and he was there in front of me, looking thoughtful.

"You are afraid. I can tell. I can sense it in you and hear your heartbeat. You are afraid, and so am I." He touched me on my face.

I pulled back, despite the gentle touch of his fingers. "You?" I scoffed. "You afraid? You are not human! You can take a bullet and live! What are you afraid of?"

Joseph pulled me close, and before I realized what he was doing, he kissed me. It was a shock, but I couldn't pull away. It was soft and quick, but it sent a jolt through my body.

He pulled away, and in the soft light of the setting sun, I saw that he was blushing.

"I'm afraid of losing you," he said. "I'm in love with you, Jeremy."

Something came over me when he said those words to me. I dropped the canteens and held him close to me. We kissed again, knowing we had only moments before anyone came to see why we hadn't returned.

"I feel the same way for you." I said to him. "But we have to get back to camp, if we are caught..."

"One moment." He touched my arm to stop me. "I noticed you in training, and I was attracted to you almost immediately. You were friendly to me and so handsome."

He stopped and looked over my shoulder. A soldier was coming up from our camp. Joseph held up his finger to his lips and winked at me as he gathered up his share of the water canteens.

"We can talk tonight. Please, can we?" he asked, smiling.

"Yes, when it is our turn for the watch. I promise."

Now I recognized Sgt. Jameson as the man climbing the hill, and he scoffed at us. "Here now, here now! Enough gazing at the sunset! The men are thirsty! Get the canteens back to them or else! March!"

"Yes sir," we said in unison. We walked back to the camp, each lost in our thoughts.

❄

THAT NIGHT we were marching around the perimeter of camp. The woods around us were quiet, and the moon was waxing at a crescent in the sky with a few clouds going overhead. The stars were shining.

We were quiet, not looking at each other much. Maybe we were nervous, or maybe it was just me. But as we got to an area that made it where we were away from peering eyes, he took my hand and led me into the nearby woods. The sky was beautiful with the moon, and the stars were shining as we kissed again.

"Joseph," I said as he began to unbutton my shirt. "We can't! We could get caught!"

He smiled at me and touched my check. "Have no fear and trust me."

He opened his mouth and I saw his throat vibrate as he inhaled deeply. He closed his eyes, tilted his head to one side and smiled again when he opened his eyes.

"There is no one near us, trust me. I will protect you." He kissed me again.

We quickly took off as much of our clothes as dared. He was gentle and sweet as he showed me how to make love to him.

It was scary and beautiful at the same time. Being with him that way, made me feel higher in spirits than I had ever been before, both physically and mentally.

We finished quickly, because of the danger of being caught. However, it was still the most beautiful, intimate moment I had ever experienced up to that point in my life.

But I wondered, was this right? Do we stay together after the war? What about my fiancé back home? So many questions were going through my head. We dressed and once Joseph made sure the coast was clear, we left the woods and returned to marching.

He smiled at me so beautifully. "Was that your first time with a man?" he asked quietly. "If so, it was done wonderfully."

I felt myself blush and tried not to laugh. "It was my first time with anyone," I confessed. "You are my first time."

We stopped and his smile was bright in the moonlight. "I am indeed honored to be your first."

As we circled the camp, I looked in the direction of the Rhine and couldn't help but shake a little. Joseph looked toward where my eyes were fixed.

"We go in tomorrow," he said. "I heard the commander talking about it earlier. We have to try to intercept a squadron on German lands. A way to send a message to the enemy."

"I know, that's why I'm afraid." I turned away from the river. "I worried that we might be too bold. But what do I know? I am only a soldier."

Joseph frowned. "Don't worry," he said as we drew near the men again. "I will be with you. I promise I will do my best to protect you. But, you have to promise me something."

"What is that?"

"If I tell you to run, to get away from me, you will do it. Please promise."

"But why?" I asked.

"If I must, I will do what I have to do to protect you and the others. But if that happens, please remember that I do love you."

He said those words at a mere whisper as we entered the camp, with the next two men waiting to take our place on guard duty.

❅

THREE LANDING SHIPS had arrived during the night to take us across into enemy territory. The fog was heavy in the air, and storm clouds were building in a dark sky that threatened rain as we loaded into the boats. We were supposed to wait until night, but the fog was so thick that the commander decided to try to get a head start and get all of us across the river that morning.

As we made our way across the water, I felt exposed, as though at any minute we would be under heavy fire. But God must have decided to bless us that morning, as we made it across the Rhine without incident and marched into the woods.

We had gotten word that a convoy of cannons and tanks was to be transported on a road near Kehl. The supplies were headed to the front lines, and it was our job to stop them and cut off this route of the enemy. We found the road, and immediately began to get ready for the ambush.

Our men scattered out and dug in near the road. The scouts had told us that it would be night by the time the transport would be at our location, so we waited for them. It was our chance to take out a supply chain going to the front lines, and we had to win this skirmish to strike a hard blow.

Night came, and with the fog and the clouds overhead, it was dark as a cave. Not even the light of the moon could make it through such thick clouds. Joseph and I were in our foxhole together, and I was trying to remember his words that he would be there for me.

I let the night we held each other go through my mind. The gentleness he showed me, the tender way he helped guide me. It was beautiful, almost magical in its own small way.

Now we were waiting to kill men we never knew. I hated how life had led us to this point.

Near eleven o'clock, I could hear the sound of the transport approaching. The head lights from the trucks hauling the equipment shone bright in the murky darkness, and we waited until they were closer.

When the commander gave the order, we opened fire on the troops, and they returned fire. We heard the order to charge, but before we could make our move, we heard a new sound coming from our right flank where the transports had come from.

I could hear treads tearing into the ground, the sound of the dirt ripped by the clanking of metal. The drum of motors, and then a light hit moving metal.

"Panzers!" I heard someone yell. "What the hell?"

I felt my heart beat faster. I knew they would run us over, crushing us under the weight of the iron monsters.

The cannon on the tanks opened fire on us, and I could hear orders yelled for anti-tank guns. They hadn't thought to have them ready, and now it would be too late to use them.

Joseph had a strange mixture of fear and anger on his face. He watched the tanks get closer, his hands gripping his rifle. The metal barrel began to bend from his grip.

The tank shells impacted on my comrades, and I the sound of a big boom followed by men being blown apart filled the air. Screams of flesh being ripped to pieces filled the air. Then, a high-pitched whistling sound came overhead.

"Incoming!" Joseph yelled. He grabbed me and pulled me to the ground.

There was a sudden bright flash and the ground shook from the blast of the shell. My ears were ringing, and Joseph was still on top of me.

I rolled him over, and nearly lost what little food was left in my stomach. His leg... His poor leg was nearly blown off. It hung on by mere tatters of flesh. Blood rushed out of the wound like a river.

"Medic! Medic!" I yelled. "We have a man down!"

In the gloom of the headlights of the approaching engines of death I saw our field medic run toward us. The sound of machine guns rang out, and the medic was ripped apart by the bullets. He fell into our foxhole dead.

I couldn't stop crying. "Joseph! I'm so sorry!"

To my shock, Joseph opened his eyes. But they now had a red, haunting glow to them.

He growled like a caged animal, and he pushed me away. "Run!" he spat out. "Run now! Please!"

I watched as his leg began to reattach itself to his body, and in the dim light from the headlamps of the nearby spotlights it appeared as if he was growing larger in the shadows. He let out a roar that was barely covered by the cannon fire, and I did as he said.

I crawled out of the hole and began to run, fear gripping my heart tight as a foul smell filled the air of rooting flesh and sulfur. I took a moment to look back. Behind me, a huge shadow rose up and disappeared into the air.

I dove into the next foxhole; two dead soldiers greeted me. I said a quick prayer for them and went low to the ground. From the field came the sound of glass breaking. I peered out of the foxhole and saw something smashing out the lights of the transports, then the Panzer.

Now it truly was dark. I could hear the German soldiers shouting confused orders, and then we all heard it. It was a roar that sounded like an animal from the depths of hell, the roar of a lion as large as a mountain.

The screams came next, shouts of fear from the enemy that turned into shrieks of pain. The deep guttural sound of flesh being ripped to pieces along with metal bending and creaking filled the night air.

The gunfire had all but stopped on my side of the engagement. All my comrades were either trying to hide in the foxholes or lay on the ground frozen in fear.

I have no idea how long the screams filled the night air, but it finally stopped. As the silence replaced the screams of the dying, I felt something land in the foxhole with me.

I froze as I tried to make out the massive creature in front of me. I'd guess that it was maybe twelve feet tall. Its glowing red eyes looked at me. The thing's breath was heavy, and a soft growl came from deep within the creature's chest. Something gently touched my check, and it was wet with a warm, sticky liquid.

"Farewell," a deep voice said. "I love you."

I heard something that sounded like the beating of wings and a gust of wind, and the shadow was gone.

❄

As the sun came up the next day, the sight we saw could not be believed. The Germans were dead, ripped to pieces. Blood formed large pools of red on the field, arms and legs, ripped free of their bodies, littered the ground like leaves in fall. Some bodies had huge gouges on the chest as if a great maw had ripped into them. Some even looked like they had been half eaten, then dropped from the mouth of an animal in its quest for food. The Panzer tanks, all of them, were smashed as if a great hammer had fallen down from the sky and struck them. The entire transport was destroyed, and not one piece of equipment that the enemy was transporting remained whole.

We all stood there in the gloom of the fog, dumbfounded. We took a count of the enemy. Over three hundred soldiers, dead. On our side, we had lost five.

"Where's DeWard?" Sgt. Jameson asked. "Anyone seen him?"

"He's dead," I heard myself saying. "He took a shell to save me. I don't know what happened after that."

Men talked about the sounds we had heard, the sights before us. The commander told us to gather up, to move on, we had a war to win.

Someone told me I had blood on my face and asked me if I was injured.

"I'm fine," I answered. "I'm fine."

But I wasn't fine, not at all. My new lover had left me, and even though the creature that he was still lived, the man I had come to love was now dead. I learned on that moonless night, that monsters were real. Very real indeed.

About the Author

Jim Gillentine is a horror/romance author born and raised in Memphis, lending a southern flavor to his creatures of the night. His debut novel, *Of Blood and the Moon*, was first runner-up for the Darrell Award in 2009. His most recent release is a paranormal romantic thriller titled *Heart of the Beast* from Pro Se Publishing. He holds a bachelor's degree in English literature and philosophy from Southern Illinois University Edwardsville. He lives with his wife, author Elizabeth Donald, in Edwardsville, Illinois. Follow him online at: Jimmygillentine.com.

A WALK THROUGH THE DARK HOUSE

GREGORY L. NORRIS

LET us take a walk through the dark house! Oh, such fun we'll have, here at 12:03 on an otherwise unremarkable night while the winter wind howls around the eaves and the rest of the neighborhood sleeps! Just you and I, like it's always been since the first time you went sleep-walking all those years ago! Remember?

You were five the first time. It was early in the morning; so early, the sky was as dark as it is now. Only then it was summer, and you were in your boyhood home over a hundred and fifty miles from this front door. Times have changed. But let's not ponder that. You walked out of your bed, through the dark house, cut across the meadow, and skipped deep into the forest on the far side of the country road, a place that still haunts your dreams fifty years later, all because you believed there were cartoon friends waiting for you up in those mysterious pine groves.

It'll be like that! You don't skip so much anymore as plod, but try to lift your feet in exultation of our secret game! Ignore the temptation to flip on switches! Follow the few sparkles of light—the intermittent white flash of the CO_2 detector outside your bedroom, the red telltale from the one that sniffs the air for smoke, and the steady blue glow from the sonic mouse repellent plugged into the bathroom wall.

Now, be careful of stepping on the cat's tail! You never know where she's decided to flop down. Otherwise, it's just the two of us, skipping and singing as we frolic from one dark room to the next, stealing glimpses of the night world as it slumbers beyond the windowpanes!

Sing with me—Patsy Cline's "I Go Out Walking After Midnight." No one but the cat will hear. No, you're humming her other famous tune, "Crazy." Old Patsy couldn't have said it better. Come! Skip! Through the hallway and around the bathroom, on to the guest bedroom where the dust has piled up thick as talcum powder! Back into the hallway and through the front parlor! There's a car passing down the road, someone coming in late from work or about to engage in the walk of shame— don't let them see you!

And laugh! Giggle like when you were young, running through the dark meadow, so happy to join your cartoon friends in the thickets of our special woods. Do you remember the last time you went out walking after midnight, in your sleep? You were in your thirties. The weathermen promised the first snow of the season, and you were so excited! Too excited to sleep, though you did. You got up and made it out onto the apartment's balcony in the thick of the night. No snow fell, and by the time you roused, understanding that you were sleepwalking, you also saw that you were clad only in your birthday suit. Such fun!

Through the kitchen—don't stub your toe on the table or chairs. Sure, grab an orange from the fruit bowl! Just don't wake up while peeling it. Do a spin on the center of the floor in front of the fridge. Explore what's inside cabinets! Sing, dance, have fun! It's just us, and all your good cartoon friends from the old neighborhood waiting behind the back door!

Oh, how they've missed you!

Open the door—no, no need to flip on the porch light. Just unlock your mind and memory to the possib—

Whoops!

I should have warned you that you got turned around in the dark, and that you weren't opening the door to the backyard but the one leading down to the cellar. Those stairs are so treacherous, even with the light on! Poor broken, little lamb. I know it hurts. It would have stung, too, all those years ago if your parents hadn't caught up to you before you reached the old well. We were all waiting for you then. But this will do!

So, try to relax. All of your old friends are here! Laugh! Have fun! Above all, *bleed*!

About the Author

Raised on a healthy diet of creature double features and classic SF TV, Gregory L. Norris writes for short story anthologies, magazines, novels, and the occasional episode for TV and Film. Once when he was a boy, he did go sleepwalking into the big woods that surrounded the enchanted cottage where he grew up.

WATCH OUT FOR THE MASTER

MAGGIE HOLMAN

MARY LIKED to think she had the house to herself, out of sight of the many new owners who, unlike her, never stayed very long. She spent her endless days strolling along the corridors, her long black servant's dress swishing, her footsteps echoing in the silence.

One sunny afternoon, Mary was sitting in her favourite spot in the hallway, when she heard a car pull up outside and park, followed by the familiar click of a key in the front door. She instinctively stepped back into the doorway of the drawing room and watched from the shadows as a middle-aged man entered, followed by a young girl. The girl looked about Mary's age, although the similarity ended there. Her hair was dyed a bright red. She wore white, laced shoes and trousers with rips across the knees, bearing no resemblance at all to Mary's own sombre Victorian dress.

Mary watched the two newcomers as they brought in four large round pots with lids on and put them down by the front door, then proceeded to go in and out, bringing in some smaller tins, some paint-brushes, a stepladder, some rolled-up sheets and other things which Mary couldn't quite identify, things she hadn't seen before. Finally, they brought in a suitcase, a sleeping bag, a pillow and a cardboard box. Mary followed them when they took the box through to the kitchen.

"The house is much bigger than I expected," the girl said, as she unpacked various packets and tins. "Is there running water and electric?"

"I already had my guys out and everything's okay," the man said. "There's a kettle and a microwave for you. All the lights work so it won't be too dark and creepy at night, and all the locks are secure."

He paused.

"You will be alright here by yourself?"

Mary sensed a hint of falseness in his concern. She wondered if the girl sensed it too.

"I'll be fine," the girl replied. "Looking forward to it."

"Shame your friend couldn't come in the end," the man continued. "Still, when the house is painted, you get all the cash."

"That's right. It's her loss. I'm treating it like a little holiday before I go off to uni."

The man paused and smiled. "If you don't mind, Bella, I'll head off and leave you to explore on your own. I've always got somewhere to be! Oh, and I meant to tell you, there's still an old bed frame and a mattress on the top floor, probably was the servant's room years ago. You'll get a nice view of the garden if you sleep up there."

"Thanks," Bella said. "I'll take a look."

"Right, here's the keys. I'll try and pop by now and then, but it depends on how busy I am. Got a lot of projects on the go at the moment. You've got my number if you need anything. Bye."

"Bye, Frank."

The man smiled, that false smile again, Mary thought, and walked straight past her towards the front door. She heard the door close and, a moment later, the sound of the car roaring off down the drive. Mary was horrified. She walked straight up to Bella.

"What are you thinking of, staying here by yourself? Haven't you heard the stories about this house?" she shouted, even though she knew Bella couldn't hear her. "People come and go but they never stay! You can't be here on your own. You just can't!"

She stayed close as Bella began to explore the house. They walked together across the hallway and into the huge ballroom, which was the central point of the house, a hub of the local social scene in its heyday. The ballroom looked out onto the sprawling rear garden through a row of beautiful arched windows which let shafts of afternoon sun into the room. A large mirror, in an ornate gilt frame, hung on the opposite wall. It was easily a good six feet high and twice as wide. It reflected the sunlight and made the room seem even bigger and brighter.

Bella walked across the ballroom and went out through a side door. While Mary followed, she continued to open and close the doors to empty rooms and cupboards. She headed upstairs, where she inspected more empty rooms and the bathroom, which still contained its Victorian fixtures and fittings. When Bella finally climbed the last steep staircase and found the attic with the old iron bed frame, she peeped out of the dormer window. Mary followed her back downstairs when she went to retrieve her suitcase and sleeping bag. She was determined to stay beside Bella at all times.

Mary watched her cook herself some food and talk on a phone she kept in her pocket. She went with her when she strolled around the garden, and when Bella went to bed that night, Mary stayed by the doorway of the attic room. When she was sure Bella was asleep, she went over to the bed and lay down beside her, shielding her from the doorway, although sleep wouldn't come to Mary. Instead, she listened, lying with her back to the door, as she'd always done, so she wouldn't have to see *him* if he came in.

❄

IN THE YEARS that followed the tragic fire which took the whole household, Mary had been stuck in this house, trying her best to avoid him, caught in his cat-and-mouse game. In life, he was in the stronger and more powerful position, in their master-servant world, and death had not softened his attitude. Mary didn't know how much she could do to protect Bella, but she had to try. Bella didn't know what he was like, because she didn't even know he was there.

It wasn't long before Mary heard the familiar quiet tread on the stairs. She closed her eyes and listened to the door when it opened and closed. She listened to his footsteps approach the bed. He stopped, said nothing, but Mary felt his eyes on her. There was no mistaking it was him: Mister Edward. She remembered the fear he used to cause her and how she lay absolutely still, quaking inside. She heard him strike a match and a moment later, the aroma of cigar smoke wafted over her. She didn't dare move or turn to look. Eventually, he turned around and his footsteps went back down the stairs. Mary breathed a sigh of relief.

"You put yourself in danger by coming here, Bella, and you don't even know it," she whispered.

When Bella woke up in the morning, alone, she sniffed a distant aroma in the room.

"Cigars?" she mused out loud. "That's strange."

❄

AFTER BREAKFAST, Bella dragged one of the four large pots into the ballroom and took all the painting items through. She prised the pot lid open with a knife, poured paint into a tray, and began to work along the wall using a roller. Mary had never seen anyone paint with such a thing. In her day, everyone tied their paintbrushes onto broom shanks if they wanted a higher reach. She leaned against the wall and watched, impressed, as Bella made quick progress, hiding the old cream paint behind a layer of pastel green. One wall was almost complete when the sound of footsteps made both Bella and Mary jump. Bella put the paint roller down and wandered past Mary. Tentatively, she peeped out of the large ballroom doors.

"Hello?" she called, and when no one answered, she came back.

"Please don't look in the mirror," Mary said, because while Bella was looking elsewhere, the mirror was not reflecting the empty ballroom. In the mirror, the ballroom was full of people, men and women in elegant Victorian dress, dancing and talking. Mary's heart sank when Bella stopped and stared at the mirror, but when Mary followed her gaze, she saw that it was reflecting the real room back at her, its partly-painted wall, a dust sheet on the floor, and the two girls staring into it. Bella must have just missed the momentary image, because she calmly returned to her painting and kept busy for the rest of the day. That night, when Bella went to sleep, Mary curled up next to her again and waited. Thankfully, Mister Edward didn't come into the room, but Mary didn't think that was necessarily a good sign. Was he planning something?

Next morning, Mary sat beside Bella on the stone steps which led down from the front door. Bella stared ahead, deep in thought, at the landscaped gardens and the driveway, then she took her phone out of her pocket, dialed a number, and held the phone in front of her.

"Hello? Frank?"

Mary jumped when Frank's voice spoke out loudly from the phone.

"Hello, Bella. How's the painting going?"

"Well, that's why I'm calling. I wanted to talk to you. I don't think I can do this painting job after all."

"Oh? Why not?"

"Well, to be honest, the house is already kind of giving me the creeps."

Frank paused on the other end of the line, then began a tirade.

"You know, Bella, if you don't want to do the job, just say so. You don't have to make up stories about the house. I have to say, I'm surprised. I didn't expect you to let me down. I was so impressed with your attitude. You know how busy I am. Are you going to be another one of those unreliable young people, like your friend? I really need you to do this painting for me, now that you've promised you'll do it."

"I'm not changing my mind about wanting to do the job, and I'm not trying to mess you about," Bella replied. "It's just, the house makes me nervous. I've been...hearing things, and I feel like I'm being watched."

"That's because you are," Mary said, "and that's why you need to leave," but she knew Bella couldn't hear her advice.

"It's probably your imagination playing tricks," Frank said. "After all, it is a rambling old place, and empty. It must echo."

"Well," Bella said, speaking less confidently, "I suppose all old houses would make strange noises from time to time."

Mary picked at a thread on her cuff. She listened to Bella as she talked herself into staying.

"Exactly," he said. "Let's see how it goes over the next few days. Gotta go. Bye!"

Bella hung up and Mary followed her into the ballroom, where Bella pulled two small black boxes, attached to a wire, from one of her bags. She plugged them into a nearby wall socket and attached them to her phone.

"Right, Bella," Bella said out loud. "Time to cheer yourself up!"

Seconds later, loud music, jarring and unfamiliar to Mary, echoed around the room. Mary instantly hated it, but Bella seemed to like the song and she sang along as she poured paint into a tray. She began to paint, her roller moving in time to the beat, her hips swaying like she was on a dance floor.

It was at that moment that Mister Edward entered the room, dressed as ever in his immaculate suit, his hair combed, his smile wolfish. Mary flinched and made to speak out, but he looked across at her and put his finger to his lips. Ever the obedient servant, Mary could only watch as he pulled the plug out of the wall. The music abruptly stopped. Bella looked across at her phone and stared at the plug lying on the floor. Bemused, she walked past an unseen Mister Edward, plugged it back in, turned the music on and carried on painting. Seconds later, he pulled the plug again.

This time, Bella approached the plug more cautiously. She stared at it, unaware of Mister Edward watching from close by or of Mary wringing her hands in agitation. She bent down to pick up the plug a second time, and in that same moment, Mister Edward placed his hand gently on the small of her back as she leaned over.

Bella jumped up quickly, lost her balance and stood in the paint tray, tipping paint all over the floor. She turned and pressed her back up against the wall, her chest heaving with panic, looking around wildly for the perpetrator. Across the ballroom, Mary felt Bella's fear. Mister Edward waved to Mary and strolled out of the door. After waiting a few minutes, when nothing more happened, Bella kicked off her paint-soaked shoe, grabbed some rags, and began to clean up the mess before the paint dried.

She abandoned the painting and went to sit in the garden, where she sipped tea absent-mindedly and stared across the lawn. Mary sat nearby, watching her. Bella's hand was shaking as she held onto her mug and Mary guessed, from her own experience, how Bella was probably feeling.

Mary had spent the end of her short life trying to balance the need to get away with the weight of duty and responsibility. Her mother had needed Mary's service money and so Mary needed to work, and those commitments had kept her in the path of Mister Edward. She understood Bella's dilemma; Bella needed the extra money and had made a commitment to do this painting, but she was struggling with the realization that something was very wrong with the house. How Mary wished she could speak to Bella and tell her she wasn't alone. More to the point, she wished she could let her know it was only going to get worse.

❄

THAT NIGHT, Mary curled up next to Bella. In the darkness, the sounds of a party in full swing began to drift upstairs.

"Please don't wake up," Mary pleaded, as Bella stirred in her sleep, but Bella woke up, sat up next to her, and they both listened to the sounds of people talking and laughing, glasses clinking, and the crackling of a gramophone playing a waltz.

"An old-fashioned garden party somewhere?" Bella asked out loud, confused and half-asleep, but no, the party was here, downstairs. Bella got up to investigate, and Mary followed her.

❄

IN THE BALLROOM, the bright moonlight flooded through the sash windows and made elongated patterns on the floor. Bella turned on the light and saw her tins and brushes, the dust sheet and the step-ladder. The ballroom was empty. However, the distant sounds of the party still travelled across the empty space, and when Bella looked around, still trying to locate its source, she saw, to her horror, that there *was* a party in the ballroom, but it was inside the mirror. She stood, transfixed, watching ladies in elegant Victorian dresses and men in smart evening suits. Couples twirled to the crackling music. Other guests sat around in groups on luxurious Chesterfield sofas, chatting and laughing together, attended by young women in black dresses and crisp white aprons and caps.

Mister Edward wandered into view. He was carrying a glass in one hand and a cigar in the other. Bella didn't know Mister Edward, but Mary did, and her fear escalated when he turned and smiled in Bella's direction. Instinctively, Mary put her hand to her throat.

"Please, Bella," she whispered. "Run away."

Mister Edward put his glass down on a nearby table, stubbed out his cigar and then slowly, very slowly, he pushed his hand out of the mirror and reached towards Bella. Terrified, frozen to the spot, Bella watched as the mirror became fluid and malleable. The image of the party was distorted and stretched as Mister Edward pulled it along behind him. The gramophone music slowed to a grating, laborious grind.

Bella stepped backwards and turned to run, when suddenly she clutched her throat with both hands and made coughing, choking sounds. She struggled to breathe, while Mister Edward leered his horrible smile and continued to reach out towards her. Suddenly a woman's voice broke the tension.

"Darling? What are you doing? I've been looking for you everywhere. Come and dance. I do so love this particular song."

Without taking his eyes off Bella, Mister Edward froze and then pulled his hand back inside the mirror. The party scene was restored, and Bella saw a woman, plain, petite and round, at Mister Edward's side. Still watching Bella, he gently took hold of the woman's elbow and they strolled towards the dance floor. The party faded away, and the reflection of the empty moonlit ballroom returned. Bella fell to her hands and knees, breathing heavily and coughing violently. When she recovered enough, she got up from the floor and raced up the stairs, with Mary right behind her.

❄

MARY STOOD in the corner of the attic, wringing her hands again, glancing now and then at the open door.

"Hurry, hurry, hurry," she whispered.

Oblivious to Mary's presence, Bella got dressed, threw her things into the suitcase, and carried it down to the first floor. Mary followed her into the bathroom and watched her collect her toiletries, when suddenly a single floorboard creaked on the landing.

"He's here!" Mary screamed, and in that moment, Bella turned towards the sound of Mary's voice.

"You heard me!" Mary said.

Bella began to cry. She shook visibly as she walked towards the bathroom door, where Mister Edward, invisible to Bella, was barring her way. As she tried to leave, she walked into the shape of him. She felt a sense of his body in front of her, of the soft material and the buttons of his expensive suit, and was unable to pass through him.

"Hello, there," he said. "You're a pretty little thing."

The voice startled Bella. She dropped all her toiletries, and they clattered across the wooden floor. She bent down to pick them up.

"What's the matter?" Mister Edward whispered in a more menacing tone. "Are you afraid? You don't need to be afraid, just as long as you stay quiet."

Suddenly, an unseen hand grabbed Bella by her throat and forced her to her feet. She was pushed backwards and bumped up against the edge of the sink. In that moment, a desperate Mary, who had never stood up to Mister Edward in life, faced the object of her century-old fear.

"You are a horrible man!" she screamed, and the strength of her courage punched a hole through to the real world. Her voice echoed through the house and hit Mister Edward like a fist. "Leave her alone! You have no right to touch her. Stop it at once!"

Just as suddenly, a woman's voice called from somewhere downstairs.

"What's going on up there? What's all that shouting? Edward?"

"It's nothing, dear. I'll be down directly."

Mister Edward turned to smile at Mary. He let go of Bella and walked backwards out of the bathroom, keeping an eye on them both. For the second time that night, Bella clutched at her throat and tried to get her breath. She left her toiletries scattered on the bathroom floor, ran past her suitcase, down the stairs and out of the front door. She raced as fast as she could down the gravel drive, with Mary close on her heels. When they got to the main gates, Bella took her phone from her pocket and called a taxi.

They waited in the darkness. Bella was shaking with shock and fear, while Mary stood dutifully beside her. When the taxi arrived, Bella jumped into the back seat. She looked back once, but there was no indication that she saw her invisible friend watching as the taxi disappeared into the night. Alone again, Mary turned and walked reluctantly up the drive, back to the house, where she knew Mister Edward would be waiting.

About the Author

Originally from the North East of England, Maggie Holman now lives in Belgium. She writes speculative and supernatural fiction, both for children and older readers, and has self-published five books: *The Things We've Seen*, *The Wishing Sisters*, *Footprints in the Snow*, *The Knocking*, and *Save the White Stag*. Her writing has been longlisted for the Mogford Prize and the National Literacy Trust modern fairy tales anthology, and shortlisted for the *Stories of the Nature of Cities* anthology.

Social Media:

Twitter @runjumpjive

Facebook @maggieholmanwriter

Website: www.maggieholman.com

THE CUCKOO'S BROOD

CHRISTINA NORDLANDER

MIREILLE HAD GONE into town that afternoon to look for Christmas presents for Mum and Dad and Germaine. Blue darkness had already started falling when she went from school to the bus stop, and on her way back into Smedby, the sky was dark above the orange street lights. On the bus she sat with one boot on a radiator, and the air burnt her cheeks. She got off a couple of stops before the terraced estate. The wind instantly chilled her face.

It was December, but the air wasn't particularly cold yet, just raw with rain. Her winter clothes made her body into its own warm fortress that was cut off from the outside world. Instead of going straight home, she wandered off down the narrow winding country road that went past the Church of Dörby. Some of the villas had Christmas lights up along the edges of roofs or wound around apple trees in the gardens. Yellow light shone out of the windows, the kind that would make her feel the cold if she looked at it for more than a moment. The backpack with Germaine's present thumped against her back when she walked.

The car park in front of the church was empty. Across the graveyard she saw the whitewashed church without a tower. The steeple was barely visible; it was tarred and black against the sky. To the right the road turned and vanished between the fields with its narrow string of lights, and to the left was a farm with a deserted paddock.

The churchyard wall was low, barely up to her waist, with a grassy embankment on the inside. She could set her palm on the wet stone and swing herself onto it.

There were folk tales that you would get some sort of supernatural visions, *something* supernatural, if you walked seven times counter-clockwise around a churchyard at midnight. Around Halloween she'd thought about doing it, because if anything supernatural existed it had to be at that time of year, but she could hardly sneak out of the house at midnight, and the churchyard was big enough that seven times its circumference was a fair distance. She'd tried one lap in daytime, and of course nothing had happened. Should she try to make it now? Dad had said she shouldn't be out too long, but she was fourteen years old, and he was hardly worried about her. She'd told them she was going into town and getting a sandwich while there. Another few minutes wouldn't make a difference.

She started walking counterclockwise, along the road. The grass on the embankment sucked muddily at her boots; they would probably be filthy when she could see them again. There wasn't a lot of light here, and there would be even less when she turned her back to the road, but it wasn't dark enough that she risked falling. The church was unlit, probably locked. When she looked up, the clouds had an odd shade, almost purple. The wind shook the branches above her. She could feel it like soft fingers under the edge of her hat.

When it came, it was nothing she had invoked. She hadn't even done one lap.

She had to walk further down the embankment because some brambly thickets were in the way, and that was when she saw a light by the church. It might have been a grave candle, but it looked too big, too bright. She got closer.

The light came from a hole in the ground, as if someone had opened a lid. It was a family tomb, inside a fence comprised of hanging black-lacquered chains that wouldn't keep anyone out. The light was colourless, industrial. She thought about spiritual phenomena, but only for a moment. This light was stable—it belonged to modern times with electricity. She got close enough to get a look inside, hand supported on the enclosure in case she would see something horrific.

It was a subterranean chamber, longer than she'd expected, almost a short tunnel. There was nothing to block her view, just walls masoned from uneven stones and a floor that looked like concrete. Someone was sitting by the far end.

Mireille turned her head. There were many yards of dark church-yard between her and the road, but it was still within sight, the row of lampposts blinking when the branches swung in front of them. There was no life, no cars, but she would see the light in the houses if she ran back towards the road.

She put her hands on the concrete edge.

"Hello?" she said.

The figure hadn't moved. It looked slight, maybe closer to her own age than fully grown, wrapped in a grey blanket or coat. She had an impression that it was female, but that might have been from the long clothing and from the way it sat slumped like a draped angel on a tombstone carving. What she could make out of the face wasn't horrible.

Dead? Why would it be? You didn't place corpses in the ground without a coffin, not in crypts.

"Hello?" she called again. "Can you hear me?"

Her voice had grown stronger. A homeless woman who'd gone into the tomb for shelter, maybe?

Nobody replied, and the figure hadn't moved. She was going to have to go down. If there was any way to help them, she would do it, and if there wasn't, she wanted to see.

A line of shiny crampons led down below her. She had to turn her back to the shrouded figure while climbing.

She landed on the floor and took a couple of steps closer. The figure sat slim and tall before her. She had the ladder behind her, she could run whenever she wanted, but the terror would hurt her more than anything physical.

A voice:

"You shouldn't have come here."

There was nothing aggressive in it, as if it realised how tense she was. Even so, Mireille jumped and let out a dark shout without words.

The figure didn't laugh. It had barely moved. The voice must have been a woman's, but something had ruined it to the point where Mireille had to concentrate to make out what she was saying.

"You need help?" Mireille said.

"Yes, you can help me."

It was still cold down here, just the cold of a sheltered space. Mireille realised she wasn't breathing through her nose.

"What do I need to do?" Her voice didn't sound like she meant it.

"I'm stuck," the girl muttered.

Maybe a stone slab had fallen on her leg. (Was that something she'd seen, or just something she'd convinced herself she was seeing?)

"I don't know whether I can help," she warned. "You want me to get someone?"

"No." The girl's voice had become quick. "Try, at least. I've been here so long."

It was possible that Mireille was stronger than she: she was sturdier, she'd eaten well, she was better dressed against the cold. She stepped closer. When she looked down at the girl, she saw two slackly resting legs in the scraps of grey tights. Nothing was holding them down.

"Where are you stuck?" Mireille said and grabbed her hands.

She *felt* them through her gloves. They were cold with moisture, a sensation like when you brush against a slug. The girl had got up.

"I'm sorry," she said.

There was something new in her voice.

She ran for the ladder before Mireille had time to react. She was still staring at the far wall where there was nothing except the block where the girl had been sitting and a battery-powered metal lantern next to it.

When she turned, something moved in the opening. It wasn't the girl, it was the trapdoor, the slab. Mireille scrambled up the ladder, but when she reached the door, it had slid into place.

She heard herself call out. She put her palm into it and shoved. The slab was stuck. She took off her gloves and tried again, until her muscles swelled on the arm holding on to the crampon. She pressed until her shoulder hurt, and the slab didn't budge. Would it slide to the side instead? She got no grip on the smooth surface, and it wouldn't move.

She was starting to feel faint and light. Lack of oxygen? She jumped off the ladder and lumbered to the block. There was nothing loose there. She turned back.

"Are you up there?" she called. Her voice still sounded under control. "Can you hear me?"

The sound might not get past the trapdoor. *Good God, how thick was it?* She climbed back up and pressed her mouth as close to the crack as it could get and screamed. If the girl was there, she didn't react. Why would she be there?

Mireille made another attempt at pushing the slab. It made no difference; she couldn't even hear it scraping. She couldn't use both hands from the ladder, but would it make a difference? It would still be the same bony body lifting.

If it was possible to scrape out the edges of the opening, the slab would fall in. It would hit her head or snap an arm or a shoulder, but she would have got it out of the way. The slab rested on a hard concrete edge. It wasn't doable.

She got back down, because if she passed out on the ladder she would fall. She sank onto the block. It was cold through her trousers. She took up the lantern and looked at it. It had a pointy metal shade and glass that was a bit blurry; it must be the kind of light people put on graves. There was nothing in it that you could use as a lever or that would make a mark on the rock. When the battery ran out, she would sit in darkness. She held it close to her head and heard only a faint buzzing. The light was yellow, and it felt as if it gave off a bit of warmth. It flickered back and forth with an edge of darkness at the outskirts of her field of sight, but maybe that was her senses failing. The flickering had gone on for a while. If it was the battery, there was nothing she could do.

She tried lying down. The block was a bit too short; her legs stuck out over the side, but she needed to sleep, and when she woke up she would be lying back home. The relief made her almost nauseous. The light was a cold irritation in her eyes, but she wasn't going to turn it off. She couldn't place herself in a state where she would be able to wake. She got up again—her arms ached when she moved—and pinched the inside of her arm until it was difficult to keep going. It didn't help. The world was hard and clear in the outlines.

She scrabbled in her backpack. The present for Germaine was little tin fantasy figures and jars of model paint. As if she could have used them to force the slab...but no, she felt the thin hard pressure of the phone in her pocket. When she got it out, her fingers were so tense she could have dropped it. She had to lay it on the pitted stone block so it wouldn't fall.

She thumbed in 112, and nothing was blocking the signal, because someone replied.

"I'm stuck here... I need help! I'm in a crypt outside the Church of Dörby. I climbed down here, and the trapdoor slid shut."

The warmth had flowed back into her body. Now she could afford to feel ashamed.

"*Don't panic,*" the woman's voice said. "*Are you injured? How are you stuck?*"

"No, I'm not injured." She spoke as quickly as she could, so it wouldn't go silent. "I'm stuck in a crypt...below ground. I saw a light down there, so I climbed down, but the trapdoor slid shut and it's too heavy for me to get it open. It's a stone tile. A stone slab. But I'm not injured, I just need someone to open it for me."

When another second passed, her voice got shrill:

"I'm not joking! I can't get out!"

"*We're* going *to help you,*" the woman said like a kindly primary school teacher. "*Where did you say you are? Outside a church?*"

"The Church of Dörby, in Smedby." Her voice had become so tired, it sounded like she was about to start crying. "It's a family tomb, one of the big ones. If you enter by the gate, it's in front and to the right of the church, pretty close to the church building."

"*All right, I'm just going to check this,*" the woman said.

Some time passed.

"*Okay, now we know where it is. We're sending people to get you out. It shouldn't take more than fifteen minutes. Will you be fine, or do you want me to keep talking to you while you're waiting?*"

"No, I'll be fine."

The phone clicked.

Now, when they were on their way, now Mireille panicked. She looked at her watch. It was going to be quarter to nine when they arrived, but the next time she checked, not even a minute had passed. She kept her gaze on it to be sure that the second hand was moving, and every second brought them a little closer. It was like when she'd been sitting in primary school counting the seconds that brought her closer to her birthday.

When she looked up, she had difficulty breathing. Her heart pounded until it shook her frame. She wanted to run to the wall and scrape at the mortar until the stones came loose. She'd had attacks of claustrophobia before, but that had been in spaces that were actually tight, like when she was a kid and the bathroom door at Grandma's place had jammed. Don't think about it. There were no barriers against bad memories here. This chamber must have been longer than her bedroom.

Was air getting in? If not, she might not make it until they arrived. The trapdoor had lain flush against the concrete. She drew in long breaths and tried to taste the air. It was chilly and had a noticeable smell, not unpleasant, just alien with long containment. Was that the way it would smell when the oxygen had burnt out? It had gone so far, she couldn't tell whether it was fear or lack of oxygen that was making her dizzy.

She climbed back up and continued to struggle with the trapdoor while she waited, but if she wore herself out, she'd burn oxygen faster. Instead she clung to the uppermost crampon and held her mouth near the crack while breathing. She couldn't tell any difference in the smell, but it seemed to help. Her body had stabilised.

The tinkling ringtone cut through her. She was close to losing her footing. Her fingers were sweaty when she pulled out the phone.

"*Now we're here, outside the Church of Dörby,*" a male voice said. "*Wherever are you?*"

Then there had been no point. It felt as if she had to summon up new energy to be able to speak.

"It's a family tomb. To the right of the church, but on the front... facing the gate. One of those grave-sites, with black chains around. One of the ones closest to the church."

That wasn't going to be enough, there were many graves like that. She hadn't seen what it had said on the marker. It was a few yards away, blocked off by earth.

"It's a stone slab. A trapdoor...fairly big. It has to be bare, all the other tombs are covered with gravel. If you find one like it, can you lift it?"

And if the girl had kicked the gravel back?

"Wait? You have torches, don't you? It's possible that the gravel is still there, but in that case it'll be tramped up...all the other tombs are raked."

Another stretch of time passed, but she heard footsteps, the scrape of stone. They pushed the slab to the side, and she saw a strip of night sky on the other side. When she climbed up the ladder and put her head through the opening, it felt like she was dreaming.

Once they'd let the trapdoor fall back, they asked her what had happened. She told them she'd gone down to explore the crypt and that the trapdoor had fallen shut. They got to believe that she was stupid and tell her she needed to watch herself from now on. The less she talked about the girl, the quicker she might forget her.

"You want a drive home?" asked a female rescue worker with crinkly hair framing a kind face.

Mireille turned it down; it wasn't far to walk, and she wasn't in that much shock. She walked onto the wet road and didn't turn her head until there were house fronts and gardens in the way.

There was nothing wrong with her when she looked down at

herself: at most she might have got some damp stains on her coat, and she still felt a faint wobbling ache in her right shoulder from her struggle with the stone slab. If not for the ache, she might have thought she'd dreamt it. Her body was unharmed, and her clothes were whole, as if it hadn't been through anything worse than walking a few times around the church. Her boots had muddy stains up the sides, but they were from before it had happened.

Perhaps it was best if she went to bed as soon as she got home. Tomorrow was a school day, and she didn't know what this might have done to her brain. She could lie in bed with the Advent candlestick lit in front of its reflection in the window, reading something that would calm her down. *Jingo* usually helped; she'd read it past midnight once after waking from a nightmare.

She would have to walk back past the scout hall, past the dark field, through the underpass under the railway, up the hill past the community college, then across the main road. Perhaps she should have let them give her a lift. She'd started turning her head to see if anything walked behind her. The road was always empty, but she kept hearing the echo of her footsteps. After a while she took to stopping, just a few seconds at a time, to make sure it didn't keep going without her.

The windows of the villas were lit, but that didn't help. Her gaze went to the yellow light, but then she started imagining the things inside: kitchens and living rooms with dark figures sitting immobile. In front of one house stood a tree so overgrown with ivy you couldn't make out its shape. The ivy reflected in the windows and made everything inside into a wet garden.

The underpass was lit, and there was no-one inside. It didn't remind her of the vault, but a few steps in, she had an attack of vertigo. (*Am I still in there?*) She ran the last few yards and stopped to draw big gulps of cold air in the dark on the other side.

She continued up the slope, and soon she could cross the main road. The windows of the terraced estate glittered below the darkened school cafeteria.

The lights were out in the hallway when she came in. A bit of yellow light from Germaine's room fell into the stairway, and when she got upstairs, she could glance through the door and see Germaine sit hunched over her desk, doing her homework. Other than that, nothing moved. Mum and Dad must have gone to bed. Or were they out, had they gone looking for her? She opened the master bedroom door, quietly so as not to wake anyone. They were asleep. She could see the silhouette of Mum's nose and long hair against some of the orange light seeping in through the blinds. Maybe she should get her pyjamas and get into the wide bed next to them, the way she had when she was a little kid. They would want to know that she was there.

"Hello?" she said. "I'm home."

Mum grunted and tossed under the quilt. She sat up. Maybe she was blinking against the light in the hallway.

"What're you doing out there, Mireille?" she said.

A moment later, a slimmer shadow rose up against the blinds.

"Who is it?"

It was a woman's voice, a young woman's voice.

Mum's gaze shot between Mireille and the other girl.

"Good Lord," she said, "what are *you* doing here?"

She got out of bed and rushed towards Mireille, not for a hug. Her stance was stiff, and she halted a step away. Mireille couldn't see much behind her, but she heard Dad twitching and mumbling as he woke.

"I don't know who you are," Mum said, "but get out of here. Don't you have a home to go to?"

It was Mum: no taller than herself now, hair starting to fade with age, the mole on the bridge of her nose that Mireille had always poked at when she was little. Her gaze was flat.

"Mum, it's me!"

She'd raised her hand to put it on Mum's arm, but she didn't dare to get close enough. A fever dream—drugs? Mum's voice hadn't sounded off.

The bed creaked again as Dad sat up.

"Go to sleep, Alain," Mum said over her shoulder. "You too, Mireille. I'll sort this out."

Mum's voice was kind when she said her name, but she was

glancing into the darkness of the bedroom. *There was something in there, wasn't there?*

She flung herself past Mum in the doorway. She had to knock Mum's arm away when she tried to stop her, but perhaps it didn't hurt. Mum didn't make a noise. The light switch gave a crack when Mireille hit it.

The girl was sitting on the far side of the bed. Mireille couldn't bring herself to get closer.

"Tell them it's me," she said.

The girl turned her head.

"Should we call the police?" she said. "She doesn't seem right in the head."

Mum grabbed Mireille's arm as if she were trying to hurt it.

"Let's go downstairs so I can phone the police," she said, yanking Mireille towards the stairs. "Or the hospital, if...you've got to understand, we don't mean you any harm, but you can't just come in here, scaring my little girl. I don't know what's happened to you, but they'll take you somewhere you can get help."

If she screamed as loud as she could, someone might come. What could they do, when Mum and Dad didn't believe her? Germaine stood in the door to her room, unmoving. She didn't do anything to help her.

"Don't worry about it," Mum said over her shoulder. "It's just a girl who thought this was her house."

The hallway was narrow, and she almost pressed Mireille towards the stairs. Both of them would fall if she tried to walk down like this. She managed to twist free and turned towards Mum, hands raised. Mum took a step back. She didn't know which one of them would win.

"Is it drugs?" Mum said. "If that's the kind of thing you've been doing, get out. I'll call the police."

Mireille shook her head. A tress of brown hair fell in front of her face.

"Good God, Mum, I'm your daughter! I'm Mireille. That girl..."

She made a gesture towards Mum's and Dad's room, but it faltered. She couldn't continue.

Mum forced her way past her and hurried down the stairs: first normally, then running. When Mireille got into the kitchen, she was holding the phone.

"...tried to hurt anyone yet, but she's very upset. Yes, please."

Outside the window was only blackness and the glitter of lamp-posts. This was slipping away from her. The only thing Mireille could think of was grabbing hold of a pencil and one of the slips of paper Dad used for shopping lists.

"But it's *me*," she said and put the paper on the worktop to be able to write. "Look for yourself."

She wrote her name—she couldn't think of anything else—and it was still her handwriting, unnecessarily ornate and old-fashioned. She held it up in front of Mum's face. Mum's gaze met hers without changing.

"You need help."

"I'm fourteen years old. My birthday was the twenty-seventh of November. I have As in Maths and English. When Germaine was little, and her hair caught fire on a candle, I poured water on her from the jug..."

She rattled it off like a list; she needed to keep her voice unemotional to make sure it would get through. A reflection showed in the window, and she turned around. The girl stood in the doorway.

"Go back to bed, Mireille," Mum told her.

When the girl didn't move, Mum walked up and gave her a quick hug. Mireille could only see her from behind.

The police came and led her out into the nocturnal driveway. One of them talked about how she was going to get a nice room to sleep in while they searched for her family. It was baby-talk to comfort her.

She didn't resist as much as she could have, because if she stayed here, she might see the girl again.

About the Author

Christina Nordlander was born 1982 in Sweden, but has lived in the United Kingdom since 2001. She currently lives outside Birmingham with her husband and two cats. She has published approximately twelve short stories and other pieces of fiction, both in Swedish and English. She also holds a PhD in Classics and Ancient History from the University of Manchester.

Facebook: https://www.facebook.com/christina.nordlander.332/

Patreon: https://www.patreon.com/user?u=79474&fan_landing=true

AN ENGAGEMENT OF LONG STANDING

SPENCER KOELLE

THE SILVER and black cracker snapped like a gunshot. Christian and Evalyn Allyson staggered back in a cloud of red foil confetti.

"Well don't keep us in suspense, read the motto!" shrieked somebody who thought she was the life and soul of the party. Jennifer sighed. Pretty soon, she'd be asked to join in the fun of the Salvation Shelter (Greater Wainscotting District) Staff Party. Christian donned his lime-green paper crown and unfurled the motto while Evalyn tucked the prize, a cheap pennywhistle, into her pocket.

"What has blue lips and a green dress? A lost girl in the cold..." Christian's words trailed off into nothing. Evalyn stiffened and took the paper from his unresisting hand. This was apparently the kind with a Motto and an Inspirational Saying. Evalyn finished her glass before reading: "Whatever you did not do for one of the least of these, you did not do for *me*." There was nothing ominous about Matthew 25:45 to Jennifer's mind, but Evalyn read it like an overdraft notice.

A jolly-faced board member picked up the next Christmas cracker and pulled it with the volunteer coordinator. The Allysons did not step away from the end table with the dusty plastic bag of Christmas crackers. Evalyn stared at Christian, her face tight with rage or pain. She still held the scrap of paper. Christian showed no expression at all.

Jennifer clipped her tray of ham rolls and brownie bites to her armrest and started wheeling over. Evalyn seemed like a nice person, and she seemed less comfortable ever since she got promoted into Development and out of her night shifts as assistant shelter manager.

"Are you okay?" she asked. Evalyn opened her mouth to answer. She glanced out the window. Jennifer turned her head. She just caught the retreating flap of a large bird, maybe a barn owl.

"My wife is feeling a little ill," Christian said, firmly. Evalyn nodded, still looking at the window and clutching the cracker motto in her hand.

Jennifer wanted to say something more to them, but what? She couldn't offer any medical aid, and giving them her home phone number would be weird. "Travel safe," she said to their retreating backs. The hostess passed out some sprigs of holly as party favors. Evalyn tucked one into a discreet pocket on her midnight-blue top, but Christian politely declined, gripping his silver cross with one hand and keeping the other in his jacket. (Jennifer made a mental note to ask Mrs. Allyson where she got her clothes. It wasn't easy to get women's clothes in that size anywhere, much less ones with real pockets and a flattering color.)

She rolled up and picked up one of the toys herself. They came out of a yellowing plastic package that was once white, with "MRJ NOVEL-TIES" printed in glittery letters. There wasn't even a bar code anywhere on it. She wheeled away from the table and pulled it herself.

Jennifer got a shower of blue confetti, a whiff of lavender water and a pink crown. The toy prize was a mini jigsaw puzzle. She'd always liked doing puzzles with her grandma, God rest her soul, on rainy Sunday afternoons. The motto said "What does a man stand up to do, a woman sit down to do, and a dog lift its leg to do? Shake hands!"

Jennifer smiled, then frowned. Had Grandma told her that joke, or did she read it in a joke book? She shrugged and headed for the punch-bowl. The Inspirational Quote was just: "Let me wish you a Happy New Year."

※

WHENEVER ONE PERSON gracefully exits an office party, that provides an excuse for others to follow. So it was that Monique Rockwell looked forward to a pleasant evening of reshelving her home library, and Rodney Wurthington hoped to catch his favorite reruns of *A Ghost Story for Christmas.*

It was just as well, Monique thought, that she'd left with this group. The bitter rain had nearly died, but there were wet patches and icy slicks everywhere. Evalyn shook and trembled like a sapling in a gale. Mr. Allyson kept looking over his shoulder, and Mr. Wurthington zipped his coat up tight.

Monique steadied herself against a low stone wall and tightened her raincoat as a sharp wind tore across the street. Their footsteps echoed oddly, just audible above the cold rain and passing cars.

Wurthington bellowed in fury as his umbrella inverted for the fourth time that night. "Blast these slipshod immigrant workers! If those towel-headed layabouts had any Christian work ethic, this country wouldn't be in such a state!"

Monique hunched herself against the rain and groaned. She'd spent a lot of the night carefully steering Mr. Wurthington away from the Interfaith Liaison Director. Mr. Allyson actually smacked his head, then disguised it as an adjusting-his-paper-crown motion before the senior board member could take offense.

Evalyn faltered in her step and turned around to stare at him. "You don't have a problem with people of Pakistani origin, do you?" Somehow, she managed to tilt her umbrella into the breeze and keep it right-side out.

"Oh no, of course not!" Wurthington boomed. "Pakis are just fine. It's ruddy Mohammedians I have a problem with!"

A barn owl took off from the streetlight at the end of the block, vanishing into the dark sky. "I think the term is 'Muslim'," Monique said, drawing on all the patience that her mother had passed on to her.

Mr. Wurthington grunted and rung out his bushy mustache. Christian pressed a little closer to Evalyn. Distant strains of "God Rest Ye Merry Gentlemen" followed them on the breeze.

Monique wondered how happy the Allyson couple were. It wasn't an official policy, but the higher ups at Salvation Shelter didn't approve of people staying unmarried past a certain age, and the sooner you got hitched, the more likely you were to get a family-sized salary. Monique might be safe in coming out as bisexual to Evalyn. She was somebody who could keep a secret.

The rain had eased up and the wind had nearly died down. In the shelter of a Marks and Spencer's store front, a young man in an elf costume shivered behind a donation box for Christians Against Cancer. Mr. Allyson stopped and put a five-pound note in the box. His wife hesitated before tossing in some change. Monique walked on, reminding herself that she was signed up for monthly donations to Doctors Without Borders, Heifer International and AllOut.org, on top of her payroll deduction and tithes at church. She still felt a prickle of guilt.

The sight of a tiny mosque wedged between a three-story pub and a cathedral incensed Wurthington enough to begin another diatribe. He enumerated a number of failings in modern society brought about by pernicious Islamic influences, such as suicide bombings, excessive spiciness in food, mailbox vandalism, inferior remakes of classic movies, and chauvinistic attitudes. These subjects carried them all the way to the bus stop.

At one of Mr. Wurthington's longer pauses for breath, Monique ventured to inform him that on the subject of transgender rights, Muslim communities were a deal more progressive than some western Christian ones, and Iran was a world leader in sex reassignment surgery. Evalyn seemed very interested by this, but the subject clearly made Christian uncomfortable, and he muttered something about Gomorrah.

Mr. Wurthington began a carefully-thought-out rebuttal, but was halted by a temporary reversal of conventional gastronomic processes. Once he pulled his face out of the hedge, Wurthington blamed this interruption on "halal lamb kebabs at the party," and not on the five Hemingway cocktails he had lined his stomach with before visiting the buffet table.

When the uptown bus pulled up, Monique mouthed: "Help me."

Evalyn offered her a sympathetic grimace while her husband fumbled in his pockets for exact change.

"Are all five of you getting on?" the bus driver snarled. Monique shook her head. She waved at the couple boarding their escape vehicle.

"There's another thing you should know about Sharia Law," Wurthington said. Monique turned away and inserted her headphones, hoping the shadows of her hood would disguise them. The rumble of the bus and bluster of the board member drove recent thoughts from her mind.

❄

THE BUS DRIVER met Duane with a hostile look. It may have been a "damn kids" look, a "somebody with your skin tone once egged my bus" look, a "don't try blowing yourself up on *my* bus" look, or just an "after twenty years in this low-paying job, I view all passengers as squealing vermin" look. Duane swiped his pass, took a seat near the middle of the nearly-empty bus, and pulled out his course reading.

His foray into the exciting world of cell biology was troubled by piping Christmas music. The bus had no speakers, and the muffled sound suggested somebody had turned the volume up so high that it was audible through their headphones.

Duane bit his lip and tapped his highlighter against the window. What was the point of using headphones if you blared it to the whole bus? Didn't that cause ear damage or something?

He got as far as an introduction to mitochondria before a harsh whisper drew his attention to the back of the bus.

"That was six years ago, and *he* wasn't allowed in," a middle-aged man said.

"She wasn't a—" said a younger woman, probably his wife.

"There are plenty of men's shelters in the downtown area. You didn't change my mind then, and you won't change my mind now," the man said.

Duane tilted his head. Without appearing to stare, he studied the couple's reflection in the window. The man had a well-cut grey suit and pale skin. An adequate supply of salt-and-pepper hair framed the kind of face that reassured you as you signed a large check.

The well-dressed fat woman next to him had to be his wife. A man with that kind of suit wouldn't take his girlfriend or mistress on a bus. Her dark blue top was modest without being frumpy, with a sprig of holly for a festive touch. The woman kept her hair in a restrained single braid. She wore just enough makeup for unobservant men to think she looked good without makeup. Though she smiled at her husband, her eyes were moist, and her nails dug into the scratchy cushions of the seat.

A forest green shape hovered between the two people, framed by a golden glow. Duane blinked. He couldn't tell if this was outside the couple's window, or reflected from his window, or a light cast by an object elsewhere in the bus.

"We'll discuss it when we get home," the husband mouthed.

"You better," she said, between clenched teeth.

Was it a jogger in very unseasonal clothing, or some scrap of fabric twisting in the wind? That couldn't be. It kept pace with them as the bus sped up leaving the roundabout. He looked around the bus for a green cell phone screen or LED wristwatch to account for the strange effect. It refused to resolve into a sensible context.

The shape jerked upwards and vanished before Duane could make up his mind. He rubbed his eyes and resigned himself to enzymes and protein structures for the rest of the ride.

❄

CHRISTIAN STEADIED Evalyn as she stepped off the bus. Her teeth were still buzzing with the engine's rumble. That endless shrill loop of "God Rest Ye Merry Gentlemen" still played in her head. She was used to rich, choral voices or resonant brass for that tune, not a high piping.

Two stars shone, in between the disintegrating clouds and above the orange street lights. Here and there, colored fairy lights and blue bulbs mocked the heavens. A garland of bright white lights failed to cheer up the row of sickly yew saplings lining the street. The light passed through her husband's green paper crown, making it look like it was glowing.

Evalyn walked as fast as she could, down the row of high housing complexes and small mid-range restaurants. The silver snowflakes and strings of lights only made the shadows deeper. Christian wiggled a finger in his ear. "Do you have your iPhone on?"

Evalyn was wondering how a cheap tissue-paper crown had survived even a light rain, when she realized that the high, piping tune wasn't in her head. She also realized that the buzzing didn't come from her teeth. It came from very near her left breast.

She reached into her shirt pocket, carefully working her fingers around the holly's sharp points. She squealed as something warm buzzed against her fingers. Evalyn gripped the object. She expected to feel the repulsive squish of a beetle between her fingers. The object was intact.

Evalyn pulled out something silver and flung it away with a gasp. The penny whistle shook and trembled against the iced concrete, whining out "God Rest Ye Merry Gentlemen."

Skin crawling, knees knocking, Evalyn turned to her husband for reassurance. "What in God's name is going on?"

Christian covered his mouth in disgust and kicked the instrument into the gutter. He squeezed her hand tight enough to hurt.

"How the hell should I know?" he snapped. He glanced just over his shoulder and jerked her into a run. "It's not like I brought this on myself!"

Evalyn ran with him, struggling not to slip. The five blocks to their building's entrance seemed like five kilometers.

The wind picked up. They both swung around the corner, hands clutched tight. Both of them had something to feel guilty about.

This couldn't be happening to her. This couldn't be real. She kicked aside a Scrumpy's cider bottle. She didn't dare look over her shoulder.

"Though I walk through the valley of the shadow of death," Christian panted in between whistling breaths.

"God forgive me," Evalyn gasped out. "Please!" she added. She should have made an exception. She should have let that homeless *person* through the side entrance, or driven *her* to another shelter, Salvation Shelter bylaws be damned. Even if Christian was right, and she was just a boy in a dress, she should have let that child in long enough to warm up. Give the kid some hot soup and find out if anyone was looking for them.

The stoplight was red at this corner. Evalyn glanced left, sure that Christian was glancing to the right, and they plunged on at full speed.

A great wind howled down the alley. The trees did not sway. The Crescent Moon bar sign did not swing in it. Plastic bags and hamburger wrappers stayed still on the ground as the north wind pushed their legs out from under them.

The ice burned as it slapped their hands. Glass shards dug into Evalyn's palms. *One short entry in the local newspaper, not on a headline page, about a "cross-dresser" found on that snowy morning.* She and her husband would get a much longer article, she thought, as she slid.

They both ignored the pain. They scrabbled together, half-supporting, half-climbing, while the notes of "Merry Gentlemen" drew closer.

They turned the last corner. With numb, bloody fingers, Evalyn dug the key to their flat out of her pocket. Christian was still fumbling with his when she pulled the door open against the gale and dived into the lobby. They knocked over the big fake Christmas tree in their haste. Evalyn pushed the up button a dozen times while screaming, "The power of Christ compels you!" Christian was still looking behind her, stammering something about casting out demons.

The doors inched open. Christian shoved Evalyn through and dove in after her, then turned to face the lobby door with his silver cross in hand. Evalyn only caught a glimpse of gold-topped green outside as she stabbed the fifteen button and whispered: "I'm sorry."

Her heart slowed down a little bit. She winced and tried to pick the brown glass shard out of her right hand.

Her husband's paper crown glowed with green fire. She struggled for the moisture in her mouth to speak.

"Take off the crown," she hissed. "God's sake, take it off!"

Christian, blank-faced, tugged at the cheap tissue paper. It disintegrated, coating his hands with glowing green slime. He spat and wiped his hands on his coat furiously.

As the elevator dinged up floors, they breathed together slowly.

Christian forced a smile onto his tight, waxy face. "I think we're safe."

She wrapped her arms around him and kissed him all over his neck. "God, I hope so."

The elevator rumbled. Seasonal Muzak played, and she gave thanks to the Lord that it was only an instrumental of "Rudolph the Red-Nosed Reindeer." Her hands throbbed.

The elevator jolted to a stop. They both gasped. The doors slid open.

❇

THE HALLWAY WAS WELL-LIT and empty. This time, Christian got his keys into the lock while Evalyn recovered her dropped keychain from the bristles of the welcome mat. They slammed the door behind them. Evalyn locked the door while Christian pulled the deadbolt.

They didn't fumble for the light switch. The sparse lights of their Christmas tree and glow from outside the picture window were enough to find their way. Without speaking, they grabbed the couch. They'd needed three movers to drag that couch out of the service elevator and into place. The two of them carried it to the door in six seconds.

Only after they piled the Barcalounger and the nightstand onto the couch did Evalyn go into the bathroom to get tweezers. She didn't even feel the glass shard as she yanked it out and slapped a big bandage on the open wound.

Evalyn staggered back into the living room. The lights of distant buildings shone against the dark reflection of their gold-topped tree. Christian staggered towards her with a wine glass filled with scotch in each hand.

"Happy Christmas," he said.

Evalyn took her glass. She laughed and started crying. She lowered herself to the floor and gulped the burning liquid. She hadn't stopped shivering from the cold.

Christian knocked back his glass. She wanted to ask him if he'd read the newspaper that day. She wanted to tell him he'd been wrong. He probably knew that now, though.

Evalyn couldn't bring herself to start any trouble with him. Not right now. She was glad to just be alive. She choked down a mouthful of liquor. She needed to pee, badly, but she couldn't bring herself to stand up again. Her husband sprawled out in front of her, hiccupping. Fairy lights of the tree shone in her glass. The lights were too few, and she didn't remember putting that huge gold ornament on.

Evalyn didn't drop her glass, but she spilled it a little. She forced herself to turn. She tried to scream. She wanted to scream. She opened and closed her mouth.

Christian had already turned to face it. The green figure rose up, with a featureless gold mask for a face. Its dress flowed around broad curves, far more feminine than the figure in green they had turned away from the shelter. There were two halves to the mask, or maybe it was a huge golden walnut. Evalyn's eyes watered. She scrambled backwards.

The mask-like thing hung too low for a normal head. The brown hands ended in midnight-purple fingertips; one of them pointed straight at her.

The mask was covered in feathers. The figure in the green dress took one step forward. Evalyn backed up against the wall. It wasn't a face. It wasn't a mask. It wasn't even a head.

"Please," she gasped out. She moistened her lips. "Mercy. Oh," she struggled for breath, "oh, God." The figure stood totally still.

The specter had *wings* instead of a head.

Christian ripped the cross from his neck. "Get the hell away!" he screamed. He flung it at the apparition. The cross missed it and bounced off the window with a tiny chime.

Rising out of the green dress's neckline, the gold wings unfolded.

"I'm sorry," Evalyn sobbed. "Please don't—"

The finger touched her lips, silencing her. It chilled as gently as the first snowflake of winter. The specter touched its right index finger to Christian's Adam's apple. Without drawing blood or leaving any mark, it sunk slightly *beneath* the skin.

She felt the cold touch trace her sternum and ribs as the finger ran down her. The room swam around her, and she felt light as a feather. Her breath froze. Her heart skipped a beat. The finger stopped just above her pocket and withdrew. Evalyn collapsed, gasping, and dug her nails into the carpet.

Her husband stood up straighter. The blackened nails slid through the fabric and closed over his heart.

"God, no!" Evalyn shouted, still weak and dizzy. She staggered upright. The apparition touched the picture window with its free hand, and the door slid open. Icy wind blasted in from the balcony, knocking Evalyn down again.

Those huge wings beat once, passing through the glass and ceiling like they were water. The specter held her husband in one hand and rose. She grabbed onto his leg, tight as she could.

Christian looked like he was shouting at the top of his lungs, but only cold mist came out. The winter wind froze Evalyn's hands while the pain burned them. She could feel his lightness tugging on her like a balloon.

The fabric slid through Evalyn's blood-slicked fingers. Christian clutched at air and the gold wings beat, further away, higher and higher.

Evalyn reached out with her bleeding hands. The gold-winged figure and her husband slowly vanished into distant night.

※

EVALYN ALLYSON HAS LEFT her post at Salvation Shelter and has not remarried. She still considers herself a faithful Christian, and attends Sunday services and holidays. She takes her seat near the back of Angel of Mercy Church every Christmas Day.

In seven Christmas services, she has not once managed to sit through the hymns.

About the Author

Spencer Koelle lives in a Philadelphia rowhouse with his partner, his roommate, and four orange cats. He enjoys scary movies, fake meat, and red wine. His website is www.spencerkoelle.com and his twitter handle is @KoelleSpencer. Spencer Koelle is an out and proud bisexual who startles easily and bites when cornered.

SCHRÖDINGER'S GHOST

H.R.R. GORMAN

January 23rd, 1961

FEARING her life would be cut to a short seventeen years by Soviets targeting the nearby Fort Bragg, June tugged her blankets close and looked out the window.

Airplane lights blinked red and white in the sky. A headlight brightened, lighting up the ground beneath. White sheets billowed into parachutes and disappeared into the dark as the airplane fell.

The sky lit up, a double flash with fire and mushroom cloud.

The air thickened, pressing June's lungs shut. Her breath caught as the sharecroppers' house cracked and blew to pieces. The pine bed splintered in the wind, tossing her beneath her shabby mattress and blanket.

She gasped when the air loosened its tight grip on her chest. Her stiff hands were blackened, and her fingers were gnarled, crisp, unable to move. Her lungs burned when she tried to let out anything between a scream or a whimper. The housefire dimmed as radiation and heat destroyed her eyes. Her hair ignited, the scent foul before the inside of her nasal passages and her last sense burned away.

As soon as she'd given up hope, her pain receded. Her breath turned to screams, her skin and fingers returned to normal, and she could move her joints. Her returned sense of smell caught whiffs of smoke, her eyes saw the fire, her skin felt the heat. "Oh God," she prayed, voice shaky, "have mercy!" She stood amid the wreckage of her house and flattened tobacco fields.

She walked forward, then stumbled over something warm and alive. At her feet was a crumbling husk about her size with fingers cracking off and skin peeling from the muscles beneath. This creature, though inhuman and monstrous now, gave June a sinking feeling in the pit of her stomach. This person *was* June, just as much as she herself was June. She felt this body's agony, felt a mental connection to the flaming body's horror that she couldn't explain.

June knelt to the poor creature and tried to help her up, but the skin sloughed away, and the body trembled before vomiting. Its empty eye sockets stared as the body stood. "Please," she begged the burning June. "You gotta get up. You gotta leave this place, get to a doctor!"

There was no hope for the burning June. The healthy June shivered while burning June shambled aimlessly into the swamps and tobacco fields. Healthy June followed.

Burning June shuffled toward where the bomb had gone off. With no trees, no animals, and no people to interrupt it, the swampy farms lay silent save for the two Junes' rustling.

Then, just as healthy June saw the crater where the bomb fallen, burning June fell to the ground with a final gasp.

Healthy June screamed as she appeared barefoot in a cold, January swamp. The bomb was gone, tobacco returned. She ran through the furrows as aimlessly as burning June had.

She closed on where the center of the crater would have been. Instead of a ghastly, nuclear pit in the middle of a swamp, small fires in trees illuminated the skeletal remains of a large airplane in the tobacco field.

She hurried home.

❄

January 26th, 1961

A NAKED BULB hanging from the asbestos tile lit the cafeteria. The hot incandescence reminded June of the nuclear flash, of the fires in the imagined house.

She sipped on her carton of milk and read her ratty physics textbook. It was scrawled with underlining and phallic images, but was new enough to contain a bit of nuclear physics and a description of string theory. She bit her lip and, while wishing for something in better shape, supposed she shouldn't be so picky.

A girl with blonde curls tied back in a seafoam bow clacked a tray on the other side of the table. Peggy Sue's shriveled right arm and polio-contorted fingers frightened all the boys and the pretty girls away. "Can I sit here?" she asked, her voice dulcet.

Peggy Sue might not be popular, but she was white, and that made her dangerous to talk with. June focused on her book and fiddled with the beans and grits on her tray. Peggy Sue used her good left hand to smooth her skirts before sitting on the stool attached to the table.

After some moments of eating in silence, Peggy Sue asked, "You live on that plantation near Big Daddy's Road?"

June looked up from her food. "Why you ask?"

"The army blocked off the road a few days ago, and they just now told us why. One of them Strategic Air Command bombers crashed into the field. Heard it on the radio." She ate a spoonful of grits, then pointed the utensil at June. "You heard it crash, didn't ya?"

June remembered the flash. She stared at Peggy Sue's arm and thought about the gnarled, crackling, blackened fingers in the screaming radiation. She shook her head. "I might have thought it was part of a nightmare."

"Oh?" Peggy Sue asked. Her spoon scraped against the metal tray like nails on a chalkboard. "What you dream 'bout?"

June focused on her textbook, on words about Schrödinger and his cat and his philosophical theories based on quantum physics.

Peggy Sue tapped her spoon against June's tray. "Hey, nerd, what you dream 'bout?"

June formed fists and glared, but her muscles softened when she noted earnestness in the other girl's face. She put a finger in the book to remember where she was, then answered, "I dreamed the plane was carryin' bombs and they went off. It was like Hiroshima, with the tobacco fields on fire and radiation and ever'thing."

Peggy Sue snorted, dragged her metal spoon with a screech across the tray. "You did too see that plane. I knowed you was sneaky, and I ort to have knowed you'd seen the bombs."

June swallowed. "It had...nukes?"

"Radio said the safeties worked, so no one had to worry. Still—a SAC B-52? That's big news to have one-a them fancy planes crash on your plantation. I'd have bust my ass to see that before the Army closed it off, if I'd been at your house."

"Then maybe I did see it," she said. "I thought it was just a nightmare."

Peggy Sue ate one more bite, patted her mouth clean with a napkin. "That's nice." She cleared her throat. "Now, June, I have a favor to ask you. A little favor, nothing important."

She bit her lip, then braved enough to say, "What sort of favor?"

"No polio girl's ever gonna fly a bomber," Peggy Sue said. "This'll be the closest I'll get to one-a them planes, and I wanna see it. I got a license and a Buick, so I can drive us there if you show me how to get to Big Daddy's Road. I'll take you home and buy you candy or something after school if you help me sneak up close."

"I don't know if that's a good idea—"

"You sassin' me, girl?"

June opened her book again. "No."

"Good. Meet me after school at my car. 1950 Buick Special, red."

June nodded. "Yes, Miss Peggy."

❄

JUNE BOUNCED in the passenger seat of the Special. Rust ate away at what was once candy apple red, and the patent-leather seats had long since flaked. She'd not sat in too many cars before, and she wondered how she'd forgotten about the stench of fuel permeating the cab.

She pointed down a dirt road separating the Bixbys' tobacco plantation and the Williams' cotton. "Turn here," June said. "They've opened the road now, and folks is allowed in the Williams' cotton. We can get purty close."

Peggy Sue turned the car down the lane, and the shocks on the old Buick squealed. She pulled over, easing the car into a moist, swampy ditch just off the side of the road. Skeletons of cotton plants littered the other side of the barbed wire fence, and a few unpicked bolls floated around in the wind.

Peggy Sue took the keys out of the ignition. "We're gonna have to walk from here. I just wanna see an airplane, not get whooped by Papa for ruinin' the car."

June remained in the car. The field was calm and cool now, but the nightmare had been so real.

"You comin'?" Peggy Sue asked. "I leave you in this car, ain't a cop in the world won't pull you out and 'rest you for stealin' a white girl's Buick."

"Ain't no cops 'round here."

Peggy Sue rolled her eyes. "With a wrecked warplane? I bet any number-a cops been called out to stop people like us from sneakin' in."

June grumbled, upset Peggy Sue was right. She opened the door and stepped out.

Her foot landed on ashy, dry ground. The cotton skeletons were all gone, the tobacco fields flattened. The Buick and trees were gone, and only a crater marred the alien surface. She pinched herself—was she mad, or was she asleep?

Was this reality, the world with Peggy Sue fake?

Her lips felt dry, her skin itched.

A familiar voice called from about a hundred feet away. "June?" The woman who'd called rode a rusted old bicycle. Burns matching the floral pattern on the woman's night dress encrusted her arm. Her face was burned, and some of her hair had fallen out. She dropped the bicycle to the wayside. "June! Baby girl, what you doin'?"

June's arms started to feel inflamed, her bones aching. She shook her head and backed away. "Auntie Delia?"

Her aunt ran forward. "Dear, sweet Jesus! We thought you were dead!" When she got close enough, she reached out and grabbed June, pulling her tight into a hug. "Where were you? We went to your house, and it and all the ol' shacks was just gone. The bodies of all the chilluns and your mama an' daddy were fried, everything was gone!"

"This isn't real," June said, shaking her head. "It's not real—I don't belong here—"

Auntie Delia let June go. "Sweetie, just come home with me. We'll get you some food in your stomach, assumin' you can keep it down. Some of us cain't, but most of those folks, well..." She swallowed. "They's with Jesus now."

"No, stop," June said, waving Auntie from coming closer. Her fingers pained her when she backed away. Then skin on her arms blackened and slid off.

Auntie tried to grab June and stop her from falling, but June's cooked arm snapped at the elbow. Auntie screamed as June fell.

Fell onto brown grass in a wet ditch, facing the angry, rusted grill of the Buick.

Peggy Sue rushed over to where June lay in the ditch screaming. "June!" she shouted. She reached out with her left hand, the shriveled right still twisted. "Where'd you go? You just disappeared."

June calmed, her hands back to normal despite her skin still tingling. "I don't know," she said. "A horrible place."

Peggy Sue crossed her arms. "I saw it. You just vanished—poof!"

June wrapped her arms around herself. "I feel like Schrödinger's cat," she said. "Like I'm sitting in a box, waiting for someone to lift the lid and see if I'm alive or dead."

Peggy Sue lifted a brow. "The hell you talkin' 'bout?"

June got herself up from the cold water in the ditch. The passenger door on the car was still opened, so she easily reached in, untied the twine around her books, and drew out her physics text. She showed a yellowed page to Peggy Sue. "This Schrödinger has a theory that everything, from every decision to every freak accident, has an alternative.

That alternative exists, however unlikely, in another universe." She closed the book. "The bomb going off is an alternative to our world."

Peggy read over the words. "This is un-Christian nonsense."

"I've seen it, though!" June argued. "I saw the bomb go off, felt my skin crumble to dust, listened to my auntie cry thinkin' I was dead. You think I'm just another stupid colored girl, but the theory's right here in the textbook. Who knows what kind of holes a nuke can blow between universes?"

Peggy Sue closed the book and handed it back to June. "You're the one takin' the nerd classes. Maybe you know somethin' I don't, and I sure 'nuff did see you vanish into thin air." She swallowed before starting her way around to the driver's side of the car. "You go be Schrödinger's ghost or somethin' back home. I gotta get to my house 'fore Mama finishes dinner."

June nodded. "I'll see you at school."

The car door squealed with a need for grease on its hinges as Peggy Sue entered the Special. She reached her left hand across the wheel, stuck the keys in the steering column, and departed without response.

❄

January 29th, 1961

JUNE SCRATCHED at the crinoline beneath her skirt. Mama shot her a look that said, "Ladies don't lift their skirts at church, not even in the parking lot." She stopped going after the itch and hopped off the back of the mule cart with her younger sisters and brothers. The air was laced with the cloacal stench of blacksnakes and mold, the combination just vivid enough to hide the scent of mice that attracted the snakes into the little church's basement.

Mama opened the door, and the younger children filed in after her. June, at the back, crossed the threshold last.

The line of siblings vanished. The smell of blacksnakes grew stronger, melded with dead flesh and ever-present mold invading the wood. Light streamed in through the broken roof, and churchgoers lamented with a charismatic prayer of torment. The boards beneath her feet were weaker than normal. She feared falling into a pit of dead snakes and rodents if the structure failed.

June sat down at her normal spot in the pews. Spaces normally taken by people at the Bixby or Williams plantations remained empty.

A burned, scarred man poked June. "Hey," he said, "That was June Bixby's spot—you get out of that, you ungrateful—" He trembled when she turned to look at him. "June?"

June gulped. The cold chill of death accompanied a tingle of radiation burns, like sun so hot and blinding that she'd keel over at any moment. Her throat seized like on that night she watched herself crumble. "I don't belong here," she croaked, reaching to her throat as she choked on flaking tongue.

The man's eyes widened, his whites in brilliant contrast with his field-hand skin. "Ghost!" he cried.

Everyone turned to see what he waggled his finger at. June glanced at the faces of those in the church, from Auntie Delia to the preacher to uncles and in-laws from the Lawrence plantation.

Auntie stood. "I tole y'all!" she said. "I tole y'all I seen her spirit!" She ran up the center aisle to the preacher.

He shook his head, still shocked, and clutched his Bible to his chest.

June stood from the pew. She tripped, at first not realizing over what, then looked back to see a charred foot—her foot—had caused her to fall. Her arms blackened, her hair caught fire, and she fell to the floor. She screamed, but nothing came out—

Mama pulled her up from the floor with a smack. "What devil's gotten into you?"

June shivered and vomited. The liquid from her stomach dripped between the wooden floorboards, and snakes hissed when the acid touched them.

Her Mama pulled her up. "You get back home—you's sick! Cain't worship Jesus when you throwin' up." She popped June on the rear, then drew out a torn handkerchief from somewhere deep in her bosom.

June left, watching her arms and hands to make sure the sloughing skin and curled fingers didn't return.

❄

January 31ˢᵗ, 1961

A STEEL TRAY clacked upon the yellow Formica. The single bulb above the table flickered. June sat at the table under the light and plopped her physics textbook down.

Peggy Sue looked up from her canned apples and beef roast. "Whites only at this table."

"You sat at a Black table last week. I'm returnin' the favor." She opened the book a few pages beyond what she'd shown Peggy Sue before, then pointed to a line. "I need your help."

Peggy Sue read what June indicated. "I don't understand this gobbledygook."

"Think of it this way: I'm trapped in two worlds, one where the nuke went off, the other where the safeties worked and no one noticed it dropped. If I'm a ghost in one world and alive in another, then the lid of Schrödinger's box hasn't been lifted. This universe hasn't decided if the cat is dead—hasn't decided if the bomb went off. This timeline is metastable, and metastable always wants to become stable." June closed the book. "The bomb could still have gone off last Monday night."

Peggy lifted a brow. "Retroactively?"

"More or less."

"How we goin' to fix something we cain't even understand?"

June leaned forward and whispered, "We've got to make sure no one checks the safeties. They can't know if the bomb should have gone off."

"Why?" Peggy asked. "How's them not checkin' the bomb right gonna change anything?"

"It's like Schrödinger's cat," June said. "Once you open the box, you know if the cat is alive or dead. It's only by lookin' at the results that we can decide what happened in the past. You and me don't know how to read the switches on the bomb, so even if we look at them, we can't figure out if the bomb exploded or not—only those men can. The lid of Schrödinger's box, in our case, is the order of the switches."

Peggy Sue bit her lip, then leaned in to say just above a whisper, "Won't you be half a ghost forever if we do that?"

June mumbled, then answered more clearly, "Well, I could be a ghost full time if the soldiers find the bad answer." She took her book and her tray, leaving the white table before someone got angry. "This afternoon. Your car."

❄

PEGGY SUE STEADIED the wheel with her shriveled hand so she could reach around with her left and put the car into park. "This is stupid. Comin' all the way out here with a colored nerd."

"Shut up," June said. "We gotta stop them from checking the bomb's safeties, but we don't know how far along they are. We gotta get to the bomb first." June opened the car door when Peggy pulled the keys from the ignition. She nudged a featherless chicken out of her way with her foot, feeling sorry for the poor, friendless thing.

Once Peggy Sue exited the car and accepted she'd dirty her pumps, June led her to an old barn the Bixbys owned. The barn's red paint had been blown and peeled through hurricanes, and the boards were ridden with termites to the point where the structure leaned to one side. June went in and held her breath to avoid inhaling mold spores on the hay. A rat squeaked as it ran from the open light, and June squealed as she remembered the snakes underneath the church.

She found a large roll of baling twine and heaved it onto her shoulder. She might be a 'nerd,' but no amount of book smarts could keep a member of her family from the tobacco field at harvest. The twine wasn't heavy for her. She exited the barn and nodded her head toward the tobacco field on Big Daddy's Road. "Come on."

They walked several miles through the fields and toward the wreckage. When they could see the broken top of a tree where a bomb had already been collected, they stopped.

June handed one end of the moldy twine to Peggy and tied the other around her own waist. "Don't let go, no matter what happens," she told Peggy. "Pull on the string every few minutes."

"What's that supposed to do?"

"The string's an anchor," June said. "I'm gonna sneak in as a ghost in the other world. My clothes went with me before, so a rope around my waist should too. You *can't* travel because you live outside the kill zone. If I can make it into the other world, I'm hoping you'll anchor me back here and help me come back."

Peggy rolled her eyes. "How you gonna control gettin' to the other world?"

"By dreading it," June answered.

As her words darkened her thoughts, the sky dimmed with wintry clouds. June looked to her hands, unburned, then tugged on the rope. It stayed taut as if hooked to something unseen. She checked her hands again, finding them soft and straight. She followed a dry path toward the crater's center.

After a hundred yards, her hands hurt. June held tight to the twine and kept walking. She slowed as her skin blackened, as her limbs brittled. She pulled through the pain, held onto the twine as best she could with the hopes Peggy could give her any ounce of strength. Thirty feet, twenty feet, ten. She lunged forward.

June fell into a deep hole, landing in swampy muck. Men above her tried to get at a chunk of metal with their shovels. She looked down the length of the twisted, broken metal, noticing a boxy tail that had been warped. Sickly yellow paint showed through the mud.

"The core's here," a man shouted. He tapped on the metal. June and Peggy were cutting things close.

A man with Yankee voice shouted back down the shaft, "Arm-safe box down there?"

"Think so. I see a lil' box right there." He pointed, a shadow in the halogen light guiding June's eyes to the hunk of twisted metal.

June put her hand to the bomb and crawled through the muck

beneath hoping to reach the box first. The twine around her waist held her back as it was buried in the ground on the safe side of reality. Her fingers curled around the edge of the blackened metal and scraped out bits of mud.

A cable fell near June's head, so she ducked to hide while the men wrapped it around the tail. "Haul 'er up!" Another man reached down and pulled the first up, and they crawled out of the deep hole before a crane pulled against the bomb.

The tail snapped off, and the cable bounced up. The men around the edges scurried away while others laughed.

June got purchase on the box and pulled it close so she could see. She put her nails and fingers beneath the door and pried it open. Four switches on electrical cables sat inside, all pointed the same direction.

Was this the box they were looking for? Was this the box of arm-safe switches? She couldn't tell. The men digging up the bomb could tell, and they'd be able to see if the bomb had gone off. It was Schrödinger's box, and these switches were the cat. Which was right? What combination would save her?

She flipped one.

And the crater returned.

"No!" she shouted. She stood from the center of the blackened crater. She ran, seeking signs of life or a way out. The climb out of the pit was steep, even harder for a melting, burning girl to get out. "I don't want to die," she pleaded to God. "I was trying to save us. Don't make me be a ghost!"

She fell to the dusty ground, unable to go further. Her throat burned as she breathed, her stomach rumbled, and her vision darkened.

Something pulled around her waist.

That something kept pulling. The knot in the twine was tight, and the string dug into June's frying skin, but June felt joy inside despite the pain. She cheered Peggy for remaining faithful and real.

A few minutes later, a hand grasped June's shoulder. She opened her eyes, finding Peggy with the twine wrapped around her. Peggy's left hand was rope burned. June jumped up and hugged her.

"Did you get to the safety box?" Peggy asked.

June nodded, her skin still tingling. "I did some stuff. They can't see how it was set before I got to it."

"Then we kept the lid shut, and we're going to be okay!" Peggy hugged June back.

June sighed and secretly wished she could know what the bomb's switches had said.

About the Author

H.R.R. Gorman likes to stay up at night reading and writing dark fiction. By day, H.R.R. Gorman makes drugs. Don't worry—it's something chemical engineers are legally allowed to do as long as it's for the Dark Lord of Big Pharma. He lives in North Carolina with his nuclear engineer spouse and vicious attack Pomeranian.

TOPSIDE

GUSTAVO BONDONI

THE DRIVER *of the cement truck just laughed. A peasant who didn't know anything except that the system would keep him fed despite the fact that he was an illiterate piece of shit. He was little better than the animals his ancestors had sodomized, and yet he would live. One of life's little ironies.*

That same man was laughing at him, laughing at one of the men who had designed the system.

An outrage.

But then, when you had had an "accident," and were tied like a hog on the floor, there was little you could do to avenge yourself on the man with the cement truck.

Concrete began to fall, landing on his legs first. The man had probably been instructed to make it slow, and he wouldn't have the imagination to disobey his orders.

❄

THIS IS *what it's all about,* Elena thought as she watched the traffic flow beneath her. Even though the building was only eighteen floors high, the cars looked like ants after someone kicked a hill. And the sound dissipated, turning into a whisper. Moscow looked like a toy city, its people invisible unless she wore her glasses, its problems far beneath her. Life simply didn't get any better than this.

"Look out Elena," Vitaly cautioned. "Don't get too close to the edge. Those communist architects weren't too fussy about workers' lives, so these roofs haven't been designed for safety."

She turned, gave the stupid boy a withering look, wondering why she'd told him about this place. It was her special place.

"I've been here before," she said.

"Are you always this drunk?"

"Sometimes. Other times I'm on ecstasy. Sometimes I just leave all my clothes on the roof and walk around naked, letting the wind get into every crack." She said that just to get him excited. She wasn't going to do much more than talk with this imbecile. "And the lights that fly around the roof are incredible. You should see them when you're stoned."

"I've seen plenty of things when I'm stoned."

She didn't believe him. This little prick hadn't popped a pill in his life. He was too scared to even get close to the edge. What was the fun in that? You couldn't see anything from back there. "I think you're just chicken. You thought I would let you fuck me up here, didn't you? You just don't get it. I thought you were a roofer, but you're just an asshole."

"I'm a roofer," he replied.

"Roofers get it," Elena said.

"I get it. Look." He walked to the edge, moving quickly, making a point, and looked down at the cars. She stepped away from him, afraid that if he got belligerent, she wouldn't be able to defend herself, prick or not.

He turned with a triumphant expression, his back to the drop. "See? I can take it. The fact that I don't go all lyrical when I talk about one of the ugliest cities on the planet doesn't make you any better than I am, *bitch*." He didn't look nearly as drunk—or as friendly—as he had just half an hour before. The expression on his face could only be described as ugly.

A ball of white light swooped from the sky—she didn't see where it originated—and hit Vitaly in the chest. It did no damage whatsoever, but it pushed him back one step.

It was enough; his arms pin-wheeled and he went over, screaming like a girl as he fell.

It took Elena and her lawyers almost a year to convince the authorities that it had been an accident. The fact that Elena never believed it for a second only made it harder.

※

She'd been a filmmaker until the day they told her that a true communist could change roles, and then she'd been made a lowly construction worker. And now she was going to die. The fall from atop the construction site would turn her to jelly.

But as she fell, she remembered the wood that had splintered on the platform. Balsa wood. Paper. A sham floor, painted to look like the real thing. Despite her own experience with special effects, she hadn't even hesitated to step on it.

In a world where true believers were no longer respected, impact would be a welcome thing.

※

"Have I told you the story about this place?" Mikhail asked. He felt the warmth of the vodka coursing through him, warm in his temples, warm in his belly, but it wasn't the only warmth he felt on that cold night. The simple fact that Aliette had managed to make it had him feeling manic —even though he really hadn't drunk that much.

Aliette was nearly impossible to corner. She always had something interesting to do, somewhere interesting to be. An expats' dinner at the Hard Rock Café over on Arbat street—smart people in smart dress in a smart part of town. Junior clerks named Mikhail need not apply.

And yet she never really made him feel too bad about the fact that he was a local whose only trip outside the motherland had been one short stay at a resort in Odessa for his end-of-high-school trip. But that was just the Ukraine, it didn't really count, did it? He was thankful that she chose to tell him of the voyages to exotic places she'd made while working with the UN, places like Mali and Singapore and Cleveland. Just dots on a map to him, but she made them come alive. He was amazed that she'd been to so many places. She was only twenty-eight.

"No, you haven't. But I'm sure that it's another story of horror and someone dying, right? You Russians sure like to hear about people dying, don't you? Let me guess: the KGB used to hold clandestine interrogations on this roof." Her words were reproving, but her smile seemed teasing, her eyes bright and alive.

"No, the story is not that old. But I suppose you aren't interested in yet another Russian drama."

Now she held his gaze. He would have wanted to look into those dark brown eyes forever, but he forced himself to look away. Looking at her chest wasn't much better—even under the layers of clothing needed to be on the roof, he could see the attributes that his friends had labeled "super bonus."

He shook his head. It was impossible to look at her without being drawn in. From the waves of curly black hair all the way down to her legs, there was nothing a man could find fault with.

"You won't tell me? Then I'll have to get someone else to do it!" She stamped a foot in mock fury and looked around for candidates. None seemed to satisfy her, and she sighed. "Can't I convince you to spill it? What do I have to do?" She pouted.

And suddenly Mikhail was on dangerous ground. Had this been a Russian girl of his own social circle, he wouldn't have hesitated to make an obscenely graphic suggestion—and she would have hit him and walked away, or she would have laughed and ended up giving him a wall job in some secluded corner of the roof. A sixth sense told him that if he tried that here, he would be squandering the tiny opening she was actually giving him. He smiled. "Let me get you another drink and I'll think about it," he replied.

Her smile said *bingo*, and he stopped feeling like a wuss. "Caipiroshka," she said without hesitation. He wondered whether she did it on purpose, whether she knew that those little green lemons cost him a fortune. Fortunately, vodka was something he had plenty of.

He walked towards the table where the drinks and associated paraphernalia were arrayed. Gerry was mixing himself one of his awful concoctions consisting of, as far as one could tell, a little bit of everything with alcohol in it. "Good roof," he said.

Mikhail smiled. "Thanks. Took me a while to find it, though. Went through half the city."

It was a good roof. A damned good roof. The building was a mid-Soviet-era apartment complex: grey, concrete, and without a single curved line. Hundreds of families lived in identical shoeboxes below, and thousands of cars rumbled along Leningradsky Prospekt, towards the city center or towards the airport. What the building lacked in aesthetic appeal, however, it more than made up for in height. The structures around it were six and seven stories shorter, and the view, especially towards downtown, was magnificent.

"Pity about the people, though. Too many for them to be real roofers."

Real roofers. It was always the same thing. No one really knew where the roofer movement had sprouted—suddenly, young hipsters around Moscow were leaving the stress of the bustling city behind and gazing over it from the tops of its buildings—but everyone seemed to believe that only people who felt it the way they did could possibly be real roofers. The joke said that if you get two roofers together, both of them are imposters. "Well, as long as they don't ruin it for the rest of us," Mikhail replied. He walked back to where Aliette was waiting.

"Well, have you decided to come clean? Mmm, this is a good drink."

"I mixed it myself," he replied. "All right, I'll tell you. And I won't even have to swear you to secrecy—everyone else already knows the story."

"I was right, wasn't I? It's a story of drama and death."

"Of course. This is Russia! Are there any other stories worth telling?" He laughed. "Anyhow, it was right on this very roof, in early spring of this year. A girl came up with this guy."

"What were they up here for?" Typically loaded question—or at least that was what most Russians would have felt was typical for a French girl.

"Probably not what you're imagining. They probably just wanted to roof a bit."

She seemed to get the reference, despite the fact that she certainly wasn't a roofer, the only guest up here that he'd invited despite being certain she didn't fit in. "And what happened? Rape? Murder? Unidentified body parts dropping over Moscow from a high vantage point?"

"Well, the official story seems to be that there was an accident and he fell off. The trial is still ongoing."

She laughed. "Of course, no one believes that, do they? Over here, when people die in their sleep at the age of a hundred and forty-seven, someone goes on trial for murder. So, did she kill him?"

"Well, the prosecution certainly seems to feel that it might have happened that way."

"And why? Were they lovers? Part of an illicit ménage à trois?"

"No. They were just regular people. Roofers—or at least she was. As far as anyone could tell, she'd only just met him that night. This was their special spot before I discovered it."

"So she just pushed him over the edge because she thought it was a good idea?" She pondered this for a bit. "That really isn't much of a story."

"That's the whole point. It doesn't really make any sense. But there are other stories about the same episode. Stories that are a bit darker."

"Ah, were they having sex and she blindfolded him and led him over the edge?"

"No. The stories say that there are ghosts on this roof."

She laughed. "Ghosts? Even Russians don't believe in ghosts."

"The ghosts of the men who died putting up this building. Political prisoners. Supporters of Stalin's regime, but who were ousted when he died. Men who survived the war. Hard men. Harder women."

"If they were so hard, how come they died just doing construction work? It sounds like a silly little story to me."

How to explain to this girl the things every Russian knew? That the great projects were designed for high worker attrition. Safety regulations were lax, harnesses often suspiciously worn when they were supposed to be brand new. Daily accidents meant that, by the time a structure was complete, the undesirables among the workers had, strangely, all died out. But foreigners, with their strange tendency to let their enemies survive to drive a dagger into their backs at some later date, never understood these necessities.

"It was not a safe time to be an enemy of the state. Hundreds of workers were killed. They say their bones can still be found in the concrete of the basement."

"And their ghosts haunt the roof," she said. She laughed, but there was a nervous tremor in it; maybe it was the cold. "Don't they get tired walking up the stairs?"

Mikhail hesitated. "I've seen them," he said.

Something in his face must have told her that he was serious because she bit off her next comment before it got out. "What do they look like?" Her tone seemed half mocking, half serious.

"White balls of light. They float around the roof sometimes. I'm up here pretty often, but I've only seen them a couple of times."

"You probably saw ball lightning."

He looked her in the eye. "What I saw was not ball lightning."

She seemed to shrink down into herself, eyes darting around the roof as if, suddenly, the terrace, complete with its young, hip crowd, many of whom she already knew, was a place of menace and foreboding. He was sorry, and he held out his hand. She took it and pulled him into a hug, and he could feel her thin body—thin enough that Russians just a few years older than Mikhail would have dismissed her as ugly—shivering under her coat.

Suddenly, the woman of the world, the pillar that made him feel completely inadequate in her presence, became just another girl, a real human being with fears and feelings and insecurities. He took her chin in his right hand, gently turned her face towards him and gave her a kiss. At that moment, he had no doubts that she would kiss him back, and she didn't disappoint.

She tasted like vodka and little green lemons.

❄

He thought he could see scratch marks clawed into the wall, but it was probably just his imagination. That was a concrete wall. They were inside a concrete well—actually, this well had a roof, so it probably counted as a concrete box. He wondered what purpose the architects had designed this space for. Was it there to give structural rigidity to a group of columns? Was it a storage area that had been closed off at the last minute?

All he knew was that it probably hadn't been designed to hold ten people, especially ten people who'd been drugged and left there, packed like sardines but alive as the air slowly turned stale. He felt sleepy, probably from the lack of oxygen in his lungs. No one else moved.

He was no longer raging, no longer mourning the dream they'd lost, or the privileges that he'd enjoyed. There was no air for any of that.

He tried to scratch at the wall, but his fingernails were long gone.

❄

Aliette wasn't sure what she was doing. Maybe it was the Caipiroshkas, maybe it was the Russian autumn cold, but suddenly, she needed a warm human body to hold, something solid, something to drive the chill that had settled on her back out of her body.

She knew she was being silly, knew that the guy's ghost stories were meant to have exactly this effect, but there was nothing to be done—she felt the way she felt. She hated herself for giving in so easily, and hated herself even more for feeling grateful to him for kissing her.

Mikhail put his arms around her, led her through the crowd; there were plenty of people on the roof, but the space was big enough to make them seem like islands that loomed in the darkness. "Let's find somewhere you can sit," he said. She let herself be led. There was nothing else she could do right then.

They found a low wall, far from the limited hubbub near the sound system. *And how could you possibly fall for his ghost story with the boom, boom, boom of "Groove Armada" blaring out at you like that?* she asked herself. No answers were forthcoming.

"Are you feeling better?"

She wasn't really in the mood to talk. She would break down if he insisted, and there was no way she was going to allow that to happen. Instead, she kissed him. She kissed him hard, hard enough that he could read the promise of things to come in that kiss, but also hard enough that the rush of being kissed back just as hard buried any cold fears she might have been feeling. He ran a tentative hand along her back, trying to see what she would do, and she felt her body responding.

Good, she thought. *I hope he has the guts to move quickly. And if he doesn't, I'll help him along.* She wasn't sure how much she would allow, but being on a roof surrounded by people made it unlikely that he would overdo it. But she did want to feel that he was taking it seriously, wanted her body and the alcohol to get her mind out of the loop. Wanted to forget about buried bodies and communist ghosts and enjoy her night. And besides, Mikhail was a good-looking guy. Probably not the brightest bulb on the tree, but that was irrelevant tonight.

He pressed his body into hers, hands looking for the bottom of her shirt, sliding up her stomach and under her bra. She moaned, encouraging him.

But he paused and pulled away. His face was flushed with excitement, but suddenly alert, an incongruous combination. "Do you hear that?" he said.

"What?" She was confused, resentful. Just when it was beginning to work, he came out with this.

"The humming. That means that the ghosts are coming. Look, there's one of them!"

She knew it had to be a joke, or some kind of special effects trick played by one of this asshole's friends just to impress her. But as soon as she saw the pure-white ball of light floating a few meters in front of her, Aliette lost it. All she wanted was to get out of there, to get away from this dark terrace and these strange roofers and the ghosts of party members past. She tore herself away from Mikhail's half-hearted grip and ran towards the door.

About halfway there, she broke down, feeling the tears streaming down her cheeks as she went. She'd always thought that she could survive in any city but, as soon as she left the safety of the expats, of that clique that didn't care whether you were from Nairobi or New York, she fell apart. Even a tribe as adolescent, as needful of attention, as *pathetic* as the roofers had undone her in less than two hours.

Her fright, that stupid gut reaction, had coalesced into fury by the time she reached the door that led to the stairs. She wondered fleetingly whether anyone would let her out at the ground floor, but decided to worry about that when she got there. She wasn't going to spend another second with these losers—and she certainly wasn't going to let them see her cry. They'd never understand the real reason for it, anyway.

Her fury, however, was short-lived. It turned into a solid ball of raving, nearly lunatic panic when she realized that the ice-cold knob wouldn't budge, and that she was trapped up on the roof. She turned back.

The white balls were mingling with the crowd. And Mikhail was right: they didn't look anything at all like ball lightning.

❄

SHE COULD FEEL *the snow beneath her. That was a good sign. It meant that her nerves hadn't yet gone completely dead, that she still had sensation in her ass, at least. Her fingers and her toes had long since gone numb.*

It wouldn't snow that night, at least. It was much too cold for snow.

She wondered whether anyone would stumble upon her before she froze, some kind soul brave enough to commiserate, and competent enough to have some idea as to what could be done about the chain holding her in place.

Of course, it was unlikely that anyone would be up here. Even the night watchman would know that this area was off-limits. Maybe they might have told him that an enemy of the state who'd disguised herself—ha! As if she'd had a choice—as one of the workers was going to have an accident.

Tomorrow, her body would be discovered. It might be found by some poor worker innocently coming up to work on his little bit of building, or it might be found by someone who understood what it meant, someone who, like her, had lost everything that had made their life better than that of their neighbors when the government changed. That person would know that, sooner or later —probably sooner—this fate awaited him or her as well.

One thing was certain. Her body would not be found by a supervisor. It would not be found by any of the coworkers who'd stripped her to her undergarments and chained her to the roof of a half-built apartment complex in the middle of the Russian winter. No, they would be somewhere else, they would pretend to act surprised, horrified. And then they would report it as yet another regrettable accident.

❄

MIKHAIL WATCHED Aliette walk towards the door, but he soon forgot her. He'd never seen this many of the white lights on the roof at the same time. He'd never seen them get that close to people before. He was fascinated.

I wonder if they really are the ghosts of political prisoners? he thought, but in the next moment, all thoughts were wiped out of his head at the sheer beauty of the lights. They coursed through the crowd like tame lightning, moving in and out between the people, sometimes brushing one or another.

He watched as one of them actually went through a woman's body, watched as she laughed at it, not hurt in the least.

Soon, they were coursing through everyone, sometimes staying a few seconds, others barely clipping an arm or a leg. The guests began to reach out for them, laughing, pointing, playing tag.

But, off to one side, Mikhail saw a girl—someone's girlfriend, not one of the guests he'd invited directly—completely apart from the proceedings. She was walking with purpose, her blond hair bouncing with each step.

She was walking straight towards the edge of the roof.

He opened his mouth to shout, but something stopped him. Perhaps the calm way she was walking made him think that he would make a fool of himself if he yelled a warning, perhaps it was something else. Either way, he watched as the girl, unruffled, eyes open, and completely without fuss, walked over the ledge that led to an eighteen-story fall.

Her dimly-heard screams didn't reach him until several seconds had passed, and they cut off abruptly. She must have started screaming very close to the ground.

Off to the right another person did exactly the same thing.

And then...

Oh, my God, that was Gerry!

Mikhail stood. He had to stop them. What was happening? Had they tripped on a bad batch of pills? How could three—no, four now—people walk calmly off the edge of a skyscraper? He had to see what was going on.

He only managed a single step. Floating in front of him was one of the globes of light. It stood perfectly still, but somehow Mikhail knew that if he moved, so would the globe, following his every motion.

He wanted to turn and run. He was *going* to turn and run, but he never had a chance. After that slight hesitation, the globe went straight between his eyes.

There was no pain, there was no disorientation, but suddenly he was somewhere else. It was dark, and warm, and he couldn't move. He tried to open his eyes, but his body wasn't responding to his commands.

I have chosen to sit in judgment of your crimes. You have betrayed the revolution and all we fought for. And you have betrayed our memory—despite the fact that we devoted our lives, hard lives, to the cause. Our deaths were predictable—it is not expedient to allow the former regime to survive—but it is only because of you, and your new generation that our lives were in vain.

The voice seemed to come from far away, but at the same time it was right inside Mikhail's head. He tried to answer, tried to ask what his crimes had been, but his mouth wasn't responding. And it also seemed that there was some kind of hollow tube pushed almost to his throat. What was going on?

Ah, but perhaps you don't understand, the voice continued, ignoring Mikhail's attempts to communicate. It sounded like it would have ignored a nuclear bomb going off beside it—it was the kind of voice that clearly would not allow itself to be distracted until it had said its piece. Suddenly, images flooded his sight. A nighttime riot, looters breaking windows—and he was one of them. A factory, with starving workers sitting outside, placards ignored at their feet. A tank, burning, smoking, and a single man emerging in what looked like a German uniform from World War II, to fall on the ground at his feet, burns covering most of his left arm and marking his face. A series of snap-shots of the German being stripped, castrated with a rusty razor, and forced to swallow his genitalia, before being left for dead as the valu-able tank was investigated. A nighttime raid, secret police taking him firmly but quietly off to his waiting fate. And the sense of not knowing what that fate would be weighing on every step.

Yes, any one of us would have been worthy to judge you, but fate gave you to me. Have you anything to say for yourself?

"I..." he began, but his mouth refused to move, the cold steel of the strange tube seeming to mock him, a feeling echoed by the strange laughter that filled his mind. He thought his next words, unwilling to brave the cold steel. *Can you hear me?*

Yes. But that will not save you.

I haven't done anything wrong.

You betray the men and women who fought for your freedom every day. Do you deny this?

I am free. Why would you claim otherwise?

You are a slave, and you've been so badly enslaved that you can't even see what you are. A blind slave—despite the fact that you have a superficial freedom that would allow you to fight the greater injustice.

Mikhail tried to talk, tried to explain how he was working his way up, how he would soon be free of the need to work for the company, and could begin to work for himself. But his body wasn't responding.

So, you wish to have access to this mouth? It isn't yours, but it was mine. I grant you power over it.

And suddenly there was pain. The steel tube that had been a pres-ence, barely felt, was jammed into the roof of his mouth, and his entire body—his but subtly not his—felt as if it was being crushed by a giant hand. He opened his eyes, and they obeyed this time, but were instantly filled with an unknown liquid that stung them. He tried to close them again, but some kind of sandy residue got between his eyes and his lids. It felt someone was rubbing his eyes with sandpaper. He screamed—he tried to scream, but only managed to wedge the tube more firmly in his throat. His hands were trapped—tied with wire, he knew without knowing how he knew—behind his back. His legs barely twitched when he tried to kick.

A tiny flow of air through the tube was all that kept him from suffocating.

The voice in his head returned. *I misjudged the man, when he started pouring the concrete. I thought he had no imagination, but I was very wrong about him. He might have been a sheep-fucking peasant, but he had potential. He saw the post, and it was the work of an instant to put it in my mouth. He broke half of my teeth, but there is no doubt that he managed to keep me alive for nearly a day and a half as the concrete hardened.*

Here, I'll let you experience what it felt like to die for my beliefs.

The disembodied voice was as good as its word. Mikhail felt the cement harden, felt himself always on the verge of suffocation. Tried to scream for help through the tube, but only lodged it in further still. Felt his bladder let go and wet his pants, and the piss pool, having nowhere to go in the concrete. Felt the first pangs of the thirst that would kill him if the hardening, expanding concrete didn't crush him first. And then passed out. It seemed like seconds, but it also seemed like more than a day.

Anyhow, you have not convinced me. I find you guilty of treason.

Mikhail felt the rushing wind, opened his eyes and saw stories flashing by, people inside oblivious to the falling bodies. He started to scream, but the sound never reached his lips. The ground got to him first.

❋

ANIA HADN'T BEEN HAVING a good time. The old joke said that half the girls in Poland were named Ania, and so were the rest, and that seemed to be holding true: there was another Polish girl in the crowd, and she was also named Anna—Ania to her friends.

Both of them were being patronized by the Russians, who seemed to think that Poles were only useful to serve as a buffer between Germany and Russia—and in the case of the women, to be treated like trash.

It was so unfair. Poland was a much more modern, more civilized country than Russia. Its people were more sophisticated and happier. It was a better place to live—but it was small, and it was weak, and the Russians needed someone to feel superior to now that western Europe was becoming a serious world power again.

At least she'd managed to find some peace looking out over the city. You couldn't tell that the city was a mess from here; it all looked orderly, peaceful. A couple of quiet Russian boys spoke to her, asking her what she did for a living, telling her their equally boring life stories, eventually walking away. They were nice enough, and that was probably why they were on the fringes, just like her.

That was all she'd seen, just the typical party in Moscow, when the Russians suddenly all went mad at the same time and began jumping off the edge of the building. She screamed, and was engulfed by a light that she hadn't noticed.

Just like that, she was in a prison. It couldn't be anything else. There were bars on the doors, and the walls were made of rough-hewn stone. A semi-circular window, also crisscrossed with thick bars, let in the weak winter light. She could feel the cold rock of the floor underneath her, and her body was bruised and battered.

Keys jangled in the door, and she stirred. She would demand an explanation, ask why she was being held. She tried to move, but the aches made her sluggish. Three guards walked towards her as she struggled. Ania realized that there was something wrong with her body: she seemed to weigh much more than normal, the hair was too long and her hands...well, they weren't her hands.

The guards, though, gave her no time to puzzle this out. The nearest grabbed her roughly by the hair as the other two tore her clothes off before she really had a chance to understand what was happening. They swore at her in Russian as they did, calling her a traitor, and the minister's whore. They told her that her husband was, at that very moment, keeping an appointment with the firing squad, but that they had granted his last request—she wouldn't be killed, she would simply be put to work, building the new face of the modern Soviet Union.

Ania wasn't married.

The guards didn't really seem to hear her protestations. The one holding her hair pushed her into the ground, face first, dragging her along the floor until her body was completely stretched out behind. The second man lay on top of her, fumbling with his pants with one hand, spearing her vagina with a couple of fingers of the other. And then she felt his cock and tried to turn her mind off.

But that was impossible. It was as if some malignant force made her stay perfectly awake and aware for each and every second of the horror. For every searing thrust, stretching—and bleeding—of sensitive tissue between her legs. Kept her awake for the oil they poured into her asshole before the second man tortured her. This one wasn't content simply to rape her ass like an animal; he also pummeled her, and pinched her breasts until she screamed, hurting her much more than the mere tearing of flesh in her butt.

The man who had her hair went last. He was almost gentle by comparison, but he stopped before finishing, asked the others to hold her and released into her eyes.

A couple of final kicks later, and they were gone, laughing.

Kind of like what Germany did to Poland, isn't it? A voice in her head brought Ania out of the safe place she was trying, unsuccessfully, to create. *Something we saved you from, something we liberated you from. And how did you thank us? By being the very first to throw our love back in our faces.*

What you just felt was my compensation for wanting a world of equality. There was much worse to come, but that was the day that I discovered what it was like to be at the mercy of forces far greater than myself. Those guards were of no consequence, and neither were the dozens who came later. Most of them were probably killed in purges months later. I don't care. I don't blame them. I would have done the same to any counterrevolutionary in my time—and I'm certain that my husband ordered a few sessions like that one.

But at least it was being done for the people. What the Poles did forty years later, they did for the capitalists.

Die, you bitch.

Ania's eyes opened—she hadn't been aware of closing them—and the ledge, the very edge of the roof, was just slipping away.

Unlike Mikhail, Ania had a lot of time to scream as she fell.

❄

It's raining men! Halleluiah! Aliette thought to herself as she watched the guests disappear over the sides of the building. If the world was going to go mad, she would match it step for step. Unlike the rest, she had no questions, no confusion. The ghosts, spirits, wraiths, whatever lived inside those white balls, were killing people. That was why she'd felt the bitter cold in her stomach when Mikhail told her the story, that was why she'd nearly panicked. Somehow, she could feel the truth of his words.

She also felt resignation. There was nothing she could possibly do about it now. The spirits would do with her whatever they wanted. The door was locked with the supernatural cold, and the only other way down was quicker but less attractive.

She saw Mikhail go over, clutching at his throat, unaware that he'd walked past a line he couldn't walk back across. The worst part was that so many of them dropped without making a sound.

The light that cornered her looked just like the rest.

You are on trial for treason against our dream, Aliette heard.

It wasn't my people's dreams, she replied.

No, but it could have been. Your people betrayed it as well.

Judge me, then, not my people.

Aliette felt the pain of icy hands rummaging in her memory. She saw a flicker of her childhood in Lyon as vividly as if she were living it right at that moment, and then it disappeared, to be replaced by five seconds of sex in the back seat of Luc's battered Renault 5.

Some images, however, kept repeating themselves. She vividly saw herself lighting a wet rag, feeling the heat of the flame, and throwing the Molotov cocktail against the window of the bank office in Davos. She saw herself being clubbed, not brutally, but efficiently, by the Swiss police and deported back to France. She saw herself arguing against rampant capitalism in the university forum. She got to watch as she joined the UN committee for resources and attempted to ensure that the same amount of food went to the people of Mali as to the warlord's family.

The last image she saw was of a tent hospital in a refugee camp, as the doctor told her they'd extracted the bullet, and that her leg looked like it was healing cleanly.

Aliette opened her eyes. She hadn't realized they'd been closed.

The city of Moscow spread out before her; it was all she could see. The pink glow told her she was facing east, maybe half an hour before dawn. The music, unheeded, had stopped. She could feel the wind in her hair, and the solid feel of the roof beneath her feet. But if she'd taken one more step...

The voice in her head came back. *You may go.*

She didn't. She only went as far as the nearest chimney, a thin affair, probably an air vent for the sewage system. Aliette put her arms around it as hard as she could, anchored herself there and cried.

She was still there, and still crying, when the police came through the door. She thought she'd never seen policemen looking quite as green around the gills as these did. They were white as sheets, and one of them, as they led her down the stairs wrapped in a blanket, smelled of vomit. She imagined that the scene down below must not be a pretty sight.

But it would always pale beside her memories of what had happened eighteen floors above, and that was a memory she would have to bear alone.

About the Author

Gustavo Bondoni is a novelist and short story writer with over three hundred stories published in fifteen countries, in seven languages. He is a member of Codex and an Active Member of SFWA. His latest novel is a dark historic fantasy entitled *The Swords of Rasna* (2022). He has also published five science fiction novels, four monster books and a thriller entitled *Timeless*.

BY HER HAND, SHE DRAWS YOU DOWN

DOUGLAS SMITH

By her hand, she draws you down.
With her mouth, she breathes you in.
Hope and dreams and soul devoured.
Lost to you, what might have been.

BY HER HAND, *she draws you down...*

Joe swore when he saw Cath doing a kid. He had left her for just a minute, to get a beer from the booth on the pier before it closed for the night. Walking back now, he could see Cath on her stool, sketchpad on a knee, ocean breeze blowing her pale hair. A small girl sat on another stool facing her, a man and a woman, parents he guessed, beside the child.

Kid's not more than seven, he thought. *Cath promised me no kids. She promised.*

The sun was long set, and the air had turned cool, but people still filled the boardwalk. Joe wove through the crowd as fast as he could without attracting attention. Cath had set up farther from the beach tonight, at the bottom of a grassy slope that ran up to the highway where their old grey Ford waited.

"Last night tonight," Cath had said when they had parked the car earlier. "*It* wants to move on. I can feel the change."

Joe had swallowed and turned off the ignition. He was never comfortable talking about it. "Where's it headed?"

Cath had just shaken her head, grinning. "Dunno. That's part of the fun, isn't it? Not knowing where we're going next? That's fun, isn't it, Joe?"

Yeah, loads of fun, he thought now as he approached Cath and her customers. It *had* been fun once, when they'd met, before he learned what Cath did, what she had to do. When his love for her wasn't all mixed up with fear of what she would do to someone.

Or to him.

The child's parents looked up as Joe came to stand beside Cath. The father frowned. Joe smiled, trying to hide the dread digging like cold fingers into his gut. Turning his back to them, he bent to whisper in Cath's ear. That flowery scent she had switched to recently rose warm and sweet in his face. *Funeral parlors,* he thought. *She smells like a goddam funeral parlor.*

"Cath, she's just a kid," he rasped in her ear.

Cath shook her head. Her eyes flitted from the girl to her pad. "Bad night. I'm hungry," she muttered, ignoring Joe.

Joe looked at the drawing. It was good. But they were always good. Cath had real talent, more than Joe ever had. She would set up each night where people strolled, her sketches beside her like trophies from a hunt. People would stop to look, sometimes moving on, sometimes sitting for a portrait.

Eventually Joe and Cath would move on, too. When the town was empty, Cath said. When the thing inside her wanted to move on. They had spent this week at a little New England vacation spot. At least they were heading south lately. Summer was dying, and Joe longed to winter in the sun. Sleep for Joe was rare enough since he'd met Cath. Winters up north meant long nights in bars. Things closed in then, closed in around him. On those nights, he would lie awake in their motel bed, feeling Cath's eyes on him, feeling her hunger.

He looked at the sketch, at the child captured there, perfect except for the emptiness that spoke from the eyes, from any eyes that Cath drew. And the mouth.

Where the mouth should have been, empty paper gaped. Cath left the mouth until the end. The portraits always bothered Joe when they looked like that. To him, the pictures weren't waiting to be completed, waiting for a last piece to be added. To Joe, something vital had been ripped from what had once been whole, leaving behind a void that threatened to suck in the world around it. An empty thing but insatiable. Waiting to suck him in, too.

"Cath," he whispered. "You promised."

She ignored him again. Joe wrapped his fingers around the thin wrist of her hand that held the sketchpad. "You promised."

Cath snapped her head around to glare up at him. Joe caught his breath as anger met hunger in her grey eyes, becoming something alive, something that leapt for him.

The father cleared his throat, and the thing in Cath's eyes retreated. Cath turned to the parents. "Sorry, can't get her right. You can have this." Tearing the sketch from her pad, she shoved it at the mother. "We gotta go." Cath stood and folded her stool as the child ran to peek from behind the father's legs. Joe grabbed the other stool and the canvas bag that held Cath's supplies. He put an arm around Cath's waist, leading her away.

The father started to protest. "But you're almost done. You just need to draw in the mouth."

Cath stopped, and Joe swore. He just wanted to get her out of there. She walked back to the man who exchanged glances with his wife. Cath touched a finger to her lips. "Mouths are the hardest part. The most important part," she said. "Everyone—they say, 'the eyes are the windows of the soul.' They say, 'Oh, you got the eyes just right.' They don't know. They don't know it's the mouth you gotta get just right. That's what makes a picture come alive. Like it's gonna just start...breathing."

The father cleared his throat, but the mother tugged at his shirt. Joe grabbed Cath's arm and pulled her away. The man muttered something, but Joe didn't care.

He led Cath to a gravel path that switched back and forth up the steep hill to the highway above. Halfway up, an observation area looked down on the pier and the beach and the boardwalk. Cath twisted away from him there. A low stone wall ran around the area's edge, and two lampposts stood at either end. Putting her stool down under the nearest light, she began setting out her sketches against the wall.

Joe dropped the other stool and sat down. The fatigue that lived with him always now rose to engulf him. He felt dead inside, all used up, like the way Cath's pictures made him feel, waiting to be sucked into the void. "We had a deal," he said.

Cath sat, looking up and down the path. "I'm hungry."

"No kids, remember?" Joe said. "And nobody with a family depending on them." He tried to make his voice sound strong, but his hands were shaking.

She opened her pad. "Kind of cuts down the field, Joe."

"Use one of the sketches you've got put away."

Cath laughed. A bitter, empty sound. Joe imagined the mouths she drew making that kind of sound. Cath looked at him finally. "All gone. Used 'em all."

Joe felt the emptiness again, a void gaping below, drawing him down. He leaned forward, head between his hands, fingers pressing hard on his temples, trying to make his fear go away. "Jeez, Cath. All of them?" He searched her face for some hope.

Cath shrugged. "Girl's gotta eat." She stared past him, and he heard gravel crunching underfoot. Joe turned, his hand slipping by reflex to touch the switchblade inside his boot top.

A fat man in black pants, white shirt, and paisley tie loosened at the neck was struggling down the steep path from the highway, a beach chair in each arm. He walked over to the stone wall and put down the chairs to rest. Nodding at Joe and Cath, he glanced at her sketches. He began to turn away but then looked back. His eyes ran over the portraits lined against the low wall like prisoners before a firing squad. The man whistled.

Joe sighed, from regret and relief. Cath would eat tonight.

❄

WITH HER MOUTH, she breathes you in...

The man's name was Harry. He haggled with Cath over the price then he sat down, and Cath started sketching. Joe glanced at the two chairs that Harry had carried, but he couldn't see a wedding ring, so he kept silent.

Cath worked quickly, her hand slashing at the page, pausing only to switch the color of her pencil. When only the mouth remained unfinished, she put the pad down on her lap.

Harry looked down at the sketch. "There's no mouth."

"Mouths are special, Har," Cath said. She puckered at him, and Harry laughed, a nervous squeaky sound. Cath touched a finger of her drawing hand to Harry's lips. He gave that little laugh again but didn't pull away. Cath ran her fingertips slowly over his lips, tracing each curve and contour. Sitting on the stone wall, Joe thought of her fingers on his own skin at night in bed, tracing the lines of his body. Love and fear and lust—with Cath, they all mixed together, colors in a picture flowing into each other, until you couldn't separate one from another.

She lowered her hand to the paper, her eyes still on Harry's mouth. Picking up a red pencil and dropping her eyes, her hand began to stab at the paper in short urgent strokes. The mouth grew under her fingers as Joe watched. She finished in seconds. Removing the sketch sheet, Cath handed it to Harry. He regarded it for a moment, grunted his approval, and paid her. Portrait under his arm, he picked up his chairs and nodded a good-bye.

After watching Harry labor down the path toward the boardwalk below, Joe walked to where Cath sat cross-legged on the ground, her sketch pad on her lap. She carefully lifted a sheet of carbon paper from the top of the pad. A copy of the sketch she had just rendered of Harry stared up at Joe in black and white. *No color*, thought Joe. *As if all the life's been sucked out of it. No*, he thought. *Not all of it. Not yet.*

From her canvas bag, Cath removed a small rosewood box, its hinged cover carved with letters in a script Joe thought was Arabic. He'd never checked, wanting to know as little as possible about the thing. Cath opened the lid and withdrew what looked like a child's crayon but without any paper covering.

The crayon was as long as Joe's middle finger but thicker, and a red so dark it was almost black. Joe remembered drawing as a kid, the crayons, the names of the colors. Midnight blue, leaf green, sunshine yellow. He knew the name that this one would have carried: blood red. It glinted in the overhead light as if it would be sticky to the touch, but Joe had never touched it, so he didn't know for sure. He didn't want to know.

Hunched over the portrait copy, Cath began to retrace the lines of the mouth with the red crayon, adding color and shading. She worked with almost painful slowness. Joe remembered how once she had made a mistake at this stage, how the fury had burst from her like a wild thing caged too long.

At last, Cath straightened. She gave the mouth one last appraising look then returned the crayon to the rosewood box. Joe walked back to the low stone wall. He knew he would turn back to watch her. He always did.

Below, Harry had reached the boardwalk. The big man put down one chair to wave to someone on the beach. Joe's stomach tightened. A woman waved back at Harry, and a small boy and girl ran to hug him. *Jesus, no*, thought Joe.

He turned back. Cath sat hunched over the portrait of Harry on her lap. Joe rushed to her, praying that it wasn't too late, a prayer that died when he saw the picture. It had started.

The portrait's mouth was moving, fat lips squirming like slick red worms on the paper. A pale vapor rose thin and wispy from those lips. Cath bent her head over the mouth and sucked in that misty thing that Joe never wanted to name.

A scream rose from the beach. A woman's cry, a thing of pain and fear. Between her sobs, Joe could hear children crying.

He walked back to the low stone wall and looked down at the crowd gathered where Harry had fallen. Joe stood there, eyes locked on Harry's still form, feeling the void opening below him again. "Cath, we have to get out of here."

Cath didn't answer him. Joe tore his eyes from the scene below and turned back to her. She was standing now, looking south, down the coastline. "It wants to move on," she said.

❄

HOPE AND DREAMS and soul devoured...

Joe drove, staring at the white lane markers slicing the dark two-lane one after another, like brush strokes by God on a long black canvas. White on black. The negative image of Cath's secret portraits. Black on white, white on black. Just the red missing. Just that blood red.

How long before some cop put it together? A string of deaths, all the victims drawn by a young woman with a male companion. Christ, Harry died with a sketch in his hand.

Cath stirred beside him, and then he felt her eyes on him. He could always feel her gaze, like a physical touch, like a brush dipping into him, drawing something from him. *Is that how you do it, Cath? How you take the thing you take? Capture it in your eyes, then cage it through your fingers onto the page? Have you been feeding on me, too?*

"I'm still hungry," Cath said. Her voice was small, almost child-like in the dark.

He knew what she meant. "We'll hit town soon," he said. But it would be three in the morning when they arrived. No one around. No one to draw. And she had no pictures left. Cath said nothing but looked away. After a while, he figured she was asleep. Then he felt her eyes again.

"I don't *want* to hurt people, Joe."

He swallowed. This was new. She never talked about it, even when he did. He should say something now, something smart, something that would lead them out of this. He should, but he had nothing left to say. He could only nod. "I know, babe."

"It just gets so hungry. I get so hungry."

"I know."

"I can't stop it. It keeps pulling me, making me..."

Joe could feel her pain in those words. And his fear.

"I'm tired," she said. "So tired I wish I could just go to sleep and never wake up. Ever been that tired, Joe?"

He swallowed again. *All the time*, he thought, but he just nodded. Cath looked away, and he took a breath as if he was coming up for air.

"I'm hungry," she said again.

"I know."

Her eyes settled on him again like a beast on his chest.

"I could draw *you*, Joe."

Joe's hands tightened on the wheel. Cath had said it the way a kid told you she could ride a bike or tie her shoe. The lines flashed by in the headlights. White on black, no red.

"Don't even need to see you," she said. "Know you so well."

Joe stared at the road. *Don't look*, he thought.

"Know your face like I know my own," she said.

The burden of her gaze lifted. He looked at her.

Her eyes were shut, and her hand moved in her lap, mimicking drawing motions. "Don't even need light. Could draw you with my eyes closed." Her hand stopped, and she leaned her head back. A few minutes later, Joe heard her breathing slow and deepen.

So there it was. He always knew it would come to this. This was why he had stayed, even after he learned what Cath did, what she was. Afraid that when he left, when Cath no longer needed him, she would draw him down. Draw him down onto the page from memory, then drink him in like all the others.

The road lines flew at him like white knives out of the night. White knives and blackness. Just the blood red missing. Taking a hand from the wheel, he felt inside the top of his boot, running his fingers over the bone handle of his switchblade.

A few miles down the road, he found a wide shoulder and pulled over, turning off the engine and the lights.

Cath still slept. Hands shaking, Joe pulled the knife from his boot. *It's self-defense*, he thought. But he just sat holding the knife. It was for the best. How many more would she kill? But he still loved her. Could he do it? He was tired, so tired. He leaned back. He only slept now when Cath did, when he didn't feel her eyes. He closed his eyes. Her breathing brushed his ears, soft and deep, soft and deep, soft...

He awoke to the sound of scratching on paper. He looked over. Framed against the moonlight, Cath sat hunched over her sketchpad, her hand moving in short, sure strokes.

"Kind of late for drawing, isn't it, Cath?" Joe asked. His throat was dry. He fumbled in his lap for the knife.

"Hungry," she said, her voice barely audible.

"Dark, too," he said, blood pounding in his ears.

"Don't need light. Drawin' from memory," she whispered.

Drawing from memory. Drawing him. He knew she was drawing him. "Don't, Cath." His thumb found the blade's button.

"Tired of being hungry." She sat back, eyes on the sketch.

He couldn't see the picture, but he saw the red crayon in her hand. She'd finished the mouth. "Please, don't do it," he said. His cheeks felt cool and wet. He realized he was crying.

Cath lifted the paper to her face. She was crying, too.

"Don't!" Joe screamed. The knife blade clicked open.

"Bye, Joe. Sorry." Cath breathed in through her lips.

Joe saw a pale wisp rise from the paper and move toward her mouth. Saw his hand gripping the knife flash forward. Saw the blade slice her white T-shirt and slide between her ribs.

Saw the red, the blood red, flow over the white of her shirt to blend with the black of the night and the shadows.

Cath spasmed and fell sideways onto him. Surprise mixed with peace in her face. "Thanks...Joe," she whispered. Her eyes closed and her head slumped back. A wisp of mist escaped her lips.

That's me, Joe thought. Sobbing, he pressed his lips to hers, sucking in the breath and the grey mist from her mouth.

Bitter and sour, the thing burned his throat as he breathed it in. Something was wrong. Joe felt a presence of something dark, some-thing...*hungry.*

His head spinning, Joe flicked on the dome light. Blood soaked into his shirt where Cath slumped against him, the picture still clenched in her hand. Joe stared at the sketch, a scream forming in his mind.

A familiar face stared back at him from the page, a face that Cath knew from memory. The face she knew best of all.

Not Joe's face.

It was Cath.

She hadn't been drawing him. She'd been feeding herself to the thing that had lived in her. Cath had been killing herself.

The emptiness that was the mouth in Cath's pictures gaped beneath him, and Joe felt himself being drawn down.

❄

LOST TO YOU, *what might have been...*

A February evening, St. Pete's Beach. Joe sat on his stool, his back to the beauty of a Gulf sunset. His portraits lay strewn on the sand around him like the dead on a battlefield. A woman and man looked them over while Joe waited. The woman held the hand of a little girl and boy. Twins, Joe guessed. *Couldn't be much more than seven,* he thought. He remembered when that would have meant something to him, before Cath died, before...

The little girl tugged on the mother's hand. "They all look so sad, Mommy." The mother hushed the child while the father haggled with Joe over the price. The day had been slow, so Joe agreed to do both kids for the price of one.

Joe started sketching. His hand leapt over the paper, and the images of the children grew around the emptiness where their mouths should have been. A tear ran down his cheek, but he kept drawing.

He had to. He was hungry.

About the Author

Described by *Library Journal* as "one of Canada's most original writers of speculative fiction," Douglas Smith is a 4-time winner of Canada's Aurora Award and a finalist for the Astounding Award, CBC's Bookies Award, Canada's juried Sunburst Award, and France's juried Prix Masterton and Prix Bob Morane.

His books include the YA urban fantasy trilogy, The Dream Rider Saga (*The Hollow Boys*, *The Crystal Key*, and *The Lost Expedition*), the novel, *The Wolf at the End of the World*, and the collections, *Chimerascope* and *Impossibilia*.

ABOUT CRONE GIRLS PRESS

Crone Girls Press originally began as a Facebook group for fans of speculative fiction, hosted by speculative fiction author and writing coach Rachel A. Brune. As the idea took hold to publish an anthology of horror fiction in honor of her favorite fall holiday, Rachel began soliciting stories of dread, despair, and doom, all of which made for some uplifting reading. Upon receiving some truly terrifying—and excellent—material, she decided to go for broke and start working on an anthology series that would feature work by established and debut authors...from the darker side of speculative fiction.

We've now published five full-length anthologies and are always adding to our series of three-novella mini-anthologies, Midnight Bites. *Tangle & Fen* represents the latest publication in our efforts to publish chilling horror from the widest variety of voices that we can include in our pages. Enjoy—but don't stay up *too* late past midnight...

Thank you, Fiends!

We so hope you enjoyed your stay with us. If the sights you have seen and the dreams you have escaped stay with you after closing these pages, wouldn't you do us the favor of warning others of what they might encounter, should they happen to open these covers?
Share your thoughts, whether they be the careful, measured words of the diligent reader, or the sobbing cry from the asylum, on Goodreads or Amazon!
We'll be seeing you soon.

Our list of other titles is always growing. To stay in touch, join us on Facebook, and sign up for the Crone Girls Press newsletter: http://eepurl.com/gPT5sI.

IF YOU LIKED…

If you liked *Tangle & Fen*, you may also enjoy:

Other Titles from Crone Girls Press:

Stories We Tell After Midnight 1

Stories We Tell After Midnight 2

Stories We Tell After Midnight 3

Coppice & Brake

A Woman Unbecoming

Midnight Bites

Foul Womb of Night

Mother Krampus

Hard for Hope to Flourish

Memorial Station

Objectified

Milton Keynes UK
Ingram Content Group UK Ltd.
UKHW051423270524
443319UK00002B/207

9 781952 388149